SEARCHING FOR BRISTOL

Eagle Point Search & Rescue, Book 3

SUSAN STOKER

Edited by Kelli Collins

Cover Design by AURA Design Group

Manufactured in the United States

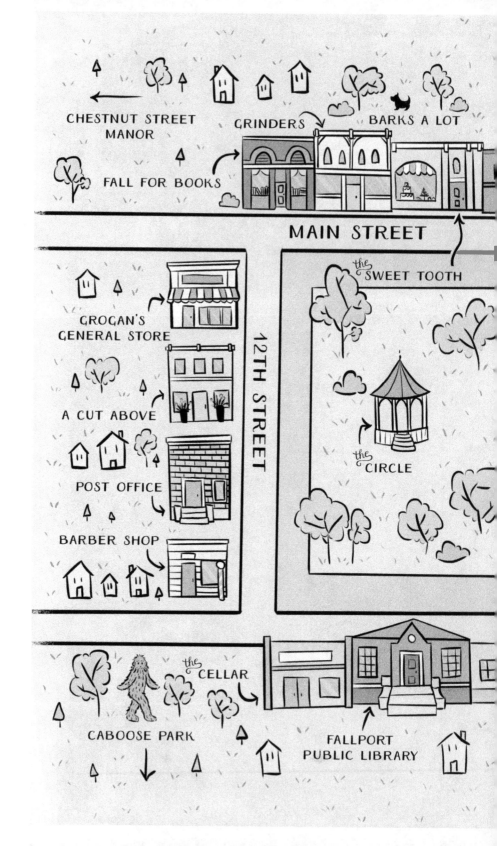

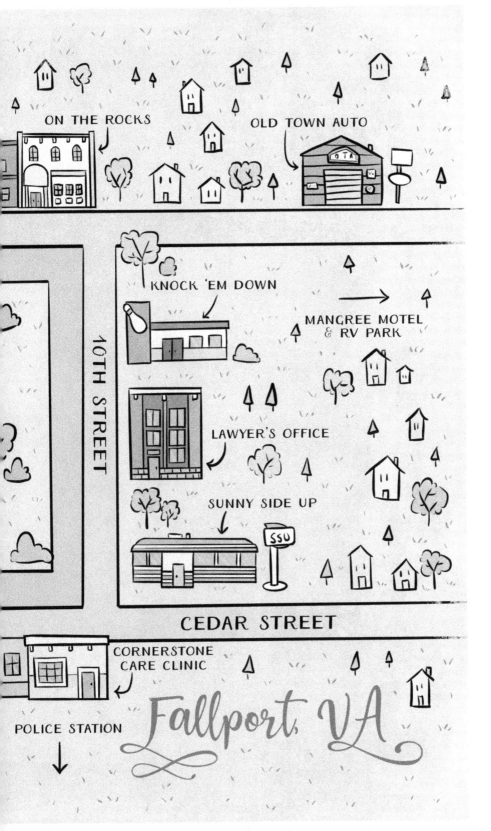

CHAPTER ONE

Bristol Wingham wanted to kick her own ass.

She'd known better than to go hiking by herself. But Mike had pissed her off so badly, there was no way she could've stomached one more night in his presence. She'd told him time and time again that she wasn't interested in being anything more than a friend, and she thought she'd finally gotten through to him.

And okay, she was kind of desperate for friends. Which was why, when he'd suggested this trip, she'd agreed in the first place.

But as soon as they'd arrived in the quaint town of Fallport, he'd once again begun pressuring her, trying to talk her into dating.

Mike was good-looking enough. Used to women falling all over him, in fact. His brown hair, chocolate-brown eyes, and muscular physique were enough to woo plenty of women, but Bristol had stopped being impressed by physical attributes a long time ago. And at twenty-nine, Mike should've been well past the time in his life when he saw all women as conquests. But apparently, he wasn't.

Sighing, Bristol closed her eyes. She should've known something was up when he'd belatedly informed her that Drake Long and Carol Page would be coming on the trip. Drake was twenty-five and Carol a young twenty-three. The last week had been spent listening to the other woman giggling and fawning all over her boyfriend...and Mike.

The plan before leaving had been to go on one last hike, to a picturesque camping area along the Falling Water Trail. It was an intermediate hike that linked up to the famous Appalachian Trail at some point, but they weren't going to be on it that long. The overlook where the campground was located was around eight miles from the trailhead.

But after only four miles, Mike had suggested they stop and camp right off the trail. Bristol had been confused...until he'd asked her to join in on a sexual interlude that he, Carol, and Drake had obviously already planned.

She'd been appalled—and had told Mike for the three-thousandth time that she wasn't interested in being more than friends, and she *certainly* wasn't having sex with the other couple either.

Mike had shrugged and said it was her loss. Then he'd calmly turned his back and began setting up camp...with one tent.

There was no way Bristol was going to sit around and listen to the threesome having sex for the rest of the afternoon and evening, so she'd turned on her heel and continued down the trail. Her plan was to camp at the overlook as they'd intended... well, as she'd *thought* they'd intended.

She'd meet up with her ex-friend in the morning, get back to Kingsport, and never talk to any of them again.

Except she hadn't made it to the campground. She'd gone off

the trail to pee, heard some rustling in the woods and decided to investigate. She wasn't exactly expecting to see Bigfoot or anything, but she would've loved to have seen some sort of wildlife, and she knew better than to go too far off trail.

But she hadn't expected the ground beneath her to suddenly give way.

She didn't remember much of what happened after that. Bristol assumed she'd hit her head in the fall and was knocked unconscious. Her head hurt—bad. She was nauseous and had a splitting headache. But that wasn't the worst of her injuries.

Somehow in the fall, she'd hurt the shin on her right leg so badly, the first time she'd attempted to stand, she'd passed out from the pain.

The next time she woke—after throwing up from the pain in her head and leg—she'd been much more careful about moving.

Looking up, she saw she was at the bottom of a very steep rock face. It was about twenty-five feet to the top, and she could see the clear trail her body took as she'd tumbled downward, aided by loose soil. Her fall had been broken by bushes at the bottom, otherwise she might not be alive at the moment...or at least would be in a lot worse shape than she was.

Her pack was still on her back, which was good, but she couldn't walk. All she could do was drag herself along the ground in an attempt to find a way to get to the top of the small cliff she'd fallen from and back to the trail. Someone would *have* to come by at some point...she hoped.

But it had now been three nights, and Bristol was getting scared. She'd yelled for what seemed like hours, but either no one was on the trail, or she was too far away from it to be heard. She'd hoped Mike and the others would notify someone that she was missing when they got back to the car and didn't find her, but it was obvious they hadn't.

They probably thought she'd hitchhiked back to town or something. But how did they think she was going to get home? Levitate?

Then again, maybe she was being too harsh. It was possible a search team was on the case but just hadn't found her yet.

Deep down though, after three nights, Bristol had a feeling Mike and his friends had left without a second thought as to what had happened to her.

The idea was disheartening and scary.

She'd crawled along the ground the first day, staying near the bottom of the cliff but away from the sharp rocks, and it had been extremely slow going. The agony in her leg kept her from doing much more than scooting on her butt. Every dip and movement of her leg sent sharp pains shooting upward, and after just a couple hours, Bristol had decided it was better to stay put and hope someone found her, rather than risk making whatever was wrong with her leg worse by moving.

She'd done her best to create a splint for her shin, but since she had no idea what she was doing, Bristol didn't know if she was helping or hurting the injury. The nausea she'd experienced when waking up at the bottom of the cliff had stuck with her, whether from her head injury or the pain from her leg, she didn't know. She'd tried to stay hydrated and had forced herself to eat some of the granola and protein bars she'd brought with her, but they tasted like chalk and it was all she could do to keep the food down.

She'd also managed to get her tent out of her pack, but hadn't been able to properly set it up, since she couldn't stand. But having some sort of shelter was better than none, and she was grateful that she had it. Going to the bathroom had been an adventure, and she felt absolutely filthy.

Looking up at the sun shining through the treetops around

her, Bristol wanted to cry, but she forced herself to take a deep breath instead. She was alive; she had to stay positive. But she had a feeling she couldn't stay at her makeshift camp much longer. If no one was looking for her, she had to do what she could to save herself.

She'd never been the kind of person to sit around feeling sorry for herself. Her parents hadn't raised her to be a quitter, and she wasn't about to start now.

No one would find her where she was, that was certain. She'd have to find a way to block out the pain and get herself back to the trail. She hadn't gone too far off it while tracking whatever animal had made the noise. If she could get to the trail, it would be much easier to move. She could eventually get back to the trailhead and someone would come by. This was a fairly popular hiking destination.

It took two hours to get her tent and everything else back into her pack, and for Bristol to be ready to start moving. She'd given herself a pep talk and re-did the bandage around her leg to immobilize it—which she knew she'd done a shit job of, but was trying to pretend otherwise. Her backpack was on her shoulders and she was ready to move once more.

Deciding that maybe it would hurt her leg less if she got on her belly and crawled that way, Bristol took a deep breath and turned over. Black spots swam in front of her eyes as she turned. Panting, she rested her forehead on the dirt under her.

"Shit. Fuck," she muttered as the world seemed to spin. Tears formed in her eyes, but she forced them back. "Suck it up," she said out loud. "You got yourself into this, and you're going to have to get yourself out."

Lifting her chin, she eyed the landscape in front of her. She was going to have to go east, around the cliff, then turn south and hopefully catch the trail. She had no idea how wide the cliff was, or how far she'd have to crawl to get back around to the trail, but ultimately the distance didn't matter. She didn't have a choice. She'd waited around for three nights hoping someone would come looking for her, but after hearing hide nor hair of anyone, she couldn't sit there any longer.

Inch by inch, Bristol began to crawl. Every foot seemed like a mile. Rocks dug into her forearms and hands, and her leg throbbed badly enough that she'd stopped to dry heave—since her belly was empty—twice. But she kept going. She did her best to throw rocks and branches out of her way so her leg wouldn't bounce over them, but the rough terrain she was dragging herself through was brutal.

After what seemed like hours, Bristol looked behind her to see how far she'd gone—and immediately wished she hadn't. The trees were thick, but she could just see where she'd spent the last three nights in the distance.

The urge to give up was strong. She wanted to blame the situation she was in on Mike, for being a horny bastard, but the reality was, she'd been the stupid one to go off trail. She'd been determined to see the overlook that had been their original destination, instead of immediately heading back to the trailhead and catching a ride to Fallport.

Taking a deep breath, Bristol clenched her teeth and began to crawl once more. She could do this. She literally had no other choice.

* * *

Cohen "Rocky" Watson walked quickly along the Falling Water Trail. There had been no other cars at the trailhead when he'd arrived, which was unusual for this time of year.

He still wasn't convinced the supposedly "missing person" he was searching for hadn't just forgotten her promise to visit Sandra Hain, the woman who owned the Sunny Side Up diner in town. People did that kind of thing all the time. Promised something, then simply forgot, not understanding how much the other person was counting on them.

But Sandra thought otherwise. She'd begged Rocky to go looking for Bristol Wingham, the tourist she'd befriended.

Rocky had no idea why Sandra had gotten so attached. She was notoriously picky about who she accepted and who she didn't, like most people who lived in the small town of Fallport. Regardless, Sandra and this Bristol person had obviously clicked, and Rocky hadn't had the heart to turn down Sandra's plea to at least check the trail to see if the woman was in trouble.

He'd left after eating breakfast at the diner, going back to his apartment to grab his go-pack he always had ready for search and rescue missions, and to change into appropriate hiking gear. He hadn't bothered to call Raiden, the other member of the Eagle Point SAR team who was in town at the moment.

The others had all gone with Zeke, Elsie, and her son, Tony, to the Eagle Point Lookout tower.

Rocky smiled to himself, knowing all about the surprise that awaited Elsie when they got there. She wasn't much of an outdoors girl, and Zeke had wanted to make her as comfortable as possible at the tower, so he'd hiked the ten miles ahead of time and outfitted it with a blowup mattress, sheets, a comforter. Rocky was pretty sure he'd brought flowers as well.

He was thrilled for his friend. Rocky genuinely liked Elsie and her son. Tony was a good kid who was starved for positive male attention. He understood a little about what the nine-year-old was feeling, as his own father had died and he'd been raised by his mother. But his situation was a bit different, since he'd had his twin, Ethan, and their sister, for company growing up.

7

Rocky scowled when he thought about what Tony's biological father had done to his own child. The scheme to kill him and collect life insurance after his death. What a fucking bastard.

He wasn't sure he wanted children himself, but if he ever did, he'd protect them with his life. There was too much evil in the world already, making it too easy for kids to be hurt or corrupted. He'd seen it with his own eyes through his former job as a Navy SEAL.

He'd gotten out of the Navy the same time as his brother, because he couldn't imagine not being close to Ethan. He didn't miss it; he'd become disillusioned with the bureaucracy that came with the military. Moving to Fallport and finding people who got lost in the Appalachian Mountains was much less dangerous than what he used to do, but no less fulfilling.

The morning was beautiful, nice and warm, and while hiking would become miserable because of the heat in the afternoon, Rocky couldn't complain at the moment. He adjusted his pack on his back—it was light compared to the loads he used to carry as a SEAL—and continued up the trail.

He'd been walking for about six miles when something caught his attention. A couple miles back, he'd seen evidence of a campsite. It was in an unauthorized area...not a place set up for camping. Rocky had been irked, but not exactly surprised. He used to be shocked when they found trash on the trail—poopy diapers, empty bottles and cans, even random items of clothing —but it was hard to surprise him anymore. Plenty of people were lazy, entitled, and didn't care about anything but themselves. Certainly not others who might come along the trail behind them, not the animals who might get hurt by eating the trash that was left behind, and definitely not whoever picked up whatever junk was left in their wake.

So seeing that someone had camped in an area that wasn't designated for it wasn't all that surprising. Rocky figured the foursome Sandra had told him about had probably camped there for the night, before heading back to the trailhead and heading home to Kingsport, Tennessee. But because it was such a nice day, and because he couldn't be certain that was their site, he'd decided to keep going to the overlook, the group's original destination. It was only another four miles or so.

But two miles later, as he stood in the middle of the trail, Rocky frowned at the trampled weeds leading into the woods to his left. If he wasn't mistaken, it was a trail left by a person.

A *recent* trail.

And just like that, his adrenaline kicked in. All thoughts of the easygoing hike he'd been on disappeared.

"It's probably nothing," Rocky muttered to himself. "Tons of people have been on this trail. Who knows how many have wandered off?"

But how recently? The trail he was looking at was maybe a few days old.

Cautiously, he stepped off the well-worn and marked hiking path to follow the trail that led into the woods. Rocky was well aware that there was a large drop-off not too far from the path. There was an outcropping of rocks that went on for half a mile or so, and every now and then, someone tumbled over the edge. It was possible to survive a fall from the cliff, as it wasn't more than thirty feet down, but the potential injuries one sustained could be serious. He and his team had rescued two people who'd fallen in the past, and Rocky expected they'd have more in the future.

He had no idea *what* enticed people off the hiking trail. If he was a superstitious man, he'd say there were creatures lurking in the trees, luring humans to the edge. But because

9

he'd seen and experienced too much to believe in such things as Bigfoot or Mothman—or worse, the being some people in Appalachia called Sheepsquatch—Rocky felt no fear as he followed the clear-as-day path someone had taken in the last few days.

He swore under his breath as the trail ended where he expected it to, right at the edge of the small cliff face. Worse, he saw scuff marks in the rocky dirt next to the edge and a chunk of earth had clearly broken off. Someone had been here—and had slipped over the edge.

He cautiously looked down, relieved when he didn't see a broken and bruised body at the bottom of the precipice. But that didn't mean someone wasn't down there, hurt and needing assistance.

"Hello?" he bellowed, listening as the word echoed off the trees around him. The loud noise scared a few birds nearby, and they took off from their perches on the branches overhead with loud complaining squawks.

Listening hard, Rocky didn't hear anything, just the sound of his own heart beating.

He swallowed hard. Most people would simply shrug and continue on their way, but the hair on his arms was standing up. His intuition told him that he'd located the missing woman Sandra had sent him to find. He had no proof, and it was unlikely she was here when her hiking companions clearly weren't, but something was telling Rocky not to give up. That he'd discover what happened to Bristol Wingham.

He waited a moment and tried to think about what *he'd* have done, had he fallen over this ledge. If he wasn't hurt, he'd probably try to climb back up at the same place he fell. But if he was injured...

Rocky looked to his right and left. If he was hurt, he'd do his best to get back up to the trail—and hopefully people—the fastest and easiest way he could.

Which meant heading east.

Walking slowly, watching where he put his own feet so he didn't fall over the edge himself, Rocky strained to catch sight of anything unusual below. It was slow going, since the ledge wasn't well defined and he had to dodge large boulders, trees, and thorns. Every now and then he yelled out, hoping Bristol—or whoever had gone over—was conscious and could hear him.

He'd walked just ten minutes before something caught his attention below. Most people would've overlooked it, but Rocky wasn't most people.

There was a large circular patch of grass that was flattened, visible thanks to the taller weeds and grass around it. If he was a betting man, he'd guess that was where someone had set up a tent or shelter.

If he thought his adrenaline had kicked in earlier, it was nothing compared to now. The urge to get down there, to find the missing woman, was coursing through his veins, but Rocky forced himself to slow down, to think.

"Hello?" he yelled again. "Bristol Wingham, can you hear me?"

He strained to listen, but all he heard was the wind.

"Damn," Rocky muttered. But determination swam through him. He was close. The signs were all here. Bristol *was* here. Or she had been.

It was possible she'd made it back to the trail and someone had found her and gotten her out of the woods...but he didn't think so. Finding an injured woman on a trail would be something the good people of Fallport wouldn't be able to resist gossiping about.

Silas, Otto, and Art, the three old coots who hung around

outside the post office on the square every single day, would've gotten word of something like that, and wouldn't have been able to resist telling literally everyone with whom they came into contact. No, if Bristol had been the one who'd fallen off the ledge, forced to camp at the bottom of the drop-off, she was still out here. And in need of help. Rocky knew it to the bottom of his boots.

He walked along the top of the small cliff, looking for a way down as he continued to search for signs of the missing woman. It took another couple of minutes, but he finally spied a way down that didn't look as steep as the rock face behind him. It wouldn't be easy, but it was hard to track someone from twenty-five feet up. He needed to get down below so he could read any signs more clearly.

Moving slowly, Rocky began the descent of the cliff face. He carefully picked his handholds as he made his way down. His friends would probably call him crazy for the risk he was taking but as each minute passed, urgency pushed at him. He didn't know why, but he felt a deep-seated need to get to the missing woman.

Admittedly, he always felt that way when he and his team were on the hunt, but this felt...different. Maybe it was because he was by himself. Maybe because Bristol had been out here for three nights already. Maybe it was the way Sandra had spoken about her, with respect and concern. The owner of the diner was sociable, yes, but as far as Rocky knew, she didn't go out of her way to befriend strangers like she had with Bristol.

Whatever the reason, Rocky knew he needed to find her. Fast.

He made it to the bottom of the cliff face and brushed his hands off on his pants. His palms stung with small cuts from the rock he'd just climbed, but he barely felt the tiny hurts. Studying the terrain, he saw what he'd missed from his vantage point twenty-plus feet up.

Drag marks.

And immediately, fear struck.

It may not have been a legendary creature who'd lured Bristol from the trail...but it could've been a flesh-and-blood man. Or woman. Maybe one of the people she'd been hiking with had it out for her and had brought her to the overlook and shoved her off, then gone down to make sure she was dead. He or she could've dragged her body, looking for a place to conceal it.

Rocky reflectively reached for his weapon—a weapon he no longer carried because he wasn't a SEAL any longer. He had a knife, and he was damn good with it, but if someone was out here who wanted to do harm to a hiker, he'd prefer a weapon that would allow him to keep his distance.

Swearing, he studied the area again and saw nothing else out of the ordinary. It wasn't likely, if someone had hurt Bristol purposely, that he or she was still anywhere nearby, but he wasn't going to take any chances.

Determination filling him, Rocky followed the marks on the ground. He wasn't going to yell anymore, just in case someone *had* hurt her and was still in the area. In that case, he'd need to sneak up on them if he was going to have the upper hand. And he *would*—there was no doubt about that. He knew these woods better than most people, and he had the training to kill with his bare hands, if necessary.

The thought of having to kill anyone turned his stomach, but Rocky didn't slow down. He'd do what was necessary to save an innocent life. He might not be a SEAL any longer, but that didn't mean he'd look the other way when someone needed help.

The longer Rocky followed the drag marks, the more sure he was that whoever had made them wasn't someone looking to stash a dead body. Mostly because no one in their right mind would drag *anyone* for so long. He'd already passed plenty of places where someone could've hidden a body, including undergrowth and small caves along the cliff wall.

No, whatever path he was following was something else—a very determined and stubborn person, doing whatever they had to do in order to survive. He could see now that the trail he was following wasn't one person dragging another, but someone scooting along the ground. And the only reason someone would do that was if they were injured and couldn't walk properly.

Respect bloomed within Rocky, and the farther he walked, the more impressed he got. If this was Bristol, she was a fighter, that was for sure. He hated that she was probably hurt, but he respected her stubbornness and will to get back to civilization.

Without hesitation he lifted his chin and yelled her name once more, no longer worried that someone was out there lying in wait. "Bristol!"

For a moment, all he heard was more silence. He sighed in frustration.

Then he heard something else. A voice in the distance.

"Help! I'm here!"

Holy shit!

He'd done it. He'd found her.

Rocky's feet were moving before he realized it. He began to jog, following the voice and the marks on the ground.

"Hello?" the female voice called out, sounding extremely stressed.

"I'm coming!" he yelled back. "Hold on!"

It took another few minutes, but when he finally saw Bristol Wingham, he almost tripped over her.

He'd turned a corner, having finally reached the end of the outcropping of rocks where the land began to gain elevation, sloping upward toward the trail once more, and suddenly there she was. Sitting on the ground, her legs pointed downhill, face flushed with exertion, long, tangled black hair in a scrunchie and tears in her eyes.

Rocky practically threw himself to the side to keep himself from stepping on her.

"Bristol?" he asked as he went down on his knees next to her.

Her dark brown eyes were wide and she was breathing way too fast. She nodded in response to his question.

"I'm Rocky. Are you all right?"

She took a deep breath and shook her head.

"What hurts?" It was obvious she was in pain, but Rocky was still impressed. She wasn't hysterical. His gaze went to her legs before she spoke. The only reason someone would be crawling through the forest was if she couldn't walk.

A rudimentary splint confirmed his suspicions.

"My leg," she said. "I don't know what's wrong with it, but I'm guessing I broke something. It hurts. Bad."

That was his thought as well. Bristol had done her best with the splint on her right shin. It was obvious she had no training, but she had the basic principle down. Immobilize the limb. Protect it. Rocky couldn't see any bones sticking through the pants she was wearing, but that didn't mean she didn't have a compound fracture beneath her clothes.

"How did you find me?" she asked quietly.

"Sandra," Rocky told her.

"The owner of Sunny Side Up?" she asked, clearly surprised.

Rocky was equally surprised she knew who he was talking about. It was his experience that most tourists didn't bother to remember the names of the locals. It wasn't as if they were trying to be rude, but with the number of names people heard in their lifetime, it just wasn't expected.

But just as he'd thought, this woman and Sandra had obviously made a connection. "Yes. She was worried when you didn't come back to say goodbye. She asked if I would come check things out and look for you."

Bristol's brow furrowed. "So you...what...just dropped everything and aimlessly started walking through the woods?"

Rocky chuckled. He was so relieved to have found her, he didn't even mind the look of disbelief on her face. "Something like that. I'm a member of our local search and rescue team," he explained. "I know these trails extremely well. That's why Sandra asked me to see what I could find."

"Oh. Wow. Okay," Bristol said. "Well, I'm grateful. More than grateful. Damn ecstatic!" She gave him a small relieved smile.

A zing of something went through Rocky at seeing that smile. She was filthy, smelled a little funky, had a possible broken leg...and despite all that, she still somehow had the ability to feel joy.

Rocky had rescued a lot of people over the years, both as a SEAL and as a member of the SAR team. He'd seen people at their best and worst. When they were found, people had cried, completely freaked out, been scared out of their minds, confused, belligerent, and even irritating. But Rocky got it; they were out of their comfort zone. He never took it personally when someone he rescued was an asshole. His job was to get them out of whatever situation they'd found themselves in, and that was it.

But something about Bristol Wingham, her fortitude, her strength, her...obviously positive personality, drew him.

Mentally, Rocky shook his head. This was no time to be thinking about his own possible connection with the woman. She was hurt. And they were still six miles from the trailhead.

That thought made him scowl.

"What?" she asked, noticing the change in his demeanor. "What's wrong?"

"Nothing," Rocky forced himself to say lightly. He wasn't about to tell her that, while he might have found her, they still had a hell of a hard road ahead of them to get her to a hospital. Like an idiot, he hadn't called Raiden to tell him what he was doing. No one knew he was out here on a possible rescue except for Sandra, and she wasn't likely to call Raid.

He didn't know when Ethan and the others would be back from the Eagle Point Tower, and while he had a phone, the cell service in the woods sucked. For the thousandth time, he wished the town had the resources to get the satellite phones Ethan kept saying they needed in order to communicate with each other and Doc Snow, Fallport's local doctor.

Pushing those thoughts away—now was no time to think about things he didn't have, or hadn't done—Rocky shrugged off his pack. "I need to get a look at that leg, see what we're working with. Then I'll get it splinted properly. Good news is that I've got some painkillers for you to take the edge off while we're getting out of here."

"I'm sorry I didn't know how to do it right."

Her soft words brought Rocky's eyes back to hers. "What?"

"My leg. I wasn't sure exactly how to splint it, so I just tried to mimic what I've seen on TV shows and movies and stuff. I used the cords from my tent to tie the sticks to my leg, but I obviously didn't know what I was doing."

"You did good," Rocky reassured her.

She snorted.

"Seriously. I'm impressed." And he was. "You have no idea how many people I've come across who haven't been able to do *anything* to help themselves. You not only did what you could to take care of your injury, you've been out here for three nights by yourself. I'm guessing you stayed in your tent for a while before deciding your better bet was to try to get to the trail, instead of staying put. And despite your injury, you painstakingly dragged yourself to this point. I don't know many people who could or *would* have done what you did."

Her eyes filled with tears once more, but she closed them before any could escape. "Thank you," she whispered.

"No. Thank *you* for not giving up," Rocky replied. "For being strong. For holding on until I could find you."

"How *did* you find me, anyway? It's not like I'm on the beaten path or anything."

Rocky pulled out a pair of shears from his pack and motioned to her leg. "I'm going to need to cut your pants to see what we're working with. That okay?"

"Of course," she said without hesitation.

It was a small request, but she'd probably be surprised to learn how many people bitched about their clothes being cut when they were found. Rocky understood; hiking gear wasn't exactly cheap. But if he was trying to find and treat injuries, it got old when people were pissy over a pair of pants.

As he carefully removed the splint she'd tied to her leg and began to slice the material of her khakis so he could see her shin, he explained how he'd noticed where she'd gone off the main trail, then about finding the spot where she'd slipped over the edge of the cliff. Finally, he mentioned the spot where she'd set up her tent, and clarified how, once he'd climbed down the rocks, he'd seen the clear trail created by her drag marks.

"I'd thought for a minute that maybe someone had pushed you and was dragging your dead body," he said without thinking. And then kicked himself for being so blunt. The last thing she needed to hear was him talking about her demise. But she surprised him once again by laughing.

"I hadn't even thought of that, but I've watched enough of those true crime shows to know you were spot-on with that line of thought. I can't believe you were able to follow my trail so easily. I had to pee," she admitted sheepishly. "Then when I was done, I thought I heard something and went to check it out. It was stupid. I know better. I didn't even notice the damn cliff until I was already sliding down. I remember throwing up and passing out, but not much else...other than the pain."

"You don't remember?" Rocky asked sharply.

"No."

"Does your head hurt? Did you hit it?"

"It's killing me," she said as nonchalantly as if she was discussing the weather.

Rocky's respect for her grew. "You could have a concussion," he said.

"I'm sure I do," she said with a small shrug. "I was throwing up for the first couple of days after I fell. The nausea's better now, but the headache is still there."

He frowned. None of that was good. But it had been three days since she'd fallen off the rocks. There wasn't much he could do about the concussion now. Studying her leg, he was relieved not to see any bones breaking through her skin. "No compound fracture," he said softly.

"That's good," Bristol said, watching as he examined her.

He probed her leg, taking note when she winced and where the pain seemed to be the worst. He wasn't a doctor, but he'd seen plenty of broken bones in his life. "It's definitely fractured. Won't know for sure how bad it is until you get an x-ray," he said as he began to wrap her leg tightly and re-splint it.

Bristol nodded but didn't reply. It wasn't until he was finished immobilizing her leg as best he could that Rocky looked up again. Her eyes were closed and her teeth were clenched. One hand was behind her, propping herself up, and the other was curled into a tight fist close to her side.

Once more, Rocky wanted to kick his own ass. He'd been so focused on wrapping her leg that he hadn't even thought to give her the painkillers before he'd started. When he was with his team, one of the other guys usually took care of that while he looked over the patient.

Another reason to regret not calling Raiden. His friend would've dropped everything to come out here with him, and Rocky really needed a partner right about now. Someone who could head back to the trailhead to contact the doctor, maybe call LifeFlight so they could get Bristol evacuated by air to Roanoke to be looked over.

But instead, he was on his own. And his fuckery was causing her pain.

"Shit," he said as he reached for his pack once more.

Her eyes opened at his curse. "What? What's wrong?"

"Nothing's wrong, I'm just an idiot," he told her honestly. "Here," he said, shaking out two pills and holding them out to her.

She simply looked at them in confusion.

"They're painkillers. I'm so sorry, I should've given these to you before I started poking and prodding at your leg. I could put in an IV, but honestly, I have no way of setting up the rig and getting you out of here at the same time. I'd rather do a scoop-and-go, and get you to a doctor as soon as possible." He was talking too fast and overexplaining, but Rocky couldn't stop himself.

"I fucked up," he admitted. "I know better than to go on a search by myself, but I honestly didn't think you were out here. I hoped you'd just forgotten to say goodbye to Sandra and were sitting at home, safe and sound. Getting out of here isn't going to be easy. It's gonna suck, in fact. Big time. And I'm kicking my own ass for that now. There's no cell reception out here, and I can't leave you to go back to the trailhead to my car to get more help."

Bristol blinked. "Why not?" she asked as she took the pills and swallowed them down with water from the canteen she had strapped around her chest.

Rocky didn't know whether to be relieved she trusted him enough to not even ask what the pills were, or pissed that she hadn't. It was a weird sensation, a feeling he'd never had with anyone else he'd rescued. He couldn't figure out why he was so off-kilter with this woman, and decided he'd worry about it later. "Why not what?" he asked.

"Why can't you leave me? Now that you know I'm here, I wouldn't be scared. Except, of course, if you got hurt on your way back to the trailhead. Or got in an accident while you were going for help. *That* would suck." She gave him a small smile.

"I'm not leaving you," Rocky said firmly. She was right, it would probably be faster if he ran back to the trailhead to get help, but just the thought of leaving her alone again wasn't something he was willing to entertain. It had been drilled into his head time after time that you didn't leave a victim. Ever. He'd seen people who looked perfectly healthy go downhill in a matter of minutes. And the last thing he wanted was to have found Bristol, only to lose her because of his boneheaded decision to search for her without help.

"So, what's the plan?" she asked with a tilt of her head. "I mean, I could keep dragging myself to the trail, but I'm not sure I can make it the whole six miles to the parking lot."

Rocky rolled his eyes. "As if I'd let you. I'm going to carry you."

Her eyes widened. "You can't do that!" she exclaimed.

"Why not?"

"Because!"

It was Rocky's turn to chuckle. "I assure you, I won't drop you. You're what…five feet tall?"

"Four-eleven," Bristol mumbled.

"Right. I'm thinking some of the packs I carried when I was in the Navy probably weighed more than you. But it's not going to be comfortable," he warned.

"Like dragging myself was?" Bristol asked with a small eye roll as she held her hands palms out for him to see.

Once more, Rocky wanted to kick his own ass. He'd been so worried about her leg, he hadn't even thought about what pulling herself over the rough terrain would've done to her palms. He gently grabbed hold of her wrists and leaned over to get a better look at the scrapes and tears on the palms of her hands.

"Don't move," he ordered, as he reached for his pack once more.

CHAPTER TWO

Bristol stared at the man who'd found her. The relief that had swamped her at hearing her name being called from somewhere behind her had been so great, she thought she would pass out. Though...the man who appeared out of the trees had scared her at first.

He was wearing a military-green T-shirt, camo pants, had a fairly long, bushy beard, and was extremely muscular. She could see the hint of a tattoo peeking beneath one of the sleeves of his shirt, and he had a large pack on his back. For a second, she was afraid she'd gone from being in trouble, to being in *deep* trouble. But then he'd introduced himself, mentioned Sandra, and got right to work trying to make her feel better.

Bristol wasn't a very worldly person. She spent most of her time by herself in her house in Kingsport, lost in her art. But there was something about this large man that had her trusting him in short order. Maybe it was because he was the first person she'd seen in days. Or because she knew, deep down to her bones, that she never would've made it back to the trail by herself. Maybe it was the look in his deep brown eyes when he'd asked permission to cut her pants, or his obvious skill when he'd re-splinted her leg.

Whatever the case, Bristol now had no doubt that this man wouldn't hurt her.

She watched as he rummaged in his pack for something to put on her hands. They hurt, but not as badly as her leg. However, whatever pills Rocky had given her were already starting to take effect. She felt kind of floaty. She was still aware of where she was and what was happening, but it sort of felt as if it was happening to someone else, and she was watching from above.

She was smiling slightly when he turned back to her with a bottle of some sort of liquid in his hands and some gauze.

"What?" he asked after seeing her face. "Are you okay?"

"I'm good," she said. "I feel great, actually. Anyone ever tell you that you kind of look like Bigfoot?"

He hesitated a moment, staring at her, before bursting into laughter.

Bristol couldn't do anything but stare back. He was a good-looking man, there was no doubt about that, but when he laughed? He was freaking *gorgeous.*

She'd never been with a man who had a beard before. She wondered if it itched. If it got in his way when he ate. Did it feel weird when he went swimming, and did he brush it in the mornings, like people did with their hair? She had so many questions, but even in her floaty state, she knew they were probably inappropriate.

"Can't say they have, but with all the fuss about Bigfoot and that damn show, I'm guessing I'll be hearing it more often now."

"I'm sorry, I didn't mean to offend you," Bristol apologized as he began to gently clean one of her hands. She hadn't realized how badly she'd damaged her skin as she pulled herself along the forest floor, but she literally didn't have a choice, so even if she *had* realized it at the time, it couldn't have been helped.

Rocky grinned. "You didn't offend me," he said. "I'm hard to offend. Besides, with my beard, and you being...pint-sized, I probably *do* look like Sasquatch."

"How tall are you?" Bristol asked. She wouldn't have been so nosy without the drugs in her system, but since he didn't seem upset, she couldn't hold back the question.

"Six feet."

"Hmmmm. Over a foot taller than me."

He smiled. "Guessing you're probably used to that, yeah?"

"Being shorter than most people? Uh-huh."

"Maybe it's a good thing Raiden didn't come with me after all."

"Why? Who's Raiden?" Bristol asked.

"My friend. He's on the SAR team with me. He's six-eight."

Bristol stared at Rocky with wide eyes. "Seriously?"

"Yup. I think his bloodhound is probably taller than you."

She frowned. "I *know* you're not making fun of my height. I mean, not poor little me. Lost in the woods. Injured and in pain." She was kidding. Mostly.

Rocky looked at her, and all humor was gone from his expression now. "I'd never make fun of you," he said seriously. "I don't give a rat's ass *how* tall or short you are. Or about your weight, your heritage, or any other superficial thing people use to discriminate these days. I care more about who you are inside. Are you the kind of person who would just walk by someone in need? Or would you stop in the middle of a busy highway to save a frightened kitten?"

"I'd stop," Bristol whispered, feeling ensnared by the intense look in his eyes.

They stared at each other for a long moment before he nodded. "I could've guessed that about you. You made quite the impression on Sandra."

Bristol blinked, feeling as if something important had just happened, but not sure what. "She's nice. She listened to my bitching about Mike. Like, *really* listened because she was interested, not just because she wanted my business."

"Mike?" Rocky asked as he continued cleaning her palm.

"Yeah, the douche I came with. The one I *thought* was my friend. The guy who calmly asked if I wanted to participate in the *ménage à trois* he was having with Carol and Drake. I don't know what it's called when there's four people, but regardless, it's definitely not my thing. Which I *told* him several times."

"That how you ended up on your own out here?" Rocky asked.

Bristol nodded. "They were too interested in sex to even make it to the campsite at the overlook. I really wanted to see it. So I decided to go on ahead. Stupid of me, I know. Then I had to pee and...you know the rest."

"I saw where they camped," Rocky told her. He'd finished cleaning her hands and was sitting next to her simply holding her wrists. She was very aware of his hands on her, but since he didn't even seem to notice, she kept still, not wanting to be a weirdo about the tingles shooting up her arms from his touch. Of course, that could be from whatever cleanser he'd used on her palms, but whatever.

"I told them it wasn't a designated camping spot, but they were too interested in getting in each other's pants to care," Bristol said with a shrug. "I figured I'd be back at the trailhead before they were the next day, to catch a ride back home with them. It would've been a very uncomfortable ride, but whatever.

I'm guessing they didn't stop to tell anyone that I might still be out here?" she asked.

Rocky shook his head. "Not that I know of. Sorry."

"I'm not surprised. Mike wasn't the best friend."

"Why'd you come with him then?" Rocky asked.

"Honestly?"

"Always."

"I needed a break...and I don't have a lot of friends. I don't get out much, and I love hiking. I figured it would at least get me out of the house for a while and I could recharge."

"Recharge?"

"I'm an artist. I make custom stained-glass windows. I also do jewelry and some sculptures, but stained glass is my passion. Still, since I rarely do anything but work, I was getting a bit burned out and decided a change of pace would do me good. This was a bit more excitement than I anticipated," she said a little sheepishly. Bristol knew she was babbling, but she couldn't seem to stop. "Rocky?"

"Yeah, Punky?"

Bristol frowned. "Punky?"

Rocky smirked. "You kinda remind me of her."

"You mean Punky Brewster, from that eighties show?"

"Yup. She's funny and spunky. And resilient. Like you."

"I guess that's better than being called Teeny or Short Stuff."

"Well, Punky was short too," Rocky said.

Bristol rolled her eyes, but secretly didn't mind the nickname. She'd been called a lot of things in her life, but she liked the reasoning behind Rocky's nickname for her.

"What did you want to ask me?"

Bristol frowned. "I have no idea."

"Your head hurt?" Rocky asked, sounding concerned.

She nodded.

"Your leg?"

Bristol nodded again.

"What else?"

"My hands. My back. My butt. My feet are squished inside my boots and feel like they're suffocating, because I haven't taken my shoes off since I fell. My elbows. And I think I scraped my side when I tumbled down the rock face."

Rocky reached for the hem of her shirt, and Bristol pulled away from him instinctively.

She might trust him, but she wasn't a complete idiot. He was still a man, after all. One who could easily overpower her. She was no match for him in her condition, especially considering how muscular and tall he was. Not to mention, she hadn't missed his reference to being in the Navy...with her luck, he was probably a SEAL or something, and knew a hundred and one ways to kill someone and not leave a trace behind afterward.

"Don't be scared of me," he said quietly, even as he leaned away from her.

Bristol took a deep inhale. "Sorry," she mumbled.

"And don't apologize either."

Now she huffed out an irritated breath. "What *can* I do then?" she asked.

"Hang tough," he said without hesitation. "I wasn't kidding, getting out of here is gonna suck. I can carry you, but it's not going to be comfortable for you."

"And it will be for *you*?" she asked.

"Nope. But I'm not the one with a hurt leg, butt, hands, elbows, side, and head."

He had a good point. "I'll be okay. The alternative is to scoot out of here for six miles on my ass, and trust me, that wasn't much fun either."

Rocky smiled and shook his head. "I can't believe I'm smiling. More, I can't believe *you're* smiling."

"Do I have a choice?" she asked seriously. "I could be crying, but that wouldn't accomplish anything. I could be pissed at myself, or at you, but that'd just be stupid, since you're the one who's gonna get me out of here. I could be freaked out, but again, that wouldn't help. I can promise I *will* do all of those things later—except be mad at you, because that's just not going to happen—if it would make you feel better."

"Naw, I think I'm good. You ready to go?"

"Yes!" But then she frowned. "How's this gonna work?"

Rocky was already moving. He gently eased her pack off her back and unzipped it.

"Rocky?"

"Yeah?" he asked, as he began to unpack her things.

"What are you doing?"

"I can't carry you while you're wearing your pack, so I need to move your stuff to mine. Give me a second."

"Leave it."

He looked up at that. "What?"

Bristol nodded. "Just leave it. The Bigfoots can have it. Or is it Bigfeet? What's the plural?"

For some reason, Rocky laughed. Hard.

"What? What's so funny?"

"It's just that my friend's fiancée's son once asked him the same thing. He asked me what I thought, and we actually had a twenty-minute conversation about the English language and plurals."

"What was your conclusion about Bigfoot?" Bristol asked with a smile.

"We still have no idea. But I'm not leaving your stuff. It'll all fit in my backpack. I didn't load it up for my trip out here

29

because, like an idiot, I figured I'd just be gone one night on an easy trip. I'm not leaving your underwear out here for some Sheepsquatch to find and perv on."

"A what?" Bristol asked, watching him pack his bag with her things.

"Sheepsquatch. I hadn't heard of them until I moved here either. Apparently, they're wooly-haired, with a long and pointed head, saber-like teeth, and of course, they have horns like a goat. They walk on two feet, have a hairless tail like a possum, are as big as a bear, and smell musky, kinda like a skunk."

"What the heck?" Bristol asked, completely confused.

Rocky chuckled. "Right? It's supposedly been seen in Kentucky, but also over in Fulks Run, Virginia. I think I'd rather Fallport be known for Bigfoot than Sheepsquatch."

"You ever seen a Bigfoot?" Bristol asked. The look Rocky gave her made her laugh. "Right. I take it that's a no."

"I've seen a lot of things in my life, Punky, but Bigfoot isn't one of them. I have no idea if such a creature exists, but if he does, I hope he stays hidden. The hell his—or her—life would become if someone actually caught one would be indescribable. The government would probably want to dissect him, the news shows would lose their minds, and it would spell doom for any others in the world. He'd probably be put in a zoo for people to gawk at, if he survived at all. No longer be able to roam free."

"I agree," Bristol said with a nod.

He finished folding up her pack and stuffing it inside his own, then stood and shrugged it on. The man acted as if he hadn't just flung fifty or more pounds of gear onto his back. She knew from firsthand experience that all her crap wasn't exactly light. But seeing him act as if the combined weight of their backpacks was nothing made her realize exactly how strong the man was.

"I bet I can walk," she offered. "I mean, if you helped me. If you put your arm around me, I could use you as a crutch. Or a cane. Whatever."

Rocky stared down at her as if trying to read her mind. Then he crouched—and it was everything Bristol could do not to look between his legs.

Yes, she was hurt, and kind of high on whatever painkillers she'd taken, but she was still a hetero woman. And he was extremely good-looking. And okay, she knew herself—she was attracted to him. She'd always loved big tall men. She wanted to see if he was big all over, but she refrained from looking. Barely.

"You're not walking. Or hopping. I've got this, Punky. I'm not going to drop you. I can get us both to my car."

"Then what?" she blurted, wishing she could take the question back the moment it was out. "Never mind. It doesn't matter," she said quickly. "I appreciate you being here and helping me."

"Then I'll take you to Fallport and Doc Snow. He's the resident doctor in town. I'll have him look you over and see what his professional opinion is about that leg. He's got an x-ray, but I'm guessing with that fall you took, and with your concussion, he's going to want you to be checked out by a level one or two trauma center. Especially if you need surgery. If that's the case, depending on your pain level, we'll either drive you to Roanoke or call LifeFlight. But to start, we'll concentrate on getting you back to Fallport and, after hearing what the doctor thinks, go from there."

"We'll?" Bristol frowned.

Rocky didn't respond right away, just stared at her. But after a long pause, he nodded. "Yeah. If you think I'm going to put you on a chopper, or drop you at the hospital and walk away...that ain't happening."

She wanted to ask why. But she was so relieved, so grateful—doctors really weren't her thing—all Bristol could do was nod.

"You okay with that?" he asked.

"Yes," she said simply.

"Good." He smiled slightly. "Because there's something about you, Bristol Wingham, that's already got me hooked."

His words made goose bumps break out pretty much everywhere. "Me too," she said softly.

Another smile formed on his face. "Now, this is gonna suck. I'm sorry, but there's no other way to say it. Your only job is to hang on to me, understand? I'm not going to drop you. Not going to let you fall. I'm gonna lean over and pick you up. One arm under your knees and the other at your back. We'll take lots of breaks, because your legs will eventually go numb from my arm under your knees. I've got more pain pills, and we'll keep you topped off, but that doesn't mean you aren't going to be sore and uncomfortable. Okay?"

"Okay," she breathed, even though she wasn't at all sure about this. But Rocky carrying her was a hell of a lot better than her crawling through the forest. Remembering the kind of pain she'd already endured as she'd done just that was enough for her to straighten her spine and tell herself to suck it up.

"That'a girl," Rocky said softly. "Here we go."

Bristol tensed as he leaned over her, but she put an arm around his neck and held her breath as he stood with her in his arms. He didn't grunt with the effort it must have taken to dead lift her. He made it seem easy.

But the pain that shot up her leg made *Bristol* inhale sharply.

"Breathe through it, Punky," Rocky said quietly, standing still. "I know it hurts, but you can do it."

She did her best not to throw up all over the man who held her and eventually the pain lessened a bit. It felt good not to be sitting on her ass on the hard ground anymore. She opened her eyes and turned her head slightly to look at him. Their faces were close. Extremely close now. But Bristol wasn't scared. Not of him. "I'm okay."

"You sure?" he asked.

Bristol nodded. "Let's do this."

A look of respect and admiration crept over Rocky's features as he nodded and started walking.

CHAPTER THREE

Rocky was trying to walk as lightly as possible, but he knew he was hurting the woman in his arms with every step. It wasn't easy to hike through the forest without hitting her feet on any bushes or tree limbs along their way. And with every brush of a limb against her legs, she winced and sucked in a breath.

But he'd never been as impressed with someone as he was Bristol. She didn't cry. Didn't yell out in pain. Hell, a part of him wished she would, if only to release some of her stress. When they finally reached the trail, he sighed in relief. He kept his eyes open for a place to take a short break and when he saw a flat rock alongside the trail, he knew he'd found it.

"You ready for a break?" he asked.

They hadn't talked much as he carried her up and around the outcropping of rocks she'd fallen off. She wasn't very heavy, all things considered, but with the combined weight of their packs on his back, trying to be careful about where he stepped, and not hurting her as he trekked through the woods, he could use a ten-minute break himself. And Bristol had to be hurting pretty badly by now.

"Yes," she said without prevaricating.

He liked that about her. Liked that she wasn't afraid to admit she needed to stop.

"All right. There's a rock here. I'm going to lean over and put your butt down on it. Do *not* try to move your legs yourself. Catch your balance with your hands, then I'll lower your legs straight out. Got it?"

She nodded.

Rocky had bandaged her hands, but they too were probably still sore. A sour feeling swirled in his belly. He didn't like the thought of her hurting at all. But like she'd said earlier, everything was painful at the moment. She'd been very lucky, all things considered, that all she had was a possible broken leg and various scrapes and bruises. She most likely had a concussion, if her symptoms she'd told him about were anything to go by, but now that three days had passed, she was over the worst of that.

"Okay, here we go. Deep breath." When she inhaled deeply, Rocky did just as he'd described, placing her ass on the rock and waiting until she had her balance. Then he carefully lowered her legs, resting her heels on the dirt in front of her.

Bristol's face was white and her teeth were biting into her lower lip, but she didn't cry out in pain. Just did as he asked and let him move her where he thought she'd be most comfortable.

"On a scale of one to ten, with ten being the worst pain you've ever felt in your life, where do you stand?" he asked.

"Five," she said between clenched teeth.

Rocky blinked in surprise. "Seriously?" he blurted. He would've thought she'd say at least an eight.

"Yes."

"When have you been a ten?" he couldn't help but ask.

Her eyes opened, and he realized the painkillers he'd given her were definitely doing their job. He should've thought about that.

"There's pain, then there's *pain*," she said with a sigh. "The most pain I've felt was the day my dad died from colon cancer. I was completely helpless to do anything for him.

"My parents did an amazing job raising me. Never complained when it was obvious I was more into the arts than something more *useful*, like math or science. They encouraged me to take as many art classes as I could fit into my schedule. Then when I majored in art in college, they still didn't say one damn thing to discourage me. And believe me, plenty of other people told me I'd never make a living as an artist. Said I needed a fallback plan. But all I've ever wanted to do was create pretty things. My mom was my first paying customer when I opened my online store. She even used a fake name, so I wouldn't know it was her. She only told me years later." She smiled fondly at the memory.

"Anyway, when Daddy told me he had cancer...I wanted so badly to fix it. Use some of the money I'd made to get him the best doctor in the world. I've never felt the kind of pain I did at that moment, knowing my big strong father was dying. He tried the chemo and radiation and stuff, but it didn't work. All I could do was hold his hand as he took his last breath. Nothing physical can ever compare."

Rocky felt awful. He hadn't meant to bring up such a painful memory. "I'm sorry."

"Thanks," she said without hesitation. "The seventh anniversary of his death is coming up, and it still hurts just as badly as it did when he passed. But...life goes on, you know? You can't go back and change things, no matter how much you wish you could."

"I know."

Bristol looked him in the eye then, and he felt as if she could somehow read his mind. But instead of asking any questions, she just nodded.

"My dad died when I was young," Rocky said, feeling a compulsion to share. "I didn't know him all that well, not like you knew yours. My mom raised me, my brother and our sister. She's awesome. I couldn't imagine losing her like you lost your dad."

"You have a brother?" she asked. "And a sister?"

Rocky eased the pack off his back and lay down right in the middle of the trail. He stretched his back and enjoyed being off his feet for a moment. Bristol wasn't exactly heavy, but carrying someone while hiking through the woods wasn't something he normally did, and his muscles were already telling him he was going to pay for the exertion over the next few days.

Looking up at the treetops, he nodded. "Yup. And my brother, Ethan, lives in Fallport too. We're twins."

"Twins? Lord save us all if there are two of you walking around!" Bristol exclaimed.

Rocky chuckled. "Unfortunately, he's the good-looking one. We're fraternal twins, so we don't exactly look alike."

"You're kidding, right?"

Rocky frowned and turned his head to look at her. "About the fact we're twins? No."

She shook her head. "No, about you thinking you're not good-looking."

Electricity seemed to arc between them. Rocky wasn't oblivious to the looks he got from women when he was out and about, but for the most part, he ignored them. And those looks had lessened somewhat since he'd grown his beard. Women were much more drawn to Ethan and his clean-cut ruggedness, than

Rocky's scruffy lumberjack look. But he wasn't looking for love. He was content to do his contracting work and live in his somewhat crappy apartment.

But Bristol's admission that she liked his looks made him realize just how attracted he was to *her*. She had some Asian ancestry for sure, which was definitely appealing. Even with her mussed and dirty hair, the sweat on her face, and the dirt covering practically every inch of her body, she was pretty.

"Seriously, Rocky. Yeah, you've got the Bigfoot thing going on, but you make it look good. Really good," she told him. A hint of color bloomed in her cheeks as she spoke, but she didn't look away from him.

"Never thought about it much. As long as my body does what it needs to do when I ask it to do it, I'm good," he told her honestly.

"Like carry damsels in distress?" she asked.

He smiled at her and sat up, propping himself up with his hands behind him. "Yup. Although I'm not sure I'd call you a damsel in distress. You did a hell of a good job of taking care of yourself in the three days before I found you."

She snorted. "Well, there's a difference between three days and actually getting myself back to the trail."

"You would've made it," Rocky said, believing the words wholeheartedly.

She shrugged. "What do you do when you're not in the woods rescuing injured hikers?" she asked.

Recognizing the change of subject, Rocky didn't object. If she didn't want to talk about how he thought she was pretty damn tough, he'd let it go. "I'm basically a general contractor. I work on old houses, build decks, put in new floors, that kind of thing."

She nodded. "Your comment a moment ago about your body

doing what you want it to do makes more sense now. No wonder you're so in shape."

"My old team leader in the Navy would kick my butt if I gained weight and went soft," he told her.

"How long were you in?" she asked.

Rocky liked this. Getting to know each other. He also liked that he had her full attention. She wasn't fiddling with a phone. Wasn't attempting to figure out a way to get out of the conversation, or only talking about herself. She was looking him in the eye, seemingly curious for more information about him. He was just as interested to know more about her too.

"Seemed like a lifetime," he finally told her. "But I enjoyed being a SEAL, for the most part. Wouldn't have enjoyed it as much if it wasn't for Ethan being right there with me. We weren't on the same team, but we frequently worked the same missions together. The special forces world is small, so at one time or another, we worked with most of the US SEAL teams... and a lot of the Delta Force teams, as well."

Bristol laughed.

"What's funny?" Rocky asked. He loved watching her laugh. She did so wholeheartedly and without reservation.

"I was thinking earlier that with my luck, you were a SEAL and knew a hundred ways to kill someone and not leave a trace. It kind of freaked me out for a second, but I told myself I was being silly."

Rocky's grin faded. "I'm not going to hurt you."

"I know."

"Do you?" he couldn't help but ask. "I'm a big man. You're right, I *do* know several ways to kill without any kind of weapon. I was a damn good SEAL and the government taught me well."

"Are you trying to scare me?" she asked quietly.

Rocky thought about it for a second, then shrugged. "Maybe."

"Why?"

"Because you scare the *hell* out of me."

She looked shocked. "Me? Come on. I'm as harmless as a puppy. Besides, as you said, you're a big man. The second I tried anything, you'd thump me into the ground."

"Never," Rocky told her fervently.

"Then why do I scare you?" she asked.

Rocky decided honesty was his best bet. "Because there's something about you that's different from anyone else I've ever met. I have no idea what it is, or why, but now I understand why Sandra got attached to you so quickly. The thought of you being in pain or hurt makes me kind of crazy. I want to fix it. Want to kick the shit out of Mike and his dopey friends for leaving you without a second thought."

They stared at each other for a long moment, and Rocky knew this was insane. They'd just met. But he couldn't lie. There was just something about her.

"I'm not sure what to say about that."

"You don't have to say anything," Rocky replied. "I didn't tell you to make you uncomfortable. I just want to reassure you that I'd no sooner do something to hurt you than I would my brother. How do your legs feel?"

"Besides the right one being broken? Not bad," she quipped.

There. That. She had every reason to bitch and moan about the pain she was in, but instead she downplayed it and made a joke. It was something *he* might do, or his close friends. Maybe that was why he felt so comfortable with her.

"Any tingling in your feet? Carrying you with my arm under your knees can cut off the circulation if we aren't careful."

"I'm good. How are *you*? It can't be easy carrying me, even if I'm not that tall."

"I'm all right. But yeah, this would be easier if I had my team with me, of course. You ready to go?"

She nodded. "Will you tell me about your team?"

"Sure." Rocky stood, arched his back, then leaned over and touched his toes. He twisted to the right, then to the left, before heading over to where he'd dumped the backpack. He shrugged it back on before returning to Bristol. "Okay, same routine as last time. I'll pick you up, wrap your arm around my neck, and don't move your legs at all. Let me do all the work."

"Okay. I'm ready."

Rocky picked her up as if she was made of glass, and having her in his arms again felt...right. Which was irrational.

Best to concentrate on the here and now. She was hurt, and the slightest move could possibly lead to pain for the rest of her life if he knocked her leg the wrong way. The absolute trust she offered made him even more determined not to do anything to cause her discomfort.

He could move faster now that they were on the trail. He still had a ways to go to get back to the trailhead, where he'd have cell phone reception. His first call was going to be to Raiden, even if his friend would give him hell for fucking up so badly by going out on a search alone...despite Rocky thinking there likely wasn't anything to search for. Then he'd call Doc Snow and make sure he was available to meet him and Bristol at the clinic in town.

"Rocky?" Bristol asked. "What are you thinking about so hard?"

"Getting you help when we get off the trail," he told her. "But you wanted to hear about my team, right?"

"Yes, please."

Rocky had no problem talking about his friends. "Well, you know about my brother. Ethan's the de facto leader of the Eagle Point Search and Rescue team. He pretty much had the idea to get us started, and he recruited me and the others. Best decision I ever made was to come to Fallport. Not only do I get to keep working with my brother, but he managed to put together a team of like-minded men."

"How old are you and your twin?"

"Thirty-five. Why? How old are you? Oh, shit—I'm not supposed to ask that, am I? Never mind, forget I asked," he told her.

Bristol giggled, and Rocky felt the laughter vibrate through him, since he was holding her against his chest.

"I don't mind. I'm not ashamed of my age. I'm thirty-seven. Although some days it feels as if I'm old as dirt, and other days I swear it was just yesterday I was graduating from high school."

"I know the feeling. Anyway, Ethan met an amazing woman, Lilly, earlier this year. They're engaged and planning on a Halloween wedding."

"How'd they meet?" Bristol asked. "Please tell me it wasn't because she was lost in the woods and he found her."

It was Rocky's turn to chuckle. "Not quite. She was a videographer in town to film that Bigfoot show."

"No way!" Bristol exclaimed. "Are you serious?"

"Yup. Long story short, Ethan and her spent a bunch of time together, and she ended up staying in Fallport."

"Wow. That's crazy. I mean, that's pretty much why I'm in town too. Mike heard about the show and thought it would be fun to come up here and hunt for Bigfoot. He said it would be better to do it now, before the show aired, and everyone and their brother descended on the town."

"He's not wrong, even if he *is* still a douchebag for what he did to you."

Bristol chuckled again. "We're in agreement on that."

"Anyway, next there's Zeke. He used to be a Green Beret in the Army, and now he owns the bar in town, On the Rocks. He's with Elsie. She was a single mother who works as a server in the bar. They'd known each other a while, but things heated up between them and they just married recently. He took Elsie and her son, Tony, out to Eagle Point Tower, and most of the guys on the SAR team went with them, which is why they aren't here now.

"Drew used to be a Virginia State Police officer, and is now an accountant. He does all our taxes, and I swear the man's a genius with how much money he's saved us all."

"I wish I had a good accountant. I've gone through several through the years, and it seems as if all they're interested in is *taking* money rather than actually helping me save on my taxes," she said with a sigh.

"I'm sure he wouldn't mind sitting down and talking with you about your business and stuff. He'd give you some great tips, if nothing else."

"That'd be awesome. I might just see if we can do that, thank you," Bristol said.

"Then there's Brock, who used to work at US Customs and Border Patrol, and now he works at the local car place. There's nothing the man doesn't know about engines and everything to do with cars. Talon's from the UK, and he was in the Special Boat Service—that's a special forces branch in England. He's the pretty boy out of all of us. Probably because he's a barber. He's always immaculate, so if you ever want to give him shit, tell him how messy his hair looks or that it's too long."

Bristol smiled. "Um, since I don't know him, I don't think I'll do that."

"Hopefully you'll get to know him. He's kind of a clown too... but that can switch on a dime. I've seen him laughing one second, then ready to kick ass and take names the next."

"Then I'll definitely not be pissing him off anytime soon," Bristol told him.

"The last guy on the team is Raiden. He's tall, I told you that. He didn't have an easy time growing up. He was gangly, has kinda funny-looking ears—his words—and a pointed nose. He got made fun of a lot. He's told us more than once that his only friends when he was little were his dogs. Not surprisingly, when he went into the Coast Guard, he became a dog handler. A damn good one. He's like a dog whisperer or something. He's got a search dog, a bloodhound named Duke. Who's *amazing*. Many hounds are hard to handle because of their food drive and their stubbornness, but Duke does everything Raiden says almost before he says it."

"Ooooh, I love bloodhounds!" Bristol exclaimed. "Except for the drool. That's kind of gross."

Rocky laughed. "Yup. It is. But Duke is an incredible tracking dog. He probably would've found you in half the time it took me."

"You really sound like you respect and like all of your friends."

"I do. And more than that, I trust them with my life. If we're out here on a job, there's no one I'd rather have at my back."

"Are you going to get in trouble for coming out here by yourself?" Bristol asked, her brow wrinkling in concern.

"No. That's not how we work. There's no hierarchy with the team. Ethan's our leader, but that's just because he's willing to do things like meet with the city council and mayor when we have to discuss the budget, and he'll talk to the press if necessary. But otherwise, we're all a bunch of guys who get to serve our city and help our friends and neighbors—and tourists, when necessary— when they need it. But that's not to say they aren't going to give me shit for coming out on my own without telling anyone where I was going. I know better than to do something so boneheaded."

"Just like I knew better than to hike by myself," Bristol said quietly.

"Exactly. Raiden is the only one in town right now, and I should've called him before I headed out. Even if I wasn't sure that Sandra's concern was necessary. I definitely learned my lesson. I just hope it wasn't at your expense."

"My expense? Rocky, you *found* me."

"And we probably could've already been back at the trail-head by now if Raid was with me. I could've sent him back to call for help while I stayed with you. You wouldn't have to be going through the pain you are right now if I wasn't by myself."

"Whatever," Bristol said a little heatedly. "You need to stop beating yourself up. If we armchair quarterbacked every decision we ever made, we'd never be able to get up in the mornings. Could you have done things differently? Yes. But then again, I could've too. And you could've decided to ignore Sandra, convinced her that I was fine, and then *no one* would've found me. So get over yourself."

Rocky couldn't help but laugh. "Right, sorry."

She wasn't wrong. While he'd fucked up by coming out by himself, he *had* come.

He walked another thirty minutes before insisting on another break. This time when he put her down, she couldn't hold back the wince. Rocky got another pain pill out for her. As much as he wanted to insist she eat something, if surgery was in her near future, it wouldn't be a good idea.

So they chatted some more, and when it was time, he very carefully picked her up once again. The more time he spent holding her, the more right it felt to Rocky. She was so slight, but she still seemed to fit him perfectly, which was kind of odd, considering the difference in their heights.

By the time they reached the trailhead, they were both tired, sweaty, and hurting. It was late afternoon and he'd walked over twelve miles, half of those carrying more than twice the weight he set off with that morning. Rocky ignored his aches and pains because he knew they were nothing compared to what Bristol was feeling. She still denied she was in any more pain than a five on a scale of one to ten, but as the day wore on, Rocky had a feeling she was lying through her teeth.

He got her settled in the passenger side of his dark blue Chevy Tahoe and pulled out his cell phone. The first person he called was Robert Snow, Fallport's resident doctor. The man agreed to meet him at the clinic on the square as soon as he could get there.

Not wanting to waste any time, Rocky started his car and headed toward town. He dialed Raiden's number as he drove.

"Hey, Rocky, what's up?" Raid said when he answered.

"First, I fucked up, I *know* I fucked up, and I'd appreciate you saving the lecture for another time," Rocky told him. He was using the hands-free Bluetooth feature of the phone and gave Bristol a small shrug as he waited to hear his friend's response.

"Right. What do you need from me?"

That was why Rocky had such respect for his friends. For Raiden. He quickly went through what Sandra had said that morning and how he'd hiked out on the Falling Water Trail and found Bristol. "We're on our way to Doc Snow's right now, but we might need to go to Roanoke depending on what the x-rays say."

"All right. Again, what do you need from me?" Raid asked.

"Will you swing by Sunny Side Up and talk to Sandra? Tell her that I found Bristol and she's okay. It might be a few days before she can come see her, depending on if we have to go to Roanoke or not, but I want to make sure she knows that Bristol's safe."

"Consider it done. What else? Want me to come sit with her while you go home and shower or grab something to eat?"

"I don't need a babysitter," Bristol protested.

Rocky ignored her protest. "That'd be awesome, thank you. I'm kind of rank after everything. I'm sure Doc Snow and the staff in Roanoke would appreciate me not smelling like a dirty shoe."

"Right. I'll talk to Khloe then be on my way over to Doc's. You need me to bring anything?"

"Nope. Thanks, Raid. I appreciate it."

"Whatever, asshole. As if I'd say no. Even if you *did* fuck up by not calling me. Later."

Rocky winced as he clicked off the phone. Raid was an introvert. The fact that he hadn't hesitated to call Rocky out at the end went a long way toward letting him know how pissed his friend *really* was.

"He sounds...nice."

"That's because he is," Rocky said.

"Who's Khloe?"

"His employee."

"Where does he work?"

"Oh, I didn't tell you earlier? He's the head librarian at the Fallport Public Library."

47

"Seriously?"

"Yup. Why?"

"I don't know. I've got a picture of what he looks like in my head, and librarian is the last job that comes to mind for a former Coastie who has a bloodhound and is six-freaking-eight."

Rocky couldn't help but chuckle. "One thing about the Eagle Point Search and Rescue team...we definitely don't fit most stereotypes."

Bristol reached over and put her hand on his arm, and Rocky swore his entire body tingled from her touch. "Thank you for having him go talk to Sandra. That was very thoughtful of you."

"You made an impression on her. She's worried. It would be cruel to keep her hanging, now that you're safe."

"I agree. Which is why I'm thanking you."

"You need to *stop* thanking me," Rocky told her.

"Why?" she asked, pulling her hand back and putting it in her lap.

Her black hair was in disarray on her head—she'd put it up in a messy bun during one of their breaks, but tendrils had escaped their confines and were hanging around her face. She wore absolutely no makeup, her face was streaked with dirt, she smelled like anyone would after being out in the elements for days, and was definitely in need of a shower and clean clothes. And yet, Rocky couldn't seem to take his eyes off her.

He was beginning to understand his brother's hard and fast fall for Lilly a little better now.

"Because I don't want to spend the next however long we're together saying 'you're welcome' over and over."

"But you're going out of your way to help me," she protested.

"And you aren't used to that?" he asked, genuinely curious.

"I...No. I guess I'm like your friend Raid. I'm an introvert. I spend a lot of time by myself at home, working on my projects."

"Well, I guess you need to get used to it. Because I'm not going anywhere. I'm in this for the long haul."

"This?"

Rocky shrugged, slowing as he neared the town square. "Making sure you're really all right."

"Do you do this for everyone you rescue?"

Rocky parallel parked into a space right in front of the doctor's office on the square, then cut the engine. He turned to look Bristol in the eyes. "No. Once we find someone who's lost, our job's done. We hand them off to the police or the paramedics."

"Then why are you doing it now?" she asked.

"Because something's telling me that if I let you go, it'll be the biggest regret of my life."

With that, Rocky climbed out of the SUV and walked around to the other side. He'd probably said too much, and he knew it sounded ridiculous, but there it was. He wasn't going to shy away from the connection he felt with this woman.

Not until she made it clear she didn't want anything to do with a small-town handyman slash former military grunt slash outdoorsy guy.

CHAPTER FOUR

Bristol wasn't sure what to think about Rocky.

No, that was a lie.

She liked him. A lot. Too much. It was crazy how much she respected the man after only knowing him for hours. But in that time, he'd gone out of his way to reassure her, treat her wounds, not jostle her more than necessary, and generally treat her as if she was the most precious piece of glass he just happened to find in the middle of the woods.

Everything she'd learned about him so far, she liked.

He'd carried her into the clinic in the adorable downtown area of Fallport and the doctor had been sympathetic and concerned about what she'd gone through. He'd also been very impressed, and not afraid to say so. He'd x-rayed her leg and said that her fibula was definitely broken, declaring she was lucky it had been the small bone in her shin that she'd fractured, and not the tibia.

But since it was broken, and not just cracked, he believed the bone needed a pin to be sure it healed properly. Which meant going to Roanoke and seeing a doctor there. Doc Snow had reassured her that he'd talk to one of his colleagues at the larger hospital, and they'd be ready for her when she arrived.

While she'd been waiting for Rocky to come back—he'd left to shower and change clothes, before heading to Roanoke—Bristol met his friend Raid, who'd sat with her. Rocky was right, Raid was unusual looking, and not just because he towered over her. He had a particularly bright shade of red hair, and his ears did stick out a bit. She couldn't help but chuckle when she saw that he was also sporting a beard.

"What's funny?" Rocky had asked before leaving.

Bristol had shrugged and asked, "Do all of you have beards?"

He smiled, nodded—then shocked the shit out of her by leaning down and kissing her forehead gently. As she stared up at him with wide eyes at the intimate, but not unwelcome gesture, he'd said, "Mine's the most impressive though," before winking and heading out of the room.

"Interesting," Raid said once Rocky had left.

"What?"

"You two seemed to have gotten pretty chummy out there in the woods."

Some people might have taken his words the wrong way, but because he had a small smile on his face, Bristol couldn't get upset. She shrugged and said simply, "Yeah."

Raid's green gaze met hers, and he stared at her for a long moment before saying, "Rocky's a good man. One of the best. I'd literally give my life for his. I'm thinking after seeing his brother and Zeke fall so fast for amazing women, he's wanting the same for himself. I sure don't know what the future holds, but I'm begging you...if you don't think you can see yourself moving to Fallport and settling down with Rocky, please don't lead him on."

Again, Bristol could get upset that Raiden was assuming so

much, but since it was obvious he cared about his friend, she didn't take offense. "I have no idea what's going to happen in the future either. It seems to me that it's a bit early to be thinking about moving, or even about having a relationship with Rocky. But, for the record...I work from home, and thus can live anywhere.

"I've never screwed over any of my former boyfriends, and I wouldn't start now. If—and that's a big if—Rocky and I decide we want to see where our chemistry takes us, I'm not going to lead him on. I promise you, Raid. I've got a job I love, a wonderful parent, plenty of money in my bank accounts, and I value my independence. I'm not a mooch, I'm not desperate for a child, and if I just happen to end up single for the rest of my life, that'll be fine too."

Raiden smiled, and Bristol's breath hitched. The smile changed his entire countenance. He went from tall, dark, and grumpy, to handsome and charming in a heartbeat.

He chuckled and said under his breath, "Rocky's a goner."

Bristol opened her mouth to ask what he meant, exactly, but a woman marched into the room as if she had every right to be there, despite not being dressed like a typical nurse or doctor.

"Hi, my name's Khloe. I wanted to make sure you were all right. Does your leg hurt? What can we do to make you feel better? Where's Rocky? I think you need to get going; it's already been too long since you were injured. The sooner you get to the hospital and get into surgery, the better it'll heal. Raid, can you call Rocky and see how much longer he's going to be?"

Bristol could only stare at the woman, confused. She seemed overly concerned about her, a perfect stranger, than was normal. She was petite, like Bristol, but she still had maybe half a foot over Bristol's four-eleven height. Her and Raid's heads were practically even, although he was sitting and she was standing. She had light brown hair, hazel eyes, and Bristol hadn't missed the limp in her stride as she'd entered the room. She was pleasantly plump, filling out the jeans she was wearing as if they were painted on.

When Raid stared at the woman without moving, she said, "Fine, *I'll* call him." She pulled a phone from her back pocket.

Raid reached out and grabbed the phone from her hand. "He's going to be back momentarily. No need to stress him out by calling."

Khloe frowned and stepped toward the bed where Bristol was lying, turning her back on the tall man sitting next to her. "Are you all right? Are you in a lot of pain? Did Doc Snow give you some painkillers? I can go find him and tell him you need more if you're hurting."

"I'm okay. Thank you, though," Bristol said. And she was. Her leg throbbed, as did her palms where the doctor had cleaned them again, but she was still feeling kind of floaty from the pills Rocky had given her.

But her words didn't seem to have any effect on Khloe's concern. "I know you can't eat anything, but I can get you some more water if you need it."

Wanting to calm the clearly concerned woman, Bristol reached out a hand and touched her arm. "I'm really okay."

"Khloe?" Raiden asked behind her. Bristol could see a frown on his face. "What's wrong?"

Bristol watched as the other woman took a deep breath. She closed her eyes for a moment, then turned. "Nothing's wrong. I'm good. I...I just wanted to make sure Bristol was okay. Broken bones hurt, and you and Rocky are super soldiers who probably don't feel pain, even when you break bones. So I just wanted to check on her. Now that I have, I'll be going. Don't worry, I finished up the inventory before I left, and I'll work on labeling the books and getting them on the shelves tomorrow."

She stepped toward the door, but Raid stood and grabbed her arm. He held her gently but firmly. "I don't give a shit about the books. At the moment, I'm more worried about *you*."

"I'm fine," Khloe said quickly. Maybe too quickly.

"Something's up," Raid countered quietly.

"Nothing's up," she insisted stubbornly. "I'm good. Bristol's good. Rocky's on his way back to take her to Roanoke, so I'll be leaving."

"I'll take you home," Raid said firmly.

The look of panic on Khloe's face was obvious—and confusing. "No, you won't. You can't leave Bristol. Rocky would kick your ass if he got back and she was alone." Then she turned to the bed. "I'm glad you're all right."

"Thanks for coming to check on me," Bristol said, still thoroughly baffled.

Khloe nodded. "I'm sure Lilly and Elsie both would've been here if they were in town. They're super nice like that." Then she tugged on her arm, and while Raid continued to frown, he let go of her. She snatched her phone from his hand then strode with her uneven gait toward the door.

Raiden stood staring out the door for a long moment after she was gone, and Bristol wasn't sure what to say or do, so she stayed quiet. It was more than obvious there was some kind of tension between Raiden and his pretty co-worker, though she wasn't sure what kind. But it was none of her business, and she'd be leaving Fallport shortly anyway.

At that moment, Rocky returned. "Everything all right? I saw Khloe leaving," he said.

"She came to make sure I was okay," Bristol said after a moment, when Raid didn't respond.

"That was nice of her."

"It was," Bristol agreed.

"Since you're back, I'm going to head out. Left Duke in the library, and I need to make sure he's all right."

"I'm sure he's fine," Rocky said. "You've left him there with the other librarians plenty of times."

Raid shrugged. "Hope everything goes well in Roanoke," he told Bristol, before giving Rocky a chin lift and walking out the door.

"What was that about?" Rocky asked in confusion.

But Bristol had already forgotten about everything but the man in front of her. She'd been up close and personal with him for most of the day, but seeing him in jeans, a fresh T-shirt, and even smelling his clean scent from where he was standing a few feet away had her tongue tied. It made her own condition all the more obvious. She'd kill for a shower right about now, but knew that was impossible. She hated feeling and looking so grubby next to Rocky.

"What's wrong?" he asked, misunderstanding her silence. "Are you in pain? Doc's still here, I'll go get him. He might want to put an IV in before we head out and—"

"No!" Bristol exclaimed, interrupting him. "I'm fine."

"You aren't fine," Rocky insisted. "Something's wrong."

Hating that he was so observant, but not surprised—he *had* been a SEAL after all, and from everything she knew about the elite unit, they were extremely aware of their surroundings at all times—she gave him a sheepish look. "I just...seeing you all fresh and clean made me realize how *not* fresh and clean I am."

Rocky's face gentled and he pulled the chair Raid had been

sitting in closer to the bed. Reaching out a hand, he palmed the side of her face. His large hand was warm and she loved the feel of it against her skin. "I'm sorry."

"About what?" She whispered the words, for some reason.

"I should've thought about how taking a shower would make you feel. I've been in your shoes plenty of times, and it sucks. We'd come in from a mission and stink to high heaven, then have to meet with a few muckety-mucks. They'd be in their pressed and starched uniforms, doing all they could not to wrinkle their noses at the smell of body odor filling the room." He smiled at her, then sobered. "It doesn't bother me," he told her.

Bristol rolled her eyes. "Right, because it's so pleasant."

"You're alive. You smell like *life*," Rocky said bluntly.

She could only stare at him. He was right. The dried sweat on her skin and the dirt caked into her clothes was a direct result of her fighting for her own survival.

"You two should get going," a deep voice said from the doorway.

Bristol jerked in surprise, but Rocky didn't seem fazed by the doctor's appearance. She realized he probably wasn't. He'd most likely heard him coming. Again, that special forces training of his coming in handy.

Without removing his hand, Rocky turned to look at the doctor. "They're expecting us?"

"Yup. They'll be ready to take her back right away when you get there. Doctor Madden is one of the best surgeons in the area. He'll get her fixed right up. The break isn't awful, she was lucky, and he said after seeing the x-rays I emailed over, he thinks she'll only need one pin."

"Thanks," Rocky said, standing.

The loss of his hand on her cheek made Bristol want to cry. Which was ridiculous.

"You ready to go?" he asked, once he was standing by her bedside.

Bristol nodded.

"Doc, you'll get the door for us?" Rocky asked.

"Of course. Be careful," the older man warned as Rocky leaned over her.

As they'd done many times that day, Bristol put an arm around his neck as he gently lifted her from the bed. Grateful she hadn't been put into a horrible hospital gown, Bristol held on as Rocky carried her through the clinic and back out to his car.

Before she knew it, they were on their way, heading down I-480 toward the interstate that headed north to Roanoke. The drive would take two hours and, if she was being honest, Bristol was a little scared about the upcoming surgery.

"I forgot to ask Raiden if he talked to Sandra," Bristol said after a few minutes of silence had passed.

"He did," Rocky said. "I'd just gotten out of the shower when she called me to confirm that you were all right. Then she proceeded to tell me 'I told you so.'"

Bristol smiled. "Well, as far as I'm concerned, she can have a crown that says 'Queen of I Told You So.'"

Rocky chuckled. "Right, I'll have that made up as soon as I can."

Bristol felt her throat getting tight, and she did her best to swallow the overwhelming emotion. "Thank you."

"Although if you give her a crown, it'll go to her head. And she'll probably give Silas, Otto, and Art a run for their money as far as being the kings of gossips around here," Rocky added.

He glanced over at her when he was done speaking, and his

face gentled. "Bristol," he said softly, upon seeing how hard she was trying not to lose it.

Bristol turned away and buried her face in one of her hands as she lost her battle to stay strong.

"Shhhh, you're okay," Rocky soothed. One of his large hands rubbed her back as she silently sobbed.

Bristol had no idea how long she'd been crying when she finally swallowed hard and tried to compose herself. She realized that Rocky hadn't stopped murmuring to her the entire time. He was telling her how brave and strong she was. That the surgery was going to be a piece of cake and he wasn't going to leave until she was discharged.

At that, she turned to look at him. "What?"

He seemed surprised she was speaking again. "What, *what?*" he asked.

"You can't stay in Roanoke while I'm in the hospital," she said.

"Why not?" he asked with a small tilt of his head. His hand moved to her lower thigh. He didn't squeeze, didn't move his fingers to inappropriate territory. It was just a heavy reminder that she wasn't alone. Which Bristol needed after everything that she'd been through.

"Because," she said. "You have a life. A job. Two jobs, actually. And we don't know how long I'm going to be there. And you don't have an overnight bag."

"Actually I do," he said calmly. "Packed one when I went home. And I work for myself. My clients will understand when I call to tell them why I need to reschedule. Ethan and the rest of the guys should be home from their camping trip tomorrow. And it doesn't matter how long you're going to be in the hospital—I'm staying."

"I...thank you. I'm still amazed that you're even driving me yourself."

"You don't have to thank me. You fascinate me, Bristol. And impress me. As I said before, you've remained positive about your entire situation. You could've been bitter, grumbling about your discomfort and badmouthing your friends who left you out there. But, other than a few comments while explaining what happened, you haven't. You made an impression on Sandra, and that's hard to do. But listen...if you don't *want* me to stay, if you're uncomfortable around me, then all you have to do is say so."

"No!" she exclaimed a little too forcefully. "It's not that. I'm just...scared."

"Of what? Me?" Rocky asked.

"I'd never be afraid of you," Bristol said honestly. "I'm just out of my comfort zone. I've never had surgery before. I've never been to Roanoke. I don't know anyone there, and I don't know what's going to happen after the surgery. I'm guessing I won't be able to walk for a while, so I also have no idea how that's going to work when I'm home. Hell, I don't even know how I'm going to *get* home. I keep to myself, I don't have a lot of friends to help me when I get back to Kingsport. I can call my mom, but she lives out in California, and as much as I love her, she'd smother me and we'd want to kill each other within a few days. I'm just...I'm overwhelmed. You've already helped me so much. I have no idea why you're going out of your way for a stranger. And...Raid warned me not to lead you on."

"Shit. He did? I'll have a talk with him," Rocky said, his voice hard.

"No, please don't. I think it's wonderful that you have such good friends who will look out for you like that."

Rocky sighed, then his hand tightened on her thigh for a

moment before he spoke. "How about we take things one day at a time? Doc Snow said he didn't think your surgery was going to be bad. He guessed you might be in the hospital a day or so, but then you'd be discharged. You're right, you probably aren't going to be able to be on that leg for a while. You could always stay in Fallport while you recuperate."

Bristol blinked at him, frowning. "Fallport?"

"Yeah. Once you feel better, I could take you to Kingsport and we could get some things for you. You said you're an artist, right? We could grab some of your materials. You can work on them in Virginia just as easily as you could in Tennessee. You said you don't have a lot of friends in Kingsport. Well, you already know lots of people in Fallport. Sandra will hover, because that's what she does. You know Khloe now, who seems especially concerned about you. I'm sure Lilly and Elsie will love to meet you and you'll hit it off just fine. Tony, Elsie's son, will also probably be happy to entertain you as well. He's always looking for someone to read to him.

"Not to mention, the rest of the guys will want to meet you, because we're always impressed by people who can hold their own in the woods. And you, Bristol, are at the top of the 'hold your own' heap. Hell, you would've rescued yourself if I hadn't come along. Whatever happens after the surgery, I'll help you figure it out and you'll be just fine."

Bristol's head swam, and not just because of the painkillers. "Where would I stay?" she wondered quietly, more to herself than anything.

Rocky's hand left her thigh and he put it back on the steering wheel. It was crazy, but she missed the comforting weight of his palm.

And if she wasn't mistaken, the man next to her looked uncomfortable for the first time.

"Well, Elsie and Zeke just moved into a house, they've got a couple extra rooms. I know they wouldn't mind you bunking with them until you can get around on your own. Whitney Crawford owns a kickass bed and breakfast. We'd have to see if she has any space between reservations, but that's an option. The apartment Elsie was staying in near mine is empty at the moment, it hasn't been re-rented, but I'm not sure you should be by yourself right off the bat. It'll be hard for you to get around on your own. Sandra would probably love to have you, as well."

He looked over at her for a long moment before turning his attention back to the road. Then he said nonchalantly, "And I've got an extra room in my apartment. It's not the best, but it's clean, and you can absolutely trust me. I'm not a half-bad cook, and if something happens, I've got plenty of first-aid experience. I'm basically a medic, but never got the official certifications after I left the Navy. You'd have your own space and the lighting is fairly good in my place when the curtains are open, so you could do your art stuff. I wouldn't be around all the time because I'd be out doing my job, but if you needed something, any of the other women—hell, anyone in Fallport—would be more than willing to check in on you and help with anything you might need when I'm not there."

Bristol had a feeling her mouth was hanging open, but she couldn't help it. Had this man just invited her to stay with him? And maybe she was hearing things, but it sounded as if he was trying to make his apartment seem like the best option, as well.

She was even more surprised to realize she wasn't opposed to the idea. The more he talked, the more ideal it seemed. Except for the fact that she'd literally just met this man. It was completely insane to think about moving in with someone she didn't know. Yes, she was hurt, and would need some help at least for a little while, but still.

"Right. Too soon," he said as if he could read her mind and her concerns. "All I'm saying is that there are plenty of people who'd be willing to help you after your surgery. You shouldn't be alone. That's just not safe. And the last thing you need to do right this second is worry. You're going to be fine. The surgery is going to go well. Don't be scared about anything, Punky. One thing at a time. All right?"

Shit. She was going to cry again. Bristol nodded and rested her head on the seat back behind her. "Thank you," she whispered again. "For everything. I seriously have no idea what I would've done if you hadn't found me."

She wasn't surprised when he shrugged off her thanks. "You would've made it, Punky. I have no doubt."

This man. She'd never met anyone like him. Generous, self-less, gorgeous, and he seemed to have absolutely no idea how appealing he was. "I've got money," she blurted.

Rocky chuckled. "Okay?"

"I mean, I've got insurance and whatever isn't covered, I can pay. And I can contribute to rent or food or whatever afterward too."

Rocky nodded. "That's good."

She wanted to laugh. Most people would want to know more. Maybe how much money she had, how she earned a living being an artist, and maybe would try to take advantage of her situation. But not Rocky.

He probably wouldn't even care about the fact she had several million dollars in investments and six figures in her bank account right this moment.

"Close your eyes, Punky," he ordered. "I know you have to be exhausted. I've got this, you're safe. You can relax."

As if his words were all her body had been waiting for, Bristol suddenly felt like her eyes were way too heavy to keep open.

Without thinking about it, she reached over with her left hand for his. The second she touched him, he turned his hand and intertwined their fingers. He rested their clasped hands on the console between them. She felt him squeeze her hand once, then she fell into a deep sleep, secure in the knowledge that she wasn't alone. That Rocky would take care of her.

CHAPTER FIVE

Rocky paced the waiting room anxiously. Bristol had been taken back to surgery an hour ago and he was waiting to hear something about how she was doing.

He mentally kicked his own ass for saying all that shit in the car. The last thing she needed was for him to pressure her to come back to Fallport. She was obviously used to being on her own and could take care of herself. But he hated to imagine her all alone after her surgery, trying to hop around to do anything. Not only would that be painful, it would be dangerous. If she fell on that leg, she could do more damage.

He'd gone on and on like an idiot, trying to sway her to stay with him. Which was crazy. They'd just met. But something deep inside him didn't care. She enthralled him with her bravery and strength. She hadn't given up in the woods. She'd done whatever she could to try to save herself. He hadn't been placating her; if Rocky hadn't found her, or if he'd ignored Sandra's misgivings, he had no doubt she would've dragged herself to the trail and all the way back to the trailhead if she had to.

Bristol Wingham was a fighter. A survivor. She was a mighty force in a tiny little body.

And he wanted her. Which was insane. Completely ridiculous. But there it was.

His phone rang as he paced, and Rocky paused to pull it out of his pocket. He saw it was his brother on the other end.

"Hey, bro," he said as he answered.

"What the fuck?" Ethan asked in response.

Rocky couldn't help but sigh. "Right, so...Sandra was worried about a tourist who said she was going camping and never returned to say goodbye when she was supposed to. I went out on my own—yes, I know that was stupid—and found her. She'd fallen off a cliff and had a broken leg. I carried her to the trailhead, brought her to Doc Snow, now we're in Roanoke and she's in surgery to have a pin put in her leg."

"Seriously—what the *fuck*?" Ethan repeated.

"I would've called you, but you were out of range," Rocky said.

"We're getting those damn satellite phones. I don't care if the city council says they don't have the budget."

Rocky sighed, not realizing how much he'd needed to hear his brother's voice, even though Ethan was obviously pissed he'd not been available for Bristol's rescue. Talking to him calmed something deep inside Rocky.

"How is she?" Ethan asked.

"In surgery. I'm waiting to hear more."

"You need us to come up there?" Ethan asked.

Rocky appreciated the offer more than his brother knew. "Right now, no. There's nothing any of us can do."

"You staying there with her?"

"Yes."

Ethan didn't even question why he was so determined to stay

by Bristol's side. "What do you need from Lilly and me?" Ethan asked.

Again, his brother was the best. "All Bristol's got is what was in her pack. Do you think you can go over to the hotel and see about getting the stuff she left there? I'm guessing the staff there would've collected it when they cleaned her room. And if Lilly can pick up some things to tide her over until we can go to Kingsport to get some of her stuff, that would be good too."

"Of course. I'm sure Elsie and Lil will both be happy to help."

"Thanks. She's tiny. Like, not even five feet tall. And slender. I have no idea what size she is though."

"Lilly'll figure it out."

"She's got long hair. I'm guessing my shampoo isn't going to cut it. So she'll need toiletries and womanly stuff too."

"No problem. What's the plan for when she's discharged? She going home?" Ethan asked.

Rocky inhaled deeply, then let out the breath in a long sigh. "I don't know. She doesn't have anyone in Kingsport, and she won't be able to get around well on her own. I told her she'd be welcome in Fallport, that she had lots of options for places to stay while she's recuperating."

There was silence on the other end of the line for a moment before Ethan asked, "She's your Lilly, isn't she?"

"I don't know. How did you know Lilly was it for you?" Rocky asked.

"I just knew," Ethan replied. "I know that isn't much of an answer, but it's not something I can explain. It was the horrible thought of her leaving after her job was over. It was her sense of humor. Her loyalty. But mostly it was just a feeling deep inside me that said if I let her go, I'd regret it."

Rocky nodded. He knew what his brother was talking about.

The thought of saying goodbye to Bristol was physically painful. "It's only been a day since I met her," he mused.

"Doesn't matter. When you know, you know. Of course, that doesn't mean things will turn out the way you want. Or that you'll fall madly in love. Or that she'll feel the same way about you. Life's a bitch sometimes, and if you think she's it for you, you might have to fight like hell to make it work. She's got a life, as do you."

"I know," Rocky said. And he did. He hadn't stopped thinking about the logistics of possibly dating Bristol. And how, after she'd had some time to think, she might realize that any feelings she had were a result of being rescued by him. The very last thing Rocky wanted was someone being with him because they were grateful for his help.

"Call me in the morning," Ethan ordered. "Let me know what's up. How long she'll be there and what you need. I'll send Lilly out in the morning to pick up some things for her and we can either bring everything up there, or we can meet you here in Fallport, wherever you've convinced her to stay. And for the record, you know she's welcome here. We've got room."

"Thanks. Your place was already one of the options I gave her."

"Anything you need, anytime you need it," Ethan said fervently.

God, Rocky loved his brother. "How was Elsie on the trail? Assuming she made it and liked the surprise Zeke had for her?" he asked, needing to talk about something other than his confusing feelings for the woman he'd just met.

"She did great. Hiking is never going to be her thing, but knowing she did it for her son...that's pretty awesome. And yeah, Zeke did an amazing job of transforming the tower. Blow-up mattress, flowers, the whole shebang. We all helped him carry everything back out so he doesn't have to return in the near future to clean up."

"Cool. And Tony? He enjoy it?"

Ethan chuckled. "Enjoy is an understatement. Zeke and Elsie showed him the paperwork to change his name to Calhoun, like theirs, and I think his shriek of excitement was heard in the next county."

Rocky smiled. "She's good people," he said softly.

"Yeah. And for the record? We're gonna have more words about you going out on your own on a search, brother."

Rocky sighed. It was wishful thinking that Ethan wouldn't give him shit about his fuckup. "I figured we would. I know I messed up, and it certainly won't happen again. But...having those sat phones would go a long way toward making us all safer. Even when we're searching at the same time, we can't all stay together. It'd be a big help if we could communicate with each other while we're out there."

"Agreed. I've been talking with the mayor about seeing if he can put pressure on the cell phone companies to get another tower out here too. It's not safe that cells don't work on 480 or in the forest. But it's apparently a political thing...and complicated. It's irritating as hell."

Rocky didn't envy his brother, and he was glad he wasn't the one who had to talk to the mayor. Jonathan Coleman was an asshole, and trying to get him to open the purse strings for any reason was just about impossible.

"I'm gonna let you go. But I expect a call in the morning. I'll reach out to the other guys and let them know what's up. Assuming you've talked to Raiden?"

"Yeah. He was the first call I made once I had cell service."

"Right. Then I'll talk to you tomorrow and see you soon. Love you, bro."

"Love you too. Send my regards to Lilly."

"Will do. Later."

Rocky hung up and resumed his pacing. He was glad to have his brother's support, as well as that of the rest of the team, but at the moment, all he could think about was Bristol. Was the surgery going okay? Was the break as minimal as Doc Snow had thought?

Just when he was working himself into a small panic, imagining all sorts of things that could've gone wrong with the surgery, the door to the small waiting room opened.

"Mr. Watson?"

"That's me."

"Your fiancée's surgery went extremely well."

Rocky didn't even feel bad about the deception. He knew the doctors wouldn't talk to him if he didn't have some sort of familial relationship with Bristol. And the fact that she didn't even blink when he'd called her his fiancée made him feel just fine about the lie. He forced his attention back to the doctor.

"It was a simple break, and I was able to use just one pin to connect the bones back together again. She's in recovery now, but shouldn't need to spend any time in ICU. She's in good shape and healthy. Would you like to see her before you head home?"

"I'm not going home until she is, and yes, I'd like to see her as soon as possible, please," Rocky said.

"All right. As soon as she's settled in a room, I'll send someone to notify you. I'll also arrange for a cot to be put in her room for you, as well."

Rocky nodded at the man, and he turned to leave.

"Doc?"

"Yes?" he asked with one hand on the door.

"Thank you."

The man shrugged. "It's my job." Then he was gone.

Rocky chuckled. He had the thought that was probably what *he* sounded like when people tried to thank him for finding them in the forest.

Relief swam through his veins. Bristol was all right. She'd heal up and be back on her feet in no time.

An hour later, a nurse poked her head into the waiting room and told him Bristol was settled. He followed her eagerly up to another floor and when they walked into the small hospital room, he only had eyes for the woman lying in the bed. Her hair was still dirty but it looked as if her skin had been cleaned a bit. She had an IV in her arm, her cheeks were pale, and he'd never been so happy to see someone.

She had stitches in her leg and a semi-rigid cast. In a week or so, the nurse explained, the stitches would be removed and she'd probably get a regular plaster cast.

He thanked the woman, who said she'd be in and out all night checking on Bristol, and he pulled a chair closer to the bed. He carefully picked up her hand and stroked it. "Hey," he said quietly.

To his surprise, Bristol's head turned his way. "Rocky?"

"Yeah, it's me."

"They didn't cut it off, did they?"

"Your leg? No! Why would you think that?"

"Can't feel it."

Rocky chuckled. "It's still there. The doctor said it was a clean break. One pin. You'll be up and dancing in no time."

"Can't dance," she mumbled. "Tired."

"Sleep, Punky."

Her hand tightened in his. "You won't leave?"

Rocky's heart leapt in his chest. "No. I'm staying in here with you tonight."

"Bed's kinda small to sleep with me."

Rocky laughed again. "You're no bigger than a bug. We'd fit. But they brought in a cot for me."

"'Kay. Rocky?"

"Yeah, baby?" he asked, the endearment just slipping out.

"If it's still okay, I wanna stay with you. You know...until I can walk."

Rocky closed his eyes. The relief he felt was almost overwhelming. "You got it, Punky. Sleep. We'll talk in the morning."

She nodded and closed her eyes. He sat next to her, holding her hand until it went slack in his own. He didn't move until the nurse came in an hour later to check her IV and the level of her painkillers, and to make sure her vitals were good.

Rocky moved to the cot and lay down. He had an overnight bag in his trunk, but didn't want to leave to retrieve it. He'd be fine sleeping in his clothes. Lord knew he'd slept in a lot worse places in his lifetime. It took him a while to nod off, but as he did, the last thing he saw was Bristol's face as she slept in the bed next to him.

* * *

It took Bristol a moment to remember where she was and what had happened when she woke up, but when she did, she opened her eyes—and the first thing she saw was Rocky, sleeping on a cot next to her bed, his feet sticking over the end of the mattress. Just knowing he'd stayed with her made butterflies kick up in her belly.

She didn't remember anything after being wheeled away for surgery the night before. Looking down, she saw her broken leg was slightly elevated under the sheet. She wasn't in any pain and figured that was because of the drugs flowing through the IV connected to her arm.

She felt surprisingly good for everything she'd been through. She wasn't a big fan of hospitals—who was?— but having Rocky by her side went a long way toward keeping her calm.

She watched him sleep for a while. Light was coming in the window, letting her know it had to be morning. His mouth was open slightly and he had one arm over his head while the other rested on his belly. He was still wearing the same clothes he'd changed into before he'd driven her to Roanoke.

Bristol still couldn't believe he'd done that. He'd definitely gone over and above what most people would've done for a complete stranger. But they'd bonded in the woods. She couldn't and *wouldn't* deny that. Something had sparked between them as he'd held her gently against his chest and made the six-mile trek back to his car. There was a lot she still didn't know about the man sleeping next to her, but what she *did* know, she liked. More than was probably smart.

A loud clang sounded from outside her room, making Bristol jump. It sounded like someone dropped a bed pan or something. The movement jostled her leg, and a small moan escaped her lips. It didn't really hurt so much as it surprised her, making her aware that she'd just had surgery on that leg the evening before.

By the time she turned her attention back to Rocky, he was sitting on the side of his cot looking adorably mussed. His hair was sticking up and, surprisingly, even his beard looked as if it could use a good brushing.

As she watched, he ran a hand down his face, as if he was doing his best to wake up, then his brown eyes lifted and met her gaze. "Morning," he said gruffly in a low, rumbly tone.

"Hi," she replied, feeling somewhat shy for some reason. Maybe it was because she was wearing nothing but a hospital gown. Maybe it was because they'd kind of slept together, even if she'd been completely out of it and in a different bed. Or maybe it was because the more time she spent around this man, the more attracted to him she became.

"How do you feel?" he asked as he stood.

Bristol's chin lifted so she could keep him in her sights. He really was tall, especially compared to her. He turned to the cot he'd slept on and began making the bed as she answered him. "I'm okay."

Rocky chuckled and turned back to her. "You'd say that even if your leg was hanging on by a tendon, wouldn't you?" he asked.

Bristol shrugged. "It seems silly to complain about anything, considering what the alternative could've been."

"Right, I get that, but at the same time, there's no need for you to be in pain or uncomfortable. If you're hurting, I'll get a nurse in here to give you something, or up the drugs being delivered through your IV."

He was very thoughtful. "Honestly, I'm all right. I don't particularly like the way I feel when I'm completely doped up. My leg throbs a bit, but nothing I can't handle. I'm okay. Promise."

Rocky nodded. "All right. Let me know if that changes." He wandered over to the chair and pulled it closer before sitting. He reached for her hand, and the contentment that swept over her when he brushed his thumb over the back of it was heady...and confusing.

"I talked to the nurse last night, and she said the doctor thinks you should be ready to be discharged tomorrow or the day after...depending on how you feel, of course. He's gonna talk to Doc Snow about getting the stitches out shortly after, and changing your cast. I'm gonna call Ethan, my brother, in a bit, maybe when the nurse comes in to get you ready for the day. He and Lilly will drive up here and bring you some clean clothes and some toiletries. I'll get Zeke to go by my apartment and see what he can do to set up the guest room for you, so you can get around more easily once you're able to be up on crutches. Anything you like to eat? I'm sure Drew or one of the other guys would be happy to go to the store to stock up for us."

Bristol stared at him in confusion. "Um...your guest room?" she asked quietly.

Rocky froze. There was no other word for it. He had been fairly relaxed a second ago, but now he was stiff as he stared at her. "What do you remember from last night?" he asked.

"Nothing. I mean, I remember everything up until the surgery. Seeing the doctor and being wheeled away. But I don't recall going into the operating room or anything afterward until waking up this morning."

Rocky sighed.

"Why? Did something happen?" she asked, suddenly nervous.

"No, nothing happened," he said soothingly. He squeezed her hand, then stood suddenly and headed for the small bathroom in the corner.

Bristol bit her lip. She thought about what Rocky had said, about her staying in his apartment and getting her clothes and food. She racked her brain, doing her best to remember if they'd had a conversation about what would happen once she got out of the hospital, but it was no use. Everything was a blank.

Rocky came out of the bathroom, the hair at his temples wet and little drops of water in his beard. He'd obviously washed his face. To wake up? Or to give him time to figure out what to say to her? Bristol wasn't sure. But she guessed it was probably a combination of both.

He sat back down on the chair next to her bed, but this time he didn't reach for her hand. A pang of disappointment hit Bristol, and she mentally scolded herself for being ridiculous. "I'm guessing we had some sort of conversation about after my release from the hospital?" she asked, not willing to beat around the bush.

Rocky nodded. "Yeah. As I told you before, you've got options." He took a breath, likely about to repeat all the choices he'd mentioned the day before, but Bristol stopped him.

"I said I'd stay with you?" she asked bluntly.

He stared at her for a moment before nodding. "But if you're not comfortable with that, it's not a big deal."

"I don't remember the conversation."

He chuckled, but it wasn't a humorous sound. "Yeah, I got that, Punky. I should've realized you were so out of it and that you wouldn't remember what we talked about."

"Is it going to put you out if I stay with you?"

"No. As I told you, I have a guest room. It's nothing fancy, and the walls in the apartment complex are kind of thin. But if you stay with me, you'll have your own room. We'll have to share a bathroom though. I do live on the second floor, so you'll need help getting up and down the stairs for a while, I'm guessing. I'll need to get back to work soon after we return, so you might get bored sitting in the apartment, but I'm sure both Lilly and Elsie will visit as much as they can. Not to mention, when Sandra hears where you are, she'll probably be a regular guest." He snorted. "Who am I kidding? Once the people of Fallport hear where you are, and that you're kind of stuck until you can walk again, you'll probably be bombarded with visitors."

Bristol tilted her head and studied him. "Why?"

"Why what?" he asked.

"Why would anyone care?"

"You aren't familiar with small towns, are you?"

Bristol shrugged. "Not really. Kingsport isn't huge, but it's bigger than Fallport. I've met my neighbors a couple of times, though I don't really *know* them. I was impressed when Sandra remembered my name after only one visit to the diner."

"Everyone knows everyone in small towns. It can be great, as in the case of Sandra knowing who you were the second time you came in, and asking me to go find you. It can also be a pain in the butt, as everyone knows everyone's business. I can't believe Zeke was able to keep it a secret from Elsie that he'd turned the Eagle Point Watch Tower into a comfortable love nest for the two of them. Hell, when I went to the post office the day everyone left for the hike, Art and his cronies asked me about it, and if I'd heard anything about how she liked it yet."

"Art?" Bristol asked.

"He's one of three men who sit outside the post office on the square every day. They love gossiping and are damn good at it. Anyway, all I'm saying is that small towns aren't like any other place. People care. Yeah, they might be nosy Nellies looking for information, but they'll still bring over a casserole while they're ferreting out your secrets." He chuckled. "So, to answer your first question about why people care...it's just how they are in Fallport. Not being conceited, but my friends and I are held in pretty high esteem, simply because of the people we've found. And if you're staying with me, they'll want to help out however they can."

Bristol nodded. She could understand that. Rocky was a like-able guy, there was no doubt. And if his friends on his search and rescue team were half as accommodating and generous as Rocky had been, she wasn't surprised that the good people of Fallport would bend over backward to help someone he was championing.

"For the record, I don't do this," he said, gesturing between them. "My role is to find people, not nurse them back to health. Not to drive them to Roanoke to the hospital." He shrugged a little self-consciously. "And if the Eagle Point SAR team *did* offer this kind of service to the people we rescue, I'd probably be the last person someone would want at their side."

Bristol frowned. But he went on before she could comment.

"I'm too...rough around the edges. My looks scare people off sometimes. Not to mention the lumberjack jokes I have to suffer through."

That bothered Bristol. "Well, those people are stupid," she said with a huff.

Rocky smiled, then sobered. "Anyway, the next couple of weeks are gonna be tough for you. The thought of you leaving and trying to do things on your own in Kingsport, and possibly getting hurt in the process, doesn't sit well with me. We get along well, I enjoy talking to you, and I can help while you're healing." He shrugged. "I'm not making my case very well."

"Actually, you are," Bristol told him. "I'm not mad at all that you already seem to have everything planned. I'm relieved, to tell you the truth. And for the record, I don't usually go around accepting offers to live with men I just met." She smiled at him shyly. "But it feels as if I've known you for months, rather than for only a day."

"Right?" he asked with a grin. "It's kind of weird."

"It's *so* weird," she agreed.

They smiled at each other, and Bristol couldn't stop the sigh of relief when he once more reached for her hand.

"So...your brother and his fiancée will be coming by this morning?" she asked.

"Most likely. I do still need to call after you see the doctor, to update them on how you're doing and how long you'll be here."

"I know you don't like to hear it, but I have to say thank you again," Bristol said. "Seriously, you being here is keeping me from freaking out. And knowing I have somewhere to go—and a way to get there, since I don't have my car—makes me feel much better."

"You're welcome to stay with me as long as it takes for you to heal, Punky," Rocky said. "There are no strings with my offer. If you get uncomfortable and want to stay somewhere else, that's okay. I'm not going to get pissed if you want a change of pace. Again, my apartment's not terribly fancy, and I spend most of my time when I'm not working chilling in front of the TV or hanging out with my friends."

"Sounds a lot like what I do," she told him honestly. "Minus the friends part."

He smiled at her, and his thumb brushed the back of her hand once more, making the hair on the back of her neck stand up. Rocky opened his mouth to say something, but was interrupted by the door opening and a nurse coming into the room.

"Good morning!" she said cheerily. "It's good to see you awake. How do you feel?"

Rocky let go of her hand and stood, giving the nurse room to approach the side of the bed. Bristol felt a little resentful that they were interrupted, but smiled at the woman anyway.

Rocky folded up the cot he'd slept on, then stepped out of the room, giving her privacy as the nurse gave her a sponge bath. Bristol would give anything to be able to wash her hair and take a real shower, but when the nurse moved her leg, the pain made Bristol break out in a cold sweat, despite the painkillers. It was obvious it would be a while before she could shower on her own. The thought should've been depressing, but because she didn't have to worry about being alone as she recovered, she was surprisingly all right with everything.

The doctor came into the room shortly after her bath, Rocky on his heels. He asked the doctor what seemed like hundreds of questions, but they were mostly things Bristol would've forgotten or not known to ask herself, so she was relieved he was there. The doctor wasn't ready to commit to a time when she could leave, but as the nurse had told Rocky, he suspected she'd be good to go in a day or so...but only because she wasn't going to be on her own, and because he knew Fallport's doctor personally.

Translation: without Rocky's offer to stay with him, she'd likely have to remain in the hospital longer, since she was single and lived by herself.

After the doctor left, the nurse reminded her about how the pain meds worked in her IV, that she should push the button when she got too uncomfortable. Then she headed out to see other patients around the time breakfast was delivered.

Bristol realized she was starving, but after only finishing half the meal on the tray, she found it almost impossible to keep her eyes open.

"I'm gonna go and call my brother," Rocky told her.

Bristol nodded, blinking to stay awake.

"Sleep, Punky. Stop fighting it."

"I shouldn't be so tired," she complained.

Rocky rolled his eyes, and Bristol couldn't help but laugh at the sight of the muscular man making such a ridiculous facial expression.

"Cut yourself some slack. You've had a hard few days," he told her. "Anything you want the guys to get for you at the store, food-wise?" he asked.

Bristol shook her head. "I'm not that picky. I'll eat whatever you do."

"Okay. You want me to put the rest of your breakfast to the side so you can eat it later?"

Bristol's eyes shut, and she forced them open again. "No, I'm good."

In response, Rocky wheeled the tray out of the way of her bed and pushed the button to lower the mattress so she was lying semi-flat instead of sitting up. Then he surprised her by leaning over and kissing her forehead gently. His beard tickled her skin, and she smiled a bit even as her eyes slid shut once more.

"I'll be back later," he said quietly.

For some reason, panic suddenly struck. Her eyes flew open and her hand reached for him. She grabbed hold of his forearm and held on tight, but no words came out.

"Bristol?" he asked, concern lacing the word.

"You promise you'll be back?"

His face relaxed, and he covered her hand with his. "Yes. I'm not leaving."

Bristol took a deep breath. "Right, okay. Sorry...just had a mini panic attack for a second."

Rocky leaned in, resting his weight on his hands, flat on the mattress next to her. She didn't let go of his arm and felt the muscles shifting under her palm. "I'm just going to go call Ethan. I need to go to the parking lot and get my overnight bag, so I can change. I'll probably stop by the cafeteria and grab some breakfast too. I'm one hundred percent not leaving you, Punky. When you wake up, I'll be sitting right here, catching up on work, seeing which projects I want to accept and which I can push off for a while. Okay?"

"Okay," she said immediately. "I just...being out in the woods by myself...it wasn't great. And for a second I was scared of being alone. But that's stupid because I'm *not* alone. I can push the call button anytime I need to. I'm sorry. Go. Do your thing. I'll just be here...sleeping."

"Don't discount your feelings. You were in a very scary situation. But I promise that I'm not going anywhere."

"Thanks," she whispered.

Rocky stared at her for a long moment, as if trying to read her mind. Eventually, he nodded, smoothed a lock of hair behind her ear, then stood and turned for the door. Almost before he reached it, Bristol's eyes were closed once more.

CHAPTER SIX

The doctor decided that it was smart to keep her for an extra night, so Rocky didn't get to spring her from the hospital until Thursday. The last few days had been...relaxing. He didn't have to worry about the phone ringing and going out into the forest on a search. He didn't have to think about what materials he needed to order for a job or much of anything else, other than entertaining Bristol.

And after the first day, when she'd slept a lot of the time, she was remarkably easy to amuse. He was afraid time spent in the hospital would drag, but getting to know Bristol was fascinating and made time fly, instead.

Her leg was healing well, and she'd weened herself off the hard-core painkillers. She was just using the over-the-counter stuff now. She wasn't allowed to put any weight on her leg for two weeks, and then she could use crutches or a knee walker, which the doctor recommended as being more comfortable for most people, even though it could take some getting used to.

Rocky had called Doc Snow, and he'd been happy to agree to

come to the apartment to check on her and take out her stitches when it was time to do so. He would also put on the plaster cast she'd need to help make sure the bone healed properly after the stitches were removed.

Ethan had driven up the first day Bristol was in the hospital. Lilly had been asked to photograph a surprise engagement at the last minute, so she hadn't been able to come, much to her disappointment. He'd brought clothes that Lilly and Elsie had shopped for the evening before, and Lilly had told him to apologize for them not being too fancy.

But Bristol had beamed at the soft sweatshirt and loose flannel pants. Rocky helped her cut off the right leg so she could wear them comfortably and they'd fit over the cast.

The three of them had talked for a short while, until a nurse had come in to help her shower and wash her hair. When she'd returned to bed, Bristol couldn't keep her eyes open. Rocky sat next to her and watched her sleep for way longer than he was willing to admit. He had no idea what it was about her that had him so...hooked.

Now she'd been cleared to leave the hospital. She couldn't walk on her leg yet, so someone was tasked with wheeling her out to his SUV, which he'd already pulled up to the entrance to the hospital.

Rocky easily lifted her into his truck and helped the nurse's assistant load her things into the car. When they were finally on their way back to Fallport, he looked over and saw Bristol sitting next to him with a small smile on her face.

"What's that grin for?" he asked.

Bristol turned to face him and shrugged. "Life can really take it out of you sometimes. Be so hard that it's all you can do to breathe. But then something changes, and you realize whatever had you so upset or depressed somehow doesn't seem so awful anymore. When I was crawling through the forest, I had doubts that I'd make it to the trail or that anyone would find me. My leg hurt worse than any injury I'd had before. I started having a hard time imagining I'd make it out of the woods, let alone ever feeling happy again."

She shrugged. "And now, here I am...my leg's been fixed, you're going out of your way to help me, and even though I've only talked to them through texts, I feel as if I've known Lilly and Elsie for years. Not to mention all the other people from Fallport who've sent their well-wishes. To top it off...the sun's shining today and my leg feels pretty darn good, all things considered. I'm a very lucky woman, and I know it."

"You're an optimist," Rocky said after a moment.

"Yup," Bristol said happily. "There are definitely times I get depressed, but generally, I try to look on the bright side of things. Life could always be worse, and I try to concentrate on all the good going on around me, rather than dwell on the bad."

Rocky was usually annoyed by overly chipper people like Bristol, but she didn't try to shove her optimism down anyone else's throat. She just oozed positivity, which made her glow. "It's a good way to live," he said after a moment.

"I'm not an idiot. I know so many bad things happen in the world," she said solemnly. "But I truly feel as if having a good attitude when things go wrong helps make them more bearable. And when truly awful things happen, like me falling off a cliff in the middle of nowhere with no one knowing where I was...trying to be positive keeps me from drowning in a pit of despair so deep, it'll suck me down and never let me go. If I'd stayed where I'd fallen, you might not have found me," Bristol said. "I believe that everything in our lives happens for a reason...even the bad things."

Rocky thought about that for a long moment. He wasn't sure

he agreed. He'd been in situations as a SEAL that he couldn't justify, unable to come up with a single reason for why they'd happened. Had seen children killed for absolutely nothing. Had struggled to help his military friends deal with career-ending injuries. He still couldn't come up with one good reason why his dad had to die.

But...he couldn't deny that being around Bristol was a breath of fresh air, and he truly liked being with her partly *because of* her sunny disposition.

"It's okay if you don't feel the same," she said quietly. "I'll believe enough for both of us."

"Okay," he said. There was so much more he could've said on the topic, but he didn't want to talk her out of her positive attitude.

"Okay," she echoed with a smile.

They chitchatted about nothing in particular as they drove toward Fallport, and with each mile that passed, Rocky had a feeling eventually letting her go was going to be the hardest thing he'd ever done. And if he felt that way *now*, saying goodbye after having her in his space for however long it took her to get back on her feet...It was going to destroy him.

He was beginning to think having her stay with him wasn't a good idea after all, but he couldn't, and wouldn't, take it back now. He forced himself to push the uneasy feelings to the back of his mind.

"I thought we'd make a quick stop before heading to my apartment, if you're feeling up to it," he said.

"Sure," Bristol answered with a shrug.

"How's the leg?"

"Pretty good."

"We'll prop it up when we get there. Your hands hurt?"

"No."

"All right. But if you start feeling too tired, just let me know and we'll leave."

"You've got me extremely curious now," Bristol said, the excitement easy to hear in her tone.

Rocky chuckled. "It's not a big deal. It's Fallport, after all. I don't want you to be disappointed when you find out where we're going."

Bristol reached out and touched his arm. "Before I decided to go on this trip with Mike, the biggest excitement in my life was going out to get the mail," she said with a small smile.

"Well, here's to hoping this will rank above that," Rocky said as he chuckled.

He pointed out the Mangree Motel and RV Park as they passed, and told her about Elsie and her son living there. Mentioned Edna, the woman who ran the place with her husband, was ornery and gruff, but had a heart of gold. He showed her where Brock worked as a mechanic. Asked if she'd seen Caboose Park, and when she said she hadn't, promised to take her there once her leg healed up a bit more.

He pointed out as many of the quirky things about the town as he could as they drove, and when they got to the square downtown, quickly parallel parked right in front of Sunny Side Up.

"Oooh, are we going to see Sandra?" Bristol asked.

Rocky smiled. "Yeah. She's been driving me nuts with texts, wanting to know how you were doing, and since the food in the hospital wasn't all that great, I figured you wouldn't mind getting a decent meal and calming her fears at the same time."

Bristol smiled at him...but then her lip began to quiver.

"What? What's wrong?" he asked, somewhat alarmed.

"It's just that, if it wasn't for her, you wouldn't have come looking for me. And I know you didn't really think you'd find me, but still. I owe her so much!"

Wishing the console wasn't between them, Rocky reached out and put his hand on her nape and turned her toward him. He rested his forehead against hers. "Don't cry," he ordered. "If you do, Sandra will absolutely lose it."

Bristol gave him a watery chuckle.

"I've already told you Sandra doesn't take to people very easily. And she's notoriously cranky when it comes to tourists. They're a necessary evil for her, but she much prefers the locals. For her to take such a shine to you means you're special."

"I'm just me," Bristol said softly.

"So, just keep on being you," Rocky suggested. He took a deep breath and leaned back, but kept his hand on her. He loved touching her. Didn't want to let go until he absolutely had to. "Deep breath, Punky. And remember, when you've had enough, just let me know. I'll take you home...er...to my place to get settled in."

She smiled, and he couldn't read the expression on her face. "I know you told me not to thank you, but it's really hard at times like this."

"Stay put," he ordered. "I'll come around and get you." Rocky knew he sounded a little gruff, but he was feeling off-kilter. This little spitfire of a woman had him tied up in knots. He caressed her nape with his thumb and felt her shiver, then forced himself to let go and climb out of his side of the car. He was at the passenger door in seconds. Bristol had unbuckled her seat belt and was waiting patiently for him.

"A girl could get used to this," she quipped as he leaned over and easily picked her up.

Rocky was extremely careful not to bang her leg on the door-frame as he straightened. He turned and kicked the door shut as he strode toward the entrance to the diner. "Anytime you want me to carry you around, just let me know," he said seriously.

"Whatever," Bristol mumbled. "Just because I'm short doesn't mean my legs don't work." She took a breath to say something else, but the door to the diner opened just then and Rocky strode inside.

As he expected, the place was packed. The small reunion between Bristol and Sandra had turned into a full-on welcome home party.

Rocky saw his search and rescue team, along with Lilly, Elsie and her son Tony, Sandra, Finley Norris—who owned The Sweet Tooth, a bakery across the square—Nissi O'Neill, the lawyer whose office was next to the diner, Whitney Crawford, the owner of Chestnut Street Manor Bed and Breakfast, and Tiana and Reina, waitresses who worked with Elsie at Zeke's bar.

Doc Snow and his partner, Craig, were at a small table. He also saw Fallport Police Chief Simon Hill; Davis Woolford, a homeless veteran; Dorothea, Cora, Ruth, and Clara, four close friends who loved to be in on everything happening in Fallport; and to round out the crowd, Silas, Otto, and Art, who'd given up their seats outside the post office to come check out the woman everyone in town was talking about.

The small diner was filled with people wanting to meet Bristol, and witness her and Sandra's reunion firsthand. The story about how Sandra had been the one to alert Rocky to the possibility that Bristol might be missing had spread through Fallport like wildfire.

"Rocky...I think someone's having a party. Maybe we shouldn't interrupt," Bristol said, looking at him with a furrowed brow.

He couldn't help but laugh. "Punky, the party's for you."

Her frown deepened. "What?"

"Everyone's here to meet you. To let you know they're glad you're all right."

She looked around and said, "But I don't know...oh...is that the woman who runs the bakery?"

"Finley, yes."

"And I recognize those older guys...they always waved to me from outside the post office." She looked up at him again. "Are they really here for *me*?"

"Yup."

"Shoot," she said, and closed her eyes. "I'm gonna cry again!"

"No crying, Punky," he chastised. "Here comes Sandra."

The owner of the diner was very definitely headed their way. Rocky had stopped just inside the front door, but she wasn't wasting any time. Sandra was in her forties, close to six feet tall, had beautiful dark, flawless skin, and her afro bounced with every step she took.

Bristol opened her eyes and saw the woman coming toward them. She let out an excited squeak, and it was a good thing Rocky was holding onto her tightly, because Bristol almost threw herself at Sandra as soon as she was close enough.

Being careful not to jostle her leg more than necessary, Rocky held her carefully as Bristol hugged the other woman.

"Thank you so much," Bristol said into Sandra's shoulder.

"I'm so glad you're all right," she replied.

The two women clung to each other for a long moment, the connection they had obvious to everyone in attendance. Finally, Sandra pulled back and gently wiped the wetness on her face with her fingers.

"Lord, I'm a mess!" she exclaimed. Then she started ordering people around. "Rocky, Bristol needs to sit. Go over there, I pushed a chair close to the booth so she could rest her leg. Watch it!" she barked as one of the waitresses came close to bumping into Bristol, as Rocky leaned over to place her on the seat.

"You're hungry, right? Of course you are. Hospital food sucks. I'll have something out in a moment." Sandra turned to glare at everyone watching, clearly eager to meet Fallport's newest resident, even if her stay would be temporary. "This isn't a zoo," she told them all. "Stop staring at the poor girl!" Then she walked toward the kitchen, mumbling to herself as she went.

Bristol giggled, and Rocky couldn't help but smile back. He squeezed her shoulder then took a seat on the other side of the booth.

For the next fifteen minutes, Bristol held court. There was no other way to put it. Everyone came up to say hello, letting her know how relieved they were that she was all right. Slowly, the crowd in the diner thinned out as people headed back to their jobs and regular Thursday-afternoon routines.

"Glad to see our Rocky found you, girl," Otto told her after introducing himself.

"Me too," Bristol agreed for what had to have been the fiftieth time since arriving.

"From what I heard, you held your own out there though," Silas said.

"I'd like to think so, but that doesn't mean I'm not grateful I didn't have to crawl all the way to the trailhead," Bristol said.

"The people you were with should be whipped," Art grumbled. "Don't know what happened and don't care. No respectable person leaves someone in the woods like they did."

Rocky agreed, but he sat up straighter, ready to step in if Art got disrespectful. He liked the three older men, but they sometimes had a tendency to be too blunt, to the point of being harsh.

"Easy, Art," Drew said, stepping in before Rocky could.

"Easy?" Art scoffed, turning his irritation on Drew. "You think it's right for a young lady to come to town for a nice vacation, only to be left in the middle of nowhere? Hurt and unable to get back to the trailhead? And if she did make it back there, with no transportation?"

"Of course not, but we don't know the circumstances, so we shouldn't judge," Drew said calmly.

"Oh, I'm judging," Art mumbled.

Rocky was done with the conversation, and about to tell Art to cut it out, when he heard Bristol laughing from across the table. His gaze swung to her. She seemed highly amused by the conversation.

"Well, you're right. Mike was a jerk. But I'm thinking he might like a whipping a bit too much."

There was silence for a beat, before Art's lips curled into a sly grin. "He's like that, huh?" he asked.

Bristol shrugged. "I don't know, and I definitely don't care. We were friends—*just* friends—but now I'm thinking we aren't even that anymore."

"Probably smart," Otto agreed.

"It's a good thing they're already out of town. If they were still here, they'd be getting a pretty cold shoulder from everyone by now," Silas muttered.

"Move over!" Sandra called from behind them, and the three men parted, giving her access to the table. "Isn't it about time for you to get back to your stations?" she asked. "You wouldn't want to miss the afternoon post office rush, would you?"

The three men grumbled a bit, but it was obvious they were indeed ready to get back to their routine. They said their goodbyes, and then the only people left around the booth were Rocky's teammates and Lilly, Elsie, and Tony.

Talon pulled a couple of nearby tables closer to the booth,

and everyone grabbed chairs. Rocky wasn't upset they were all planning on joining him and Bristol. He was excited for her to get to know his friends.

Lilly took the seat closest to Bristol, Elsie beside her. Raiden took the seat next to Rocky in the booth, Duke settling in under the table at his master's feet. The rest of the guys were scattered around the tables.

"Chicken-fried steak," Sandra said as she pushed the plate she'd put on the table closer to Bristol. "With asparagus and mashed potatoes. Save room for my lemon meringue pie for dessert. Karen'll be here in a moment with the rest of your meals." Then Sandra smiled at Bristol before heading back to the kitchen.

"How does she even know what we want?" Elsie asked.

"She doesn't," Zeke said, smiling at his wife. "But it doesn't matter what she brings, it's gonna be delicious."

"True," Elsie agreed, then turned to Bristol. "Hi. I'm Elsie. And this is my husband, Zeke. I feel really awful that we were all on a hike when you were lost."

"You couldn't have known," Bristol said easily. "And it's nice to meet you. I've heard a lot about you. And about your son. Hi," she said, grinning at Tony. "Rocky told me all about how awesome *you* are."

"He did?" the little boy asked.

"Yup."

"He tell you that I'm gonna be a race car driver when I grow up? And a professional fisherman and firefighter?"

"Wow. No, he didn't. But I'm thinking I should get your autograph, so when you're famous I can say I knew you when you were a kid."

Tony sat up straighter in his chair and beamed. "Cool!" Bristol pushed a clean napkin toward him, and Elsie chuckled as she reached into her purse and pulled out a pen. The boy carefully wrote his name on the napkin, his tongue sticking out as he concentrated. When he was done, he held it up and smiled. "It's a little lopsided, but that's because the napkin kept moving. But here you go!"

"Thank you," Bristol said. "I'll keep it forever."

Rocky watched the exchange, not surprised that Bristol had Tony wrapped around her little finger already. He also didn't miss the approving looks from his friends. Whether she knew it or not, she'd scored huge points with all of them.

Bristol then focused on Lilly and Elsie. "Thanks for the clothes. They were a lifesaver. Hospital gowns are the worst."

"You're welcome," Lilly said with a smile. "Let us know what else you need, and we'll be happy to get it for you."

"Oh, no, I'm good. I mean, I don't have a lot here, but what I do have—thanks to your generosity, and what I had with me when I came to town—should be enough to tide me over. I've got way too many clothes at home as it is."

"Kingsport, right?" Drew asked. "By the way, I'm Drew."

"Hi," Bristol said, giving him a warm smile. "And yes, Kingsport."

"I'm Talon. Rocky told us you're an artist. I looked up your website and store, you're very talented."

"Wow, um...thanks. And yeah, my specialty is stained glass, but I also dabble in jewelry and small sculptures. I probably need to go online and update my customers about what's going on. I put a note up that I'd be taking a short break, but didn't say why or for how long," Bristol mused.

"I'm sure they'll understand," Lilly said.

"And if they get pissy about you not being around, fuck 'em," Brock said. "If they can't understand your life was in danger and you were laid up because of surgery, they're idiots."

"That's Brock," Zeke said dryly. "Tell us what you really think," he said with a shake of his head at his friend. "And... watch your language." He gestured toward Tony. Luckily, the boy seemed to be engrossed in a book he'd laid out on the tabletop. Elsie always carried one in her purse for her son, to keep him occupied in situations like this.

"Sorry," Brock said with a shrug. "Had to deal with a not-so-nice customer at work today. My tolerance level is low."

"It's okay," Elsie told him.

"And you're right," Bristol added. "Luckily, I don't actually need to rely on the webstore customers. My work with churches, as well as other large commissions, keeps a roof over my head and food on my plate."

"The stained-glass industry is that good?" Raiden asked.

"I'm thinking interrogating Bristol on how much money she makes isn't exactly appropriate conversation," Rocky warned.

"I'm just curious," Raid argued.

"It's okay," Bristol said. "And to answer your question, no, the stained-glass industry isn't that good...but I am."

There was silence for a beat, then everyone laughed.

"You walked right into that one, Raid."

"She told you."

"Right on, sister."

Rocky grinned, loving Bristol's confidence in what she did, but liking the way she seemed to fit in with their group even more.

Karen walked up to the table then with a huge tray on her shoulder and began unloading food. Sandra had chosen a family-style meal for them, with large bowls and plates of food everyone could share. Rocky noticed that she hadn't brought anyone else chicken-fried steak. Bristol was the only one who received her specialty.

Everyone began to help themselves to the food, and the mood was happy and relaxed. They all ate, the banter flowing nonstop. Rocky didn't even get upset when the topic changed to his idiotic decision to head into the forest by himself, without letting Raid know where he was going.

"We really need those satellite phones," Brock muttered. "If Rocky'd had one, he could've called Raid, or even one of us. He could've stayed put with Bristol and let us come to him."

"I've got a meeting set up with the mayor and the city council to see if I can convince them to put in a bid," Ethan told the group.

"How long will that take?" Bristol asked, joining the conversation.

"Who the heck knows?" Ethan said in disgust. "I thought I'd left the bureaucracy behind when I left the military, but even small towns have hoops that have to be jumped through when it comes to stuff like this."

"I'll happily get them for the team," Bristol said.

Silence settled over the table for a heartbeat, then everyone started talking at once.

"No, you won't."

"The city council will pony up the money eventually."

"That's generous of you, but it's all right."

"Awesome!"

The last came from Lilly.

Rocky held up a hand to silence his friends, then met Bristol's gaze head on. "We appreciate it, but it's not necessary."

"It sounds to me as if it's *definitely* necessary," Bristol countered. "And I want to. I *need* to. You barely let me say 'thank you.' And it's obvious you guys need a better way to communicate when you're in the woods. If it'll help someone else who's lost, I want to donate them. I can afford it."

Rocky didn't know why her offer didn't sit well with him. "We weren't talking about this to make you feel guilty or to get you to offer to buy phones," he said.

"I know you didn't. Please let me do this for you guys. For the town. I've never felt as at home anywhere like I have here. Not even in Kingsport. Please, Rocky. I want to do my part to help someone else who might get into the same situation as me."

Rocky sighed. "Can we talk about it later?" he asked.

Bristol nodded. "But I'm not going to change my mind," she warned him.

"I like her," Brock said from his seat at the table next to theirs.

The rest of the meal was relatively uneventful. Friendly conversation continued, and it felt as if Bristol had been a part of their group for years rather than a couple of days. They'd all finished eating, and everyone was talking about nothing important, prolonging their time together, when Rocky noticed Bristol's eyes getting heavy. He looked at his watch and was surprised to realize how late it was.

"We need to get going," he announced.

Bristol's gaze swung to his. She gave him a tiny nod.

Relieved that she wasn't protesting, Rocky gestured for Raid to scoot out of the booth. He did so without complaint, and soon he had Bristol in his arms once more. It took longer than he would've liked for her to say goodbye to his friends—and now hers—but also to Sandra and the other locals who were eating in the diner.

Lilly promised to come over the next day to visit. Elsie and Bristol spoke for a moment about what books Bristol might like to read, and Elsie promised to pick up a few novels at the library and drop them off after her shift was over at the bar tomorrow.

The rest of the guys also said they'd stop by to see if they needed anything.

Rocky was grateful for the support, but he was also a touch exasperated. He couldn't help but want to spend some time alone with Bristol. He'd enjoyed their time together as they walked through the forest, even if it wasn't the best situation. He couldn't wait to learn even more about her, now that she was feeling better.

He carried her out of the diner and back to his car, settling her in gently, then jogged around to the driver's side. The drive to his apartment wasn't long, and as he took Bristol back into his arms, Rocky couldn't help but sigh in contentment.

He walked up the stairs to the second floor of the complex. His apartment was on the far end of one side, and Ethan's had been three doors down. It was empty once again, now that Elsie and Tony had moved into Zeke's place.

There were six apartments on the lower level and six on the second. A single staircase led to the second-floor walkway. All the doors faced the parking lot. It was nothing special, but Rocky had never really minded the slightly rundown look of the place. The apartments were clean and his neighbors all pretty much kept to themselves.

He leaned over at his door, letting Bristol unlock the bolt and turn the knob before he carried her inside. He gave her a quick tour of his place, which literally took five seconds, pointing out the kitchen, living room, master bedroom, and the bathroom in the hall they'd be sharing. Then he brought her into the guest room, surprised and grateful at the homey feel. Zeke and Elsie had outdone themselves in making the space welcoming for Bristol.

The full-size bed had a comforter Rocky had never seen before, and there was a small lamp on the table next to the bed.

They'd cleaned the space entirely; the boxes and random workout equipment he'd stored in the room were nowhere in sight. Rocky assumed they were either in his room or the closets. He made a mental note to thank his friends.

He gently placed Bristol on the bed and took a step back, feeling awkward now that she was no longer in his arms. "Um... do you need help with anything?"

She smiled gently. "I could use my bag with my stuff."

"Right. Sorry. Yeah, I'll go get that now," Rocky said with a small shake of his head as he backed toward the door.

"Rocky?"

Her voice stopped him. "Yeah?"

"I appreciate what you're doing for me."

He grinned and shook his head.

"Hey, I didn't say thank you," she protested with a twinkle in her eye.

"I'll be right back. Don't go anywhere," he joked.

Bristol laughed. "I won't. I'll be right here when you get back."

Rocky loved seeing her happy. He stopped with a hand on the door and turned back. "Thank *you* for trusting me, Bristol. I swear you're safe with me."

"I know. I wouldn't be here if I didn't trust you."

Feeling good, Rocky gave her another nod, then left, heading for the front door so he could go and collect their bags from the car.

An hour later, after Bristol swore she didn't need him to call Lilly or Elsie to help her get ready for a nap, Rocky peeked into the guest bedroom. Bristol was on her back, her leg propped up on a pillow, and she was dead to the world. She'd probably overdone it today, but Rocky couldn't be sorry. He'd loved seeing how comfortable she was around his friends.

He closed the door almost all the way, leaving it open about five inches so he could hear if she called out and needed anything, then wandered back out to his living room. Sitting on the couch, he realized he was content.

Usually when he came home at the end of a long day, he was fidgety. He didn't spend a lot of time in his apartment because it didn't feel like home to him. But tonight, knowing Bristol was down the hall, and would require help with her basic needs for at least the next few days, made Rocky feel needed.

He enjoyed his job. Loved what he did as a part of the Eagle Point Search and Rescue team. But he'd been increasingly lonely. Having Bristol here felt...nice.

Shaking his head, Rocky rolled his eyes at himself. He was being ridiculous. Seeing his brother and Zeke find women who were so perfect for them had made him mushy. Bristol was only here until she was back on her feet. Then she'd go back to Kingsport.

But a small part of Rocky objected. Wanted to make her love Fallport and being around him and his friends so much, she wouldn't want to leave. It was unlikely, but not impossible. Lilly had decided to stay.

With that thought in mind, Rocky reached for the remote and turned on the TV. He kept the volume down so it wouldn't wake his guest, and relaxed as he found a baseball game. Time would tell what would happen with him and Bristol. And if all that happened was that he'd found a new friend, he'd do his best to be content with that.

But at the back of his mind, he couldn't help but think about the connection they had blooming into more.

* * *

"Where is she?" the man mumbled to himself as he sat in his car outside of Bristol Wingham's house in Kingsport, Tennessee.

She'd left almost two weeks ago, and not knowing where she was ate at him more with each passing day. She hadn't packed more than a large backpack, so he'd assumed she wouldn't be gone long. Now here it was, nearly two weeks later, and she still wasn't home.

Worse, the man who'd picked her up, Mike Moran, had returned nearly a week ago—without Bristol. He lived not far from Bristol's place, and the man had been watching for his return, as well. Had he hurt her? Done something to her? It made no sense that she'd leave with him, but not come back.

He felt his heart rate increase. Worry for Bristol almost overwhelmed him. But under that was anger, as well. How *dare* she leave without telling her customers when she'd be back. How dare she worry him like this! If she was his, he'd make sure she never stepped foot out of the house without telling him where she was going. It was a safety issue.

He couldn't protect her if he didn't know where she was.

He was her most loyal customer. The first time he'd seen one of her stained-glass windows, he'd known she was meant to be his. People might call him crazy for thinking so, but he didn't care. Her art had spoken to his soul, as if she'd made the piece just for him.

He'd bought it on the spot and became obsessed with learning as much as he could about Bristol. He'd even moved to Kingsport, just to be closer to her. Eventually, she'd realize she was meant to be his, and she'd want him just as much as he wanted her.

He was certain he'd bought far more of her beautiful creations than anyone else. Jewelry, sculptures...he'd even pretended to be the pastor of a church and had commissioned a large stained-glass window, which was now his greatest pride and joy.

He needed to find her. Had to know if she was all right, if she was safe. And when she came back, he'd make sure she understood she should *never* scare him like this again.

It was time.

Time she knew how much he loved her.

That he'd do whatever it took to keep her safe from all the crazies in the world, from anyone who might want to hurt her.

But first, he needed to find her.

CHAPTER SEVEN

Bristol sighed in frustration. It had been four days since she'd gotten out of the hospital and moved into Rocky's guest room. When she'd first arrived, she'd been overly optimistic about how well she'd be able to get around. Probably because the painkillers she'd been given in the hospital hadn't worn off.

But now that they had, she found moving to be extremely painful.

The morning after her arrival, she'd insisted on attempting a shower. It had been fast and awkward. Rocky had placed her on a plastic stool beneath the shower, with her leg propped on the side of the tub, before reluctantly leaving her to do what she needed to do—though he'd hovered outside the bathroom, ready to burst in if she needed anything. By the time she'd dried off, dressed herself, and called out for Rocky, she'd been almost light-headed with the pain from the throbbing in her leg and regretted trying to do so much on her own.

Meanwhile, Rocky had been the perfect host...and friend. He hadn't gone back to work yet. Had been sticking to his apartment, making sure she was all right and keeping her company. She'd had a steady stream of guests too, which was surprising, but they made her feel really good.

This morning, however, she was cranky. And extremely frustrated. She wanted to be able to get up and go to the bathroom without having to be carried. She wanted to stand in front of the sink and brush her teeth instead of doing it while sitting on the toilet. Wanted to go out into the fresh air. Wanted to wear real pants instead of ones with only one leg.

So when Rocky knocked on her door that morning and cheerfully called out, "Good morning," Bristol wanted to tell him to go away so she could wallow in self-pity. But that would be rude. He was doing her a huge favor. If she'd gone home to Kingsport, she would've been in big trouble. She couldn't get around on her own until her leg healed up a bit more. The doctor estimated two weeks before she'd be able to get up and hobble around with crutches or a knee walker.

Rocky poked his head inside her room, and the second Bristol's gaze met his, she felt her impatience and irritation rising. She didn't want to be someone this man had to babysit. Didn't want to be a patient. She wanted him to see her as...*more*. In fact, the thoughts running through her head were startling...yet not. The connection they shared had been there from the moment they'd met in the woods.

This was *not* how she wanted to spend her time with Rocky.

She felt grubby, pathetic, and angry.

"What's wrong?" he asked as he came into the room.

Figured he'd be able to tell she was in a bad mood. "Nothing."

Rocky snorted. "I might be single, but even I know when a woman says she's 'fine' or 'nothing's wrong,' she's not fine and something is *definitely* wrong. You want to talk about it?"

Bristol sighed and shook her head. "I'm good."

"You aren't. Talk to me, Punky. Did I do something? Or *not* do something? What can I do to help you?"

"Not do something?" Bristol exclaimed. "Rocky, you've been nothing but amazing. Feeding me. Giving me a place to stay. You've practically glued yourself to my side ever since you found me."

"So you need space?"

Bristol made a frustrated sound in the back of her throat, shaking her head once more.

Rocky walked closer and sat on the edge of the bed. Bristol thought that it was impressive he wasn't afraid to enter the lion's den, so to speak. Most men she knew would've retreated at the first sign of a woman in a bad mood. But of *course* Rocky hadn't.

"Let me guess. You're feeling claustrophobic. You hate that you can't get up and do things for yourself. You're appreciative of me being here, but also resentful. Am I close?"

She stared at him in confusion. "How do you know that?"

He chuckled. "I've been there. Laid up while injured. Took a bullet to the shoulder on a mission once. I was shipped to Germany while the rest of my team continued on without me. I was alone, and while the nurses were pleasant and nice, I was in a strange place and hurting. I wasn't allowed to get up, and all it took was a few days of me having to lie in bed all day to go stark-raving mad. Luckily, my injury wasn't that bad, and I was sent back to the States after less than a week, but still. What can I do to help?"

Bristol's stomach clenched at the thought of this man being hurt. She ran her gaze up and down his body, as if looking for any signs of injury. It was crazy, because Rocky had carried her over six miles through the woods with a heavy pack on his back...he was obviously more than healed from an old injury, but still.

"Bristol?"

She shook her head slightly, realizing he was waiting for her to answer his question. "I'll be okay. Yes, I'm feeling all of what you described, but I know I'm lucky."

He studied her for a long moment, then said, "Just because you know you're lucky, doesn't mean you aren't feeling confined and frustrated. If you could do one thing right this second, what would it be?"

Bristol didn't even have to think about it. "Take a shower. A real one. I mean, I know I took one a few days ago, but I cut it short because my leg hurt so much."

"What else?"

"Make something. A pair of earrings. A sculpture. Or better yet, work on a stained-glass piece."

"Hmmm, not sure I can help with that right this moment. I'm guessing the big box store isn't going to have the materials you need to create your art, huh?"

Amazingly, Bristol smiled. "Not really. Although that's how I got started. My mom bought me a huge box of beads as a kid, and I was hooked."

Rocky smiled back and asked gently, "You ready to get up and have me take you to the bathroom?"

Bristol did her best to shrug off her grumpiness. This situation wasn't Rocky's fault. It was her own. There were so many things she could've done differently when Mike had sprung his sex-fest idea on her. "Yeah, I'm ready," she said, pushing the covers off her legs.

As he'd done many times over the last few days, Rocky gently picked her up and carried her out of the guest room into the hall. He brought her into the bathroom and placed her down on the toilet. The first few times he'd done so, Bristol had blushed so hard, she could feel her face burning. But he was so nonchalant about it all, she'd gotten used to their routine.

The second he left the room, Bristol shimmied her underwear and sweatpants down, ignoring the twinge of pain the movement caused. She did her business, then awkwardly pulled her clothes back on. She reached for the toothbrush and toothpaste Rocky left close enough so she could reach them, and quickly brushed her teeth. She couldn't reach the sink to spit, so she had to use the small bowl Rocky had brought in for her.

Doc Snow had removed her stitches yesterday, and had put a regular plaster cast on her leg. She knew it was the next step in her recovery, but she hated the heavy cast and her leg itched almost unbearably. She had no doubt the itchiness was all in her head, but it was still annoying.

Taking a deep breath, Bristol did her best to center herself. Find her optimism once more. The room smelled like her roommate. Rocky usually showered and got ready before he came in to see if she was awake and help her start her day. Inhaling deeply, she couldn't help but feel jealous of the scent of his soap. God, what she wouldn't give to be able to stand up, step over the edge of the bathtub and wash herself. It didn't even matter if she had to use his masculine body wash instead of her usual assortment of flowery and sweet-smelling soaps she had at her house back in Kingsport.

A soft knock on the door brought her out of her musings. "I'm done," she called out. Rocky entered, and as if it was completely normal to pick up a woman who was sitting on the toilet after doing her business, he took her in his arms and headed out of the bathroom, careful not to bang her leg on the doorjamb.

Instead of bringing her back to her room, Rocky carried her into the living room and got her settled in the easy chair. He pulled up an ottoman and carefully arranged her leg. He brought some pillows and a blanket over, and when he was done tucking her in, leaned over and put his hands on the arms of the chair.

"I thought a change of pace would do you good."

"Th—" She remembered at the last second his aversion to being thanked. "I appreciate it," she told him.

He grinned, and butterflies took flight in Bristol's belly. The man was extremely good-looking, but when he smiled? It upped his hotness tenfold.

"Good. I'll go grab your phone so you can check messages and stuff. I'm going to change your sheets this morning. Can you wait a bit for breakfast?"

"Rocky, you don't have to wait on me," she protested, even though he actually *did*. It wasn't as if she could get up and change her own sheets or make her own breakfast. That was part of what was so hard about this. She was an independent person, and it felt weird and uncomfortable having someone else do literally everything for her.

"Believe it or not, I enjoy it," he said.

Bristol rolled her eyes.

"I do," he insisted. "It's been a long time since anyone has needed me." And with that, he leaned down, kissed the top of her head, and said, "Relax, Punky. I got this."

She watched him, a little bemused, as he headed for the hallway, probably to grab her phone that was still on the small table next to her bed.

Sure enough, he reappeared a few seconds later with her phone in hand. He gave it to her, then went into the kitchen and poured her a cup of coffee he'd obviously started when she was in the bathroom doing her thing. She held the cup in both hands, loving the warmth seeping into her skin. Her hands were mostly healed and the heat on her palms felt good. She inhaled the steam rising from the cup and smiled up at Rocky. "Vanilla?" she asked.

He nodded. "Yup. You mentioned that you liked flavored coffee, so before Lilly came over yesterday, I asked her to stop and pick some up for you."

Rocky was constantly trying to find ways to make her recovery more pleasant. "That was nice of you," she said in lieu of thanking him.

He chuckled and headed back down the hall.

Once again, Bristol watched him go. Lord, the man was built. He was wearing a pair of black sweatpants this morning, which molded to his ass. He was muscular, but he also had some junk in his trunk. She grinned at the thought, and sipped at the coffee in her hands. It was fair to say the longer she was around him, the more he intrigued her and the further he got under her skin.

Which was disconcerting. She lived in Kingsport, and he was here. Once she was back on her feet, she'd return to Tennessee... and then what? She didn't know. All she knew was that she would miss this small town and the people in it. They'd made her feel more than welcome. From her first meeting with Sandra in the diner, to the way people were constantly stopping by Rocky's apartment, bringing food, desserts, and staying to talk for a bit just to entertain her. It was surprising, and longing hit Bristol...hard.

What if I stayed?

Bristol blinked at the thought. What if she *did* stay? As she'd told Raid, she could work from literally anywhere. She got most of her supplies online, and Fallport had a post office so she could mail out the orders from her online store. She had more than enough money to be able to afford the move.

The longing was the most surprising part. Moving wasn't really about Rocky...okay, it wasn't *all* about Rocky. But she'd never move for a man after only knowing him for a week. The lure of Fallport itself, however, was hard to resist. She'd never been to a town that was friendlier than this one. Yes, she was well aware there were probably plenty of assholes living here, and she just hadn't met them yet. There were inconsiderate jerks everywhere in the world. But just thinking about how most of the people she'd met had been worried about her, and genuinely concerned for her well-being, made Bristol want to be a part of this community.

She didn't even know her neighbors back home very well. They certainly wouldn't have come over and sat with her in the evenings and taught her how to play Cards Against Humanity. Bristol had felt a little awkward at first, since she was the only woman last night when Drew, Brock, and Talon had come over. The five of them had played the card game and she'd laughed so hard, her stomach was still a little sore this morning.

Recalling her attitude when she'd woken up made her feel a little ashamed. She had nothing—absolutely nothing—to be grumpy about.

Pushing the thought of moving to Fallport to the back of her mind for the moment, Bristol took another sip of coffee. She had it damn good right now, and she knew it. She just needed to be patient. Her leg would heal, and then she could make some decisions about her life.

But she couldn't help but wonder what Rocky would think about her moving to Fallport. Would he be happy? Or would he feel as if she was expecting something...maybe even get irritated with her?

It was no use speculating on the what-ifs. Not until she actually made a decision.

"You look like you're thinking really hard over there," Rocky said as he came back into the room with a handful of sheets from her bed.

Bristol jerked in surprise. She'd been so lost in her head, she hadn't heard him approaching. Then again, he walked extremely quietly, probably something he'd learned as a Navy SEAL.

"Oh, you know, just trying to solve world peace and all that," she said breezily.

"Awesome. When you figure it out, let me know and I'll call the president and set up a meeting between you guys."

Bristol laughed, then tilted her head as she watched Rocky put the sheets in the washer in a closet off the living room. "Wait, do you know the president?"

He laughed as he turned the dial to start the washer, then glanced at her. "Would you freak out if I said I did?"

"Um...maybe?"

Rocky headed for the kitchen. "Then it's good you don't need to freak out. I don't know the president."

"Whew," Bristol teased, pantomiming wiping her brow.

Rocky aimed a look her way and said, "*This* president. I knew the last one."

She almost choked on her coffee and studied her host, trying to decide if he was fucking with her or not. When he gave her a sheepish grin and shrugged, she shook her head, deciding he probably really *did* know the former president.

"Oatmeal okay for breakfast? And yes, I know you like lots of brown sugar, and I thought I'd put some blueberries in it as well. I've also got some fresh melon Doc Snow brought over yesterday when he came to check out your progress."

"Sounds delicious."

As she drank her coffee, Bristol watched Rocky move around the kitchen. It wasn't a large space, and him being a big man made it even smaller, but he moved efficiently and, before she knew it, he was carrying a bowl over to her. He picked up the large coffee table book on wildlife in Alaska that she used as a pseudo tray and placed it and the bowl on her lap. "Good?" he asked.

"Perfect," she told him. It really was hard not to thank him every other second, but she was getting the hang of avoiding those words and showing her appreciation in other ways. By finishing whatever he brought her to eat, by looking him in the eyes as she accepted whatever he was doing for her, and hopefully with her body language.

"I'll get the fruit," he told her and went back toward the kitchen.

Bristol waited until he was sitting on his couch next to her with his own breakfast before digging in. He'd told her she didn't have to wait for him, but there was no way she was going to shove food in her face while he was still getting situated.

They ate in silence, and when Bristol was done, she asked him a question she'd been thinking about for a while. "Are you going back to work today?"

He looked up at her and narrowed his eyes. "Sick of me already?" he joked.

But Bristol could tell he was genuinely concerned about that exact thing. She chuckled. "Um, no. No way. But you're getting antsy. I can tell."

"Yeah?" he asked.

"Uh-huh. I'm assuming it's not normal for you to sweep and vacuum every inch of your floors like you did yesterday."

He shrugged. "I like to stay busy."

"Right. So when are you going back to work?"

He stared at her for a long moment. "If you truly don't mind, I might venture out tomorrow. I don't want to leave you alone all day, but there are a few jobs I could take that aren't too time-intensive."

"Rocky, I appreciate what you've done for me more than I can say, but you don't have to babysit me all day. Besides, there have been a steady stream of people coming by since I've been here. I'm guessing I wouldn't be alone while you're out earning a living. And if someone else gets lost in the woods, you'd have to go look for them with your team and I'd be alone anyway."

Rocky shook his head. "No, I wouldn't. I've already talked with the guys, and if we get called out, I'm not going. There's never any telling how long we'll be searching when we go out, and no one was comfortable leaving you by yourself for an indeterminate period of time."

Bristol stared at him, honestly shocked. They'd had long conversations about some of the searches he'd been on, and how much satisfaction he got from them. How he felt as if he was using some of the skills he'd learned as a SEAL and giving back to his community. Granted, it wasn't as if her being here meant he was giving up his place on the search team altogether, but still.

"What? What's that look for?" he asked, scooting down the couch a bit so he was closer to where she was sitting.

"I don't want you to give up something you love because you have to babysit me," she said after a moment.

"I'm not giving it up," he said without hesitation. "Missing one or two searches isn't a big deal. To be honest, if I went, I'd probably be worrying about you more than paying attention to what I was doing...which isn't safe. Until you're back on your feet and more mobile, I'm not willing to just leave you on your own. Even if I arranged for Lilly, Elsie, or someone else to come by, you wouldn't be able to get up to see who was at the door. You'd also be vulnerable to anyone who thought they could come by and take advantage of you because of my absence."

Wow. Bristol wasn't sure what to say about that. All she knew was that it made her feel really good.

"Besides, I don't see it as babysitting. I *like* having you here. Having the guys come over more often has been nice."

"You guys don't do that normally?" Bristol asked.

Rocky shrugged. "Not really. I mean, we get together at On the Rocks, or have lunch together, but we're all usually pretty busy with our jobs and stuff, and haven't taken a lot of time to just hang out together like we have in the past week. Thank *you* for that."

Bristol took a deep breath. She had no idea if Rocky was just saying those things to make her feel less like a burden, but she definitely felt good that she was playing a small part in reinforcing the amazing friendship the men of Eagle Point Search and Rescue shared. "Am I mistaken, or did you just thank me?" she asked, trying to lighten the mood.

It worked. Rocky chuckled. "Right, sorry, forget I said that." He met her gaze and said, "And don't think I haven't realized how hard you're trying to keep your thanks to a minimum. I like having you here, Punky. I definitely feel as if I should be thanking *you*. Not for getting hurt, never for that, but for trusting me."

"I do," she said seriously. "And I'm not the most trusting person. I mean, look what happened with Mike," she said ruefully.

"Mike's an asshole," Rocky said, the force behind his words making Bristol blink in surprise.

"Seriously, what the hell was he thinking? One, if a woman says she wants to be friends, a man needs to get with the program and move on. The *last* thing he should do is think he can change her mind by asking if she wants to participate in a damn orgy."

Bristol couldn't help but laugh. He wasn't wrong.

"And second, letting you hike off alone, and then leaving when he knew all too well that he was your ride home, is the biggest asshole move of all. Thank God you told Sandra where you were going and when you were supposed to be back," Rocky muttered.

Bristol was definitely thankful she'd done that. She might not do a ton of outdoor stuff, but she enjoyed hiking, and she knew better than to head off into the woods without letting someone know where she was going.

Leaning over the makeshift tray on her lap, Bristol touched Rocky's arm. She opened her mouth to thank him, but stopped herself at the last minute. But she didn't have to worry. Rocky immediately covered her hand with his and squeezed. They stared at each other, sparks flying between them. She connected with this man on a level she hadn't experienced with anyone else. It was a bit disconcerting, considering so much was up in the air.

He opened his mouth to say something just as there was a knock at the door.

Surprised, Bristol sat back.

"Be right there," Rocky called out before standing and reaching for the book on Bristol's lap.

He obviously knew who was here, because he didn't seem too surprised that someone was visiting so early. He took the book with her empty bowls on it to the kitchen before heading to the front door.

Elsie was on the other side, and she had a big smile on her face as she entered the apartment. "Hey, Bristol. How are you feeling this morning?"

She smiled. "I'm good. Each day gets a little better."

"Awesome! You ready to do this?"

"Um...do what?" Bristol asked, totally confused.

In response, Elsie turned to Rocky. "You haven't told her?"

"Haven't had a chance. We just finished breakfast," Rocky said.

She rolled her eyes at him. "I just figured you would've told her right away, since you called and asked me to come over as soon as I could," Elsie said. "I got Tony on the bus and headed straight here."

"And I appreciate it."

"I'm sure I would too, if someone told me what it was that I should appreciate," Bristol quipped.

Elsie chuckled and walked into the living room. She sat on the couch in the same place Rocky had just been and explained, "Rocky said you needed help with a shower. That you did your best to take one the other day but it didn't go that well. He said he should've thought about calling me to help before now, and he felt bad, thus the urgency for me to get over here as soon as I could."

Bristol knew her mouth was open, but was completely shocked. She looked over Elsie's shoulder at Rocky. "When did you call?"

"When I was in the back getting your sheets," he said with a small shrug. "You said the one thing you wanted right this moment was to shower. Getting your supplies so you can do your art will take a bit more planning, but I figured I could at least help you get clean. I should've thought about that before. I'm sorry."

Excitement rose within Bristol. She couldn't *wait* to take a long shower and not worry as much as she had when she'd been by herself. "Don't be sorry. This is awesome!" she exclaimed.

"You two sit and chat for a bit while I get things ready in the bathroom," Rocky ordered.

"Wow. I haven't known Rocky all that long, but he seems... different," Elsie said when he was out of earshot.

"Different how?" Bristol asked.

"Just *different*. I mean, he's always nice, but it's kind of been in a standoffish way. I was beginning to think maybe I irritate him, especially when he volunteered to stay here in Fallport with Raiden while the rest of us hiked out to the watch tower. But seeing him with you the last few days...it's made me see him in a new light."

Bristol was definitely interested in hearing more. "Yeah?" she asked, hoping to encourage the other woman to keep talking.

"Uh-huh. He's...softer around the edges or something. And the way he hovers over you reminds me of how Zeke is with me."

Bristol shook her head. "We're just friends. I mean, I'm grateful he found me, and I'm extremely thankful he's helping me out, but we aren't like you and your husband."

"I have no doubt you're grateful, and I'm sure Rocky is more than relieved he found you. But there's more to you guys than just gratefulness."

"It hasn't even been a week," Bristol said softly, verbalizing what she'd been telling herself for days when she tried to rationalize what she was feeling for Rocky...and failing.

"When you know, you know," Elsie said quietly.

"How long did you know Zeke before you knew you wanted to marry him?" Bristol asked.

"Well, he was my boss for a long time before we were anything more. But here's the thing—once we acknowledged the intense chemistry we had, things ramped up between us *fast*. And I'm thinking maybe you should talk to Lilly about this. She's with Rocky's brother, after all. And they're twins, so I think they probably operate a lot alike. She and Ethan moved *really* fast. And the two of them are ridiculously in love and happy."

Bristol shook her head again. She was getting way ahead of herself here. "I'm happy for you and Lilly, but my situation is completely different."

"Why?" Elsie asked.

"Well, because I'm dependent on him for everything. I can't even go pee by myself. And the fact that you're here brings my point home even more. Taking a shower without help isn't exactly easy. Rocky's taking care of me."

"Sure, I can see how that would make things more complicated, but you aren't always going to be laid up like you are now. This is your getting-to-know-each-other stage. Once you're back on your feet, literally, you can see what happens."

"I don't live here," Bristol said wistfully, ignoring the little voice inside telling her that it would be easy to move.

"Neither did Lilly. But here she is," Elsie said simply.

Bristol huffed out a breath. "You seem to have an answer for everything. It's not that easy."

"Of course it's not," Elsie agreed. "But nothing worth doing is ever easy."

Her words made sense...and increased the longing inside Bristol to make Fallport her home.

"You ladies ready?" Rocky asked from the entrance to the hallway.

"Think about it," Elsie said quietly, reaching out and patting Bristol's hand. "I'm always here if you have questions. Lilly will be too, I have no doubt." Then she turned to Rocky. "We're ready."

He nodded and walked over to where Bristol was sitting. "May I?" he asked.

Bristol suddenly realized that every time he picked her up or touched her, he asked permission. Thoughts of how her supposed *friend* Mike had constantly indulged in unwelcome touches made the differences in the two men all the more clear. "Yes," she told Rocky.

Their eyes met—and it was as if they were suddenly the only two people on the planet.

She wasn't sure how long they'd been staring at each other when Elsie chuckled and said, "I'll just meet you in the bathroom," and walked out of the room.

"What are you thinking about so hard?" Rocky asked.

"I know you don't want to hear this, but thank you for calling Elsie to help me shower."

Rocky shook his head. "Should've thought about it without you having to say anything."

"You found me, went with me to the hospital, stayed with me, brought me back here, fed me, entertained me, and have basically done everything possible to make sure I'm all right. I think I can let you off the hook for not thinking about calling someone to help me bathe," she told him dryly.

Rocky slowly reached out a hand and stroked the back of his fingers down her cheek. "What are you doing to me?" he whispered.

It sounded like a rhetorical question, but Bristol answered anyway. "The same thing you're doing to me."

The flare of desire...and hope...in his eyes mirrored Bristol's own thoughts.

"Right. Shower," Rocky said, as if trying to rein himself in.

For just a second, Bristol wondered what would happen when he let go of that iron control of his. But then he was leaning down and sliding his arms under her knees and behind her back.

"You make this seem so easy," she grumbled, needing to move

them from the intimate bubble they'd been in to something more relaxed.

"That's because it is. In case no one's told you, Punky...you're tiny."

Bristol rolled her eyes. "Wow, really? What a revelation."

He chuckled, and she could feel the rumbling against the hand that was resting on his chest. Her other arm was wrapped around his neck. If she leaned forward just a fraction, she'd be able to feel his beard against her cheek.

Just as she was contemplating doing that very thing, he walked into the bathroom.

"Here she is. Queen Bristol, ready for your assistance," Rocky teased.

"Awesome. This is gonna work great," Elsie said. "Put her on the stool, then shoo."

Rocky bent over the tub to place Bristol on the same small plastic stool she'd sat on before. "Ma'am, yes, ma'am," he said crisply.

Bristol giggled, and Elsie did the same. For just a moment, she felt Rocky's hand at her back, giving her a subtle caress, then he was stepping away from the tub. She figured she imagined it, but when she looked up and met his gaze, the heat she saw there made her inhale sharply.

"Enjoy your shower, Punky. Take your time. There's lots of hot water. The complex might look like a dump, but the manager installed kick-ass water heaters." Then Rocky nodded at Elsie and left, closing the door firmly behind him.

"Whew, *baby*," Elsie said softly, fanning herself with a hand. "That look!" she exclaimed.

Bristol didn't bother to deny the other woman's words. She'd seen a lot of promises in Rocky's eyes...promises she had no idea if either of them would ever act on. They were in a weird position. Attracted to each other, but they weren't exactly equals right now. She was dependent on Rocky, and she had a feeling he'd never act on whatever it was they were feeling when the balance of power between them wasn't even.

But once she was upright and could get around better? All bets were off.

Determination rose within Bristol at that moment. If she was going to even entertain the idea of moving to Fallport, she had to make sure whatever happened between her and Rocky wasn't going to make moving here seem weird.

Did she want to see where their attraction could lead? Yes. Hell yes.

But she didn't want things to burn hot and fast, then fizzle out and have to deal with seeing her ex everywhere she went. She'd like to think they could remain friends if a relationship between them didn't work out, but she didn't know Rocky well enough to decide if that might be the case.

"That's some deep thinking you're doing," Elsie commented.

Bristol took a deep breath. She needed to get her head out of her butt. She was moving way too fast in her mind. There was no telling what would happen in the next month or two. Or even the next week. She needed to put on the brakes, do her best to ignore the desire swimming in her belly for Rocky, and take things slowly.

Yeah, right. Slowly. She had a feeling that slow going wasn't going to be much of an option when it came to her and Rocky. They were on a collision course, and for the first time in her life, Bristol was looking forward to the crash.

"Just thinking about how this is gonna work," Bristol said honestly. Of course, she was talking about her and Rocky and not the impending shower, but Elsie didn't need to know that.

"You said you did this by yourself before?" Elsie asked.

"I did. But it was short and painful, trying to do everything by myself, so having you here will be a huge help."

"Right. Rocky left a plastic bag for us to cover your leg. We can prop your leg on the rim of the tub, under the shower curtain. It's not ideal, but it should work. I'll help you undress, which I'm guessing is the hard part, and then let you do your thing. But I can wash your hair if you want."

"Yes, please. Last time I struggled a bit, and I don't think I actually rinsed out all the bubbles."

"Of course. Arms up."

Bristol didn't feel too self-conscious as her new friend helped her get rid of her clothes. She supposed she should, but after the short stay in the hospital, where it felt as if *everyone* had seen her naked, this wasn't too bad.

Elsie turned the water on and waited until it was hot before pulling the little tab that would make the spray turn on above her head. She handed Bristol a washcloth. "Let me know when you're ready for me to wash your hair. I'll be right here."

"I will, thanks." Thankful for the privacy to clean herself, the second the shower curtain closed, Bristol lifted her head and let the warm water rain down on her face.

She'd never take a shower for granted again. This was heavenly.

CHAPTER EIGHT

Rocky sat in his living room yet again, clenching his teeth as he heard the shower turn on in the other room. It was just over a week when he'd first sat here, doing the same thing. That time, Elsie had been with Bristol, making sure she didn't fall off the stool or otherwise hurt herself as she got used to showering with a temporary handicap.

It had been hell on his libido then, just as it was now.

She was more stable every day, and no longer needed help undressing. Every time she showered, all Rocky could think about was how Bristol was naked in the same space he'd been in an hour ago. He wasn't a man who needed to masturbate every day, but lately he felt as if he was a teenager all over again. He couldn't stop thinking about the woman sharing his apartment.

She was moving better on her crutches, as well, though she preferred to use Rocky as a human crutch whenever he was home. He preferred it too, truth be told. She'd put her arm around his waist and he'd hold her tightly against him as she hobbled to the bathroom, the living room. He'd started taking short jobs around town again, but he thought about Bristol—what she was doing, whether she was all right—every minute he was away from her.

He knew she was fine. She was doing amazingly well, actually, for having a broken leg, living in a strange place, and not having any kind of normal routine that she was used to. She got cranky occasionally, but when she did, it never lasted long. She did her best to pull herself out of the doldrums. She wasn't mean to him or anyone else when she got in a mood. Knowing that about her only made Rocky like her more.

Listening to the water running in the other room, he remembered the smile on her face when she'd come out of the bathroom after that first shower with Elsie's help. It was breathtaking. And when he'd scented his own body wash on her skin, it was all he could do to hide his erection from both women.

And now, she was in his shower again, water cascading down her body, and it was taking everything in him not to join her.

The feelings coursing through him just a week later were overwhelming. Almost unwelcome. Bristol was in his care; she didn't need him lusting after her every second. That would make her feel awkward, and the last thing Rocky wanted was for her to feel uncomfortable around him.

But everything about her appealed to him...and the time was coming when he knew he wouldn't be able to hold back acting on his attraction.

The attraction he saw mirrored in Bristol's eyes when she looked at him.

"I'm ready!" she called out from the bathroom.

Rocky took a deep breath before standing and heading her way. She'd progressed to balancing on her good foot and holding onto the counter as she did what she needed to in the bathroom.

He'd installed some sturdy handholds in the shower, so she could bathe standing up without worrying about falling, though the stool remained so she could rest when needed. She was getting very adept at maneuvering in general, and it was only a matter of time before she'd be ready to go back to Kingsport.

The thought made Rocky's belly swirl uneasily. But for now, he had another surprise for her...and he hoped it would buy him some time. Of course, it could also backfire and make her want to get back to her own life sooner rather than later.

He walked toward the bathroom, the steam rolling out of the small room making him smile. His Bristol loved a long hot shower.

Shit.

Not *his* Bristol.

He needed to get a grip, otherwise he'd definitely scare her away with his over-the-top alpha personality. Living with Bristol had brought out a part of Rocky he hadn't really known about himself. He'd always thought his brother was overprotective with Lilly—but that was *nothing* compared to how he felt about this woman.

When he left for a job, he always made sure he'd arranged for someone to come and be with her while he was gone. Sandra was always happy to visit. And he'd been surprised by how willing Finley Norris, the bakery owner, had been to stay with her as well. Khloe had even come one day. When needed, Elsie would also hang out in the morning before the bar opened, and Lilly stopped by frequently.

"I freaking love your shower," Bristol said with a huge smile as Rocky came toward her. "You weren't lying when you told me how awesome the water heater was."

He grinned as he stopped beside her. He wrapped his arm around her waist and mentally sighed at how right it felt. She gripped him, and he took her weight as they headed for the living room.

He got her coffee—chocolate hazelnut this morning—and poured her a bowl of cereal. They'd eaten many different things for breakfast over the last two weeks or so, but her favorite seemed to be cereal. She was easy to please, which made Rocky happy, since he liked to please her.

"I thought we'd do something different today," he said as nonchalantly as he could as he carried the bowl of cereal and pitcher of milk into the living room.

"Yeah?" she asked, interest shining in her eyes.

Bristol never complained about being bored, even though Rocky was sure she was itching to get out of the apartment more. He'd carried her out to the walkway a few times, and they'd sat out there watching the comings and goings of the other people in the complex so she could get some fresh air. They'd watched TV, played board and card games, read quietly, and generally coexisted peacefully for the near two weeks she'd been convalescing in his apartment. But he had a feeling that today, she would feel like she was truly free for the first time since she'd been hurt.

"Uh-huh. A week ago, I asked if you could do one thing right that second, what would it be."

"I remember. I said take a shower, and not even an hour later, you'd arranged for me to do just that," Bristol told him.

"Right. And what was the other thing you said you wanted?"

She furrowed her brow, trying to recall, and finally shrugged. "I don't remember."

"You said you wanted to make something."

"That's right! Wow, I was really feeling sorry for myself, I suppose."

Rocky shrugged. "I wasn't able to help with that then, but

now that you're more mobile and that leg doesn't hurt when you're upright and moving around, I thought we'd work on your second wish."

She stared at him in confusion.

"I want to take you to Kingsport so you can get some of your art supplies. And maybe some clothes. I'm sure you're sick of wearing my shirts and the few outfits you have. We can get some of your shorts, and whatever else you want to make your life easier and more comfortable here."

Bristol stared at him for so long, Rocky shifted anxiously in his seat. He honestly had no idea what she was thinking. "If you want me to take you home and leave, that's okay too," he said softly, hating to even voice the words, but knowing he needed to say them.

"You probably want your apartment to yourself, huh?" she said after a moment.

"No!" Rocky blurted. Then took a deep breath. "No," he said a little more calmly. "I *like* having you here. And honestly, if you said you wanted to go home and stay, I'd worry like hell. You aren't quite steady on your feet at all times, and your leg still gives you trouble now and then. I just thought maybe time would go by faster, and you'd feel more like yourself, if you had some of your stuff around and you could work on some projects. And I admit to being curious to see your art and how you create it."

"You really wouldn't mind?" she asked.

"Taking you back to Kingsport? No. Having you work on your art here? Definitely not."

"Having my stuff clutter up your house?" she asked. "The stuff to make my jewelry has a tendency to get everywhere. Beads, earring backs, things like that. And I often get lost in my art when I'm working on a project. I might forget you're around while I'm engrossed in what I'm doing."

Rocky studied her, then asked, "I'm guessing someone else in your life complained about that at some point?"

She wrinkled her nose. "Yeah."

"Punky, I'm not fifteen. I can handle you concentrating on your own thing for however long it takes for you to be ready to emerge from your artistic haze."

She smiled. It lit up her face. Rocky lived to be on the receiving end of those grins. "In that case, I would *love* to go to Kingsport with you! I probably should check to make sure no stray mail has been delivered, even though I've had it forwarded here temporarily. I'm not holding out hope for the two plants I own, because I definitely don't have a green thumb, but maybe they've held on and I can water them and they'll be good to go again. And it'll be great to get some of my shorts and stuff to wear. Although, I'm telling you right now that the Navy shirt you've been letting me sleep in? I'm not giving it back," she teased.

"It's yours," Rocky told her, doing his best to tamp down the desire that hit him just remembering how she looked wearing his oversized T-shirt in the evenings.

"Okay, I've done a pretty good job of not saying it, but I have to right now. Thank you, Rocky. Seriously. This means the world to me."

"You're welcome," he told her quietly. "Eat. Then we'll head out. I need to call Ethan and let him know we're going."

"Is he going to be upset?"

Rocky frowned in confusion. "Upset that I'm leaving town? No. I told him what I wanted to do a few days ago, but I wasn't sure what you'd think. And if you decided you wanted to stay home, I told him I'd be gone at least overnight, maybe longer."

"Why?" she asked.

"Because I was going to get a hotel room in Kingsport until I was sure you were good to be on your own."

He saw her swallow hard. "Seriously?"

"Yes. There's no way I would dump you off at your doorstep and leave," Rocky said.

"Most people would."

"I'm not most people," he said firmly.

"Yeah, I've figured that out over the last two weeks," she told him.

The desire to kiss her was almost too overwhelming to resist, but Rocky managed. It wasn't quite time to show her how much he admired her. How much he enjoyed spending time with her. How badly he wanted to be more than a roommate or savior.

He cleared his throat. "If we leave after you eat, we should be able to get there and back before it gets too late."

"Right. I'm eating," she said, smiling brightly at him again before turning her attention to the bowl in front of her.

* * *

Bristol couldn't keep her eyes off the man sitting next to her as they headed south on Interstate 81 toward Kingsport. She'd kind of been waiting for two weeks for him to suggest that it was time for her to go home, but he hadn't. For a second this morning, when he'd brought up going to Kingsport, she'd thought that was it. That he'd gotten sick of having her in his space and was ready for them both to get back to their normal lives. But he'd shocked her by suggesting the trip was just to grab some of her art supplies and clothes, not to drop her off permanently.

Bristol supposed it was probably a better idea if she ripped the bandage off, so to speak. She was enjoying being with Rocky a bit too much. The longer she stayed, the more she got to know him and his friends, the harder it was going to be to leave.

The more she got to know him, and his adorable town, the more she wanted to stay.

But the big question in her mind was whether her feelings were simply a result of her being grateful she'd been rescued, or were they more?

She pretty much knew she'd never liked a guy more than she did Rocky. And just about everyone in the town had been more than welcoming. Every day when she woke up, she wondered who would visit, what funny local stories they'd have to share. The feeling of community in Fallport was something she'd never known she was missing...and something she wanted to be a part of.

Bristol didn't want to wear out her welcome. She liked Rocky. A lot. The last thing she wanted to do was fall head over heels in love with him, only to find out he was only being nice out of a sense of obligation.

But deep down, she knew that wasn't the case. She'd caught him staring at her with an electric longing in his eyes. And while he was careful not to overstep any kind of personal boundaries, she hadn't missed the fact that every now and then...he'd get an erection around her.

Of course, that could just be a natural reaction of his body and not necessarily because of *her*, but she didn't think so. And her own attraction toward him was so intense, there seemed little chance it could be one-sided. There were a few mornings when he'd taken an extraordinarily long time in the shower, and she couldn't help but wonder what he was doing in there...and if it was the same thing *she* did when she was naked in the shower, thinking about him.

"You okay over there?" Rocky asked, bringing her out of her own head.

Smiling at him she nodded. "I'm great. How could I be anything else?" A grin formed on his face, and she asked, "What's that smile for?"

"I just like being around you. You're always so cheerful... which is nice."

"I've found that it's a lot easier to look on the bright side of things than dwell on the negative. Life is short, and I don't want to spend it wanting what I can't have or focusing on all the bad stuff that's happened to me."

"Like falling off a cliff," he said dryly.

"Exactly. I mean, yes, my friend totally screwed me, didn't seem to care about my well-being, and I got hurt. But the entire situation could've been a lot worse than it was. I could've hit my head and died instead of only getting a broken leg. You found me, stayed with me, and you gave me a place to heal. And Fallport is wonderful. I've met so many great people. I love your friends. And you've got a great shower." She smiled at him again.

He divided his attention between her and the road. "You broke your leg, were abandoned by your friends, you've been practically immobile and stuck in my tiny little apartment with a stranger. You don't have your car or any of your personal stuff. You haven't been able to work for two weeks, and while you haven't talked about it, your business is probably suffering as a result. Generally, your life was turned upside down."

Bristol laughed. "Yup. But again, all the good things that have happened as a result of breaking my leg outweigh all those other things. At least in my mind."

Rocky shook his head. "I've never met anyone like you."

"Is that a good thing or a bad thing?" Bristol asked, a little trepidatious.

"Good," he said immediately, which went a long way toward making her feel better. "We're getting close to Kingsport, you want to give me directions?"

Bristol held onto the good feeling deep inside at his answer as she told him where to go, but the closer she got to her house, the more nervous she got. She hadn't considered what Rocky might think about where she lived...and now she was afraid this trip wasn't such a good idea.

They pulled onto her street, and she said, "It's the third house on the right."

She couldn't tell what he was thinking as he pulled into her driveway and turned off the ignition of his SUV.

After a long moment, he turned to her. "I'm thinking there's some things you've left out about yourself, Punky," he said dryly.

She bit her lip nervously as she studied her house, trying to see it through his eyes. She'd loved it from the moment she saw it. It was big. Probably around forty-five hundred square feet. Far too big for one person, but the second she saw the view out the back windows, she'd had to have it. There were five bedrooms, a huge kitchen, the bathrooms had been remodeled before she'd moved in, and the closet in the master bedroom was bigger than the guest room at Rocky's apartment.

"It's...just you living here?" he asked.

"Uh-huh," she said. "It's not as big as it looks." That was a lie. With the huge floor-to-ceiling windows in the living area, it seemed even bigger.

Rocky chuckled and shook his head. "You have your key?"

Bristol shifted and pulled her keyring out of her pocket. She didn't have a purse with her, because who takes a purse hiking and camping? But it was one of the many things she had on her mental list to pack to bring back to Fallport...if Rocky still wanted her to come back with him.

131

"Stay put," he ordered. "I'll come around."

Bristol watched him walk around the front of the SUV. His strides were long and confident, as usual. When he was at her door, he helped her out and, with his arm around her, served as a human crutch as they headed for her front door.

She loved when Rocky carried her. She always felt small around other people, but in his arms, she felt...cherished. But there was something to be said for being plastered against his side with his arm around her, his fingers slightly digging into her waist as he took the weight off her broken leg and she hobbled next to him.

He had no extra fat on him that she could feel. She liked having an excuse to touch him, to put her arm around him. He was warm, made her feel safe. She didn't worry that he was going to let her stumble. Rocky was strong and capable next to her.

When they reached the four steps that led up to her front porch, he didn't ask or warn her, he simply tightened his arm around her waist and easily lifted her feet off the ground before walking up the stairs.

Bristol giggled.

"What?" he asked.

"You didn't even think about that, did you?"

"About what?"

"About simply lifting me to walk up the stairs."

He looked a little sheepish. "Sorry. And no. I didn't want you to hurt yourself. I'm not sure you're up to stairs yet, so I just acted. Are you irritated?"

"No." And she wasn't. "Although I'm going to need to try stairs at some point."

"I know. But that day isn't today," he told her as he gently put her back on her feet at the door.

"You might change your mind once you see how many stairs

there are in my house," she told him as she put the key in her lock.

"Not happening, Punky," Rocky said sternly.

Bristol could only chuckle again. "All right, but if you get tired of lugging me around, just say the word. Welcome to my home," she said as she pushed open the door.

Rocky helped her inside and shut the door behind him. He looked around the large open foyer and whistled low. "Wow, Punky. This is...it's beautiful."

"Wait until you see the view," she told him, then pointed to the right. "That way."

He walked her into her living room, and she heard him draw in a sharp breath. "Wow."

"That's what I thought the first time I saw it," Bristol concurred. The houses on her side of the street backed up to a nature preserve. There were rolling hills, lots of trees, and a peacefulness that helped recharge her batteries when she got down or frustrated with a project she was working on. "It's why I bought this house. The bonus is that no one will be able to build behind me because the land is protected."

"It's beautiful," he told her. Then he looked down at her. "Again, I'm thinking there's some things you left out about yourself."

Bristol shrugged. "I told you that I did well for myself with my art. And that I could afford to get the satellite phones for your team."

"You did, but this...damn. I'm not sure what I expected, but it wasn't you living in a mansion. You must really be going stir-crazy in my little apartment."

"I love this house...but it *is* just a house," she told him softly. "I knew it was too big, and I was right. I kind of rattle around in here all by myself. Your apartment is..." Her voice faded off as she racked her brain for an appropriate adjective.

"Tiny? Cramped? Rundown?" he threw out.

"Cozy. Comfortable. Safe," she countered.

They looked at each other for a long moment before Rocky took a deep breath. But he didn't pull away.

"Rocky?" she asked, not sure why she was whispering, except the moment seemed to call for it.

"I'm going to kiss you," he said firmly. "If you don't want me to, now's your chance to tell me."

Bristol held her breath. She wanted his lips on hers. Badly. Had since almost the first moment she'd seen him.

"Did you hear me?" he asked.

She wanted to laugh. How could she *not* hear him when they had an arm wrapped around each other and were standing hip to hip? "Yes," she said, answering both his question and giving him permission at the same time.

He didn't smile, but Bristol swore she saw relief flare in his eyes. Pulling her tighter against him, turning so her front was plastered to his, Rocky used his free hand to lift her chin.

"You are so pretty. And I'm not just talking physically, although you're that too. You have a light shining in your eyes that draws everyone you come into contact with. And I'm no exception. Once we go here, Punky...there's no going back," he said.

Bristol appreciated that he was doing his best to make sure she really wanted his kiss, but she was getting impatient. She needed his lips on hers. *Now.*

She went up on her tiptoes and was annoyed that he was still too far away for her to reach. Without thinking, she reached up and grabbed a handful of his beard and tugged him down. The last thing she saw before her eyes closed was his amused grin.

The second his lips touched hers, Bristol was a goner.

She'd never kissed a man with a beard before, and the way it tickled her jaw and chin was almost as arousing as the feel of his hand moving around to her nape and his other arm tightening around her waist.

The next thing she knew, her feet were off the floor and he was lifting her, so she didn't have to strain her neck to kiss him. She was held firmly against his body, and she could feel every inch. His hard chest, the way his arm flexed around her waist. His hard cock against her core. But it was his lips on hers that had her moaning deep in her throat.

The small sound seemed to inflame them both. This was no tentative first touch. Rocky kissed her with the confidence of a man who knew what he wanted, and had no problem whatsoever taking it.

His head tilted and his tongue plunged inside her mouth, and Bristol immediately twined her own with his. She shoved her hands into his hair, holding him to her as they kissed as if their lives depended on it. Butterflies swam in her belly, goose bumps broke out on her arms, and she writhed in his grasp, wanting to get closer.

Rocky held her tightly as he kissed her. He nipped her lip, and Bristol reciprocated. She thrust her tongue into his mouth, loving that he was letting her take control of the kiss. Then it was his turn to groan as she nibbled his lip again.

She had no idea how long they'd been kissing when he lifted his head and stared at her. Because he was holding her up, they were nearly eye-to-eye. When he licked his lips, Bristol couldn't help but look down at them.

"Damn, woman," he breathed.

She couldn't help it. She giggled.

"That was..." He paused before continuing. "Will you go out with me?"

Bristol was confused. "What, like a date?"

"Yeah, a date."

"Um, *yes?*"

"I know we're doing things a little backward, you moving in with me and all before I even asked you out on a date, but I like you, Bristol. So much. I want to continue to get to know you."

Things like this didn't happen to her, and she prayed she didn't somehow mess it up. "Same, Rocky."

"So...you'll be my girlfriend?"

She giggled again, but nodded. "Yes."

"And we're exclusive?"

"Rocky, it's not as if I've had men pounding down my door, wanting to go out with me."

"Then they're idiots. And we *are* exclusive," he said firmly.

He hadn't put her down, and Bristol had to admit that she loved being held by him. He still had one of his large hands on the back of her neck while the other one was locked around her torso, keeping her secure against him.

"One thing, though," he said seriously. "I clearly don't make what you do. Is that going to be a problem?"

Bristol frowned. "If you think I'm the kind of woman who would care about something like that, maybe we should stop whatever's happening between us right now," she said, a little more harshly than she'd intended.

"I'm sorry," he apologized immediately, going a long way toward helping Bristol calm down.

"Can we sit and talk about this?" she asked.

He didn't answer verbally, just immediately stepped toward her ultra-comfy suede couch. It was big enough to fit at least six people. There were plenty of nights she'd fallen asleep on its squishy cushions. He sat, gently placing her sideways on his lap, one strong arm around her back and the other across her thighs.

It was a little distracting to be this close, but it was hardly unwelcome. Still... "Um, maybe I should sit next to you instead of *on* you for this conversation?" she suggested.

"Nope. I like you right here. You know how many times I've thought about holding you like this over the last two weeks?" he asked.

Bristol blinked in surprise. "Really?"

"Yes, really. Now, you were saying?"

"It's not a long story," she said with a shrug. "I've always loved art and being creative. I found my niche with stained-glass windows. One thing led to another, and my talent, along with a bit of luck, made me very popular in certain circles online. People who want the best, they know to come to me. I sell my stained glass for anywhere from five hundred dollars for a tiny four-by-six inch panel, to six figures and up for large windows for churches and other buildings."

Rocky blinked in surprise. "Really?"

"Really," she confirmed. "I've invested almost all of my earnings. If I'm being honest, I could retire today if I wanted and not have to work another day in my life. But I like what I do. Creating art fulfills a need in me. I make jewelry and sculptures when I want a break from the stained glass." She shrugged. "I told you I was good at what I did," she said a little quieter...and a little defensively.

To her amazement, Rocky laughed. "That you did, Punky." Then he surprised her by picking up one of her hands and kissing each of her fingertips. "If I'd known, I would've taken a little more care with making sure your hands were all right."

Bristol wanted to melt into a puddle at his feet. She didn't go around telling people how successful she was. First, they tended to think she was bragging, which she wasn't. She was matter of fact about her ability to create beautiful art. And second, when people found out she was rich, they treated her differently.

"Does this change things?"

Rocky twined his fingers with hers and rested them on her leg. "Does what change things?"

"The fact that I've got money."

He stared at her for a long moment before saying, "Do you want it to?"

Bristol frowned. "No?" It came out more as a question than a statement, but she wasn't sure what he was asking.

"Then, no, it doesn't change anything. Bristol, I like you for who you are. Not because of how much money you have. I will admit that it intimidates me a little. I'm good with budgeting, kind of had to be being in the military, though I'm guessing my bank account looks pretty pathetic compared to yours. But I promise that as long as we're together, I'll treat you as if you're the most important person in the world. And that's the kind of thing money can't buy."

Bristol closed her eyes momentarily, almost overcome with emotion.

"Bristol?"

Her eyes opened. She wanted to straddle his waist and press herself against him, but she couldn't quite manage that with her leg just yet. "That's all I've ever wanted. To be important to someone because of who I am, not because of a number in my investment account."

"You're important to *me*," he said without hesitation, then leaned in.

This time their kiss was sweet. Not quite as passionate as before, but no less earth-shattering.

Bristol tucked her head under his chin as she lay against his chest and simply soaked in the moment. Rocky's hand brushed against her hair, almost as if he was petting her. She wanted to purr, it felt so good.

After a while, he said a little self-deprecatingly, "I'm guessing your supplies aren't going to be the few boxes I envisioned, are they?"

She smiled as she lifted her head. "My workshop is in the basement, and yeah, there's no way I can do my bigger pieces in your apartment. But I don't have any commissions on my plate at the moment, and I'm thinking I should probably stick to jewelry right now. It's been a while since I've done any pendants and earrings, and my time in the woods inspired me to do some pieces with nature."

"Right. So we'll bring as much as will fit in my SUV, and if I need to make another trip, I will. We can see about finding you a bigger space to work in too."

Bristol stared at him in silence.

"What?" he asked, picking up on her quizzical look.

"I just...you're not what I expected, Rocky Watson."

"It's Cohen, actually."

"What is?" Bristol asked confused.

"My name. Rocky's a nickname. My given name is Cohen."
She smiled and relaxed against him. "I like it."

He shrugged. "I don't. You have no idea how badly I got made fun of growing up. Cohen wasn't exactly a 'fit in with the crowd' kind of name."

"How'd you get the name Rocky?" she asked.

"I was in the eighth grade and had just watched the movie. I decided I wanted to be like him, a boxer. He was badass and didn't take shit from anyone. I went to school and told everyone that was my name now, and I beat up anyone who dared call me Cohen for the next few months." He shrugged. "Not very nice of

139

me, I know...but it worked. Everyone started calling me Rocky and that was that."

"My given name is Bristol," she told him with a smile, being silly.

He returned it. "Right."

She got serious. "A part of me wants to know what the catch is with you," she told him honestly. "You're gorgeous, you save lost hikers, you were a SEAL, you stayed with me at the hospital in Roanoke then let me bunk with you, without seeming to want anything in return. Now you didn't even blink at learning that I'm rich, and you're even talking about making another trip here for my crap and finding a place for me to make my stained glass. Oh, and you kiss better than anyone I've ever been with. I just... keep waiting for the other shoe to fall. You know, for you to tell me you're married, or that you want me to be a sister wife, or that you're a leader of some sadistic cult and you're simply grooming me to be your latest sacrifice to the devil or something."

Rocky didn't even crack a smile. "I could say the same thing about you," he countered. "You're tough as nails, you're talented, gorgeous, don't need or want me for my money—which is a good thing, because I'm never going to be rich. You seem to love the small town I live in, you make friends wherever you go, and you eat my cooking without making even one face. I keep waiting to see what flaws you might have. Like you smack your lips when you eat—which you don't—or you leave your hair all over the bathroom—which you also don't—or that you're really a sadist and you're looking for a new masochist to beat on."

Bristol laughed.

"I'm just a man," Rocky told her. "I have my faults, but treating women like shit isn't one of them. I can't promise to never piss you off, and I'm sure you'll irritate me at some point, but I'd like to think we can talk about what's bothering us and work things out. It's obvious you need your art, and I'd be stupid to not do everything in my power to keep you happy. Especially considering I'm hoping this works out long-term.

"I'm willing to compromise on a lot of things, but I *would* like to stay in Fallport. It's not a deal breaker. I could move to Kingsport, since contractors can find work anywhere. But I love my job with Eagle Point Search and Rescue and it would suck to leave my friends. So going out of my way to try to make you comfortable and happy in Fallport is all a part of me hoping to convince you that one day, you might be able to make a life there with me."

"Rocky," she whispered, completely overwhelmed. He was just as blunt as she was. She'd never wonder where he stood on a topic. But no one had ever gone out of their way to see to her needs the way he was doing.

"No pressure," he said, kissing her forehead. "Who knows what the future will hold. This intense connection might fizzle out...but I hope whatever happens, we can always be friends."

Bristol nodded. She had no idea if that was possible—the fire between them burning out *or* them being just friends—but Rocky being so damn reasonable was a relief. And a turn-on. "I want to do something for you too," she said. "I'm not comfort-able being the one who receives everything and gives nothing."

At that, Rocky burst out laughing. And while slightly irri-tated that he seemed to be laughing *at* her, she still couldn't help but feel tingly at the sound.

"I'm not laughing at *you*," he said, reading her mind. "But at the idea that you think you're not giving me anything."

"I'm not. You've done everything! Bought food, carried me around, arranged for people to come over and keep me company when you're working. You fix my meals, wash my clothes, clean the apartment. I'm not doing anything but sitting around."

"Wrong," he said, all humor now gone from his tone. "You've given me more than I could ever explain. Before I met you, my life was boring, and so lonely. I'd work for way too long, come home, eat, sleep. That's it. There was some unfortunate excitement recently with both Lilly and Elsie, but generally, when my apartment door closes behind me, my life is gray.

"Then you arrived...and suddenly there's color in my life again. I've laughed more in the last couple weeks than I can remember laughing in the last year. I look forward to coming home at the end of the day, which was never the case. I used to work well into the evening simply because I didn't want to come back to an empty apartment. I know my cooking isn't exactly gourmet, but it's been fun coming up with different meals for us. You've brought more *life* to my life than anyone has before...if that makes sense. So you can stop thinking you aren't bringing anything to this relationship."

His words made her feel good—and sad at the same time. She hated thinking about him living a gray life.

"Right, so, we've had a heavy morning. We had our first kiss —which knocked my socks off, by the way—we agreed we're now exclusively dating, I found out my girlfriend is loaded, and we have a lot of packing to do. You ready to get to it so we can head back to Fallport before it gets too late? Or do you want to stay the night here? We can do that too. And since you have five bedrooms, I'm hoping I can bunk down in one of them. I know I said I'd find a hotel, but seeing this house? I'm not sure I'm comfortable leaving you alone here."

Bristol rolled her eyes. "I lived alone before I met you."

"I know. But now you *have* met me, and that's not happening."

Bristol frowned. "You don't think I can take care of myself?"

"I know you can," he retorted. "But all I can think of is how many windows and doors there are in this place. And how easy it would be for someone to get in and hurt you. At least in my apartment, there's really only one way in and out...unless someone is Spider-Man and can climb the wall to the second floor. Even then, I'd hear them before they got through the window."

Great, now she was going to be hearing prowlers with every creak of her house. "I'm not going to take all day to pack. We can be on the road before it gets dark," she told him.

"I'm not trying to be an overbearing dick," Rocky said, palming the side of her face. "I just don't want to lose you, now that I've finally found you."

"You aren't going to lose me. But you have to keep in mind that I've lived on my own for a long time now. Don't smother me, Rocky. I'd hate that."

He didn't blow off her concern, but nodded instead. "I'll do my best. Feel free to let me know when I'm getting overprotective."

"I will," she said.

"Good. Now, how about you give me a tour of this amazing house and we'll get to work?"

Bristol smiled at him and leaned forward, kissing his lips briefly before pulling back. She saw desire flare in his eyes, but liked how he was able to control himself. Some men, now that they'd established they wanted each other, would quickly push for more. But not Rocky.

He stood with her in his arms, as if she weighed nothing more than a child, and said, "All right, woman, show me your home."

* * *

The man in the car down the street frowned as he stared at Bristol's house. He just happened to be sitting there, as he did several hours a day in the hopes he'd catch her coming home, when an SUV entered the driveway.

He didn't recognize the car, noticing it had a Virginia license plate. His blood boiled when he saw the large bearded man help his Bristol to the front door. They were way too close. Touching each other way too familiarly. He saw her laugh up at him, and a film of red dropped down over his vision.

She was *his*.

She wasn't supposed to be smiling at another man.

Wasn't supposed to be touching anyone else.

She had a cast on her leg. The man she was with must have hurt her in some way. It was the only possible reason he could think of for why she hadn't been around for weeks. She'd hooked up with some guy—and he'd hurt her.

She hadn't posted anything on her social media for nearly three weeks. Hadn't put any new items in her store, and in fact had posted a note that said she was taking a break and was closing her store to new purchases for a while.

Unacceptable. The joy he felt when he held something she'd made with her own hands...something she'd touched, breathed on...was as necessary to his life as breathing. She'd denied him that.

And she was with another man.

No. Just *no*.

He sat where he was, seething and watching, all afternoon.

When the bearded stranger began hauling boxes out of her house and loading them into his SUV, he almost lost it there and then. He wanted to leap out of his car and storm down her drive and confront him. Was his Bristol moving out? Moving in with some abusive asshole?

Unacceptable!

She was *his*.

Chewing on his nails, he watched as the SUV got more and more full. When it was completely packed with boxes, both the cargo space and the back seat, he finally got to see his Bristol again—but the sight made his lip curl. The man was *carrying* her. Holding her in his arms as he brought her to the passenger side of the SUV. He carefully placed her on the seat, held out the seat belt for her, then leaned down and kissed her.

Kissed her.

Right there in front of anyone who might be watching.

No. No, no, no, no, no!

Determination welled within him. He'd waited too long. He should've made his move sooner. But he had no doubt that when Bristol saw him, she'd fall madly in love. As deeply as he loved her. She'd feel the connection between their souls. She had to.

He needed to figure out where she was going and make plans.

Bristol Wingham was *his*. No goddamn lumberjack was going to take her away from him. No way in hell.

He memorized the license plate on the SUV as it pulled out of Bristol's driveway, and after a few long seconds, followed behind the man taking his woman away. Once he figured out where she was staying, he could plan his next move.

He'd staked out her house enough to know how to get in without her neighbors seeing him. Part of his plan had always been to make sure, once they were together, that she'd be comfortable. That she'd have plenty of her own things around her. He and Bristol were meant for each other. No one and nothing was going to keep them apart.

Being sure to keep a few cars between him and his target, the man's mind spun with what needed to be done, how he could get his Bristol back. Red-hot anger spiked as the SUV got on the interstate and headed north. He hadn't expected her to be staying out of town...but it didn't matter. He'd finally found her. He had no intention of letting her get away again.

CHAPTER NINE

Rocky unlocked his apartment door and the first thing he heard was laughter. The next thing that struck him was the delicious smell emanating from his kitchen.

He closed his eyes as he let the moment wash over him. How long had it been since he'd come home after a long, sweaty day of work to the feeling of truly being *home?*

How about...never.

His apartment had always simply been a place to lay his head. Even when he'd been in the Navy, it was the same way at the different bases where he'd been stationed. But ever since Bristol moved in, he actually looked forward to calling it quits at the end of the day, and he hadn't worked past dark since bringing her home. Two things that rarely happened before her.

"Rocky!" Lilly called out, seeing him in the doorway. "Come look at what Bristol made for me!"

The other woman sounded extremely excited, and while Rocky didn't exactly care about jewelry, he *did* care about making sure his future sister-in-law felt comfortable around him, and that Bristol knew he supported her work.

As he closed his door, Rocky once again tried to wrap his mind around the fact that Bristol made an unbelievably successful living with her art. He hadn't seen her make one of her stained-glass panels yet, but after their trip to Kingsport, he'd immediately looked her up online—and was flabbergasted by what he'd seen.

She was a miracle worker. The windows she'd made were so beautiful, they'd taken his breath away. And Rocky wasn't a man who was easily impressed. His favorite piece he'd seen so far wasn't the biggest, about six feet tall and three feet wide. A man in Indiana had installed the window in his home, on the second floor. The sunrise caught it perfectly, and was a perfect complement to the beach scene Bristol had crafted out of glass. The sun coming over the horizon made it look as if the glass was coming to life. Seeing that image, Rocky had better understood why her art cost as much as it did.

"Hey, Lilly," he said, making a beeline for Bristol. It had been three days since they'd gotten back from Kingsport, and while he'd never thought his houseguest had been unhappy, it was easy to see how much creating art settled her. She seemed more... content, than she had before.

He walked over to where she was sitting on his couch and leaned over, kissing her. Rocky loved having the freedom to touch her when he felt the urge. Loved being able to show her physically how happy he was that she was with him. And the way she enthusiastically returned his kisses was soul-satisfying.

He lifted his head, but didn't stand up all the way, bracing a hand on the arm of the couch. "How do you feel?"

She smiled up at him. "Good."

"You take any painkillers today?"

Shaking her head, Bristol said, "No. I feel fine."

Rocky studied her, trying to ascertain if she was telling the truth or not. His Bristol had a high pain tolerance; he might not know everything about her yet, but he knew that much. The fact that she'd crawled through the woods and hadn't complained even once after surgery proved it.

"All right," he said after a moment. "But don't be a hero. If you hurt, take something."

"I will," she said, reaching out and running her palm up and down his biceps tenderly.

Feeling her hands on him made Rocky want her so badly, it almost hurt. But no matter how much he wanted to physically prove that he liked and admired her, she wasn't healed yet. He never wanted to hurt her, and if he got her naked, the last thing he'd be thinking about was being careful with her leg.

Not only that, he was enjoying this slow intimacy between them. The desire was always there, buzzing gently, but the anticipation of how and when they'd move their relationship to the next level was exciting. Gave him something to look forward to. Lord knew he needed that, after going from the life of a SEAL, to the last five slow—extremely slow—years here in Fallport.

"All right, enough lovey-dovey stuff," Lilly said with a laugh. "Look at the earrings Bristol made for me!" She held up a pair of dangly earrings.

Rocky stood and obediently took the jewelry from Lilly. He examined them much more carefully than he would've if they were anything other than something made by the woman he could still taste on his lips.

He had no idea what kind of flower Bristol had made out of the beads she'd brought from her house, but they were incredibly detailed. They even sparkled in the low light of the apartment. "They're very pretty," he remarked as he handed them back to Lilly.

Both women chuckled.

"Coming from a guy, that's high praise," Lilly said. "They're lilies. You know, like my name."

"At risk of sounding like a *complete* guy...the only kind of flower I'd recognize is a rose. Maybe a dandelion too," Rocky said with a small shrug. "But these *are* pretty. The blue in them will bring out the lovely blue in your eyes."

Lilly stared at him for a beat, then said, "Wow."

"Right?" Bristol agreed.

Rocky looked between the two women in confusion. "What?"

They laughed again, and he was completely lost.

Bristol obviously felt sorry for him, because once she got control of herself, she explained, "I'm guessing not many men would comment on jewelry matching someone's eyes."

"I love Ethan to death, but I know for a fact he'd never say something like that," Lilly added with a huge smile.

"Aaaaand now I'm gonna go smash a beer can against my forehead, belch, and scratch my nuts to reassert my manliness," Rocky said with a laugh.

That set the two women off again, and he watched with a big grin as they laughed hysterically. *This* was what was missing in his life. Joy. Laughter.

"While you two make fun of me, I'm gonna go shower," Rocky told them.

To his surprise, Bristol leaned forward and grabbed his hand. "We weren't making fun of you," she told him, looking serious. "I'm impressed you even made that connection, because that's exactly what I was thinking when I decided on the colors."

As he stared down into her eyes, it felt as if they were the only two people in the world. He had a feeling she and Lilly would probably still laugh at him when he went to shower, but at that moment, knowing he and Bristol were on the same page, he didn't even care.

He lifted his other hand and brushed the backs of his fingers over her cheek. "Something smells good in here."

She smiled. "It's nothing fancy. Pork roast in the Crockpot. Lilly helped, since it's still hard to stand on one foot for long."

"You shouldn't be up for long periods of time yet," Rocky scolded.

Bristol rolled her eyes. "I'm fine. I know my limits. And as I just said, that's why Lilly helped. She did the leg work. Literally."

Rocky nodded at Lilly. "Thanks."

She was sitting on the other end of the couch, watching them closely. "You're welcome."

"Been a long time since I've walked in here and had dinner waiting for me," he told Bristol.

"How long?" she asked, then wrinkled her nose. "Sorry, no. Forget I asked."

Rocky couldn't deny he liked that she sounded a little jealous. And he was on the same page. He was extremely envious of the time others got to spend with her when he was out working. It wasn't rational, but he felt it anyway. Oddly, knowing she was experiencing some of the same emotions made him feel closer to her somehow.

But he also didn't want her to think she had anything to worry about when it came to their relationship. So he whispered, "Never." Then leaned down, kissing her once more. A hard and fast kiss, before standing and heading for the hallway.

He wasn't quite in his room yet when he heard Lilly say, "Gii-iiirl. You two are hot enough to throw sparks."

Pausing to hear Bristol's response, he smiled when she said, "He's pretty amazing."

He was still smiling as he grabbed a change of clothes and headed to the bathroom. By the time he was finished and back in the living room, Lilly was gone.

"I didn't mean to chase her off," Rocky told Bristol.

"You didn't," she reassured him. "Apparently everyone who comes over takes their babysitting duties seriously. They don't like to leave me by myself until you get back. As if I'm gonna leap up and start breakdancing or something the second I'm alone."

She snorted a laugh when she was done, so Rocky knew she wasn't upset. He *had* asked people to hang out until he got back from whatever job he was working on, simply because he was leery of Bristol falling or somehow hurting herself, having to lie on the floor in pain until he got back. It was irrational, and stemmed from the knowledge of her doing that exact thing in the woods until he'd found her, but since it didn't look like Bristol was upset about having company, he didn't worry about it.

"You're getting around much better," he said.

"Yeah. Other than feeling a little lopsided and being extremely cautious not to put weight on my leg, I feel really good," she agreed. "Are you hungry? The pork roast should be done."

"Starving," he said, then offered his arm. He missed carrying her around, but he was glad to see her getting more mobility back every day. When it was just them in the apartment, she used him as a crutch instead of the unwieldy things Doc Snow had given her. She'd ordered a knee walker, a wheeled contraption that had a pad she could rest her knee on as she scooted around, but it hadn't arrived yet.

He helped her to the small table next to the kitchen area, and chuckled upon seeing it. The entire surface was covered with plastic bins full of art supplies. Beads, sparkly doodads, a pair of pliers, and small plastic squares with Bristol's logo on them, which she used to hold pairs of earrings and other jewelry for sale.

"Jeez, I'm a slob," she said with a small laugh. "Give me a second and I'll clean this up."

"It's fine," Rocky told her honestly. Being in the Navy had made him a neat freak, but seeing her things strewn across his table was a sign she was comfortable in his space, and that was exactly how he wanted her.

"Rocky, it's a disaster. I'm sorry. I'm used to leaving my crap out in my workroom at home. I didn't even think."

He helped her sit, then squatted next to the chair. He put one hand on her thigh and the other at the small of her back. "You know what seeing this makes me think?" he asked.

"That you can't wait until you get your nice clean space back?" she suggested dryly.

"No," he said with a shake of his head. "It makes me appreciate the fact that you're here. Healthy and happy. I love seeing your enthusiasm and pleasure when you're in the zone creating something. This stuff on my table? It means I get to share my space and life with a beautiful, interesting, and talented woman."

Bristol licked her lips and stared at him. "Um...okay. Wow."

"I don't care if I find beads in every nook of this place years from now. No matter what happens tomorrow, next week, or in a year, they'll remind me of you, of seeing your smile, and the feeling of not being so alone, if only for a little while. Now, what do you want to drink with dinner?"

He'd purposely lightened the conversation, because he was getting into dangerous territory. He genuinely loved having her around, but didn't want to pressure her into doing something she might not want to do. She had her own life back in Kingsport, and the last thing Rocky wanted was for her to give that up on a whim.

"I think tea. Please."

"You got it," Rocky said, leaning forward and kissing her forehead before he stood and turned to the kitchen.

* * *

Bristol watched the man who had somehow snuck under her skin before she'd even realized what was happening. Living with him was easy. She'd never shared the same space with a man before. She'd had some definite preconceived notions about what it might be like, but Rocky had blasted all of them to pieces.

He was neat, considerate, did the laundry, cleaned, cooked, and genuinely made her feel as if this was truly her home, and she wasn't just a temporary guest. The more time she spent with Rocky, and in Fallport, the more she wanted to stay.

This coming weekend was the Pickleport Festival, something Fallport held every year, and Bristol was almost giddy with excitement. She'd been making as many pieces of jewelry as she could to sell—with proceeds going toward equipment for the search and rescue team. She was still planning on purchasing the satellite phones the guys needed, but the money from the sale of her jewelry could go toward whatever else they needed.

Finley had offered some space at the table she was setting up for the parade. She was selling baked goods, of course, special pastries she didn't normally offer in the store. Bristol had adored the other woman immediately upon meeting her. She was average height, maybe around five-six or so, and gorgeously plus-sized. She'd joked that it was almost a requirement for a bakery owner to be overweight.

Bristol suspected the woman had no idea of her own appeal. Despite that, Finley seemed comfortable in her body, wearing clothes that enhanced her shape rather than attempting to hide it. Bristol had always longed to have the kind of sexy curves Finley boasted.

And she hadn't missed the way Brock watched the pretty bakery owner whenever the two were in the same room. He couldn't take his eyes off her, in fact...and Bristol wondered why he hadn't asked her out or otherwise made his attraction known. But she was new to Fallport and to the group; the last thing she wanted was to put her foot in her mouth by bringing it up. She had no idea what their history was, or if they had one at all. Maybe they'd dated and things hadn't worked out. Until she knew more about both Brock and Finley, she'd keep her mouth shut.

So many people had kept her company during her convalescence. She'd gotten to know some of the regulars at Sunny Side Up too, including those who'd greeted her when Rocky had brought her home from the hospital. One day last week, before Rocky left on a job, she'd admitted that she was feeling a little cooped up. He'd brought her to the diner, sat her at a booth, and Sandra let her hang out until he returned a few hours later.

A ton of people had stopped by to see her and chat. By the time Rocky arrived to take her back to his apartment, she'd actually been sad to go.

"This smells amazing," Rocky said, carrying a plate overflowing with roast and veggies over to her.

Bristol laughed and protested, "I can't eat all that!"

He merely shrugged. "Then eat what you can and we'll wrap up the rest." He went back to the kitchen to grab his own plate and a bottle of beer. He pushed a plastic bin of beads out of his way and smiled at her as he sat. Then he reached for her hand.

Bristol automatically clasped his, and he squeezed her fingers gently.

"I'm not a very religious man. But I've seen enough in my lifetime to believe there's some kind of higher power out there. I feel as if I need to say some sort of grace tonight."

Bristol smiled at him. "I'd like that."

Inhaling deeply through his nose, Rocky didn't close his eyes, but instead pinned her in place with his intense gaze as he spoke. "Thank you for this meal and the wonderful company. Coming home to laughter and the smell of deliciousness in my kitchen was enough to make me stop and give thanks for all that I have in my life. Friends, family, a roof over my head, food on my table, and a woman who's shown me in the short time she's been here what a relationship should be like. I promise to never take her, or anything else I have in my life, for granted."

Would this man ever stop surprising her? She hoped not.

"Amen," she said quietly.

"Amen," he echoed. He lifted their clasped hands and kissed her knuckles before squeezing her fingers gently once more and releasing her.

The brush of his beard against her skin made shivers snake up her spine. The more time she spent around Rocky, the more she *wanted* to spend with him. She was in deep, and every day just made her feelings for him grow.

Rocky talked about his current job as they ate. He was rebuilding a deck with composite materials and replacing the old worn-out wood. It wasn't difficult, but being in the sun and the heat made it more tiring than it otherwise would be.

They talked about the upcoming festival, and Bristol told him how much she was looking forward to it.

"I can't remember the last time I saw a parade. I mean, I watch the Thanksgiving one in New York every year, but I'm guessing this one is gonna be very different."

Rocky chuckled. "As night and day," he said. "There won't be any of the fancy blow-up balloons or floats. Mostly people driving their pickups and towing flatbeds that have been decorated with poster board and streamers."

"It sounds awesome," Bristol said honestly. She guessed, knowing the townspeople like she did, that they'd go all out for their local celebrations.

"The gathering in the square afterward is nuts," Rocky went on. "Fallport loves their festivals and celebrations. There's an abundance of food, and everything you can think of related to pickles will be served. Pickle ice cream, fried pickles, pickle pizza, and even pickle fries. There are also more traditional contests for the best pie, fudge, and even a watermelon seed spitting contest. I heard that old man Grogan—he owns the general store in the square—has a Bigfoot-themed float, and he's debuting the merchandise he's created for the influx of Bigfoot hunters we all expect to see, once that paranormal investigation show airs."

Bristol winced. "Kind of like why I was here, huh?" she asked.

Rocky shrugged. "You weren't really here to find Bigfoot. You came for a change of pace and to spend time in nature with someone you thought was a friend. Not your fault he was an idiot. Anyway, I was kind of against the notoriety at first. I mean, it's not exactly my idea of a good time to have to rescue inexperienced hikers who go tromping around the woods in search of something they aren't going to find. But now that I've had a chance to think about it, the amount of money the Bigfoot tourists are going to bring to the town could be a huge help. As you've seen, most of the businesses around here are locally owned and not franchises. And if we *do* have an increase in searches, it'll help the city council see how important we are to the community, and hopefully they won't be as stingy with the budget in the future."

Bristol nodded. "I have to admit I'm kind of excited to see the shirts and stuff with Bigfoot on them. I'm gonna have to get some for myself, and my mom too. She'll get a huge kick out of it."

Rocky smiled. Then said, "Oh, and did you hear about Tony?"

Bristol frowned in concern. "What about him? Is he okay?"

"He's fine. I meant that he's gonna get an award at the parade."

"Really? What kind?"

"Every year, Fallport names someone their 'Hero of the Year.' After what happened with his dad, and how he managed to get himself out of the situation he'd found himself in, driving back to Fallport all by himself to give his mom and everyone else a head's up about what his dad was planning, he was nominated for the award. And he won. As did Zeke, much to his disgust."

"Why disgust?" Bristol asked. She'd heard all about what had happened to Tony. How his dad actually tried to have him killed for a life insurance payout. When that failed, he'd taken Elsie— for whom he'd also bought a healthy policy. She'd escaped into the forest off the interstate, and Zeke had found her easily. "I mean, he's definitely a hero, as are all of you guys for what you do."

Rocky shrugged. "We're just a bunch of guys doing something we love. Using the skills we've learned from our previous jobs. We don't like being called heroes."

"Well, that's silly. You *are*. And I'm glad the town is recognizing that."

"That means a lot," Rocky said quietly. They shared a tender look before he continued. "Anyway, Tony gets to ride on a float. Well, it's not actually a float, but he gets to sit on top of the mayor's SUV, through the sunroof, and wave to everyone as he goes by. He's also pretty excited about the crown he'll get too."

Bristol smiled. "I bet."

"Zeke'll be with him, but he's a little less excited about the attention. And I hear he's gonna refuse to wear the sash and crown that goes with the title." Rocky smirked.

Bristol laughed outright at that. "Yeah, I can't really see any of you enjoying that part. But it's cool for Tony."

"Yeah. He's been a trooper. He was pretty devastated about what happened for a while Thought it was *his* fault his mom had been put in danger. But with the help of Elsie and Zeke, not to mention everyone else in the town, I think he's pretty much gotten over it. The Hero of the Year thing and getting to be in the parade will help even more."

"Oh, it definitely will."

"You asking for his autograph when you first got here was pretty awesome too," he told her.

Bristol smiled. "I was serious about keeping that napkin. He's gonna do great things, and when he's famous, I can say I knew him when."

"I'm thinking we should all be asking for *your* autograph," he said.

Bristol rolled her eyes. "Whatever."

"I'm serious. I looked up some of your stained glass, you know. I'm impressed."

He couldn't have said anything that would've pleased her more. "Thanks."

"You're talented. Very talented. How'd you get started?"

"I was in Girl Scouts when I was young, and a local artist came to one of our meetings, and we all got to make miniature stained-glass ornaments. I was fascinated by the whole process and bugged my mom to death to do another. She finally found a local lady who agreed to take me on. I think everyone thought I'd get tired of it...but I didn't."

"And now you've got your art in buildings all over the United States, and even overseas."

"Pretty much," Bristol said with a shrug. "The thing is, I'd be doing this even if I didn't make any money at it. There's just something so satisfying about taking little individual pieces of glass and putting them together to make a bigger picture that's meaningful, and that everyone can enjoy. Being able to make a living doing it is just icing on the cake."

"I agree. If only hiking in the woods paid as much." They both laughed, then he nodded at her plate. "You did a pretty good job on that."

Looking down, Bristol was surprised to see how much of a dent she'd put in the huge mound of food he'd heaped on her plate. "I guess I was hungrier than I thought," she said. "But if I get as big as a house, don't go blaming me."

To her surprise, Rocky leaned over and said in a serious tone, "I don't give a fuck *what* you weigh. I like who you are in here," he said, lifting a hand and tapping her temple. "You're funny, outgoing, talented, friendly, empathetic to others, and strong as hell. None of that's gonna change if you gain fifty pounds. I want you to be healthy so you can be around for a very long time, but life's too short to worry about that shit. Be who you are. Screw what society shoves down people's throats about the ideal body size. You, Bristol, are fucking beautiful. All four feet, ten inches of you."

She was almost overcome with emotion after he stopped talking. But she managed to say, "Four-eleven. That extra inch is important."

He chuckled. "Right, sorry. Now, you want a bowl of ice cream for dessert? I got your favorite...cookie dough with pretzel pieces."

After his impassioned declaration that he didn't care if she gained weight, there was no way Bristol was saying no. Hell, who was she kidding? She'd never say no to her favorite ice cream regardless. "Yes," she said simply.

"Awesome. Come on, I'll get you settled on the couch then bring you a bowl."

"I can help with the dishes," she protested.

"Nope. You made dinner, I'll do the dishes."

"Using the slow cooker isn't making dinner," she said wryly.

"Fine. Then I'll do the dishes because you can't reach the cabinets where everything goes when they're done, and you'll stick the bowls and plates in weird nooks and crannies that you can reach and I won't be able to find later."

Bristol burst out laughing. He wasn't wrong. The last time she'd unpacked the dishwasher, she'd put things away all willy-nilly. "It was either that or get up on a chair, which I didn't think you'd appreciate with my leg and all," she told him after a moment.

He shuddered. Actually *shuddered* at the idea. His concern for her was like a warm blanket around her shoulders after being out in the cold all day. "I'll see about getting a stool for the kitchen. One with a handle or something so you don't have to go crawling around on the counters and chairs to reach the cabinets."

"It's okay," she told him. "I'm used to it."

"Not happening," he said firmly as he scooted his chair back. "You need anything from the table to work on your jewelry?"

"No, I think I'm good for now."

Rocky nodded, then helped her up from her chair and wrapped his arm around her. She didn't really need that support to walk anymore, not with the crutches Doc Snow had given her, but she wasn't going to complain about having him smushed up against her side. He smelled awesome after his shower and if she turned her head, his beard would brush against her cheek. She loved that for some reason.

He got her settled on the couch and headed back to the kitchen. She watched as he carried their plates to the sink, rinsed them, placed them in the dishwasher, got down two bowls that she never would've been able to reach, scooped out huge helpings of ice cream, and came toward her with a smile.

"Thought you had like a hundred more earring sets to make," he said as he handed her the bowl.

"I do," she said with a shrug.

"Then why weren't you making them instead of watching *me*?" he asked.

"Because your ass is much more exciting than beads," she blurted.

He laughed. "Right. For the record, I feel the same about yours."

They grinned at each other.

"Eat that," he ordered, nodding at her bowl. "Before it melts. You want to watch something?"

"Do you?" she countered.

"There's a game on that I wouldn't mind seeing. But if you'd rather watch something else, that's cool too."

"The game's fine. I need to concentrate on these earrings. I didn't get nearly as many done today as I should've, since I was chatting with Lilly."

The look Rocky gave her was so full of...expectation and

anticipation, it was all she could do not to put her ice cream aside and scoot over next to him and climb onto his lap. But she controlled herself. She was enjoying how things were going between them. She didn't feel any pressure, as far as their physical relationship went, and the longer they waited, and the more they got to know each other, the more the flames between them would grow.

When they did come together—and she was fairly sure that was going to happen sooner rather than later—they'd both get burned...in a good way. She hoped.

"Killin' me, Punky," Rocky mumbled as he turned on the TV.

She wasn't surprised he was on the same wavelength when it came to their attraction. But he wouldn't do a damn thing about it until he was one hundred percent sure she was onboard. It was one more thing she liked about him.

Her lips twitched, and when she glanced over at Rocky, she saw that he was looking back...and smiling too.

She put a large spoonful of ice cream in her mouth and did her best to think about what she wanted to make next for the Pickleport Festival.

Mike might've actually done her a huge favor, she mused. She wasn't happy she'd gotten hurt, but she couldn't deny that being found by her own mountain man wasn't the worst thing that had ever happened to her.

CHAPTER TEN

Bristol couldn't stop smiling. She hadn't been this happy in a very long time. She was currently sitting in front of The Sweet Tooth, watching the parade. Rocky had been right, the "floats" were nothing more than pickup trucks hauling flatbed trailers, but everyone was in high spirits and having a great time.

She hadn't been to many parades, but the few she'd attended hadn't been this...neighborly. It seemed as if the entire town had shown up for the parade and the festival that would follow. All the businesses in the square had agreed to stay closed until after the festivities, other than having tables set up to sell some wares, giving the owners and employees a chance to enjoy the day. Well, all the businesses except for the pool hall.

Rocky had grumbled about the owner being a jerk who hated Fallport. Which made no sense to Bristol. If he hated it here, why in the world had he bought the business in the first place?

But everyone else was having a great time. Lilly was running around taking a million pictures, Elsie was sitting to Bristol's left, waiting anxiously for Tony and Zeke's "float" to drive by. On her right side was Finley, who was stressing about whether or not she'd made enough cookies and other goodies for the festival after the parade. The jewelry Bristol had made was all spread out on the table behind them, and she hoped to make a good amount of money for the Eagle Point Search and Rescue team.

Across the way, Bristol could see Silas, Otto, and Art sitting in their normal spot outside the post office. They were waving at everyone and generally being treated like the kings of Fallport that they were.

Little kids roamed everywhere and the atmosphere was relaxed and friendly.

"What are you smiling about?" Finley asked.

Bristol turned, directing her smile at the other woman. She'd been so welcoming, and Bristol had seen firsthand how generous Finley was...handing out extra treats to the customers, and even making sandwiches for Davis Woolford, the lone homeless man who lived in Fallport.

"I just love this," Bristol told her.

"Yeah, this is only my second year being here for it, and there's really nothing like small towns when it comes to a festival."

"I didn't realize you'd been here that long," Bristol said. "For some reason, I thought you were relatively new to the area."

The other woman shrugged. "I mean, compared to most people, I *am* new."

"What brought you here? Fallport isn't exactly on the beaten path," Bristol said.

Finley shrugged...and Bristol realized she seemed uncomfortable with the question. "I needed a change," she said simply.

Knowing better than to push, Bristol squeezed her arm affectionately before sitting back in her chair. "Thanks for letting me hang out and use some of your table space," she said, doing her best to change the subject.

"Of course. I appreciate the company," Finley said.

"Having a good time?" a deep voice asked from behind them.

Bristol jumped in her chair, and felt better when both Elsie and Finley had a similar reaction. Elsie turned and scowled at Brock, who'd walked up behind them without any of them noticing. "Jeez, Brock. You need a bell or something," she told him.

He chuckled as Bristol turned to greet him—and for the first time, she noticed the man was absolutely ripped. He wore a white tank top that showed off his arms and shoulders, and was much more muscular than Rocky.

"Sorry," he told them. "You guys thirsty? It's kind of hot out. I could go grab you a lemonade or something."

"I'm okay," Elsie said. "You guys?" she asked, turning to Bristol and Finley.

Bristol shook her head. "I just finished a water." She looked over at Finley...and saw her new friend's gaze was focused on her hands in her lap. "Finley?"

"Huh? Oh, I'm good," she said, then turned her attention back to her fidgeting fingers.

"Tony and Zeke should be driving by soon. I saw Tony earlier with his crown and sash, and he was practically bursting with pride," Brock told Elsie.

"I don't think he slept at all last night," she said with a chuckle.

Brock exchanged a bit more small talk with her and Elsie. Finley was as silent as a mouse as she listened, but didn't participate in the conversation.

"Where's Rocky?" he asked at one point.

Bristol pointed over to the other side of the square, where Rocky, Raid, and Tal were sitting behind a table. They'd volunteered to be the judges in the watermelon seed spitting contest. It wouldn't start until after the parade was over, but they were busy signing people up and giving directions on when and where the participants should show up for their turn.

"That's right, I forgot they were suckered—er...*volunteered* for that," Brock said with a grin. "Well, if you need anything, just give me or any of the rest of the guys a yell. Have fun." He walked off...and Bristol saw Finley watching him leave with a longing in her eyes she could totally understand.

Elsie's cell rang, and she sent an apologetic look toward Bristol and Finley. "It's Zeke. He said he'd call when they got close to make sure I didn't miss them."

"No problem. Tell him we can't wait to show our adoration," Bristol teased.

Elsie chuckled and stood to answer the phone, taking a few steps toward the building behind her to get some privacy as she spoke to her husband.

Knowing she didn't have much time before Elsie was back, and not wanting to embarrass Finley, she said quickly, "He's pretty awesome."

"Who? Zeke? Yeah, Elsie's lucky."

"No. I mean, yes, he's awesome too. But I was talking about Brock."

Finley looked surprised for a moment, but quickly hid the emotion. "You like him?"

Bristol rolled her eyes. "Come on, give me a break. I think it's pretty obvious the only guy I like is the one I'm currently living with."

"What's up with that?" Finley asked. "Are you guys dating yet?"

Bristol shook her head. "Nope, I'm not going to let you change the subject. What's up with you and Brock?"

Finley sighed. "Nothing."

Bristol raised an eyebrow, showing her skepticism.

"Seriously. You saw. He doesn't even know I exist. The only reason he stopped was because you and Elsie are here."

"You didn't talk to him though," Bristol pushed, but in a gentle way.

"I don't know what to say," Finley replied with a sigh. "He's... he's lived this amazing life and has done all these awesome things. I'm just me. Besides, he'd never look twice at me. I mean, look at me, then look at *him*."

"There's nothing wrong with you," Bristol said.

Finley scoffed. "Yeah, right. I'm fat," she said bluntly. "And I own a bakery. What a stereotype. Don't get me wrong, I'm old enough to know I'm never going to look like the women in magazines. I like sweets too much to even care what I weigh. I've always been big, it is what it is. But there's no way he'd ever be interested. You saw him. He's so...*built*. He could literally have any woman he wanted. He needs someone elegant. Exotic. Not someone like me."

"I think you're wrong," Bristol said with a shake of her head. "I don't know him all that well, but from what I've seen, none of the guys are superficial enough to base their attraction to a woman simply on looks. Besides...he can't take his eyes off you when you're around."

"What? That's not true," Finley insisted.

"It is," Bristol told her.

"Whatever," she sighed. "I'm telling you, Brock Mabrey is never going to look at me as anything other than the frumpy, shy woman who smells like cinnamon and works at the bakery."

Bristol frowned. "You don't know that."

Finley gave her a rueful look. "I do. But I love that you think I'd even have a chance with him."

Bristol wanted to continue the conversation. To assure Finley that she was definitely pretty enough to catch any guy's eye and that she'd make an amazing partner, but this wasn't exactly the time or place. She also yearned to take Brock aside to find out what he thought of Finley...subtly, of course.

"They're almost here!" Elsie said as she returned to Bristol and Finley. She didn't sit, just shuffled excitedly from foot to foot as she stared down Main Street, where the SUV carrying her son and husband would appear.

Three minutes later, there they were. Tony was waving like crazy to everyone lined up on the sidewalk, while Zeke was sitting with a half-smile on his face as he kept one hand on Tony's back to make sure he didn't fall off the roof of the SUV. There were streamers trailing from the vehicle, and a large posterboard on the side proclaiming Tony and Zeke "Heroes of the Year." Tony was wearing a crown that kept slipping forward over his forehead with his exuberant movements.

Elsie squealed a little in excitement and waved just as excit-edly as her son. She blew a kiss to her men, and Bristol had to admit that her heart fluttered a bit when Zeke gave her a small chin lift and put his hand over his heart as he stared back at her.

They passed by them in seconds, but it was obvious this moment would last a long time in the family's memory. Since the heroes' "float" was one of the last in the parade, the people around them began to move off the sidewalks and cross the street to head into the grassy area of the square, finding places to sit for the rest of the afternoon's festivities.

"Go on," Bristol urged Elsie. "I'm sure Tony is going to want to tell you all about it. And Lilly will want to take pictures of you guys all together."

"Will you be all right?" Elsie asked.

"Of course. My leg is broken, not my head," she said with a laugh.

"Leave your chair. I'll put it behind the table and you can grab it when you're ready," Finley threw in.

"Thanks. You guys are the best!" Elsie exclaimed. She leaned down and gave Bristol a short hug and waved at Finley before she hurried across the street to hunt down her family.

"Please tell me you're open," a harried-looking young mother asked as she approached Finley and gestured to the table heaping with cookies and other goodies behind them. "This one," she said, gesturing to the toddler at her side, "is cranky and all he wants is a cookie with sprinkles."

Finley smiled at her. "Of course. I've got just the thing. Bristol? You okay?"

She nodded at Finley. "I'm good. Go on. I'm going to take a short spin around the square with my knee walker before I sit again for the rest of the day, if that's okay."

"Of course. Go," Finley said. "But don't overdo it." She helped Bristol to her feet and made sure she was steady before she headed for the table, taking the chairs they'd been sitting in with her.

Bristol arched her back, stretching. She'd done a lot of sitting and lying down in the last few weeks, and she was itching to start moving once again. Making her stained glass wasn't a sedentary kind of hobby, and she had a ways to go before she'd be ready to get back to it.

She started off down the sidewalk, nodding at people she knew as she went. The coffee shop, Grinders, was right next to the bakery, and there was a used bookstore next to that, which Bristol hadn't had a chance to check out yet. She carefully crossed Main Street and headed past Grogan's General Store, toward a few ladies sitting outside the hair salon.

Rocky had introduced her to them once before. He mentioned they loved gossiping, but they weren't anywhere near as informed as their arch nemeses, Otto, Silas, and Art.

"Hi," she said shyly as she wheeled past.

"Bristol, right?" one of the women asked.

She stopped, since it would be rude not to. "That's me," she said with a smile.

"You're living with Rocky," another woman said.

Bristol wasn't sure who was who. All she knew was their names. Dorothea, Cora, Ruth, and Clara. All four looked to be in their sixties or seventies, and she didn't take offense to the question that wasn't phrased as a question. She was beginning to understand that was just how the residents of Fallport were.

"Yes, he was kind enough to offer me a place to stay while I healed from my broken leg," she told them.

"Ignore Dorothea," said the youngest of the women—as far as Bristol could tell. "I'm Ruth. This is Clara and Cora. We're glad Rocky found you and that you're okay."

"Thanks," Bristol said. "Me too."

"And you're an artist?" Clara asked.

Bristol nodded. "Yes."

"I'm gonna have to check out some of your stuff," Clara said with a smile. "I see you're selling some jewelry to raise funds for our search and rescue team."

"I am. I'm very thankful Fallport has such a team. My outcome might've been very different otherwise. And I'm sure there are things they could use that they don't have the budget for. It's my way of saying thanks."

She could tell her words had an effect on the women. All four seemed to relax a bit, especially Dorothea. "Very generous of you," she said.

"If you'll all excuse me, I'm going to continue walking a bit," Bristol said as politely as she could.

"Of course," Ruth replied. "I'm guessing you want to say hello to your young man."

Bristol merely smiled and pushed forward.

Of course, Silas, Otto, and Art hadn't missed her short conversation with the four ladies, and when she approached, they couldn't let her walk by without talking to her as well.

"Good to see you up and about," Otto said.

"You kind of look like we *feel*, hobbling around with that bum leg," Art said.

Bristol burst out laughing. He wasn't exactly wrong. "There have been a few days in the last couple of weeks that I feel as if I'm double my age."

"Which still wouldn't be as old as me," Art said.

"How old *are* you?" Bristol couldn't help asking.

"Ninety-one," the older man said proudly.

"Wow. What's the secret?"

"Stubbornness," Silas answered for Art.

"In that case, *you* should live to be a hundred and fifty," Art returned.

Bristol loved hearing their banter. It was obvious the men cared about each other, even if they sniped a lot.

"You remind me a little bit of my granddaughter," Art said after a moment.

"Yeah?" Bristol asked. This she had to hear.

"Uh-huh. Although you're a tiny thing compared to her. She's tall, almost six feet. And strong. You look like a stiff wind would blow you over. She's a firefighter in New York City. Just the other day she had to walk up thirty-four floors to get to a fire in one of them high-rise buildings. Carrying forty pounds of equipment while she was at it."

Bristol couldn't help it. She burst out laughing again. "She doesn't sound *anything* like me," she said when she could talk again.

Art was smiling as he shrugged. "She's tough. Like you."

Bristol couldn't deny that felt good. Although she wasn't sure she'd hold a candle to a firefighter in a big city.

"She's a good girl," Art continued. "Her mom, my daughter, didn't do right by her, and the best times in our lives were when she spent the summers with me. But she didn't let anything get her down. As soon as she graduated high school, she fled to the city and has showed all them men what she's made of."

"Is she married?" Bristol asked, intrigued.

"She was. But things didn't work out and they went their separate ways."

She nodded, kind of at a loss as to what to say next.

"Anyway, maybe you guys can meet one day. She comes to visit me sometimes."

"It's been a while," Silas said.

"I know," Art said sadly. "But she's busy."

"Shouldn't be too busy for family," Otto said softly.

It was obvious all three men missed their loved ones. Bristol was glad they had each other to keep themselves occupied.

Talk changed to the weather. Then to Tony and his award, and how he deserved it after driving his father's Mercedes all the way down I-480 back to Fallport without wrecking.

By the time she managed to extricate herself from the conversation, Bristol was getting tired and she hadn't even made it halfway around the square. She crossed Cedar Street and wheeled herself as fast as she could past The Cellar, the local pool hall, which had loud music playing from inside.

Khloe was sitting outside the library by herself. Feeling

chagrined that she needed a break already, Bristol stopped to talk to her.

"Isn't that music annoying to the people visiting the library?" she blurted. Then immediately shook her head. "Sorry, don't answer that. Hi, Khloe. Nice day, huh? How are you?"

Khloe chuckled and stood. "Sit," she ordered, pointing to the chair she'd just vacated.

"What?" Bristol asked.

"Sit. Your leg hurts, I can tell. Take a break for a moment."

"But what about you?" Bristol asked.

The other woman held up a key. "Lots more chairs where that one came from. Here, let me help you, then I'll go grab another one real fast."

Feeling thankful, even if she was pissed at herself for not even being able to walk halfway around the downtown area without needing a break, Bristol did as Khloe ordered. Gratefully, she sat in the chair and propped her leg up on the knee walker.

Khloe was gone only a minute or two before she returned, plopping another chair down next to Bristol and sinking into it.

"I heard the break wasn't that bad," Khloe said after a minute, gesturing to Bristol's leg with her head.

"It wasn't," she agreed. "Only one pin, and the doctor said it probably really didn't even need that, but because of how much time had gone by between the break and when I got to the hospital, he wanted to be safe rather than sorry." She paused, then asked, "Can I ask what happened to *your* leg?"

Khloe shrugged, but didn't turn to look at Bristol. "Broken in four places, including a compound fracture. Was in traction for a while, and spent some time in a nursing home until I could walk again."

"I'm so sorry," Bristol said. "I can't imagine how awful that would've been."

"It wasn't fun," Khloe agreed.

Bristol figured that was the understatement of the year. She wanted to ask if anyone had been there for her while she was healing, but she really didn't know the woman well enough.

"You should take it easy for a while. I'm sure you're itching to get back to normal, but even a small fracture like you had can take it out of you. You're probably gonna be able to tell when a storm's comin' in the future."

Bristol smiled at that. "Maybe. You probably know when it's supposed to rain four counties over then, huh?"

Khloe turned to Bristol then, and her wide grin completely changed her countenance. "Pretty much," she agreed.

A loud whistle sounded over the crowd, and Khloe immediately looked up. Bristol saw Raiden's bloodhound weaving his way through the locals, heading toward them. Raid lifted his chin in their direction, and Khloe waved a hand in response.

"Wow," Bristol said.

"What?" Khloe asked as Duke walked right up to her and put his slobbery face on her lap.

"You guys just had a whole conversation with a chin lift and a hand wave."

Khloe smirked. "He's annoyed because Duke here likes *me* almost as much as he likes his owner." She leaned over and snuggled the big dog's head, scratching his ears.

"From what Rocky said, Duke doesn't bond with anyone... other than Raid, that is."

"Animals like me," she said with a shrug.

Bristol swore she heard a note of wistfulness in her tone, but when she spoke again, figured she was wrong.

"Anyway, he was asking if I'd keep an eye out for Duke while he did his thing over there with the contest. I told him it was fine, and of course I would." The bloodhound heaved out a sigh and collapsed at Khloe's feet. "Raid doesn't like me much, but when it's convenient, he doesn't hesitate to use me."

Bristol frowned in surprise. "I'm sure that's not true. You guys work together."

"Well, he sure *acts* like he doesn't like me. But whatever. He's got a cute dog, so I put up with him."

Bristol couldn't help but chuckle at that. "Raiden's kind of cute himself," she said. "Although too tall for me."

Khloe laughed. "*Everyone's* tall for you."

"True," Bristol agreed, glad that the other woman seemed to be a little more relaxed now. "What's up with the SAR guys and beards?" she asked. "Except for Brock, they've all got one."

"No clue," Khloe said with a shrug. "But you have to admit, they all rock the hairy look."

"You aren't lying," Bristol agreed.

"Rocky's staring over here," Khloe said, nodding toward the square.

Looking over at the contest sign-up table, Bristol saw that he was indeed staring in their direction. When she caught his eye, he smiled and lifted a hand and crooked his finger at her.

"Guess he wants me to go over there," Bristol said apologetically. "Hey, I know I don't live here, but would it be possible for me to check out some books sometime?"

"Yet," Khloe said with a small smile.

"What?"

"You don't live here *yet*," she repeated.

"Oh, but...I don't...I'm not..." Bristol was flustered and not sure what to say. She hadn't discussed her thoughts on staying with anyone.

"Sorry. That was rude of me. You need a local address to get a library card, but I'm sure Rocky wouldn't mind opening an account and letting you use it. And just sayin'...you and Rocky fit. I'm sure he can help you find a place big enough for a workshop so you can do your stained-glass stuff, if you wanted to move here. If you had your own place, then you could get your own library card," Khloe teased.

"Yeah."

"Rocky's looking worried, you'd better start that way, otherwise he'll be over here, hovering and worrying." Khloe met her gaze. "And don't rush things with that leg," she warned. "You can reinjure it fairly easily at this point."

"I'll be careful," Bristol said. It felt good that the other woman was so concerned. She was beginning to think there was a lot more to Khloe than what she showed the world. Before today, she'd gotten the impression Khloe was shy and didn't say much. Her one visit to the apartment had been friendly but short. Today, however, she had plenty to say, and it was all pretty damn helpful.

"Thanks for the chair," Bristol told her as she stood and pulled the knee walker over and got herself situated.

"You're welcome. Be careful," she said, as Bristol began to wheel herself away.

Looking back, she saw Khloe was absently petting Duke's side with one of her feet and an aloof look was back on her face. She could be a little intimidating, but now that Bristol had seen beneath her veneer, she wanted to get to know her better.

She didn't want to jaywalk, so she headed to the end of the row of businesses, past Doc Snow's clinic, and once more crossed Cedar Street. She was about to cross Tenth to the grassy square when a kid of around five or six of age, darted into her path.

Bristol jerked the handlebars of her knee walker to the side to avoid hitting him and let out a small screech as she felt herself tip off balance. But she didn't land in an undignified heap in the middle of the street because someone caught her elbow, allowing her to regain her balance.

Looking up, Bristol saw an older man, maybe in his late forties or early fifties, holding on to her arm. He was dressed casually, in a pair of jeans and a polo shirt. He had gray hair at his temples and a dimple in his cheek. He was also tall, about the same height as Rocky, but not nearly as muscular. "Easy there," he said as he steered her to the other side of the street.

"Thank you so much. I thought for sure I was a goner there for a second."

He chuckled. "Glad I could help."

"Me too."

"I'm Lance. Lance Zaun."

"Bristol Wingham," she said, holding out her hand.

They shook, and by the time he dropped her hand, Rocky was by her side.

"Are you all right? I saw you almost lose it and my heart stopped. I was too far away to get to you in time."

"I'm okay. Lance caught me before I embarrassed myself. I'm still getting used to this knee walker thing."

"Thanks, man," Rocky said, giving Lance a chin lift. "Haven't seen you around before."

"I just moved here. Saw the signs about the parade and thought I'd check it out. It's been fun. People are very friendly around here."

"They are," Rocky agreed as he wrapped his arm around Bristol's waist.

"You needed me?" she asked, looking up at him.

"I just wanted to know how you were doing. Wanted to check on you."

Bristol smiled. "It's been, what, an hour since you last talked to me?" she asked.

Rocky shrugged. "Missed you," he said without any embarrassment.

Lance cleared his throat. "Well, it was nice meeting you both. Be careful, I might not always be there to catch you," he said with a small chuckle.

"Right," Bristol said, laughing with him. "I guess we'll see you around."

"Yup. Later." Then he turned and walked into the square, wandering from table to table.

"You sure you're all right?" Rocky asked.

"I'm sure. Although I'm guessing wheeling around the grass probably wouldn't be smart."

"Right. How about I walk you back to your table. You hungry? Sandra's made some lunch boxes that I'm guessing will sell out pretty quickly."

"That sounds great."

"All right. I'll get you settled with Finley and bring one to you. You and Khloe get along okay?" he asked.

"Of course. Why wouldn't we?"

"Raiden says she's prickly."

"She's not," Bristol said, defending her new friend. "I'm not sure what's between those two, but she's really nice. She also seems kinda sad."

"Why?"

"I don't know. It's just a feeling I get."

"Hmm."

"Yeah. Anyway, I'm thinking I need to get back and sit down."

"Should I grab Doc Snow?"

"No. I'm just tired. Not used to all this walking and being

upright. I obviously need to get out and about a bit more than I have."

"Don't rush it," Rocky said as he turned them to walk down the skinny sidewalk next to the road and the grassy square.

"That's what Khloe told me too."

"She's right."

Eyeing the line that was forming at Sunny Side Up's table, Bristol said, "Maybe you should get in line for lunch. I don't want to miss whatever Sandra's serving. I'll meet you in front of the bakery."

"You aren't going to miss out," Rocky said confidently.

"You don't know that," Bristol told him.

"Punky, I do. I'm not even going to have to wait in line. All I have to do is tell Sandra you're hungry and she'll make sure you're covered."

Bristol's lips twitched. Rocky probably wasn't wrong. Sandra had been doing her best to mother her since she'd been found. And Bristol had no problem with that. "Right," she said after a moment.

"There are perks to having you as my girlfriend," Rocky said, humor easy to hear in his tone.

"Seriously?" she asked with a small shake of her head.

He stopped them next to Main Street and smiled at her. "Yup."

"Dating me to get food. Nice," she said in a fake irritated tone.

He laughed and put his hands on her face as he tilted it up. "Not to mention, you're easy on the eyes. And you make me laugh. And you've made my apartment a home."

"Better," she told him, grabbing hold of his wrists and doing her best to suppress the smile that wanted to form on her lips.

"And the kisses are pretty damn amazing."

"Now you're talking," she said, going up on her tiptoes.

He lowered his head, meeting her halfway, and kissed her right there in front of what seemed like the entire town of Fallport. If anyone didn't know they were officially together before, they did now.

By the time he lifted his head from hers, they were both out of breath. "Damn, woman," he complained.

"What is it about you that makes me feel this way?"

"As if you've known me for your entire life?"

"Yes, that," she whispered.

"I don't know, but I feel the same. Come on, let's get you settled so I can feed you."

Bristol loved the feel of his hand on her back as they headed to the table in front of the bakery. There were five people waiting in line, and more stopping to look over people's shoulders to see what was so interesting.

"You hungry, Finley?" Rocky asked the other woman. "I'm going to grab Bristol a Sunny Side Up lunch box. You want one?"

"You don't mind?" she asked.

"Not at all."

"If it's not too much trouble, then yes please."

"Of course." Rocky leaned down, kissed the top of Bristol's head and said, "I'll be right back."

He walked away, and Finley fanned her face with her hand. "That kiss...whew!"

Bristol could only smile in return.

"I've sold three pairs of earrings for you already! I have a feeling we're both going to be sold out sooner rather than later," Finley told her.

"Good. Then we can relax and enjoy the rest of the afternoon."

"Ha, right. I've got more cookies and stuff to bake if we're going to make any sales later, when all the shops open again."

"You work too hard," Bristol told her.

"I'm thinking that's the pot calling the kettle black. When you aren't injured, I'm guessing you work long hours too."

"Maybe," Bristol admitted.

"These are beautiful!" a woman exclaimed as she picked up an earring and bracelet set. "How much?"

Bristol turned to the woman, feeling incredibly content. Fallport had grown on her as much as Rocky and his friends. Thinking about going back to Kingsport, to her lonely life, wasn't appealing in the least. Would Rocky still approve of her relocating here if she brought it up already? Or would he think she was moving too fast?

Shrugging her thoughts aside, Bristol told herself she had plenty of time to make decisions about her future...later. Today was a day for fun, making money for a good cause, and laughing with new friends.

* * *

Lance Zaun watched Bristol from across the square. He'd bought a corndog and was absently eating it without really tasting the damn thing.

He'd touched her. Actually felt her soft skin against his own. All he could think about was doing it again.

She felt so right next to him. They fit together perfectly. Not only that, but she needed him. Where was that asshole when she'd almost face-planted in the middle of the street? Not with Bristol.

When she was his, he wouldn't let her get hurt. He'd protect her, feed her, make sure all her personal needs were met. She'd be completely dependent on him. As it should be. He was the man; it was his duty to provide and look out for his woman.

But not here.

This town was shit.

He hated everything about it.

He'd grown up in a town exactly like Fallport. A town where the locals thought they knew everything about everyone. Where every little thing he did got back to his parents, who frequently beat him for absolutely no reason. Just because some nosy biddies saw him doing something they didn't like.

He'd have to be careful. Stay under the gossip radar. But that wasn't a problem. He'd learned to do just that years ago. He didn't stand out in any way, and he made sure not to draw attention to himself. He blended into the background.

No one was going to keep him from his Bristol. Seeing her look at him with such gratitude when he'd kept her from falling made him want to snatch her up right then and there. Take her home and love her the way she was meant to be loved.

As for that asshole...he didn't deserve her. He'd left her to slave away behind her table while he had fun with his friends. And the people around here didn't deserve her jewelry. It was way too fine for the likes of them. She needed to sell it solely on her website, like she had before. It had been too long since she'd put up anything new. And now he knew why. Because she'd gotten distracted.

The world needed her beauty in the form of her stained glass and jewelry. Once he had her home, in *his* home, he'd remedy that. Maybe even sooner.

Glaring at the man who obviously thought he'd won *his* woman, Lance sneered. After a while, the guy wouldn't even remember her. His type never did. He'd think she up and left, went back to her old life. And the guy would move on to the next woman.

That's what Lance was betting on. He had a plan, and now that he was here in Fallport, now that he'd found Bristol again, he was going to put it in motion. He'd already broken into her house back in Kingsport and collected some of the things he knew she'd want to have when he made his move. Sheets, soap, shampoo, panties...

Just thinking about her underwear, the things he'd done with them, made him smile.

"Soon, sweetheart," he muttered.

"I'm sorry, what?" a man said from the other end of the bench. "Did you say something?"

Obviously homeless, the man smelled disgusting. His hair was also matted, and clearly hadn't been washed or brushed in quite a while.

"I wasn't talking to you," Lance sneered.

"Whatever," the man grumbled, then got up and walked away.

Once more, Lance looked across the square at his love. He resented even the few seconds his attention was taken away from her. Being patient would be the hardest thing he'd ever had to do in his life. But he would. If it meant having Bristol as his very own...he'd do whatever it took.

No matter who got hurt in the process.

Bristol Wingham was his. Period.

CHAPTER ELEVEN

With every day that passed, Rocky fell harder for Bristol. It wasn't so much anything she did, and more how she made him feel. Happy. Content. Protective. And physically, he'd never wanted anyone the way he wanted her.

Though he didn't feel any great need to rush her into his bed. Maybe it was because she was sleeping under his roof every night already. Maybe it was the assurance he saw in her eyes that she wanted him just as much. The "why" didn't really matter. He was just enjoying the anticipation.

In the past, he hadn't really liked dating. He didn't like dancing around an attraction. But with Bristol, he was loving it. The way she shivered when he wrapped his arm around her to help her walk. The way goose bumps broke out on her arms when he carried her. How his bathroom smelled like her lemon body wash. All of it.

Today, she'd gone with him to a house where he'd been rebuilding another deck. He was almost done, and when he'd asked if she wanted to go with him, she hadn't hesitated to agree. She'd sat in the shade and talked to him while he worked. About her mom, currently out in California. Apparently the woman moved every couple of years, simply because she got bored. She was a self-professed hippie who didn't care what anyone thought of her. She'd never gotten remarried after her husband died and was content to date with no strings or expectations.

Rocky told her about his own mother, how she was apparently the opposite of Bristol's. She never dated even once after his father died, and would probably never sell the house they'd grown up in. The house she'd shared with her husband.

They talked a little about his time in the SEALs, and he'd told her about some of his missions without any specific details. He'd even found himself opening up and talking about the mission that had gone so wrong for his brother, which was the catalyst for Ethan wanting to get out of the military.

Then talk had switched to lighter topics. Food they loved. What she was like as a teenager. Tony. Art and his cronies. All in all, it was a great day. They were now both sitting on his couch. Bristol had made them a delicious dinner after they'd arrived back at the apartment. He'd put the dishes away and they were watching a cooking show on TV.

But he had a feeling neither of them were really paying attention. At least, Rocky knew *he* wasn't. He was focused on how good it felt to have Bristol lying against him. He was hyper aware of each breath she took. His arm was around her shoulders, his fingers lightly brushing against the bare skin of her upper arm. Her head was tucked into the space between his shoulder and neck, and she had one arm thrown across his belly.

Not able to stop himself, Rocky turned his head and kissed her forehead gently.

She glanced up at him, and the look in her eyes was impossible to resist. His head lowered without thought. They'd kissed plenty already...but somehow, this time seemed different.

Her hand brushed against his beard, then she began to stroke it. He couldn't help the chuckle that escaped even as he kissed her.

"What?" she asked, smiling a little herself.

"You're petting me," he said.

"Can't help it. Your beard is actually really soft. And I like how it feels against my face when you kiss me," she said.

"Yeah?" he asked, secretly delighted.

"Uh-huh."

"I'd cut it off if you asked me to," he admitted.

Her eyes opened wide in alarm. "What? No! I mean, first of all, it's your face, I have no right to say something like that. But second, I'm not sure I'd recognize you without it."

"I dated a woman once who hated it. Said it made me look *ignorant*. That if I cleaned myself up, people would take me more seriously."

"Fuck her!" Bristol said in a vicious tone.

Rocky blinked in surprise. He hadn't heard her swear like that before. But the fact that she'd done so in defense of *him* made Rocky feel good.

"I mean, seriously, could she be any dumber? Or is it more dumb? Anyway, I think you are incredibly handsome exactly the way you are. And if you wanted to grow your beard down to your knees, you should do it."

Rocky chuckled. "Not gonna happen, Punky."

She smiled up at him. "Right. Anyway, you be you, Rocky. I like your beard. It fits you."

In response, he nuzzled the sensitive spot near her ear. Bristol tilted her head, giving him more room and letting out an adorable and sexy-as-hell moan. The hand that had been petting his beard tightened, holding onto him as if he was the only thing keeping her from melting away. The slight pain from her pulling his beard morphed into a desire so intense, it was all he could do to keep from throwing her back on the couch and stripping her completely naked and having his wicked way with her.

His cock thickened, and he closed his lips around her earlobe and sucked. Hard.

"Rocky!" she exclaimed.

He nibbled on the little piece of flesh, loving how she squirmed against him. He lifted his head and asked, "Yeah?"

She stared up at him for a beat and said bluntly, "I want you."

It was almost scary how quickly he responded to those three little words. He wanted to throw her over his shoulder and bring her to his room to show her how far she'd buried herself under his skin, but he forced himself to remain calm. "I want you too, Bristol."

She smiled shyly, and Rocky was relieved he hadn't done anything rash. She might have been brave enough to admit she wanted him, but she still seemed a little timid. He palmed the side of her neck. His thumb rested in the hollow of her throat, and his fingers speared into her hair as he leaned down once more.

He took his time with the next kiss. Nibbling. Brushing his lips against her own. Teasing her until she was arching against him and once again pulling on his beard to try to get him to kiss her like he meant it.

Giving in to her demands, because he'd pretty much reached the limits of his own control, Rocky slanted his mouth over hers and showed her with his lips and tongue how much he desired her.

He had no idea how long they'd been kissing, but when he finally lifted his lips to take a break, Bristol was lying flat on her back on the couch, and he was pressed against her side, his back to the cushions. He was glad he hadn't flattened her in his desire-fueled haze. One of her hands was shoved under his T-shirt, where she was caressing his bare chest, and the fingers of her other hand were under the waist of his jeans, playing with the skin of his upper ass.

His own hand was clutching her nape, holding her tightly against him. The other was holding one of her perfect tits, squeezing and caressing over his cotton T-shirt that she'd been wearing every night.

The feel of her under him, against him, was pure bliss. She was tiny, but packed so much sexual allure in her small stature that he knew they would be combustible.

"Don't stop," she said in a soft, low voice he barely recognized.

Smiling, he lowered his head to continue where they'd left off...when he realized what had made him pause in the first place. The sound of his phone ringing.

"Shit," he muttered.

Bristol looked adorably confused. "What?"

"My phone. I need to get it."

It took a second, but she nodded. The slide of her hands out from under his clothes made him groan. "Hold that thought, Punky."

She gave him a lazy smile and nodded. Rocky lifted himself off her and sighed with the loss of her body heat.

He strode over to the table where he'd left his phone earlier and picked it up. "This had better be important," he growled after he answered.

"It is," Ethan said. "Simon called. We're needed for a search."

It took a moment for his brain to switch gears from desire to work mode. Rocky took a deep breath. "Right. Details?"

"One of the deputies pulled a car over for speeding and the guy took off into the woods. They were out near the Rock Creek Trail, but this guy's not going to be following any trail, if he is who they think he is."

"Shit. Who is he?"

"Theodore Lorenzo Allen."

"Is that name supposed to mean anything to me? Except the fact that since you used his middle name, he's probably extremely awful, because no one uses a middle name except if he's a serial killer or something," Rocky said. He was well aware he wasn't making much sense, but he was still off-kilter from the adrenaline and passion coursing through his veins.

Ethan snorted. "Bad enough. If he was driving that car, and it's likely he was, he's got a warrant out of Norfolk for sexual assault of his eight-year-old stepdaughter. Simon thinks based on the amount of camping and survival gear in his car, he was heading for the mountains to disappear."

"So he's got experience in the woods," Rocky said, running a hand through his hair. The more he heard, the faster the pleasure he was feeling a moment ago dissipated.

"Yup."

"What's the plan?"

"We're going to meet where the man was pulled over. Raiden's going to take lead with Duke. The officer didn't chase him into the woods very far. Decided since he didn't know why the man was running and whether he was armed or not—which he very likely is—that he wasn't going to take the chance. You want me to pick you up?"

"Sounds good."

"I'll be there in five," Ethan told him.

"I'll be ready," Rocky reassured him.

They hung up without saying anything else. Rocky knew he

needed to get moving. His search-and-rescue pack was in the closet by the front door; he always kept it ready to grab at a moment's notice. He just needed to get changed.

But first...Rocky turned and saw Bristol sitting up, looking over the back of the couch at him. Her normally straight hair was in disarray on her head, her lips were slightly swollen from his kisses, and he could just see a bit of beard burn on her neck. She was so damn gorgeous—and it physically hurt to leave her right now.

"You're going out on a search," she said.

Rocky nodded and headed her way. He sat on the cushion beside her and cupped her cheek. "I'd stay if I could," he said softly.

To his surprise, she frowned and shook her head. "I know, but this is more important. Go, Rocky. Do your thing. I'll be here waiting."

"I don't know how long I'll be," he warned.

"I realize that."

"Call Lilly. Or Elsie. Hell, or any of the other half dozen women you've befriended over the last couple of weeks. Finley, Khloe, Sandra...even Whitney."

"Why?" she asked.

"So they can come be with you."

"Rocky, I don't need a babysitter. I can get around fairly well on my own now. I'll be fine here by myself."

"Are you sure?" he asked.

"Very."

"I hate to leave you."

"If you're saying that because you enjoy my company and will miss me, great. But if you're saying that because you don't think I can't manage by myself, you need to get over it. Yes, I needed your help when I first got here, but even Doc Snow says I'm healing very well. I'm good, Rocky. Go."

She was right. She was doing amazingly well. The time was coming when she wouldn't even need the knee walker anymore. She'd be able to put weight on her leg and just have the cast. Still... "We haven't gone more than a few hours at a time without seeing each other since you got hurt."

"We haven't, have we?" she said with a small smile. "I promise I'll be here when you get back. Go do your thing. But be careful. I don't know the details, but I got the gist that you'll be looking for someone who doesn't want to be found."

"Won't be the first time," he told her.

"I realize that. But it doesn't mean I'm not going to worry about you just the same," she said.

She never failed to surprise him. In a good way. "I dated a woman who hated what I did. Didn't like that I could get called away at a moment's notice."

"Was this the same woman who didn't like your beard? Because we've already established that she was stupid."

Rocky chuckled. "Right." Then he reached for her, holding her against his chest.

She wrapped her arms around him and hugged him tightly in return.

"I need to get ready," he murmured into her hair. He was cutting this close. Ethan was going to be here any minute now. But he couldn't bring himself to let go of her.

It was Bristol who made the first move. She pulled back and shoved lightly against his chest. "Go," she ordered.

"We're gonna finish what we started here," Rocky told her.

"I sure as hell hope so," she said with a shy smile.

"Fuck, I don't deserve you," Rocky said.

"Yes, you do. We deserve each other."

He memorized her face for a long second, then stood. He headed straight for his bedroom and changed into his cargo pants, hiking boots, and a long-sleeve wicking shirt. He sheathed the KBAR knife he'd gotten as a SEAL and carried with him on every mission, and now every search, and walked back out into the living room.

Bristol hadn't moved from the couch, but was now sitting with her feet on the floor. He knew if he went to her, it would be even harder to leave, so Rocky forced himself to head toward the front closet. He grabbed his pack and took a deep breath before turning back toward the woman who'd quickly become extremely important to him.

"Do me a favor?" he asked.

"Anything," she said without hesitation.

Damn, she slayed him. "Sleep in my bed tonight."

She frowned in confusion.

"It's likely I won't be back. Not with how late it is and this guy not wanting to be found. When I'm hot, tired, and frustrated tonight, it'll make me feel better to know you're here, safe and sound, sleeping in my bed."

"Okay," she said with a small nod.

"Thank you." Wanting to say so much more, but knowing he was out of time, Rocky took one last long look at her, then turned away. He left, making sure to lock both the knob and deadbolt after he'd shut the door behind him.

His brother was waiting in the parking lot below, and probably impatient as hell because it had been more than five minutes since they'd talked on the phone.

With every step Rocky took away from his apartment, his determination to find this Theodore guy increased. He'd been reluctant to leave a second ago, but now he was proud to be called out. The man they were hunting wasn't a good guy. He wanted to get him off the streets, out of his forest, and put away so he couldn't hurt anyone else. What if Bristol, or Lilly, or Elsie, or anyone else he knew ran into a man like him?

Feeling his energy surge, Rocky jogged past the three apartments beyond his own and turned to head down the stairwell. He took the stairs two at a time and threw his pack in the back seat of Ethan's car before climbing into the front passenger seat.

"What else do we know?" he asked as his brother immediately pulled out of the parking lot and headed for the meeting point.

* * *

Bristol lay in Rocky's bed, but she wasn't sleeping. She couldn't. She was too worried about him and the rest of his SAR team. She was proud of them for not even hesitating to help the police look for whoever it was who'd escaped into the woods, but she was also extremely fearful of what might happen. The fugitive could have a gun, might start shooting at the guys if they got too close.

The thought of losing Rocky, when it felt as if they were finally moving from a roommate situation to something more, was scary. Remembering how she'd felt when Rocky lifted her with ease and gently lay her on her back on the couch made her shiver. She had no idea if he was even conscious of moving her at the time; they hadn't even stopped kissing while repositioning. Yet he'd still been very careful not to jostle her leg.

The care he took with her, the way he seemed to surround her when she was in his arms, was something she'd dreamed about her entire life. Despite her dad dying and her mom not wanting another long-term relationship, Bristol couldn't

194

remember a time when she hadn't wanted to find a man she could love and settle down with.

The problem in the past was that she'd never known where to meet men. She stayed in her house creating art most of the time, and finding men on a dating app didn't appeal. She'd met Mike at the grocery store, of all places. It was a little cliché, but she'd enjoyed his company. She realized quickly that she wasn't sexually attracted to him, and his frequent requests for more had almost ended their friendship. When he'd invited her to go hiking, she should've known better. And of course, as if to prove her right, that trip had gone bad in a huge way.

But she still couldn't regret it. Because she'd met Rocky in the process, and found Fallport. A place where she felt more at home than anywhere she'd ever lived.

She'd also discovered what true passion felt like for the first time. She thought she'd known everything there was to know about sex and pleasure and want. She'd been so wrong.

The feelings that coursed through her veins tonight with Rocky, on his couch, had been overwhelming. Almost scary. But also *right*. She could still feel his smooth skin against her fingers. From what she'd felt, his chest had the perfect amount of hair. Not too much, not too smooth. She might have been embarrassed at how she'd stuck her hand down the back of his pants, but the erection she'd felt against her leg had reassured her that she wasn't overstepping her bounds.

Bristol had never been overly impressed with her own body, considering her height. The feel of Rocky's hand engulfing her breast, the way his fingers had curled around her possessively, had gone a long way toward making her feel sexy as hell.

And his beard? Good Lord. She'd had no idea what a turn-on it could be. The feel of it against her neck and face made her wonder what it would feel like on her inner thighs as he feasted on her. It was a carnal thought, made all the more exciting because it was looking like that was exactly where they were headed.

Then his phone had rung and he'd had to leave. Bristol was proud of him, but it still sucked that he'd had to leave right when things were getting good.

She hadn't really thought about him having to look for people who *didn't* want to be found. When she thought about a search and rescue team, her own situation was the first that came to mind. Finding people who were lost.

Suddenly more than a little freaked out as her thoughts returned to the potential danger of the search, Bristol rolled over and picked up her cell from the small table next to Rocky's bed. It was close to midnight, but she didn't even think before clicking on Lilly's name.

The phone rang twice before she answered.

"Hello?"

"Hi. It's Bristol. Did I wake you up?" It was a stupid question. It was the middle of the night. Of course she woke the other woman.

But Lilly immediately reassured her by saying, "No. I'm in bed but I can't sleep."

"Me either. I'm scared for them."

She didn't have to explain who "them" was. Lilly knew. "Me too."

"I didn't hear a lot about who they're searching for, but Rocky said something about a serial killer," Bristol said worriedly.

"I don't know about that, but the guy molested his eight-year-old stepdaughter and has a warrant out for his arrest," Lilly told her. "I guess he's got some survival training, if the stuff Simon found in his car is any indication. But Duke and Raiden are gonna meet them there. Duke will catch his scent and hopefully lead them right to the guy. And he doesn't have any of his stuff with him, so that'll hinder what he can do in the woods."

Bristol still didn't like hearing any of that. "Shit," she said. "Will Duke really be able to track him?"

"Hopefully," Lilly said.

"Does it get easier?" she asked softly.

"Worrying about them?" She sighed. "No."

Bristol sighed as well. She'd had a feeling that's what Lilly was going to say, but she had to ask anyway.

"But the guys are good at what they do. They've got a leg up on other search and rescue teams because of their military experience. There's no way this guy will be able to surprise them or get the jump on them."

That made Bristol feel a lot better. "Rocky told me about some of the missions he'd been on when he was a SEAL."

"He did?"

"Yeah. Is that bad?"

"No, not at all. I'm just surprised. I've been with Ethan for a while now, and he doesn't talk too much about his time as a SEAL. I know about the mission that made him want to get out, but he doesn't like to talk about his military experience much."

Warmth spread throughout Bristol at the thought of Rocky opening up to her like he had.

"You're good for him," Lilly continued. "I've noticed since you've moved in, Rocky's a lot more social. I mean, that's not really the word I'm looking for, but it kind of is. He doesn't hang out with everyone as much as the other guys do. I don't think it's because he doesn't like crowds, it's more like he isn't able to stomach people in general. That's changed since he met you."

Bristol couldn't help but laugh a little. "I'm not sure I have anything to do with that. I'm not exactly the most extroverted person. You know, crazy loner artist and all that."

Lilly huffed out an amused sound. "That's not how I see you at all. You draw people to you with ease, Bristol. I mean that. Look at Sandra. She was so worried about you after only knowing you a week that she went out of her way to say something to Rocky, begging him to go look for you. And then there's Khloe and Finley."

"What about them?" Bristol asked.

"They certainly didn't take to *me* like they have you. I even saw Khloe laughing with you at the festival last Saturday."

"That's unusual?"

"Um, *yeah*. She sticks to herself. Doesn't talk to many people and certainly doesn't go out of her way to socialize. And Finley's so shy, she usually stays in the bakery kitchen and doesn't care to mingle. Seeing you guys hanging out at the festival was awesome. You might think you're an introvert, but you really aren't."

Bristol thought about what Lilly said for a moment, then admitted, "I think it's Fallport. There's something about this town that makes me so relaxed. I don't even know my neighbors in Kingsport."

"Or maybe it's because a complete stranger—a handsome and good man, at that—invited you to recuperate in his home," Lilly said, laughing.

"Okay, probably," Bristol agreed. The thought of Rocky had her biting her lip and worrying all over again. "Do you think they'll be back tonight?"

"I don't know. Sometimes they're only gone a few hours, and other times they're searching for days."

Bristol inhaled sharply. Days? For some reason, it hadn't occurred to her that they'd be gone longer than overnight.

"They'll stay out for as long as it takes. If the search drags on for too long, they'll take turns coming in to sleep and take a break. When they were looking for my missing co-worker—you know, from the TV show?—they were out searching for weeks. Not all at one time, but they refused to stop until they found him."

"I'm sorry about your friend," Bristol said. She'd heard all about the missing TV personality, how one of her other co-workers had killed him, dumped his body in the woods, then tried to frame Lilly for the murder and make it look like she'd committed suicide.

"Thank you. Anyway, there's no telling how this search will go. I haven't been with Ethan when they've had a search like this one, though. Looking for someone who's actively trying *not* to be found."

Bristol shivered.

"But I'm sure they'll be fine," Lilly added in a firm tone.

"Yeah."

"What are your plans for tomorrow?"

Bristol had no idea. She'd kind of been letting Rocky's schedule dictate her own. "I'm not sure."

"You want to meet for breakfast? I can pick you up."

"I'd love that."

"Sunny Side Up?"

"Is there any other place to eat breakfast in Fallport?" Bristol asked.

Lilly laughed. "Well, yeah, but none as good. We can stop at The Sweet Tooth and see Finley afterward if you want."

"Sounds good."

"And, Bristol?"

"Yeah?"

"I'm glad you called. I was lying here worrying, but talking to you made me realize that I really *do* believe they'll be fine.

Simon's not going to put them in danger, and they definitely know what they're doing. They were the best of the best in their fields in the military. So no cowardly child molester is going to get the best of *them*."

Her reassurance made Bristol feel a lot better. "You're right."

"I know."

Both women chuckled.

"I'll see you in the morning. Is nine o'clock too early?"

"No, it's perfect."

"Right, then I'll see you then."

"Bye."

"Bye."

Bristol clicked off the phone and put it back on the table next to her. She lay back then turned on her side, burying her nose into the pillow under her. Rocky's scent filled her senses. She loved being in his huge bed. She felt dwarfed, lying in a ball in the middle of the king-size mattress, but she knew Rocky was large enough to need the space.

She imagined him scooting up behind her, putting his heavy arm around her waist and pulling her against him. He'd completely surround her, as usual, and that thought alone made her sigh. She'd always been a little resentful of her small stature, but imagining being in Rocky's embrace made her love herself exactly as she was. She fit against him perfectly.

Inhaling once more, she closed her eyes. Even without him here, she still felt surrounded by him. It was comforting. The hum of desire still swam in her veins, but it was muted now, ready to be stoked to life by his hands and lips when she was with him again.

Life had its twists and turns for sure. The lows sucked. Thinking back to when she was alone in the woods, scared to death that she was going to die out there without anyone finding her body for months, years, Bristol shivered. But somehow, one of the lowest times in her life had turned on a dime, and now here she was. Happy and excited about what the future might hold.

The longer she stayed in Fallport, the more she *wanted* to stay. It had taken her thirty-seven years to find the small town, and Rocky, but now that she had, she never wanted to leave.

Her experience was a reminder that when life sucked the most, that was when you had to hold on the hardest. Time would keep spinning and eventually the bad would turn back to good. She was living proof of that.

She fell asleep with a smile on her face, Rocky's scent in her nose and seeping into her skin, and more content than she'd been in a long time. Even lost in the creation of her art, she'd never been this fulfilled.

CHAPTER TWELVE

The next morning, Bristol awoke disappointed that Rocky hadn't returned, even though after her talk with Lilly, she hadn't really expected him to. But she was looking forward to breakfast with her new friend.

It was weird to be in the apartment without him. She didn't need him to get around anymore, but she missed the way he always came to her after she'd showered and wandered into the living area. He'd put his hand on her arm, or around her waist, making sure she was steady as he led her to the table or couch and handed her a coffee to start her day.

It was too quiet now. Too empty in the apartment without him. It was crazy how quickly she'd gotten used to being around someone, to the point she now craved it. Especially when she'd been perfectly happy alone in her house in Kingsport.

She'd just finished a second cup of coffee when her phone vibrated with a text. Looking down, Bristol saw it was Lilly, saying she was downstairs. She asked if she needed assistance getting down the steps, and Bristol reassured her that she didn't.

She was going to use her crutches today, instead of the knee walker, and while it might take her longer to get down the stairs, and they were kind of awkward, she was determined to get back on both legs sooner than later.

She headed out of the apartment, her purse slung over her torso, thumping against her with each step she took. She had almost reached the stairs when the apartment door just to the left of the stairwell opened. It was the same apartment Ethan had lived in, where he'd generously let Elsie and her son stay after he'd moved. They, of course, hadn't stayed there long, as she'd married Zeke and moved in with him.

Obviously the apartment had been rented again, and this was the first time Bristol had met the tenant. To her surprise, it was Lance. The nice man who'd prevented her from falling in the middle of the street during the festival the week before.

"Good morning," he said in a friendly tone.

"Morning," she told him as she attempted to hold onto the railing and her crutches at the same time.

"Let me help you," he said quickly, coming to her side.

He hovered next to her for a moment, as if not sure how exactly he could help and not wanting to touch her without permission. Something Bristol appreciated. "If you can hold this crutch, I can use the other one to brace myself, along with the railing, as I go down."

"Of course," Lance said.

Bristol gratefully handed the single crutch over and found it much easier than she thought to hop her way down the stairs.

"It's nice to see a familiar face," Lance said, making small talk as they made their way slowly.

"I didn't know you'd moved in," Bristol said. "My boyfriend and I would've helped in some way with the boxes and stuff, if we'd known."

Lance shrugged. "Not a big deal. The apartment came partially furnished, so I didn't have a lot of stuff I needed to carry."

Bristol nodded, figuring the manager of the complex must've left the furniture and stuff the town had donated to Elsie when she'd moved in. "What're you doing in Fallport?" she asked.

"I'm only here for a little while, which is also why I was grateful for the furnished apartment. I'm a writer, and I'm on a deadline. I could've gone to a hotel or something, but that didn't appeal to me. I read about Fallport in a magazine, in an article about the best small towns in America, and since it wasn't too far away, I figured I'd give changing venues a shot, to try to boost my muse."

"Where are you from?" she asked, taking the last step to the parking lot.

"I'm not sure you'll have heard of it, but a small town in Tennessee, just across the border, called Bluff City."

"I know exactly where that is," Bristol told him, smiling widely. "I'm from Kingsport. Isn't there a dinosaur park near Bluff City?"

Lance beamed. "Yeah. It's called Backyard Terrors and Dinosaur Park. It's a little hokey, but fun."

"Cool. Well, thanks for the help. My ride is here. Good luck with the writing."

"Thanks. See you around."

"Looking forward to it."

Bristol got the crutches situated under her and headed for Lilly's Outback. Her friend had gotten out and was holding the front passenger door open for her.

"New friend?" she asked as she put Bristol's crutches in the back seat.

Bristol shrugged. "His name is Lance. I guess he's an author, and he's renting Ethan's old apartment while he finishes up his book."

Lilly frowned.

"What?" Bristol asked after Lilly had walked around and gotten behind the wheel.

"I was just hoping maybe it would stay vacant, and you could move in there. It's kind of a good luck charm for the ladies of the Eagle Point Search and Rescue team."

Bristol laughed.

"I'm serious," Lilly insisted. "I mean, I didn't live there, but Ethan did. And of course, Elsie moved in and then, *boom*, she got more than serious with Zeke. I just thought maybe once you were up and about without the crutches, you could move in and...you know...since you'd only be three doors down from Rocky, you guys could move your relationship forward."

"I'm thinking I don't need to move out to do that," Bristol said kind of shyly.

Lilly's head whipped in her direction. "What? Oh, please please *please* tell me you and Rocky are doing the nasty!"

Bristol burst out laughing. "Well, no...but we *might've* if Ethan hadn't called and interrupted us."

Lilly groaned. "Dang it!"

Bristol loved this. She'd never really had close girlfriends to talk to. "And..." she said suggestively. "I'm not sure an apartment would work for me anyway. I'm thinking a house that has a small barn or outbuilding I can convert to a workshop would work out better."

Lilly's eyes almost bugged out of her head. "Seriously?" she asked.

Bristol nodded. "Yeah. I really love it here. But the last thing I want is to freak out Rocky by telling him I might want to move already. I mean, things are so new with us, I wouldn't want to put any pressure on him, or myself."

"You know Ethan and Rocky are twins, right?" Lilly asked as she pulled into a parking space behind the buildings on the main square.

"Yeah. Fraternal, not identical."

"Yes. But they're a lot more alike than anyone probably thinks. And seeing how fast things between me and Ethan moved, I'm guessing Rocky's not going to have *any* problem with you telling him you want to move to town. He's gonna be excited. And relieved."

"Will it be weird if I ask *him* to move in with *me*?" Bristol asked.

Lilly shifted in her seat after she'd turned off the engine and shook her head. "No."

"You sound so sure," Bristol said with a small wrinkle of her nose.

"Look, the Watson brothers know what they want, and they don't mess around when it comes to getting it. Rocky hates that apartment, but it's easy. He'll jump at the chance to move out. Not in a he-wants-to-mooch-off-someone-else kind of way. But more in a way that he'll be relieved you aren't living in a shithole anymore."

"His apartment isn't a shithole," Bristol said, defending Rocky's home.

Lilly simply raised an eyebrow.

"Okay, it's not the Taj Mahal, but it's not awful. The water heater rocks."

Lilly laughed.

"I just don't want to flaunt the fact that I have plenty of money. I don't want him to feel bad about that."

"Then find a house that needs work," Lilly said with a shrug.

"Something that he can fix up. He'll feel as if he's contributing in a way other men wouldn't be able to, and he's really excellent at what he does. But also, there's more to life than money."

That was actually a really good idea. Bristol had always found older homes held more charm than the newer cookie-cutter houses anyway. She smiled widely at her friend.

"Right. So, after breakfast, and seeing Finley...you want to drive around and see what Fallport has to offer in the way of houses and future Bristol Wingham original stained-glass workshops?" Lilly asked.

Bristol couldn't keep the smile off her face. "Yes!"

"Cool."

It *was* cool.

* * *

Later that night, Bristol's good mood from the morning had slipped away. She'd been so excited about the prospect of moving to Fallport and thrilled with Lilly's support. In fact, Lilly had insisted on calling Elsie and telling her all about how Bristol was thinking about moving to their town permanently. Bristol heard Elsie's screech of excitement through the phone.

She and Lilly had a great time driving around looking at houses, and making notes about what was most important in any house she might consider purchasing. They'd stopped at On the Rocks for a late lunch, and Elsie had sat with them and added her own encouragement about Bristol's potential move.

But now she was back in Rocky's apartment, and he still wasn't home. And she hadn't heard from him either. The worry she'd been able to push away for most of the day was back full force. He'd been gone almost twenty-four hours now, and she was concerned about whether he'd been able to get a good meal.

If he'd slept at all. And, of course, if he and his team had been able to track down the bad guy.

She wanted to pace, but that wasn't possible with crutches. And since that wasn't an option, she wanted to get lost in making stained glass. But she couldn't do that either. Trying to work with small beads hadn't reduced her anxiety. So all she could do was sit on the couch and stress.

Just when she was about to lose her mind, her phone vibrated. Picking it up, Bristol's breath caught in her throat when she saw a text from Rocky on the screen.

Rocky: Cell service sucks, so I hope you get this. We're wrapping things up. Should be home in an hour or so. Everything okay?

The smile on her face was probably extremely sappy and goofy, but Bristol didn't care. She was so relieved to hear from Rocky, her hands were shaking. She took a deep breath to try to calm herself before texting back.

Bristol: Everything's perfect now that I know you're all right. You are all right, aren't you? Are you hungry? I could make something for dinner.

Rocky: I'm fine. I could eat. But don't go out of your way. Anything sounds good right about now.

His message just made her more determined to make something filling and healthy.

. . .

Bristol: Can't wait to see you. Drive safe. See you when you get home.

Rocky: Home. Funny, I've never seen that apartment as home until you moved in. See you soon.

She stared at his words for a long moment, happiness spreading through her. Then she forced herself to get up. If she was going to have dinner waiting for him, she needed to get her butt in gear.

* * *

Rocky parked his Tahoe in the parking lot at his apartment complex and ran a hand over his face. He was exhausted. More so than usual after a search. He and his team had been on alert the entire time. They'd had no idea where their target might be or what he might do to avoid capture. Tensions had been high as they'd constantly watched their backs while hiking through the thick underbrush in the forest.

It was still summer. The day was hot and humid. The foliage was thick this time of year, and it was almost impossible to see more than a few feet in front of yourself in places. The man they'd been hunting could've hidden in the underbrush, or even high in the trees above them. It didn't help their anxiety that no one had any idea if he was armed or not.

So it had been a long twenty-four hours.

In the end, they'd gotten lucky. Their target had panicked when they'd gotten too close and tried to flee. Which wasn't exactly possible in the woods. If he'd stayed still, there was a possibility—a slim one, since they had Duke—that he might've been overlooked.

As they'd subdued the fugitive, the guy absolutely lost it.

Screaming obscenities and threats. He'd claimed to have some very scary friends, and he was going to send them all "to this backwater town to take out each and every one of you and anyone you love."

Rocky wasn't too worried about the threat. He'd heard worse from terrorists he'd apprehended. A child molester's threats couldn't compare.

He'd been too busy to think too much about Bristol, or to eat more than the protein bars he'd choked down while on the trail. But as soon as the team had gotten back to the trailhead, he, Ethan, and Zeke had all pulled out their phones to text their women.

Rocky wondered how Bristol had managed without him. If her leg was hurting. What she'd done to pass the time. If she'd missed him.

That last thought made him laugh at himself a little sheepishly. The truth was, now that he had a second to think about something other than being ambushed in the forest, he couldn't wait to see her. To hear all about what she'd been doing in the last day.

He'd definitely missed *her*. If that didn't prove how different she was from anyone else he'd dated, nothing would.

Taking a breath, Rocky got out of his car. He grabbed his pack from the back seat and slammed the door, then took the stairs up to the second floor two at a time. He'd been exhausted a second ago, but now excitement filled him at the thought of seeing Bristol.

The second he opened the door, the scent of garlic greeted him and his stomach immediately growled impatiently. Smiling, he shut and locked the door behind him, dropped his pack—making a mental note to restock it in the morning—and headed toward the living area and the small kitchen.

Bristol hadn't heard him enter, which was a little concerning, considering the apartment wasn't that big. But he couldn't be upset about it. Not when he saw her shimmying and shaking in the kitchen. She had music playing from her phone. Not too loudly, but enough that she'd missed his entrance.

She was standing at the counter chopping vegetables, probably for the large salad in a bowl next to her. She was dancing without moving her feet, bobbing her head, swaying her luscious hips, and clearly lost in the music.

Not wanting to startle her, causing her to chop a finger instead of the pepper she was cutting, Rocky cleared his throat.

She immediately looked up. The second she saw him, a huge smile spread across her face and she put down the knife. "Rocky! You're back!"

"I'm back," he agreed, not able to keep from returning her grin. He walked toward her, even as she used the counter as a crutch to hop closer. Making a mental note to bring her to see Doc Snow—as it seemed she was healing up quick enough that she could probably move on to the next phase of her recovery—Rocky pulled her into his arms the second he got close.

She didn't complain about him being dirty and smelly. She grabbed hold of him as if he'd been gone for weeks rather than only a day.

They stood there for several moments, neither saying a word, just soaking in the joy of being back in each other's presence. Finally, Rocky pulled away just enough to run his gaze from her head to her toes. Wanting to make sure she was truly all right.

She did the same thing, rubbing her hands up and down his biceps as she eyed him just as closely. Finally, she met his gaze and her wide smile faltered a bit. "You look exhausted," she blurted.

Rocky couldn't help but chuckle. "That's because I am."

"Did you get any sleep at all?" she asked.

His smile didn't dim. "Can't exactly call a time-out for a nap, Punky," he said dryly.

She scrunched her nose. "True. All right. Go shower. By the time you get out, dinner will be ready. You can eat, then go to bed."

Rocky'd never been the kind of man who needed coddling. He'd been on missions as a SEAL that were many times worse than this search. But he couldn't deny it felt good—damn good—to have Bristol worried about him.

"How was your day?" he asked.

"No," she said sternly with a shake of her head.

"No?" he asked, confused.

"We aren't talking about me until you've showered and have something in your belly."

Rocky chuckled. "I had no idea you were so bossy."

"I'm not usually. But I was worried about you. Still am, actually. And you getting a shower, food, and sleep is more important than anything else that might be going on."

It took a moment for Rocky to respond, because his throat suddenly closed up with emotion.

As if she realized he was struggling, Bristol ducked her head and lay her cheek on his chest once more, giving him a moment of quiet to get himself under control.

"Thank you, sweetheart. For caring."

She lifted her head and nodded. "I care," she said solemnly. "A lot. Now...kiss me, then go get clean so you can *really* kiss me. And eat. Then sleep."

He grinned at that, and her hand came up to brush over his beard. "I *am* a bit stinky."

She smiled. "Yup. But for a good cause. You got him?"

"We got him," Rocky confirmed.

"Good."

Deciding he'd held himself back long enough from kissing her as if his life depended on it, and remembering her order from a second ago, Rocky lowered his head. The last thing he saw before he closed his eyes was satisfaction and relief in Bristol's gaze.

He kissed her softly, wanting to deepen the kiss more than he'd wanted just about anything in his life. But she was right, he was a mess. And he could smell himself. The last thing he wanted was to disgust the woman in his arms, although the way she clung to him made him think it wouldn't matter *what* he looked or smelled like when he got home from a search. Bristol would welcome him anyway.

A small sound of protest escaped her throat when he pulled back, and Rocky grinned. "You ordered me to the shower," he reminded her.

"I know," she said with a small pout. "But I missed you."

"I missed you too," Rocky told her seriously. "More than you know."

They stared at each other for a moment, their connection sizzling between them, before she gave him a small push. "Go," she ordered.

Rocky nodded and, after making sure she was steady and had a hand on the counter, stepped away from her.

"The garlic basil chicken with asparagus and linguine will be ready when you're done," she told him.

Rocky could only shake his head. "Seriously?"

"Yes. Unless you shower and get dressed in three minutes. Then it'll take probably a bit longer for me to finish everything."

Not wanting to correct her and explain he was commenting more on the absolutely delicious meal she'd prepared, Rocky nodded and backed away. He didn't take his eyes off her until he'd reached the hallway. Then he spun and strode toward his bedroom to grab a change of clothes.

Fifteen minutes later—he'd taken an extra-long time in the shower because he felt especially grubby, and he was giving Bristol time to finish up dinner—he walked back into the living area of his apartment. If anything, it smelled even better now than when he'd first walked in. He wasn't sure how she'd done it, but the table held two steaming plates of food, there was a bottle of beer sitting at his place and she was waiting patiently for him to sit down with her.

Before going to his chair, Rocky leaned over and kissed her once more. This time he tasted her deeply, wanting to absorb her essence through his lips and skin.

Her face was flushed when he finally forced himself to let go.

"What was that for?" she asked breathlessly as he sat.

"Because you're amazing. And awesome. And you smell good. And I'm so hungry I could literally eat my own hand and you made this delicious dinner for me. And because having you here makes me so happy."

"Oh," she said, blushing adorably.

Rocky smiled and picked up his fork. "Can I ask how your day went now?" he said as he swirled some noodles around his fork.

Bristol nodded. "As long as you eat while I talk," she sassed.

Obediently, Rocky put a large bite of food in his mouth and moaned as the spices and flavor exploded on his tongue. He chewed, swallowed, then said, "Lord, woman. Are you a secret chef or something?"

Bristol rolled her eyes as she took a smaller bite of her own. "Not even close. But I figured you'd want something that would stick to your bones, and a creamy sauce always does just that.

I've always found garlic makes everything taste better too. I'm glad to see you don't disagree."

"Not at all," Rocky told her, eagerly cutting a piece of tender chicken. "Protein bars have nothing on this. Now...your day?" he asked.

He loved how normal it felt to listen to Bristol talk about hanging out with Lilly and everything she'd done while he was gone. He was glad she'd been able to get out and made a mental note to thank Lilly for realizing she might be nervous, since this was the first search he'd been called out on since she'd been here.

"And...I should probably tell you, because I'm guessing nothing is a secret in Fallport for long. I had Lilly drive me around today, so I could get a better feel for where things were... and to see what kind of houses are for sale."

Rocky froze with his fork halfway to his mouth as he stared at Bristol. "What? Why?"

Bristol shrugged and blushed. "I like Fallport. A lot. Everyone's been so nice and welcoming. I know it's not always that way, and eventually some people will show their true colors. But spending time at the festival, hanging out with Lilly and Elsie, getting to know Finley, Khloe, Sandra...and everyone else...I like it here. I haven't been here that long, but Fallport already feels more like home than Kingsport ever did."

Rocky's heart was thumping hard in his chest. "You want to move here?" he asked, wanting to make sure he was hearing her correctly.

"Well...yes. If you don't mind?" she said, a little uncertainly.

It was a good thing he was mostly done eating before she'd sprung this tidbit of information on him. Rocky pushed his chair back and took the single step it required to get to her side.

"Rocky?" she asked—before he leaned over and picked her up.

She let out a little shriek, but threw an arm around his shoulder and didn't protest as he carried her to the couch. He sat, holding her on his lap as he buried his nose into the space between her neck and shoulder.

It took him a moment to gain his composure. He inhaled her scent, wanting to imprint her on his psyche, then lifted his head to meet her gaze.

"If I don't mind?" he said. "Bristol, there's *nothing* I want more than to move you to Fallport. I didn't want to bring it up yet because I didn't want to freak you out. I was going to give you some more time, and when you eventually talked about going back to Kingsport, I was planning on bringing up the fact that you could make your art here just as easily as you could in Tennessee. If that didn't work, I was going to recruit Lilly and the others to help me convince you."

She smiled shyly. "I didn't freak *you* out?" she asked.

"Not even close, Punky," he said firmly. "We've got something special here. I might not completely understand how it happened so fast, but I'm not upset that it has."

"Me either," she said.

"Did you find anything?" Rocky asked.

"Not yet. But I'm guessing that if I talk to a realtor, they might know about more properties than we could find by driving around."

"Right. And you're going to need a good-size workshop. So a barn or something. Too much land won't be good, because then you'd have that upkeep, but a few acres wouldn't be bad. And you need an attached garage. They're safer, especially if you're living on some acreage," Rocky said, his mind spinning with ideas.

Bristol put a hand over his, which was resting on her thigh.

"Breathe, Rocky. I don't have to buy anything immediately... unless you're eager to get rid of me."

"No!" he blurted. "Not at all."

"I mean, I'd understand. I know I've been here longer than you probably thought I would be when you volunteered to let me stay."

"I love having you here. It's wonderful to come home to you instead of an empty apartment."

They smiled at each other for a beat.

"You're really going to move to Fallport?" he asked softly.

Bristol nodded. "I don't know when, because I don't want to rush, and I want to find the perfect place. But yeah...I think I am."

"Best homecoming ever," Rocky sighed. "I won't lie. Last night and today *sucked*. It's been a while since we've been on a hunt like this one. The guy we were after was a piece of shit, but he wasn't a novice when it came to being out in the woods."

"But you got him."

"We did. He wasn't happy about it either," Rocky admitted. "Even tried to scare us by throwing around all sorts of threats."

Bristol frowned. "Threats?"

He nodded. "But it was obvious he was just spouting off. He's on his way to Roanoke, to the jail there, it's more secure than the local one. He's gonna have a heap of charges after what he did to his stepdaughter and for running from the cops."

"Good."

"Yup." A yawn snuck up on Rocky before he could stop it.

Bristol put a hand on his cheek. "You should go get some sleep," she said.

"Did you sleep in my bed last night?" he couldn't help but ask.

The blush returned to her cheeks. "Yes."

"Can't wait to smell your lemony scent on my sheets," he told her.

She smiled and licked her lips. "Have to admit, being surrounded by *your* scent last night was both relaxing and *not* at the same time."

He chuckled. "Yeah. Tonight's not the night...but I want to finish what we started last night before we were interrupted."

"Me too," she agreed without hesitation.

Rocky desperately wanted to make love to Bristol, but was content to wait. "I'm probably being presumptuous, but...any chance I can convince you to sleep with me tonight?" he asked. "Just sleep," he added quickly.

Bristol stared at him for a long, heart-stopping moment before she nodded.

"I'm gonna go crash, but it's probably too early for you. Join me when you're ready," he told her.

"Okay."

"I'm beyond happy right now, Punky. We got the bad guy, I came home to a delicious meal. Learned you want to move here, and I'm gonna get to hold you all night. The day ended a lot better than it started, that's for sure."

She smiled at him.

Rocky lowered his head and kissed her hard. He'd meant it to be a short, heartfelt sharing of his emotions, but it turned out to be much more. Her hand slipped under his shirt, and he couldn't stop himself from covering one of her breasts, then palming her ass as she sat on his lap. His cock was hard, and he hoped it wasn't disturbing her. He didn't think so, if the way she was squirming on him was any indication.

As much as he loved what they were doing, he could feel himself tiring. Not even his desire for Bristol could keep him awake for long. The adrenaline dump, the hot shower, the food in his belly, the contentment in his soul...it was a recipe for him to crash, and crash hard.

It was Bristol who pulled back first. "You need to sleep."

He nodded in agreement. Moved his hands away from dangerous territory just as she did the same. He kissed her forehead gently.

"I'll take care of the dishes before I go," he told her.

Bristol shook her head. "No, you won't. I've got it."

"But your leg—" he began, and she interrupted him.

"My leg is fine. It actually feels pretty good. I've been putting a tiny bit of weight on it—not a lot, so don't worry—and it doesn't hurt. It feels great to be up and about and able to help out around here."

"All right, but don't overdo it."

"I won't. Rocky?"

"Yeah?"

"You're sure you don't mind that I'm moving here? I mean, things between us might not work out, and I don't want anything to be awkward for either of us if they don't."

"I wish I could say for sure that any kind of relationship between us will absolutely last. That we'll be together even when we're in our eighties and have taken over Silas, Otto, and Art's seats outside the post office. But I can't. However, I *can* promise that no matter what happens between us, I won't begrudge you making your home here. I can't see you turning into a raging bitch and making me hate the fact that you're here. Just as I'm not all of a sudden going to turn into an abusive asshole and make you regret uprooting your entire life to move to Fallport.

"With the way I feel right now, I can't imagine you ever *not* being in my life, but we'll take one day at a time. And I swear, no matter what the future holds, to respect the right for you to make this your home."

Bristol sighed and nodded. "Thank you. And I'm not going to turn into a raging bitch. Promise."

Rocky couldn't resist kissing her once more, but he made sure to keep this one light and easy. Then he stood with Bristol in his arms, ignoring her protests that she could walk and carrying her back into the kitchen. It was harder than he thought to leave her standing next to the counter with her crutches nearby. But it helped to know that she'd be sleeping next to him soon.

Four hours later, Rocky heard Bristol come into the bedroom. It didn't matter how quiet she was, his SEAL training prevented him from sleeping so deeply that he didn't hear when someone was nearby.

She gently lifted the sheet and blanket and slid underneath. Rocky immediately pulled her into his arms. She sighed and snuggled closer. He'd kept his T-shirt on and a pair of boxers, and she was wearing the T-shirt he'd given her that she loved so much.

Her hand landed on his chest and her head on his shoulder. Once again, Rocky marveled at how well they fit together.

"You good?" he asked quietly.

"Perfect," she whispered back. "I didn't mean to wake you."

Rocky didn't respond verbally, just kissed the top of her head.

She sighed once more, and he could feel her warm breath even through his T-shirt. He wished they were skin-to-skin, but that time would come. For now, he was going to soak in the feeling of her being in his arms.

His eyes closed and he let himself drift off once more.

CHAPTER THIRTEEN

A week later, Bristol had to laugh at how every single person she met while she was out and about in Fallport gave her advice about which house she should purchase. Word about her staying had spread fast, and now everyone seemed to be a housing market expert.

It was hard to get irritated with anyone when she was feeling so damn happy. She and Rocky hadn't made love yet, but they'd slept in each other's arms every night since he'd returned from his latest search. They'd also gone just a little further and further each night, exploring each other physically.

The night before, she'd slept in only her underwear after Rocky had taken her shirt off and made her come with his fingers and mouth. Sex had never felt so good before, and Bristol was more than ready for the real thing.

Tonight was going to be their night, no matter how much Rocky tried to put the brakes on. She knew he was doing it because he wanted her to be sure of their relationship, of him.

And she was. Hell, she was going to move to Fallport, that's how sure she was.

It was time. *Past* time. And Bristol couldn't wait.

Today, Rocky was working with his brother on a house that had a leak, and black mold had completely overtaken one wall of the home. He'd had to take the wall down to the studs to completely remove the mold, and now he was building it back up. When he'd taken out the wall, he'd discovered that whoever had built the house years ago had taken so many shortcuts when it came to the electrical wiring, it was a miracle it had passed inspection at all. So Ethan was there to work on that part of the remodel, while Rocky did the drywall and the other reconstruction.

Bristol had seen Doc Snow a few days ago, and the x-ray of her leg showed the fracture wasn't quite healed and she would need another few weeks in a cast, but he kindly cut off the old one and gave her a brand-new, bright pink cast to wear for the remainder of the time. Not only that, he agreed that she no longer needed the knee walker or crutches at all times, and could put weight on her foot, as long as she didn't overdo it.

So while Bristol wasn't thrilled she still had to wear the cast —it made things in bed with Rocky a bit more cumbersome— she was happy with the progress she was making and the fact she could hobble around without the crutches.

Today, she had some errands to do, including picking up a package at the post office filled with more materials for her jewelry, as well as some colored glass she'd seen online and hadn't been able to resist. The urge to create a stained-glass piece was pushing at her hard, and Bristol was looking forward to the time when she could get back into a workshop.

Rocky had asked Drew to pick her up and take her where she needed to go today. She was glad for the ride, but soon it would be time to arrange to get her own vehicle to Fallport. It was sitting in her garage in Kingsport, and now that she could walk, she didn't want to put anyone else out by having to drive her everywhere.

A knock on the door alerted her to Drew's arrival. She limped to the door and opened it. "Hey! I'm almost ready," she told Rocky's friend. She hadn't hung out with the former police officer much, and was looking forward to getting to know him better.

She turned to grab her purse and make sure the lights were off in the apartment, and when she started for the door again, noticed Drew was still standing just outside on the walkway.

"Why didn't you come in?" she asked as he backed up to give her room to close and lock the apartment door.

"I wasn't invited," he said simply.

Bristol frowned up at him. "Yes, you were," she said in confusion.

"Just opening the door and saying 'hello' isn't inviting me in," he said calmly, without any trace of irritation in his tone.

"Well, it was implied," she insisted.

Drew shrugged. "I don't do implied."

At that, Bristol had what seemed like a million questions. It wasn't that she didn't appreciate his respectfulness, she just wondered what had made him so...cautious.

He opened the passenger-side door of his black Jeep Wrangler and helped her get settled, then walked back around to his side.

After sitting, he glanced over at her and his lips twitched. "You gonna burst if you don't ask me the questions you've got rolling around in your head?" he asked.

"Maybe," Bristol admitted with a grin. "But I want you to like me and not think I'm a nosy busybody."

Drew chuckled. "I'm thinking Art and his friends have cornered the market on that around here. And if they don't, Dorothea and her crew are a close second. Go ahead and ask."

"You're different from your friends."

He tilted his head. "In what way?"

Bristol thought about what she wanted to say for a moment before she spoke. "You're more watchful. More careful about what you say to others. More judgmental—and I don't mean that in a bad way."

"I know what you mean, and you're right. My job as a cop taught me that people can and *will* misconstrue anything and everything you say. They'll take every opportunity to throw it back in your face if it fits their agenda."

"That has to be exhausting," Bristol said.

"It is."

"For what it's worth...thank you for your service."

Drew nodded.

"Also, for the record, you're welcome to come into the apartment when you arrive. I know it's not mine, but I'm granting you an open invitation anyway. And when and if I find a house I like, you're welcome there too. I feel safe with you, and I'd like to think you're my friend now, almost as much as you're Rocky's."

"Thank you," Drew said softly. "The thing is...there are some awful police officers out there. They're bigoted, jaded, and power hungry. They make it twice as hard for the good ones to do their jobs effectively."

"Is that why you got out?" Bristol got up the nerve to ask.

"Partly. I have a lot of guilt about it though. Police forces need all the good officers they can get. But we're being pushed out by the assholes, by the scorn aimed our way by citizens, and the intense scrutiny. And while I actually think that scrutiny is good, it's still overwhelming."

Bristol reached over and touched Drew's arm, squeezing it before letting go.

"And you were right about the fact that I'm watchful. Rocky and the others are too, but in a different way. I'm not looking for roadside bombs or people popping out of a house with an AK-47."

When he didn't continue, Bristol couldn't help but ask, "What *are* you looking for?"

"I don't know."

Bristol frowned in confusion.

"I'm just watching. A car I see today might end up being the breaking clue Simon needs in a robbery he learns about tomorrow. What someone says might not make sense one day, but might fall into place on another."

"That *also* sounds exhausting," Bristol blurted.

Drew grinned. "It's who I am."

"Well, if you don't mind me saying so...Rocky and the others are really lucky to have you as a friend," Bristol told him.

He raised an eyebrow at her.

"You see the world differently, which is a good thing. You think about what people *mean* when they speak, rather than simply hearing what they say. You've got your friends' backs in a way most people don't. I think it's awesome."

Drew didn't speak for a long moment, and when he did, it was only to say, "Thank you."

Bristol could tell he wasn't exactly comfortable with the conversation, so she changed the subject. "So...you're an accountant."

His lips twitched. "Yup. Boring, huh?"

"Not if you like numbers, which I'm assuming you do, since you're doing people's taxes and stuff."

"True."

"Are you taking on new clients?"

He glanced her way, and she continued quickly. "If I move here, I'm going to need someone who knows Virginia tax laws. Tennessee doesn't have any state taxes, and the last thing I want is to screw something up and have the IRS on my case."

"You don't know if I'm any good," he said.

Bristol laughed. Hard. When she finally had herself under control, she said simply, "You're good."

Drew shook his head in exasperation.

"Drew, you do *everyone's* taxes. Sandra, Whitney, Elsie—and I know you charge Elsie half what you do everyone else, which is super nice by the way. And you do taxes for Rocky and everyone on your team for free."

"You've asked around about me," he stated.

Bristol didn't hear any irritation in his tone, but it wouldn't matter to her if she did. "Of course I did. Look, I make a lot of money with my art. A *lot*," she emphasized. "I'd be stupid not to get references when looking for a new accountant. If Rocky trusts you, and I know he does, and I trust you with Rocky's *life*, why wouldn't I trust you with my money?"

Drew didn't say anything until he'd pulled into a parking lot behind the square so she could run in and get her package at the post office. He turned to her when he'd shut off the engine. "You're gonna stay in Fallport?" he asked.

"That's the plan."

"Do you love Rocky?"

Bristol wasn't sure she was comfortable with *this* conversation, and she had a feeling Drew already knew the answer to that question, but she met his eyes and answered anyway. "I'm not prepared to tell you about my feelings for Rocky before I tell *him*, but to answer your question another way...do you really think I'd uproot my life, buy a house, move to Fallport, if I didn't think this was where I wanted my life to be? Where I wanted any children I might have to grow up? Would I ask you to get intimately involved in my financial situation if I didn't have very deep feelings for Rocky?"

"Just checking," Drew said with a small smile.

Bristol rolled her eyes and waited.

"What?" he asked.

"You didn't answer my question."

"About being your accountant?" he asked.

She nodded.

"How much did you make last year?"

"One-point-two million," Bristol said without flinching.

He whistled. "How much did you pay in taxes?"

She told him—and he frowned. "That's way too much. Do you have a defined benefit plan?"

"A what?" she asked.

He sighed. "Shit. Yes, I'll be your accountant. I want to see your taxes from the last three years and any paperwork you have for investment accounts."

Bristol beamed. "Okay."

Drew's lips twitched yet again. "Why do I feel as if I'm a fly who walked right into the spider's lair?" he asked.

Bristol giggled. "I have no idea. I'm harmless though."

"That's what all women say. Stay put. I'll come around."

"I can get out by myself," Bristol protested.

"If you hurt that leg when you're with me, Rocky will pound me into the ground, friend or not. And I apparently just landed a huge account...I'd be stupid to want to hurt the hand that's gonna feed me." He winked at her, then turned to climb out of the Jeep.

Bristol couldn't help but snort. She had a feeling there were hidden depths to this man that he didn't show the world. Some woman was going to have to work hard to get under his shields. But when she did...she'd have a champion for life.

Drew opened her door and took her elbow to help ease her to the ground. He kept his hand on her as she limped around the building to the front door of the post office.

As usual, Art, Otto, and Silas were there, playing chess.

Otto raised a brow at seeing them approach. "Does Rocky know you're stepping out on him?"

Bristol shook her head in exasperation at the older man. "Do Silas and Art know you go to the assisted living facility on Sunday mornings after church to play chess with some of the residents?" she fired back.

A dull sheen of pink bloomed on his cheeks as both Art and Silas turned on him.

"What?"

"You do?"

"Just because Drew is helping me today, doesn't mean I'm cheating on Rocky," Bristol said. She wasn't worried she'd hurt Otto's feelings. He was a tough old coot, and maybe being taken down a peg would be good for him.

"Touché," Otto said after a moment.

"How come you never told us about going over there?" Silas asked.

"Maybe he's trying to learn some tricks to beat us," Art said.

"Not gonna happen," Silas said sternly.

"I'm thinking maybe we should go with him this Sunday to see what the fuss is about," Art threw in. "Not that I'm ever gonna live there. I'm gonna die in my own house, not wasting away in a place like that."

"Impressive," Drew said as he steered her into the post office. "You handled that well."

"If I hadn't turned it around, they would've been gossiping

about you and me for who knows how long. And there's no telling who would've overheard it and made assumptions."

"So you were protecting Rocky *and* me," Drew said.

"Duh," Bristol returned.

There were two people ahead of them in line, and neither said anything as they waited for their turn. It didn't take long for Guy, the post office employee, to find her package. Drew took the large, heavy box and carried it as if it was full of feathers instead of heavy pieces of glass. They both nodded at the three men still arguing about whether Otto was somehow cheating by playing chess with the residents in the assisted living home.

Drew chuckled when they were out of earshot. "Remind me never to piss you off," he said. "They're gonna be talking about that for weeks."

"I'm an angel," Bristol insisted.

"Uh-huh. Sure you are."

She grinned up at him.

"Tiny, but damn mighty," Drew muttered as he opened the passenger door of his Jeep for her when they arrived. He put her package in the back after getting her settled then climbed behind the wheel. "Where to now?" he asked.

"Are you sure you don't mind driving me around?" Bristol asked.

"Nope. Again...new rich client. Why would I mind?"

She didn't take offense, just laughed. "I want to go to the grocery store and grab some stuff, but first, there's a house that just went on the market. I saw it online last night, I wanted to drive by and look at it."

"You really are serious about moving here, aren't you?" Drew asked.

"Yes."

He studied her for a moment, then nodded. "Right. Let's go look at this house."

* * *

When Rocky opened the door to his apartment later that after-noon, once again, delicious smells assaulted his senses. He'd heard from Bristol on and off during the day about what she'd been doing. She'd told him she really liked Drew and thanked him for asking his friend to help her today.

What she *didn't* know was that Drew had made a comment the other day, questioning if Rocky wasn't moving too fast and getting in too deep with Bristol without really knowing her. Since he had complete faith in Bristol to win him over, he'd purposely asked Drew to drive her around.

And apparently his plan had worked. Not only did Bristol seem to hit it off with his friend, but Drew sent him a text that said simply, *She's perfect for you.*

The only thing bothering Rocky was a nagging sense that things were...*too* good. That might seem silly to most people, but it was his experience that when things seemed too good to be true, the shit was about to hit the fan.

Of course, he'd never experienced the phenomenon when it came to a relationship, but he'd seen it time and time again while he was a SEAL. Things seemed to be quiet in regard to a terrorist or a particular country...then *boom!* An explosion would shake things up. A mission was going off without a hitch? *Wham!* Their chopper pilot would get lost and wouldn't be able to extract them on time.

He had more than enough examples of that kind of thing happening, and the last thing he wanted was for it to happen to him and Bristol.

Doing his best to push any paranoid thoughts from his head, Rocky inhaled deeply. The apartment smelled like something spicy. He couldn't wait to see what Bristol had cooked up for them tonight.

He walked into the kitchen and couldn't keep the smile off his face at seeing her. Desire hit him so hard, it was all he could do not to walk right up to her and carry her off to bed.

"Hi!" she said when she noticed him standing there. "How was work? Did you get rid of the mold? Oh! You should go shower, just in case some of that nasty stuff is sticking to you."

"Do you think I'd bring that shit back to you?" Rocky asked.

She blinked. "Well, no, but it's not like you can wag your finger at the mold spores and tell them to attach to someone else."

Rocky burst out laughing. When he could talk, he said, "You're right. But I can wear a protective suit and take it off and get rid of it when I'm done."

"True. But I'm sure a shower would feel good anyway. And some of those spores are sneaky little shits and could've gotten under your protective suit."

She wasn't exactly wrong. To buy him some time and to help him get control over his desire to strip her naked right then and there in the middle of his kitchen, he nodded. "Right. I'm gonna go shower."

"I don't get a kiss yet?" she pouted.

"Sneaky little spores, remember?" he said with a grin. "Don't want them attaching to you, Punky."

"All right."

"Sounds like you had a good day," he said, finding it hard to leave her even though he really did want to shower before he stunk up their space.

"I did," she agreed. "I like Drew."

"Good."

"He agreed to be my accountant," she said.

The words were like a bombshell to his insides.

"Fuck," Rocky swore lightly. It was taking every ounce of his control to stay where he was. To not march over to Bristol and prove how much he loved the idea of her moving to Fallport.

She smiled as if she knew exactly what her words had done.

Glad she wasn't offended by his swearing, that she somehow knew what he was thinking, Rocky turned and headed for the bathroom without another word. He needed to get clean so he could show her just how happy he was with her decision to stay.

CHAPTER FOURTEEN

Six and a half minutes after finishing his shower and getting dressed, Rocky strode into the living area. His hair was still wet and he'd barely taken the time to dry his beard. He wore a comfy pair of gray sweats and a T-shirt. Bristol had her back to him, still standing at the stove and stirring something in a large pot.

He didn't hesitate to wrap both arms around her. He pulled the spoon out of her hand, turned off the heat on the burner, picked her up and plopped her on a clear space on the counter. They were eye level as he wrapped his hands around either side of her neck. His thumbs rested in the hollow of her throat and he lowered his head without saying a word.

She met him halfway eagerly, grabbing his shirt with both hands.

Their tongues dueled and their heads instinctively tilted as they devoured each other. When he couldn't stand it any longer, Rocky let go of her head and wrapped his arms around her. Without taking his lips from hers, he picked her up. Her thighs clung to him as he walked out of the kitchen, toward the bedroom.

He couldn't stop. He was addicted to her scent. Her taste. And he wanted all of her. Needed her. Right now.

Putting one knee on his bed, he lay her out on his comforter, not taking his lips from hers. He felt her hands pulling at his shirt. He lifted his head long enough to whip the material up and off before falling on her again. Luckily, she'd taken the opportunity to remove her own shirt when he'd been busy for those three seconds, so when they came back together, they were skin to skin.

The feeling of her hard nipples against his chest made a shudder go through Rocky. This was going too fast, but he couldn't stop. It was as if they were moving toward a head-on collision but neither could slow down. Neither wanted to.

He moved to the side so he didn't crush her and brought a hand up to her breast. He lightly pinched her nipple as he nibbled on her lower lip.

Bristol gasped and arched her back, pushing herself harder into his hand.

"You like that." It wasn't a question.

But she answered anyway. "Yessssss. More, Rocky. I need more."

"I'm gonna give you everything you want and need, Punky."

Rocky kissed her again. Hard. She gave as good as she got. Squirming under him, her hands were busy caressing every inch of his bare chest. She even petted his beard as he kissed her. When her hands went to the waistband of his sweats, he lifted his head. He needed to slow down, but he wasn't sure he could. He wanted to make this good for her, and at the speed they were going, he wasn't sure it would be.

"As much as I love you in these...they have to go," she muttered.

Rocky grinned. "So the rumor about ladies liking men in sweats is true?"

"No clue. I just know I like seeing *you*."

"Why?"

She blinked up at him in surprise. "Why?" she echoed.

"Yeah. I don't get it. They're just sweats."

"Because they highlight the size of your dick. They're covering you, but teasing at the same time. Makes me want to strip them off and see if what you're packing lives up to the hype."

Rocky almost choked, laughing at her words. "Seriously?"

"Yup."

"I'm never wearing these out of the house again," he vowed.

"Probably smart. Because I'd kill any woman who looked at you in them," she said, sounding completely serious.

Rocky grinned. "I guess I know what to wear when I want to turn you on."

"Yup. Less words, more action," she complained.

"For the record...it doesn't matter what you wear...I'm always turned on when I look at you," he told her.

He saw the compliment sink in before a happy smile formed on her face.

"How about this...you take your sweats off, and I'll take my leggings off at the same time?"

"Deal," Rocky said. He turned over onto his hip and shoved at the elastic around his waist. By the time he rolled back over, Bristol was as naked as he was.

Inhaling sharply, he paused to run his gaze over every inch of her body. She was petite, he'd known that, but seeing her nude was...everything. She had small tits with large nipples that were currently begging to be sucked. He could see her hip bones, but she still had a small belly pooch. Her thighs were full and the hair between her legs trimmed.

All of a sudden, he wasn't sure what to do. Where to start.

But Bristol didn't hesitate, she reached for one of his hands and brought it back up to her chest. His fingers tweaked her nipple without thought.

She sighed, then reached for him. Her fingers closed around his beard and she tugged. Hard.

Rocky couldn't keep the smile off his face. God, he loved when she manhandled him. If possible, it turned him on even more.

Obediently, he leaned toward her, but instead of kissing her on the lips again, he aimed for her nipple. She let go of his beard and her fingernails dug into the skin of his shoulder as she moaned.

Rocky feasted on her nipples for a moment, loving how sensitive she seemed to be. But he was too turned on to continue for long. His left hand trailed down her belly, loving when she squirmed against him when his facial hair apparently tickled her. His hand was big enough to completely cover her pussy...and for just a moment, his excitement dimmed. She was so small, and he wasn't. He had no idea if he could take her without pain. And the very last thing he'd ever do was cause her one second of discomfort.

As if she could read his mind, she said, "We'll fit."

He wanted to laugh. Usually, he was the one telling women that. Leave it to his Bristol to reassure him.

"Damn straight we will," he moaned. "I'm gonna fill you so full."

"Oh my God, yes...please, Rocky. Do it."

"You aren't ready yet," he said, even though he could feel wetness against his fingers.

She groaned and opened her legs, giving him more room. Rocky wanted to push them even farther apart. Get down between her thighs and suck her to a monster orgasm. But he was on the edge. His cock was so hard, he knew if he so much as rubbed against the bed, he was gonna blow.

So he'd have to make sure she was ready with his hand. Later, he'd eat her out, show her once more how amazing his beard could feel between her legs, but for now...

He curled his middle finger down and slowly entered her body. She was wet, but she'd need to be even wetter to take him.

Bristol moaned and tilted her hips up. Moving quickly, Rocky grabbed one of his pillows and shoved it under her ass.

"More, Rocky. Please," she begged as she grabbed hold of his wrist. She wasn't trying to pull him away. She was holding on.

Rocky slowly pumped his middle finger in and out of her body, amazed at how tight and small she was. Gritting his teeth, he forced himself to take things slow.

Using the heel of his hand, he ground against her clit as he finger-fucked her. It was hard to take his gaze away from her pussy, but when he looked up at her face, he was transfixed. Instead of her eyes being closed, she was staring at him.

She licked her lips and smiled when he met her gaze. Her hips thrust up against his fingers, and it was the most carnal moment Rocky had ever found himself in. This woman was obviously comfortable in her sexuality, and it was a massive turn-on. She wasn't afraid to show him she was enjoying what he was doing.

Her nipples were hard on her chest and she was breathing hard.

"I need you to come for me before we move forward," he said.

Bristol nodded. "Okay."

"Shit, we didn't talk about this before." His hand stopped moving, his finger deep inside her. "I'm clean. Got tested when I got out of the Navy. I've only been with two women since then, and I wore condoms both times."

Bristol blushed, but didn't shy away from the conversation. "I haven't been with anyone in four and a half years."

"Shit. Really?"

She shrugged. "Yeah. I don't need a man to orgasm. I've got a vibrator."

The thought of her fucking herself with a toy made a small spurt of precome leak out of Rocky's cock. "Damn, woman."

She smiled, and it was sexy as hell. "I'm also on birth control. I had an ovarian cyst when I was in my twenties and my doctor put me on the pill to keep them from reforming."

Was she saying what he thought she was saying?

"I trust you, Rocky. I know some would say I'm being stupid, but you aren't going to hurt me. I'm protected, and we're both clean."

He inhaled deeply, which didn't help his libido, since he could smell her arousal. It was all he could do not to climb over her and fuck her right that second.

"Make love to me, Rocky. I need you."

Make love.

She was right. That's what this was. It wasn't fucking. No way would he ever consider taking a woman bare if it was. And he trusted her as much as she apparently trusted him. He'd known SEALs who'd been taken for a ride by women. Promised they were safe and the next thing they knew, the women were pregnant, and the men on the hook for child support for the next eighteen years. He didn't have a ton of sympathy for them, really. They were just as much to blame as the women, since it wasn't like anyone was forcing them *not* to use a condom.

Still, he'd always been careful. But there was a level of trust with Bristol that he felt to his soul. If said she was on birth control, he believed her.

He shifted his hand, using his thumb to manipulate her clit while sinking his pinky and ring finger inside her.

"Rocky!" she exclaimed.

"You're going to come, then I'm going to be inside you. I'm gonna fill you up with my come, Punky. I've never done that before. Ever. And I can't wait to share that with you for the first time."

His words meant something to her, he could tell.

"I've never let a man come inside me before," she admitted.

That was it. Rocky was done. He needed this woman more than he needed to breathe.

He pressed harder on her clit as his fingers worked her pussy.

It took a moment, but soon she was thrusting up against him, her hips moving involuntarily as she strained to reach the pinnacle. Leaning down, Rocky took one of her nipples into his mouth. He sucked on it, hard. Harder than he usually would the first time he was with a woman. But his Bristol could take it. Needed it.

Her hand rested on the back of his head, fingers tangled in his hair as she gasped for breath. His fingers between her legs were soaked, and he couldn't wait to lap up her juices and get them in his beard so he'd smell her all night.

Some people would think that was gross. Before Bristol, *he* was one of those people. But the thought of having her lemony-musky scent on him, marking him, was almost a primal need.

Just when he didn't think he could hold on a second longer,

Bristol's thighs began to shake and her belly tightened. She let out the cutest little screech as she flew over the edge.

Even before she'd finished, Rocky moved. He got between her legs, grabbed his cock, and lined it up with her pussy.

He pushed in slowly, resolutely. She was so tight, he wasn't sure he was going to be able to get all the way inside. When his pubic hair meshed with hers, Rocky took a deep breath. He was two seconds away from coming. This felt like nothing he'd ever experienced before. Not even his first time. He could feel Bristol's inner muscles fluttering along his bare cock as if trying to milk his come from his balls.

He inhaled deeply again, looking at the woman under him. Her cheeks were flushed, as was her upper chest. She was staring down where they were connected with her mouth open in a little o as she panted.

* * *

Bristol couldn't breathe.

She couldn't think.

All she could do was feel.

She'd just experienced an extremely intense orgasm and now she was stretched full by Rocky's cock. It didn't hurt...exactly. But it had been quite a while since she'd taken a man, and Rocky was extremely well endowed.

She stared down their bodies at where he was buried inside her and did her best to take in oxygen.

"Bristol?" he asked in a breathy tone. "You okay?"

She nodded immediately. "Yeah, I just...that was intense."

"You need a second?"

Did she? Bristol didn't think so. The few seconds they'd been talking had been enough for her desire to ramp back up. She'd just orgasmed, but she felt as if she was on the verge of another one. "No," she said, looking up into his eyes.

"Thank fuck," he said, and began to move.

Bristol had never felt this way before. She didn't usually like being under a guy when they had sex. Since she was so small, it made her feel overpowered, and not in a good way. But with Rocky above her, she felt not even a smidge of unease. He wouldn't hurt her, she knew that down to the marrow of her bones.

Lifting her legs, she tried to wrap them around him, but let out a small sound of annoyance when her cast stopped her.

Rocky adjusted immediately, putting his arms under her knees and bracing his hands next to her hips as he continued to fuck her. His pace wasn't slow, but he wasn't pounding into her either. He was completely in control, and the slide of his cock against nerve endings that hadn't been stimulated in far too long felt amazing.

"This okay?" he asked.

She might've been irritated at how he kept asking if she was okay, but she *was* practically bent in half, her legs positioned in the crook of his elbows.

"Good," she breathed. She stared up at him as he made love to her. He was frowning in concentration and his beard swayed with each thrust. Everything below her waist tingled, and Bristol could feel that she was on the edge once more.

"Touch yourself," Rocky ordered. "I can't while I'm holding myself up."

Bristol didn't even hesitate. Nothing seemed awkward or weird with Rocky. Her right hand slipped between them and the second her fingers touched her clit, she jerked. She was still sensitive from earlier.

"Shit, I felt that," Rocky groaned. "You just squeezed my cock so hard."

"Like this?" Bristol asked, tightening her inner muscles once more.

Her man grunted and his next thrust was a teensy bit harder. She loved knowing she could affect him that way.

"I'm not gonna last, Punky. I want to feel you go off while I'm inside you. You're gonna squeeze me so damn hard I won't be able to hold back. You know you want my come. Push yourself over, Bristol. Now."

His words were crude, but he wasn't wrong. She *did* want his come. She wanted everything from this man. Instead of freaking her out, that fact empowered her. Flicking her clit faster, Bristol kept her eyes on Rocky's face. This was new to her, but she sensed it was new for him too. And she wanted to see him, imprint him on her mind when she came.

It didn't take long. The way he felt, filling her so completely, was incredibly sexy. And it was so different being full when she was getting close to coming. Her dildo had never felt like this before. Ever.

"That's it. God, you are so damn beautiful. You were made for me. We fit perfectly together."

His words sank into her psyche, making Bristol *feel* beautiful. And he wasn't wrong. They did fit together perfectly. Looking at them, you wouldn't think so, but having him inside her was as right as anything she'd ever felt before.

"Please, Bristol. I can't hold off much longer. You're so wet. And tight. I can feel your juices on my balls...*Shit*."

That did it. Bristol pressed harder on her clit and tried to tilt her hips, but she was pinned in place by Rocky. She exploded, and it felt so very good with him inside her as she flew over the edge.

He obviously felt the same way, because a sound came out of his mouth and throat that Bristol had never heard from anyone before. Part grunt, part moan, and part curse word.

He shoved himself inside her to the hilt and held himself there as he came.

They were both breathing extremely hard as they came down from their orgasmic highs. But Rocky never lost track of where he was. He didn't fall on top of her. He gently released her legs and rolled to his back, taking her with him, holding her ass as close to him as he could so he didn't slip out of her body.

Instinctively, Bristol sat up when he was on his back.

He groaned at the movement.

"Sorry," she apologized.

"No, don't be sorry," he said. "It just feels so damn good being inside you, I can't explain it."

Squirming a bit into a more comfortable position, Bristol couldn't do anything but smile down at him.

"I like this," he murmured.

"What?"

"Not having to pull out immediately to get rid of the condom. I can stay right where I am. Where my cock wants to be. Warm and safe inside you."

Bristol rolled her eyes. "That's weird."

"Don't care."

She could see in his eyes that he didn't.

His hands ran up her thighs. "Is this hurting your leg?" he asked.

"What leg?" she responded.

Rocky grinned. "That was..." He paused, and Bristol held her breath waiting for whatever he was going to say.

"Right," he finally said after a moment.

It was. It so was.

Moving carefully so as not to lose his softened cock, Bristol lowered herself until she was lying on Rocky's chest. She nuzzled the skin of his neck and petted his beard. She heard him chuckle, but didn't care. She loved this. Loved *him*.

The thought didn't even faze her. Not in the least. She'd known, at least subconsciously, that she loved this man before she'd gone to bed with him. She never would've let him take her bare if she didn't. Wouldn't be planning on moving to Fallport if she didn't. It might be too soon to say the words, but she damn well thought them.

"Something smelled good when I got home," Rocky said, running his fingers up and down her back lazily.

She smiled against him. "Baked potatoes, although the gravy I was making is probably ruined. At least you turned off the heat before you jumped me."

He chuckled. "Hey, don't want to burn the apartment complex down. What else?"

"Shrimp and sausage with peppers and broccoli."

His belly rumbled, and Bristol laughed. The movement made his cock slip out from between her legs. They both moaned at the loss.

Rocky immediately rolled once more until Bristol was under him. He took her face in his hands as he'd done when he'd gotten home. It was hot as hell and made her shiver when he held her like that, looking deep into her eyes.

"Best I've ever had," he said solemnly. "And if I hadn't skipped lunch, I'd be ready for round two."

For a moment, Bristol resented the fact that he hadn't stopped to eat. But then again, if he had, it was likely he wouldn't even be home yet. Her man liked to work until he got to a good stopping point, even if that meant he didn't get home until after seven or eight at night. Admittedly, something he did rarely these days.

"So here's what we're gonna do. Get outta bed, clean up, eat, then I'm gonna bring you back here and eat *you*. I'm kicking myself for not doing that the first time, but seriously, I couldn't wait to get inside you. Then I'm gonna let you be on top and take me, because seeing you straddling me? Hot as fuck, Punky. We'll sleep, and then have morning sex before I head off to finish the job I started today."

"You have it all planned out, huh?" Bristol asked, but she wasn't opposed to anything he'd said. Not at all.

"I've got nothing planned," he admitted. "But now that I've been inside you bare, all I can think about is getting back in there. I'm going to try not to overwhelm you, and if I do, just tell me to back off. Holding you is going to be just as satisfying as being inside you."

That was sweet in its own way. "I have a feeling it's going to be hard for us to keep our hands off each other for a while," she told him honestly.

"Agreed. But I'm not exactly small, and the last thing I want to do is hurt you. So change of plans...you can take a hot bath after we eat, then I'll eat you out and you can fuck me."

Bristol giggled. "Deal."

Rocky stared at her for a long moment.

"What?" she asked when she couldn't take his intense scrutiny for another second.

"I'm just wondering how in the hell I got here. How you're here with me."

"Guess I'm just lucky."

"Wrong, I'm the lucky one." He leaned down, kissed her long, hard and deep, then rolled off. He walked over to the closet without one iota of self-consciousness. And why would he? He was built.

Determined to display the same confidence, Bristol scooted over to the edge of the mattress and stood. And his come immediately began to leak down her inner thigh.

Surprised—because she hadn't lied earlier, this was the first time she'd let anyone come inside her—she could only stand there, staring at her legs.

"Sorry, but that's *damn* sexy," Rocky said. He went down on his knees in front of her and watched as his come continued to leak out of her.

"It's gross, Rocky. Get me something to wipe it up."

"It's gonna do that for a while, huh?" he asked, instead of doing what she asked.

"No clue. Probably."

He smiled wider. "Fuck, I'm a caveman. Knowing I'm the first to see this, and it's the first time it's ever happened for you, turns me on so bad."

"I can see that," Bristol retorted, eyeing his hardening cock between his legs.

He reached out and ran his thumb between her pussy lips, sighing in contentment when he easily slipped through the folds because of her own juices and his come. Then he leaned over and grabbed the T-shirt he'd thrown on the floor earlier. He gently wiped her thighs and between her legs. He straightened on his knees and kissed her hard once more.

"Can't lie. Thinking about that while we're eating dinner is gonna make it hard to not haul you right back into this bed."

"Try," she said dryly. "I'm hungry, and I know you are too."

He smiled, then sobered. "I'm going to do everything in my power not to fuck this up."

"Me too," Bristol told him.

"I'm serious. You're literally the best thing that's ever happened to me, and I'm gonna guard that with my life."

"I don't want you to do that," she told him.

"Too bad." He then stood, threw the dirty T-shirt into the hamper and strode over to his dresser. He grabbed a pair of boxers and two T-shirts. He snagged his sweats from the edge of the bed where he'd removed them earlier and grabbed her hand. He towed her to the bathroom, where he grabbed a washcloth, wet it with warm water, and handed it to her.

This should be weird, but somehow with Rocky, it wasn't. Bristol cleaned up and put on the T-shirt Rocky had grabbed for her. After he'd washed himself and gotten dressed, she started to go back to the room to find a pair of underwear, but Rocky grabbed her hand once more.

"Hey! I need to go put on some undies."

"Nope. You're perfect just how you are."

"Rocky, seriously."

"I *am* serious. You don't need 'em. I'm just gonna take them off later."

"But you put on boxers—and those sexy sweats, I might add. And I'm gonna take *them* off later."

He pulled her to him and leaned down to whisper in her ear. "But I want you to sit on my lap while we eat so I can feel if any more of me leaks out of you."

Bristol rolled her eyes. "You're so weird."

"I know. I'm sorry. But you'll do it anyway, right?"

"This once. Yes. Since it's the first time."

"Okay."

Their dinner was waiting for them in the oven she'd set to warm before he'd gotten home. The gravy was a lost cause, but the rest of the meal was delicious. Bristol sat on Rocky's lap, as he'd asked, and she didn't even feel too self-conscious about it.

The shirt she had on was large enough to completely cover her, so she didn't feel naked.

"Sorry I skipped lunch," he said as he ate. "I just got busy and wanted to finish up the drywall so it had time to dry before I went in tomorrow."

"It's okay. You haven't seen me when I'm completely lost in my stained glass. I forget to eat all the time."

"We're a lot alike," Rocky said.

Bristol nodded. "Yeah."

"I can't wait to see you lost in your creativity," he said, pausing from eating to kiss her temple. "I bet it's hot."

Bristol rolled her eyes. "It's not. I get sweaty and dirty, and probably smell a little funky."

"As I said—hot."

Bristol laughed. They finished eating and when he helped her stand, she couldn't help but notice the small wet spot on his sweats. He saw it too, and grinned at her, but didn't say anything. "Leave the dishes, I'm gonna go start your bath," he told her.

Bristol waited in the living room, feeling just a little off-kilter. She loved that their relationship had shifted, but couldn't help but worry a bit, wondering if it would continue to be this good between them.

Then Rocky was there, taking her hand and leading her back into the bathroom. He kissed her forehead and said firmly, "This is gonna work."

Bristol pushed her misgivings to the side. "Yes. It is."

"Relax, take your time, Punky. I'll be in our bed waiting to eat my dessert when you're done."

"Jeez, Rocky. If you wanted me to take my time, that wasn't the way to do it," she complained.

He grinned, clearly unrepentant. "Can't wait to taste you, sweetheart. Don't get that cast wet." Then he kissed her once more on the lips and left the bathroom, closing the door behind him as he went.

Blowing out a breath and shaking her head, Bristol turned and caught her reflection in the mirror. She had a huge smile on her face and her cheeks were flushed. She looked happy.

Rocky was good for her, and she hoped he felt the same way about her.

She was looking forward to her future for the first time in a long while. It wasn't that she was unhappy before coming to Fallport, and her art was fulfilling. But with no one to share her life, she was just...existing.

That had definitely changed. She felt as if she was experiencing a brand-new life.

Quickly stripping off her shirt, Bristol sat on the edge of the tub. She eased herself into the water, keeping her leg propped up on the side. She sighed. The water felt heavenly and Rocky had even put something flowery in the water, so it smelled amazing.

Yes, she had a good man. And Bristol was determined to treat him as wonderful as he treated her.

CHAPTER FIFTEEN

Bristol couldn't stop smiling. When she lived in Kingsport, there had been days where she'd laid in bed in the morning wondering where her life was going. Her routine had been the same day in and day out. Most days she didn't talk to anyone, just got up, ate breakfast, and immediately started to work. She loved her art and her home, was financially secure...but her existence was pretty lonely.

Now, her days were filled with texts, phone calls, and visits with friends. She'd been over to Ethan and Lilly's house several times, had visited Zeke and Elsie, been to a soccer game of Tony's, and even gone with Rocky on more of his jobs.

She was still making jewelry now and then, but honestly, she found she loved being with other people more than she liked being inside by herself, making her art. The urge to create would never go away, but she'd built up a large enough nest egg that she didn't have to push herself as hard as she had in the past. Thanks to Rocky and her new friends, Bristol wanted to experience life, not be tied to a website or a worktable.

That said, she was still looking forward to creating stained glass again. She'd had lots of ideas for new projects she wanted to make since being in Fallport, and couldn't wait to find a place she could purchase to get started.

Smiling as ideas swam in her brain for a huge stained-glass piece featuring a forest—with Bigfoot sticking his head out from behind a tree—she jerked in surprise when Rocky touched her hand.

"Sorry, what?" she asked.

"I just asked what you were thinking about," he said softly. They were sitting at his table, finishing breakfast. For once, Bristol didn't have a full day planned. She'd gotten in touch with a realtor and she was meeting her today to go over her wants and desires, so the woman could start on the hunt for a piece of property and house. Afterward, she was going to come back to the apartment and relax. She was also going to make a cake for Rocky. For no specific reason; just because she wanted to spoil him.

He was starting work on a new project today. Something about the foundation of a house. Bristol didn't know the details, but since Rocky was happy about the job, and the money it would bring in, she was too.

"I was just thinking about getting back in the workshop with my stained glass," Bristol told Rocky.

"Do you miss it?" he asked, frowning. "I'm sure we could figure something out so you could get back to it before you buy a place."

"I'm okay," she told him. "I mean, yeah, I miss it, but I'm not going to die if I can't make something immediately."

"Are you sure?"

"I'm sure. Besides, this break gives me a chance to plan what I want to do."

"Yeah?" Rocky asked with a lift of an eyebrow.

"Uh-huh. What do you suppose Sandra would think of replacing one of the front windows of the diner with a stained-glass forest...with Bigfoot of course?"

Rocky burst out laughing. When he had himself under control he said, "She'd jump at the chance to have one of your designs at her diner. But seriously? Bigfoot?"

"It's either that, or a hot, bearded search and rescue guy in the trees," she said with a grin.

"Bigfoot it is," Rocky said firmly.

Bristol knew he'd say that. Rocky—and the rest of the team, actually—disliked any kind of attention. They enjoyed their work, and they didn't do it for recognition or pats on the back.

"You plan anything else for the day while I was in the shower?" Rocky asked.

Bristol frowned. "Like what?"

"I don't know. Bungee jumping with Finley, rearranging all the books in the used bookstore downtown, or meeting up with Sandra to taste test a new menu?"

Bristol giggled. "No! I'm meeting with the realtor then coming back here to chill."

Rocky smiled at her affectionately. "Just checking. For the record? I think it's adorable how everyone you come into contact with wants to be your bestie."

"That's not true," Bristol protested.

"It is. You've fit in here seamlessly. It took a year of me living here for people to even remember my name."

"Whatever," Bristol said with a roll of her eyes. But inside, she was secretly delighted.

They finished their breakfast and then it was time for Rocky to head out. He took her into his arms near the front door and kissed her deeply. They were both breathing hard by the time he pulled away. "What time do you think you'll be done with the realtor today?"

"I'm not sure," she told him. "Before lunch though. She's picking me up around nine, and I can't imagine we'll talk for more than two hours or so."

He laughed gently. "Don't bet on it. I'm guessing by the time your meeting is up, you'll have another best friend."

Bristol just shook her head at him.

"As happy as I am that you want to settle here in Fallport, I have to admit that I'm going to miss you," Rocky said softly.

"Miss me?" Bristol asked in confusion.

"Yeah. I like having you in my apartment. Even if you didn't come to be here because of a good thing, you've filled my space with all your good energy."

"Oh, um..." Bristol wasn't sure how to respond.

"What? What'd I say?" Rocky asked.

"Nothing. I mean...yeah, I've loved being here too."

He wrapped a hand around the side of her neck. "Look at me, Punky." When she did so, he asked, "What's wrong?"

Taking a deep breath, Bristol said, "I just thought...when I found a house I liked...that maybe you'd want to move in with me."

Rocky stared at her for so long, Bristol felt the need to backtrack. It was either that or she might throw up.

"But I know that's silly. I mean, we're dating. I was just here until I got better and my leg is almost as good as new. Of course you don't want to leave your place."

His thumb brushed against her lips, stopping her nervous words.

"You want me to move in with you?" he asked quietly, ignoring her babbling.

Bristol shrugged self-consciously. Then nodded. "Well...yeah.

At least, that's what I was hoping. But if you don't want to, that's okay too."

"I want to," he said fervently. "I've been dreading the day you're back on your feet...and I know that makes me a dick. I didn't lie, Bristol. I've loved having you here. And now that you're sleeping in my bed every night, the idea of you moving out seems even more repugnant."

"I feel the same," she said softly.

"Damn...I hate that I have to go right now," Rocky said.

Bristol could see the desire in his gaze. "The sooner you go, the sooner you can come back," she said cheekily.

He grinned. "True." Then he tilted her head up and lowered his own. He kissed her once more, a gentle, intimate meshing of lips, before he straightened. "Looking forward to hearing what the realtor says."

"Me too."

"Fuck. You make me happy," Rocky said, his gaze roaming her face.

"Same," Bristol told him.

Taking a deep breath, he dropped his hand. "Right. If I'm going to go, I need to go now. Have a good day."

"I will. I'll text you after I meet with the realtor and let you know what she says."

"And if she sends you any interesting properties, email me the links...that is, if you want my opinion on them."

"Of course I do!" Bristol exclaimed. "And I will."

Rocky nodded and turned for the door. He smiled at her once more, then was gone. Bristol stood in the doorway and watched him walk down the corridor outside the complex, toward the stairs. He headed for his Tahoe and waved to her when he was behind the wheel, before he backed out of his parking space and headed for the exit.

Bristol closed the door and leaned against it once she'd locked it behind her. She smiled into space for a full minute before forcing herself to get on with her day.

* * *

As it turned out, Bristol didn't return to Rocky's apartment until early afternoon. She'd hit it off immediately with the realtor, who'd ended up taking her to see two properties that she thought might work, even though that hadn't been in the plan for the morning.

Bristol wasn't as sure about either of them, but her enthusiasm hadn't dimmed. She had no doubt she'd find the perfect property and house.

She texted Rocky to see how his day was going.

Bristol: Hi! I'm back. Things with the realtor went great! We went and looked at two houses, but neither were exactly what I'm looking for. But I think she has a better idea now so I'm sure I'll find something soon. How're things there?

Rocky answered by sending her a picture of a huge hole in the ground filled with brown, muddy water. She had no idea what the problem was, but it was obvious he wasn't exactly having an easy first day on the new job.

Bristol: Oh my. That doesn't look good.
Rocky: It's not. I might be a bit later than I thought getting back tonight.

Bristol: It's okay. It'll give me time to get your surprise finished.

Rocky: Surprise?

Bristol: A sweet one.

Rocky: You, naked on our bed, waiting for me when I get home?

Bristol: lol. No, but that can be arranged too.

Rocky: For the record, you don't need to give me any surprises. I just need you.

Bristol closed her eyes for a moment, absorbing the way he always made her feel so good.

Bristol: Just for that, I might have to break out the new underwear I bought for a special occasion.

Rocky: It's impossible to work with a hard-on, Punky.

Bristol: Sorry. Not. Be careful today. Let me know when you're on your way home?

Rocky: I will. Glad you had a good meeting.

Bristol: Me too.

Rocky: Although I had no doubt that you would. You fit here, Bristol. I'll see you in a few hours.

Bristol: Later.

It was so hard not to type "I love you." The words were on the tip of her tongue, and she wasn't sure why she was holding back. Hell, they were planning on officially moving in together. Saying she loved him didn't seem too fast compared to that. But since he hadn't said it yet, she didn't want to either. Again, stupid. She was an adult.

Shaking her head in disgust with herself, Bristol threw her phone on the counter and opened the cabinet. She had plenty of time to make the cake, but she wanted to make sure it cooled completely before she put on the frosting, otherwise it would melt and look funny. She might not be as good a baker as Finley, but she was determined to have something amazing waiting for Rocky when he got home from what was obviously a tough day at work.

An hour and a half later, she'd just taken the cake from the oven when there was a knock on her door. The apartment smelled wonderful; there was nothing like the scent of a fresh-baked cake...except maybe fresh-baked bread.

Bristol wiped her hands on a dishtowel then headed for the door. She had no idea who it could be, but wouldn't be surprised to see Lilly or maybe even Sandra. The diner owner had stopped by a few times with new dishes she wanted to try out for the diner. It was somewhat of a lame excuse, but Bristol didn't mind. If Sandra wanted to come see her, she was always happy for a visit.

She opened the door, her brows furrowing briefly. Luke...? No, Lance. That was his name.

"Hi! Sorry to bug you," he said cheerfully. "And I know this sounds completely cheesy and trite, but I was putting together a roast for my dinner and realized I didn't have any carrots to go in the stew. I could go down to the store, but I thought maybe I'd see if you had any I could throw in? I've been lost in my manuscript and forgot to stock up. I can give you a couple bucks, if you're able to help me out."

"Oh, that's not necessary, I'm sure I can spare a few. We just went to the store yesterday." Bristol smiled at her neighbor. She hadn't talked to him in a couple of weeks, but she'd seen him around. He lived three doors down, after all, and since Fallport wasn't exactly a huge city, she saw him out and about as well.

"Thank you so much," he said with a huge smile. "Here, let me give you some money for your trouble."

"No, really, it's okay," Bristol said as he reached for his back pocket.

But he didn't pull out his wallet; he had a piece of fabric in his hand.

Before she could even wrap her mind around what he was doing, Lance stepped forward and grabbed her around the waist. He covered her nose and mouth with the fabric, pressing down hard.

Bristol immediately began to struggle, but it was useless. Lance was too big. She tried to kick him with her casted leg, but he merely widened his stance. He pushed her against the wall just inside the apartment and smiled down at her.

It was an eerie, serene grin. He didn't seem stressed out or anxious in any way.

"Just let it happen," he said in a low tone. "Breathe in, poppet. That's it. I've got you."

Too late, Bristol realized what was happening. The cloth against her face was wet. It was such a cliché to be knocked out by chloroform, or whatever drug her neighbor had soaked into the fabric. But it was happening right now. She felt lethargic and her limbs suddenly seemed as if they weighed twenty pounds each. When she blinked, it took all her strength to force her eyes to open again.

"You really shouldn't open your door to strangers, poppet. It's just not safe."

She wanted to laugh in derision. Scream at the man and ask him what the hell he was doing, but she couldn't speak at all with his hand over her mouth, and she was losing consciousness.

Lance lifted her off her feet but didn't remove the cloth from over her nose and mouth. He backed out of her apartment and headed down the walkway.

When they reached his apartment, he opened the door and carried her inside. The last thing Bristol was aware of was Lance murmuring to her as he entered a room that was dark as night. He lay her on a bed and leaned down to kiss her forehead.

"Sleep, poppet. I'm here. Your new life has started."

* * *

Rocky was hot, tired, and irritated. The foundation he was working on was more screwed up than he'd realized. It was going to take a lot of work to fix what time and nature had done to the old house. But he was also proud of what he'd been able to accomplish so far. He'd need to ask Ethan to help in the near future, as there were some things he couldn't do by himself, but he knew his brother wouldn't have any problem lending a hand.

After starting his Tahoe and blasting the air conditioning, Rocky reached for his phone. He shot off a text to Bristol, asking how the rest of her day had gone and telling her he was about to head back to the apartment.

To his surprise, she didn't respond. Not only that, but he didn't see a read receipt pop up under his message.

He waited a full minute, then sent another text.

Rocky: Hey, Punky, you there?

Another minute passed with no response and no indication she'd seen his text.

The hair on the back of Rocky's neck stood up and he put his vehicle into gear. It was silly to think something was wrong. Bristol was at the apartment, right where she'd been earlier. The last time he'd heard from her was when she'd gotten home from her meeting with the realtor. She had no plans for the rest of the day, and if she'd changed her mind and gone out, she would've told him.

Rocky wasn't usually a man who jumped to conclusions... about anything. But he couldn't help feeling a pit of dread expanding in his stomach. It was likely he'd get home and Bristol would be lost in the creative process. Or listening to music so loudly, she hadn't heard his messages come through.

Deep down, Rocky didn't believe either option. She hadn't once failed to respond to a text. It wasn't that he expected her to stop whatever she was doing to pay attention to him when he called or sent her a message, but his gut told him something wasn't right.

He prayed he was wrong. That he'd get back to the apart- ment and Bristol would tell him he was being overprotective and ridiculous. Maybe they'd even have their first fight and she'd tell him he needed to chill out or something. He actually *wanted* that to happen.

Because the alternatives filling his head were unacceptable.

It felt as if it took way longer than normal to drive through Fallport to get to the apartment. His gaze roamed the complex and nothing seemed amiss. There were no strange cars in the lot, and no one was out and about. He parked and jumped out of the car, jogging for the stairs. He took them two at a time and ran down the walkway toward his door. He turned the knob, but it was locked.

Telling himself that was a good sign, it took precious seconds for him to find the right key and fit it into the lock. Rocky pushed the door open, the scent of a freshly baked cake slamming into him.

A sweet surprise, Bristol had said. Relief swam through his veins as Rocky closed the door behind him. "Bristol?" he called out.

There was no answer.

He walked into the apartment and looked toward the kitchen, where he sometimes found her when he got home from work. She wasn't there. He saw the cake she'd made sitting on the stovetop on a cooling rack. It wasn't iced, which made him frown.

"Bristol?" he said again. But as before—no answer.

Turning, Rocky froze when he saw Bristol's cell phone on the counter.

He picked it up and hit the home button. Previews of the texts he'd sent immediately popped up on the screen. Along with messages from Lilly, Elsie, Sandra, and even Khloe.

He put the phone back on the counter and headed for the hallway. The bathroom door was open and Bristol wasn't inside. His hand shook as he opened the master bedroom door. It was a weird feeling to both be *dreading* finding her there, hurt somehow and unable to move, and *hoping* he found her that way. If she was hurt, he could get her help. But if she wasn't there...

His worst fears were realized when the room was exactly how they'd left it that morning. He hadn't been able to keep his hands off her, had bent her over the mattress and taken her from behind. The sheet had gotten pulled off the mattress in their exuberance, and Bristol had mock complained about making the bed. Rocky had kissed her and promised to make it when he got home.

But as he stared at the askew sheets, he knew. Even without checking the room she'd slept in when she'd first arrived, he knew Bristol wasn't there. She would've changed the sheets herself. Wouldn't have actually waited for him do it.

Spinning on his heel, Rocky went back into the living area and opened the door to his apartment. He ran outside and leaned over the railing. He had no idea what he was looking for.

No, that wasn't true. He was looking for any sign of where Bristol might be. Any kind of clue. But all he saw was the same thing he did every time he left his apartment. Turning, Rocky ran his gaze over his door. It had been locked when he'd gotten home, but her phone, keys, and purse were still inside the house.

Shit. Rocky was damn good in the woods. At following tracks. At recognizing a roadside bomb from a hundred yards away. Could spot snipers in buildings in a hostile town. But he wasn't a crime tech. Didn't know what to start looking for in his house to help him find the woman he loved.

He clenched his teeth hard as he pulled his phone out once more. He *loved* Bristol...and hadn't told her. If something happened to her, and he never got the opportunity to let her know how deeply she was loved, he'd never forgive himself.

He might be overreacting, but his gut still said otherwise.

He clicked on a contact and waited impatiently for his friend to answer.

"Hey, Rocky, what's up?" Drew said as he answered.

"I need you."

"Why? What's wrong?"

"Bristol's gone and I need your help. I need everyone's help."

"I'm on my way," Drew said.

Rocky could hear his friend moving in the background. He closed his eyes and did his best not to panic. He was relieved Drew hadn't asked if he was sure. Rocky knew Bristol was in trouble as surely as he knew his name. It was a bone-deep feeling. The same one he'd had when he was seven and Ethan had crashed his bike. He hadn't been there, but he knew his twin was hurt. The same feeling he had when Ethan had almost been blown to pieces by a bomb when they were SEALs.

"Where are you? At your apartment?" Drew asked.

"Yes." The word came out more as a whisper than anything else.

"Do not touch anything. Understand? There could be DNA and other evidence."

"I'm standing outside," Rocky said.

"Good. I'll be there in a few minutes. I'm gonna hang up and call the others. Will you be okay until we get there?"

Would he be okay? No. Not knowing Bristol was somewhere out there, probably scared, maybe hurt. He was well aware of the statistics that said the first hours after someone was taken were the most important. How if someone wasn't found within those first critical two days, it was likely they'd never be.

He couldn't think of his Bristol not being in this world. She was his shining light. She made him want to be a better person.

Putting a hand over his heart, Rocky inhaled deeply. She wasn't dead yet. He *knew* it. Felt it deep inside. He still had a chance to find her. To bring her home. And whoever had dared touch her would regret it.

"Rocky? I need you with me. Do not lose it!" Drew barked.

"I'm here," he told his friend.

"Good. I'm hanging up to call everyone else. Stay put."

Rocky nodded and heard the line go dead. He turned around and stared into his apartment. There was a chance she'd simply forgotten her phone, purse, and keys, and had gone to hang out with one of her new friends, but Rocky dismissed that thought immediately. She'd never leave without her phone. After her experience, she understood more than most the importance of having a way to communicate with others.

No, this was bad.

More than bad. And all Rocky could do was stand there and pray Bristol was strong enough to get through whatever it was life had thrown at her now.

CHAPTER SIXTEEN

When Bristol woke up, she was extremely confused. The room she was in was dim. The only light came from a very low-wattage bulb in the lamp next to the bed she was lying on. A bed that didn't smell or feel familiar.

As awareness returned, she realized that she had a raging headache...and that her leg hurt so bad, tears immediately sprang to her eyes. It didn't make sense. Her leg was mostly healed. Doc Snow had said so just the other day.

"Hello, Bristol," a deep voice said from her immediate right.

Turning her head, she blinked through the tears and recognized her neighbor...Lance.

And just like that, everything came back to her. Instinctively, she tried to jerk away from him, but the pain in her leg came back tenfold. She cried out in pain.

"Easy," Lance said, as he reached out to grab hold of her arm. "You need to stay still, otherwise you'll hurt yourself even more."

Looking down, Bristol saw her right ankle had a chain around it that disappeared off the end of the bed. But more than that—her pink cast was gone. Her leg was stark white, the skin peeling and badly in need of cleaning. But that wasn't what had her staring in disbelief.

She was bleeding, badly, and if the pain she was feeling was any indication, her leg was re-fractured.

"I'm sorry about that," Lance said, not sounding sorry at all. "I had to take the cast off in order to properly restrain you, to make sure you wouldn't be able to leave me. And in the process, you got hurt again."

Visions of the movie *Misery* flashed in Bristol's mind. Had Lance purposely broken her leg so she couldn't walk?

"But you'll heal. I'll make sure of it. I'll bring you everything you need...food, water, and the stuff you need to make your jewelry. I went to your house, you know." His voice was even and smooth, as if he was talking about the weather, not about chaining her up and keeping her captive.

"My house?" Bristol asked, doing her best not to freak out. She needed to stay calm. Figure out what the hell was going on and how to get the fuck out of there.

"Yes. When you were gone for so long, I got worried. You weren't online, you weren't fulfilling orders from your website. I knew something bad had happened. And I was right. When you finally came home, I was so relieved...but you were with *him*. He's not good for you, Bristol. You haven't paid attention to messages from your followers and customers at all, or to your website. You haven't put up any new merchandise. That's not good.

"When you left, I followed you here. To this awful fucking town. Where everyone is in everyone's business. It's disgusting," he spat, sounding angry for the first time, before calming again. "When I went home, I planned. I went back to your house and got some of your things. Stuff you'll need until I can take you back to *my* home, where we'll be so happy together. I have your soap, your books...and look, even a picture of your mother."

Lance gestured to the room, and Bristol obediently looked around in horror. He was right. She saw a pillow that she'd last seen on her couch back in Kingsport. A picture of her mom and her from Christmas a few years ago. A mug from her kitchen cabinet with the image of a wildflower.

In the corner of the room was a small table that held plastic containers filled with some of the beads and other materials she used to make jewelry. She'd last seen those in her house as well, when she'd been there with Rocky. She'd decided not to bring them to Fallport because she'd already packed enough materials for the short term.

Tears leaked nonstop from Bristol's eyes. It was bad enough she'd been kidnapped from Rocky's apartment by someone she kind of knew, and her leg was bashed in so she couldn't walk. To know Lance had violated her private space back in Kingsport was almost too much.

"Don't cry," Lance said, sounding agitated.

Bristol turned to look at him. His face was red, and he was frowning at her.

"Don't cry!" he repeated, more forcefully this time. "You should be *happy*. You love me! We're meant to be together. I have so many things you made at my house. You made them for *me*!"

Bristol held her breath. She was scared—so damn scared. Lance was completely unhinged. If he'd ordered things from her store, she certainly didn't remember.

She was breathing way too fast, but if she was going to survive this, she needed to make Lance think she was glad to be here. She couldn't fight him. He was bigger and stronger, and with her leg hurting like it was, she couldn't exactly walk out of here.

Bristol thought back to a true-crime show she'd seen once. There were five or six young women who'd been kidnapped and held for long periods of time. Some of them had been held for years. The thought of being with this man for a day, let alone forever, made Bristol want to cry once more, but she did her best to keep all her innermost thoughts off her face.

In the show, the women talked about how they'd befriended their captors. How they remained compliant and did everything asked of them. The interviewer had asked if they'd ever wanted to fight. The response from every single woman was that of *course* they did, but they instinctively knew if they'd tried, he would have killed them.

Bristol hadn't really understood at the time. She'd thought to herself that if someone ever did that to her, she'd fight like hell. She'd *never* give in. Never let a kidnapper think for a second that she was all right with what they'd done.

But lying there, vulnerable, chained to the bed, her leg throbbing and her head pounding from whatever he'd used to knock her out, Bristol got it.

Her only goal was to survive. And if that meant being docile and not letting this man know how much she hated him and how badly she wanted to get away, so be it.

Rocky would find her. He had to. She just had to be smart and stay alive until then. Just like she'd done back in the forest. She'd done what was necessary in order to survive until he came for her. She hadn't known he was looking, of course, but now, she knew without a shadow of a doubt that Rocky and his friends— hell, the entire town of Fallport—would turn over every rock and look under every bush to find her.

A small voice in the back of her head warned that looking

under rocks and bushes wasn't going to cut it, but she shoved that thought away. She needed to stay positive.

"I'm glad you liked the things I made for you," Bristol said tentatively.

It was the right thing to say. Lance beamed. "I loved them. Ever since I saw one of your designs, I knew. You were mine. I moved to Kingsport to be near you, and I knew it was only a matter of time before you felt our connection like I did. We were meant to be together. I love you, poppet."

Bristol smiled. It was strained, but she did her best as she wiped the tears off her cheeks. He'd moved to Kingsport because she was there? How long had he been watching her? She didn't even want to think about it. She took a deep breath. "Where are we?"

"In my apartment."

She blinked in surprise. "We are?"

"Uh-huh. But don't worry, they aren't going to find you. No way. I made the room soundproof. The walls here are way too thin. They'd hear you for sure if I didn't."

Looking around, Bristol realized why it was so dark. He'd tacked blankets to the walls and over the window. She wasn't sure how many there were, but it looked like enough to at least muffle any noises that might come from the room.

It took everything she had to smile at Lance. "Smart," she said softly.

"I know. We're right under his nose and he won't ever real-ize," Lance crowed. "We'll stay here for a while, until they stop looking for you. Then I'll take you home, to *my* home, where you belong, and we'll live happily ever after. You'll make your windows for me, and I'll love you, and we'll never need anyone but each other."

Bristol's blood ran cold. If Lance took her away from Fallport, the chances of anyone ever finding her would be slim to none.

"I'm sorry about your leg," Lance said again, frowning. "I wasn't going to hurt you, but when I was taking off the cast, I got to thinking that you might try to leave me. I couldn't have that. Before I knew what I was doing, I was hitting you with a hammer. I thought it would be better if I did it while you were sleeping, so you couldn't feel it."

Bristol wanted to throw up. No wonder her leg hurt so badly. He'd hit her with a *hammer*? She gave him what she hoped was a pitiful look. "It really hurts."

But instead of Lance being worried or doing something to stop the bleeding, he shrugged. "I know, but now you can't leave me," he said, as nonchalantly as if he was talking about what was for dinner.

As she stared at the man sitting next to her, Bristol realized he was more than just delusional. Something else was seriously wrong with him...and she'd have to tread carefully.

He wouldn't be able to stay with her every minute of every day. She'd find a way to get out of this room. If she could get to the door and get outside, she'd be free.

Knowing she was so close to Rocky, and so far at the same time, was reassuring and depressing at the same time.

Lance leaned forward and casually put his hand over the split skin of her shin—and squeezed. Bristol couldn't stop the screech of pain.

"Don't think about leaving me, Bristol," he said, as if he could read her mind. "I've worked too hard to have you. I'm not giving you up. I'll kill us *both* before that happens. He doesn't get you. You're mine. Understand?"

Bristol nodded frantically.

Lance sat back with a huge smile on his face, as if he wasn't just hurting her a second ago. He leaned an elbow on the bed and rested his chin in his hand. In his *bloody* hand. The one he was just using to squeeze the wound on her leg. "Good. Now, are you hungry? Maybe you want to work on some jewelry? I know it relaxes you. You can make me something, then we'll work on replenishing the inventory for your store. Your fans have missed you, and it's time you reopened for business."

Bristol swallowed the bile that had risen in her throat. She wanted to scream. Wanted to rail against what was happening to her. But instead, she simply nodded.

* * *

Rocky tried to stay calm as Raiden and Duke worked. He was standing in the parking lot, watching as the bloodhound went back and forth on the walkway in front of the apartments on the second floor. It was obvious the dog had Bristol's scent, but he also seemed confused about where it was coming from. He walked from Rocky's apartment down the walkway to the stairs. He went down the stairs, then back up. Sniffed at each of the apartment doors on the second level, then went back down and sniffed all the way around the parking lot.

Eventually, Raiden approached Rocky and the rest of the team. Simon and two of his officers were there too. "I'm sorry, but because she's been up and down the stairs and in and out of your apartment so much, Duke can't lock onto the most recent scent. The most likely scenario is that she came down here and got in a car."

"Fuck," Rocky muttered.

"I've got my other two officers setting up a checkpoint on I-480," Simon said. "They'll stop every car leaving Fallport and search it for Bristol."

Rocky appreciated the police chief's effort, but if someone had taken Bristol and fled town, they were probably long gone. Five hours had passed since he'd last heard from her. Five hours during which absolutely anything could've happened.

He felt sick.

"I called Sandra and asked her to spread the word that Bristol's missing," Ethan said. "Everyone in Fallport will be on the lookout for her."

Rocky appreciated that, but it didn't stop the dread overwhelming his entire body.

"We'll spread out here and comb the area around the complex," Talon offered.

Rocky nodded.

"We'll find her," Brock told him.

"We won't give up until she's home," Zeke added.

"Go on and get started. I'll be with you in a second," Ethan told the rest of the Eagle Point Search and Rescue team.

Both of Simon's officers went back up the stairs to his apartment, to have a closer look inside for any clues they might've missed in their initial search of the place.

"Talk to me," Ethan ordered his brother.

Rocky lifted his gaze to his twin's. "About what?" he said brokenly. "She's gone."

"Did you guys have a fight?" Simon asked.

Rocky practically growled at the other man. "No," he said with a firm shake of his head. "No fight. We're good. Solid. I didn't do this, Simon. You fucking know me. You *know* I wouldn't do this."

"I had to ask," Simon said with a shrug, his hands up in capitulation.

Rocky knew that, but he didn't like it. "She's buying a house here. She met with a realtor just this morning. She asked me to *move in* with her. I wouldn't hurt one hair on her head, Simon. I swear it. I texted her at lunch, and she said she was making me a surprise. That's the last time we communicated. She didn't sound weird. Nothing happened. I came home and she was just...gone."

The look of sympathy on Simon's face was almost unbearable.

Rocky had been where Simon was right now, too many times to count. Talking with a loved one about a missing family member. Wanting to know the last time they were seen, the last words they'd said...trying to get any indication of where to start looking. And now here he was, on the other side. It sucked more than he ever could have imagined.

"Could anyone in town have found out about her financial situation and maybe want that money for themselves?" Simon asked.

Rocky sighed in frustration. "I don't know. But shit, Simon, you know Bristol. Everyone loves her. And the last thing she'd ever do was flaunt the fact that she's rich. *You* didn't even know until I mentioned it earlier."

Simon shrugged. "I know. Just trying to figure out a motive."

"What about Theodore Lorenzo Allen?" Rocky asked. "Could he have done this? Hired one of the people he claimed to know to grab her?"

Simon's lips pressed together. "I'll look into it."

"Or maybe that Mike guy. You know, the asshole who left her in the woods in the first place? Maybe he still can't accept no for an answer when it comes to being with her." Rocky knew he was grasping at straws, but he was having a hard time believing this was happening.

"He's on my list of people to check out," Simon reassured him.

Rocky struggled to force himself to think. "All her stuff's still in the apartment. Her phone, purse...shoes are still by the door. I think she had to have opened the door. Maybe she knew whoever it was."

"I don't know," Ethan said. "This is Fallport. Even if she didn't know the person, she might've still opened the door."

Rocky knew his brother was right.

"When my officers are done looking over your apartment, we'll canvas the neighborhood. See if anyone in the complex saw or heard anything. Then we'll spread out to the businesses and homes nearby," Simon said.

Rocky nodded, but inside, a deep, intense anger was beginning to burn through the shock and fear. Someone had taken his woman. He had no doubt that she hadn't gone willingly. She would never just up and leave without a word.

He and Bristol were on the cusp of a wonderful life together. A life he never thought he could have. And he wouldn't stop searching for her, ever.

"When I call the Kingsport police to ask about this Mike character, I'll see if they can do a welfare check of her house. Maybe, just maybe, she decided she was homesick and went back there," Simon said.

Rocky didn't believe that for a second. Bristol was already considering Fallport her home. She wouldn't go back to Kingsport without telling him. And certainly not without her phone, purse, and fucking shoes.

No, someone took her. Rocky was sure of that.

He didn't want to think about what that someone was doing to her right now. That wasn't something he could deal with at the moment. Once he found her, they'd deal with whatever she'd gone through together. He would be there for her no matter what.

For now, he needed to *do* something, anything.

Rocky turned to Ethan. "I need you to coordinate the search."

His brother nodded. "Already planned to."

"And I have to be involved. I can't sit home and wait."

"Don't blame you."

"I'm not sure that's a good idea," Simon started, but Rocky turned on him.

"I'm doing this," he said between clenched teeth. "You're not stopping me."

"It's not smart. Your presence could hurt a criminal case down the line."

"Someone will be with him at all times," Ethan assured him. "If we find anything, Rocky won't touch it."

Simon sighed. "All right. The criminal case thing...that's mostly just an excuse. I'm trying to protect you, Rocky. If she's found...not alive, I don't want you to see her that way."

The chief's words turned Rocky's blood to ice, but he didn't show what he was feeling. "I'm not a noob," he told him. "I know there's a possibility that we're looking for her body. But I have to do this."

He didn't tell Simon that he didn't think Bristol was dead. That he'd somehow feel it deep inside if she was. The man wouldn't believe him, but Rocky didn't care. He believed enough for both him and Bristol.

"Fine. But do not touch any evidence you might find. I mean it," Simon warned.

"This isn't our first search," Ethan said, the irritation loud and clear in his tone. "We know how DNA works."

"All right. Stay in touch. If you find anything, let me know."

"We will," Ethan said, grabbing Rocky's arm. "Thanks." He took a few steps to the right, away from Simon. Then Ethan wrapped his arm around Rocky's neck and pulled him close. Rocky rested his forehead against his brother's. They stood like that for a long moment. Rocky absorbing the love and support from his twin, needing it more than he'd needed anything in a long time.

"We're gonna find her, bro," Ethan said softly after a minute had passed.

"I'm scared," Rocky whispered.

"Me too."

"Someone's got her. She didn't walk away," Rocky said.

"You're right. We won't quit until we've got her back."

Rocky closed his eyes. His heart was pounding and so much adrenaline was coursing through his veins, he was shaking. "I love her," he admitted out loud for the first time.

"You aren't telling me anything I don't already know," Ethan said. "She loves you too. No matter where she is or what's happening, she's hanging on...for you. She's a tough cookie. She might be tiny, but she's got more determination in her little finger than people twice her size."

Rocky nodded and took a deep breath as he straightened. Ethan's hands went to his shoulders as they stared at each other. His brother was right. Bristol *was* tough. Not only that, she was smart. He had no idea what happened, but he knew she wouldn't give up. Ever.

"You ready to search?" Ethan asked.

He was more than ready. "Yes."

"Come on. Let's go find your woman," Ethan said.

CHAPTER SEVENTEEN

Bristol had no idea how much time had passed since she'd been taken. With the room kept dark all the time, she couldn't tell when it was daytime and when it was night. She had a feeling she slept a lot the first few days, to mentally escape her situation and to have a reprieve from the pain in her leg.

When she needed to use the bathroom, Lance brought her a bucket and placed it next to the bed. It was humiliating and disgusting, but she literally had no other choice but to use it. It was either that, or soil her bed and herself. Lance had to help her out of the bed, since she couldn't move her leg without pain. Bristol had been surprised the first time he'd actually left her alone to do her business, but he always returned right after she finished, taking the bucket away. He was probably watching her, which disgusted her even more.

He brought her food and drink regularly. The food wasn't great, but Bristol ate it anyway. She needed to keep up her energy, and the only way to do that was to eat.

Lance was obsessed with her jewelry and art. He bemoaned

the fact that she couldn't create her stained glass in bed, but was full of promises that when they got to his home, she'd be able to get back to it.

Leaving here was literally Bristol's worst nightmare. The last thing she wanted to do was go back to Tennessee.

Apparently, the entire town of Fallport was banding together to find her. It broke her heart and frustrated her anytime Lance offered updates on the search. There were missing posters and organized searches through every inch of the town and surrounding forest.

It made her feel good that everyone cared so much, but it also made her extremely sad. She was *here*. Right here! Three doors down from where she'd been taken. Still, as the search continued, it was her only bit of hope.

Lance didn't feel the same way, of course. He was outraged over the concern for her. He ranted and raved about how she was new here, how no one should care as much as they did. She was *his*—no one else had the right to love her like he did.

His moods constantly swung from being lovey-dovey toward her, to scarily pissed off at the situation he claimed *she'd* put him in.

Despite his anger over the search, Bristol knew he was still smugly proud that he'd hidden her right under everyone's noses. He'd told her several times about how the police had knocked on his door the evening of her abduction, questioning him about anything he may have seen or heard. He boasted about keeping the door to the apartment wide open, and they'd had no idea the woman they were looking for was literally in a room fifteen feet away.

He told her over and over that she was *his*, that no one would take her from him. Ever.

It was getting harder and harder to stay positive. To play his game. Every day, Bristol had to force herself to smile rather than scream at him. Avoid telling him how sadistic and horrible he was, and that she'd never, *ever*, love him.

If she told him how she truly felt, he'd hurt her. Maybe even kill her. She still couldn't move her leg all that much. She had no idea if the pin the surgeon had put in a couple of months ago had been knocked loose or what. All she knew was that even if she didn't have a chain on her ankle, she wasn't walking out of the apartment.

But that didn't mean she couldn't crawl. She'd done it in the forest, and she'd do it again now. Gladly.

The worst part of her captivity wasn't the embarrassment of having to relieve herself in a bucket, or pretending to enjoy Lance's company. It was when he left. No matter how much she begged and promised that she'd be quiet, he didn't trust her. He handcuffed her hands to the chain attached to her leg, strapped a ball gag around her head, and told her to be good.

It was hard to breathe with the ball in her mouth, and every second he was gone, Bristol felt as if she was going to gag on her own spit. It would run down her chin because she couldn't swallow very well, and no matter how hard she tried, she couldn't reach the buckle at the back of her head with her hands cuffed to the chain. Not to mention, moving too much hurt her leg like hell.

Once, Lance came back after being gone for an inordinately long period of time, telling her with obvious delight how he'd joined one of the searches for her. How inside, he was laughing at everyone's useless efforts the whole time.

Her captor was evil, and the small twinges of pity she'd experienced for this obviously lonely and sick man had long since disappeared.

Her days were endless and boring, since the only thing Lance allowed her to do was make earrings, bracelets, and necklaces. He didn't let her watch TV, read books, or do anything other than sleep, eat, and make jewelry. He'd brought in a laptop once, and Bristol had gotten excited, thinking she could somehow send a message to Rocky or anyone else, but he'd quickly quashed that hope by not letting her get anywhere near the keyboard.

He'd wanted the password to her website. Wanted her to teach him how to upload pictures and update the descriptions of her wares. When she'd tried to put him off, saying she wasn't sure she remembered her password, he'd grabbed the hammer from the table across the room and slammed it down on the mattress—right next to her leg.

She'd immediately given him the information he wanted.

Now, every day she made jewelry. Lance put up each listing on her website. And she had to listen to him talk about how great their life was going to be together, how much she was going to love the room he'd set up for her back in Kingsport.

The first time one of the new pieces sold, Lance was ecstatic. He'd gone on and on for at least an hour about how happy her customer was going to be, then went into detail about every single thing he'd bought from her. Bristol hadn't remembered any of the items...and she *certainly* hadn't included "love notes" with the purchases, as Lance claimed she had.

Knowing that he'd been out there, watching and idolizing her for so long, made Bristol sick. If only she'd paid more attention to her customers—and their addresses. But she hadn't. There were simply too many. She just packaged things and sent them off without a second thought.

As the long hours of an untold number of days went by, depression and despair began to set in. She had no way of knowing how much time had passed, but with each day, it was likely the search for her would die down. Eventually, people would assume she was dead and stop looking. The missing posters would come down and everyone would go back to their normal lives.

The thought of Rocky doing the same made the carefully constructed mental wall she'd put up for her own sanity start to crumble. She loved him so much, and the thought of him suffering, wondering what had happened to her, almost tore her apart.

But it was the thought of him eventually moving on that had the power to break her.

She wanted to yell, "I'm here! I'm right here!" over and over until someone heard her. Surely the blankets on the wall weren't *that* good at soundproofing the room. But of course, that was why Lance always gagged her before he left the apartment. She could try screaming when he was there, but the hammer on the table across the room always made her think twice.

Taking a deep breath, Bristol forced her mind to blank. She had to hold on. Just a little longer. Lance would mess up sooner or later. He had to. He was so unbalanced, it wasn't even funny. Someone would notice and start asking questions. He spent most of his time in the apartment with her, but he had to leave to buy food. To mail the jewelry she sold.

The people of Fallport were nosy. They'd figure out there was a wolf in sheep's clothing in their midst. She was counting on it.

* * *

Two weeks. Rocky couldn't believe it had been so long.

He wasn't eating. Wasn't sleeping. Couldn't do much of anything but think of Bristol.

Was she all right?

Was she in pain?

Did she think he'd stopped looking?

Because he wouldn't. Not even if it took years, he'd find her.

She was alive. He knew it.

He saw the pitying looks people gave him. He was well aware many had given up. That they thought Bristol was dead and buried in the forest somewhere. But just as he knew anytime his brother was hurt, he knew Bristol was still alive.

Yet, with every day that passed, he could *feel* her resolve faltering. The spark that had always flared bright between them was dimming. His window to find her was narrowing, and he knew it.

He was missing something. But Rocky couldn't figure out what.

It didn't help that less than a week after she'd disappeared, a large box was delivered to the apartment. Seven brand-new, top-of-the-line satellite phones. Bristol had obviously ordered them, probably wanting to surprise him. She would've been so excited. As much as he appreciated the gift, opening the box made him so fucking sad, it just about killed him.

Thinking about her was bittersweet and frustrating. There were no leads as to where she might be or who could've taken her. Mike, the douche who'd tried to get Bristol to have an orgy in the woods, had an iron-tight alibi. The child-molesting asshole they'd helped put away had also been cleared. He'd laughed when he'd been questioned, after hearing Bristol was missing, but there was absolutely no evidence he'd been talking to someone to organize a kidnapping.

Rocky and his team had searched every inch of the neighborhoods around the apartment complex, with no luck. The townspeople had taken turns hiking the trails around Fallport and hadn't seen or heard anything out of the ordinary. Every day, people gathered in the square to get their assignments on where to search next.

Ethan had been working nonstop, organizing and coordinating the search for Bristol. Rocky could never repay him for his unwavering support, but the truth was...he knew they weren't going to find the woman he loved sitting in the middle of the woods. He might've found her that way once, but deep in his gut, he knew someone was hiding her. The only question was— where? Here in Fallport? In a cabin in the woods? Had she been taken out of town, out of the state? There was no telling.

It was time to change things up. No longer was this a physical search. He knew it in his heart. It was now a search for information. Someone knew *something*. Had seen or heard something.

Rocky couldn't bring himself to sleep in his bed, not without Bristol there to share it with him, so he'd been spending the nights on his couch. Sleeping in short spurts. Any tiny noise made him jerk awake, thinking it was Bristol coming home. But he was disappointed every time.

He looked like hell, but didn't even care. He hadn't brushed his hair or beard in days. Couldn't remember when he'd last eaten or changed clothes. How could he worry about shit like that when his woman might be starving? Or wearing the same clothes she'd been taken in? Or not allowed to bathe?

When it got close to the time Ethan would be meeting with the people in the square, Rocky left his apartment to attend. He wanted to say something to the townspeople. Needed them to be aware on a different level than they'd been before.

He was halfway down the stairs, heading to his car, when one of the apartment doors opened behind him.

Looking up, Rocky saw Lance closing his door.

"Morning," Lance told him as he started down the stairs. "Any luck finding your girlfriend?"

"Not yet," Rocky said, as they both reached the parking lot.

"I'm sorry. That has to hurt."

Hurt what an understatement. "Yeah," he said absently.

"Well, I hope you find her. I'm off to the grocery store and the post office." He gestured to a package under his arm, giving Rocky a small smile.

"Thanks. Have a good day," he returned without thought. He couldn't remember the last time he'd run mundane errands like grocery shopping. The cake Bristol had made for him the day she'd disappeared had sat on his counter for a week, before Ethan had wrapped it up and taken it away. His brother knew without asking that throwing it away was something Rocky couldn't do. He was sure Ethan had dumped it once he'd gotten home, but would never do something so heartless in front of his twin.

Rocky didn't even remember the drive to the square. He knew that was extremely dangerous, but lately, he couldn't muster up the energy to care about his own safety.

There were several dozen people milling around the Circle, the gazebo in the middle of the square. He couldn't help but be heartened that so many were still trying to find his Bristol.

He walked up to where Ethan was standing in the Circle, and the crowd around them got silent. Rocky didn't always show up to the meetings when Ethan organized searches, but when he did, people had been sympathetic and positive, which he appreciated.

He immediately addressed the crowd. "Thanks for coming out again today. I know Bristol would be so happy and surprised with all the support people have shown her. But...here's the thing...I think we need to alter our thoughts on the search," he told the locals.

Rocky could feel his brother looking at him, but he kept his eyes on the volunteers. "If she was hurt in the woods or anywhere in the town, we would've found her by now. I don't think we can escape the fact that someone is keeping her hidden. I think we need to start talking about things we've seen not while searching, but when we're just out and about. I've never been a fan of gossip...but that's what we need right now. What have you seen or heard that seems out of place or unusual? Have any of your neighbors been acting strangely? Furtively? Did someone leave town suddenly without notice? Anyone bought a ton of cleaning supplies lately?

"Whoever took Bristol can't hide her forever. And before anyone gets crazy, I'm not suggesting you should make accusations about your neighbors and friends. I simply want you to change your way of thinking...from looking for Bristol around every corner, to dissecting any information you might have about something you saw or heard, and putting those pieces together.

"I miss her. So much. She needs us. Needs us to band together and *talk* to each other. She's out there somewhere. Waiting to be found. Please...think hard about anything out of the ordinary that you've seen, and call the police. Even if it's something small, it could be the clue we need to find Bristol. Thank you."

Rocky's gaze swept the crowd. He saw Silas, Otto, and Art. They'd left their spot in front of the post office to join in the search, or at least to listen to whatever Ethan had to say each morning. Sandra was there. As were most of the owners of the businesses in the square. Hell, even the owner of the pool hall, Whip, stood a short distance from the rest of the crowd, and he was a standoffish son-of-a-bitch. But Rocky wasn't going to turn away anyone who was interested in helping to find Bristol.

Davis was there, looking scruffy as ever, as were the servers from On the Rocks. His friend's bar didn't open for a few hours, and they were here on their free time, wanting to help. Nissi O'Neill, the town's lawyer, Finley, Khloe...even Edna Brown, the woman who owned the motel where Elsie and Tony had lived for so long. There were teachers from Tony's school, and even people Rocky didn't know.

Fallport was a community, and when something happened to one of their own, everyone took it personally.

Ethan ended the meeting by announcing there would be no official searches organized today, and instead urged everyone to do just as his brother had suggested—talk to each other. Think about the things they'd seen and heard recently, and if anything seemed to be suspect in any way, to call Simon at the police station.

When everyone had left, and it was just Rocky and Ethan left standing in the Circle, Rocky turned to his brother. "She's losing time," he said quietly.

"We aren't giving up," Ethan said sternly.

"I know, but...it's been two weeks."

"You know as well as I do that sometimes our searches take even longer than this," Ethan said.

"I do, but in almost one hundred percent of the cases that take this long, we find a body, not a person," Rocky said, admitting for the first time what he was beginning to fear deep in his heart. He hadn't wanted to think his Bristol was dead, he hadn't *felt* like she was dead, but he had to consider the most obvious scenario.

"No," Ethan said, getting up in his brother's face. "She is *not* dead. You'd know it."

"Would I?" Rocky asked.

"Yes! You know that as well as I do."

Rocky closed his eyes and said in a low, tortured tone, "I find people for a living. What good are my skills if I can't find the one person who means the most to me in the world?"

"For the record, I think you're on the right track with what you said today. We got too focused on a physical search. This isn't like the missing people we track down in the forests. She didn't walk out of your apartment of her own free will. Actually asking the townspeople to gossip is exactly what we need right now."

"Simon's not going to be happy," Rocky said, opening his eyes.

"So what," Ethan retorted with a shrug. "He'll deal. I have a good feeling about this. The one thing small towns do best, *Fallport* does best, is gossip. Someone saw something. I know it. Hang on, brother. Just a little longer."

"Bristol needs to hear that, not me," Rocky replied.

Ethan clapped a hand on his shoulder. They stood like that for a moment, soaking in the love and support they had for each other, before Rocky said, "I have a meeting with the realtor Bristol saw before she disappeared."

"You do?" Ethan asked in surprise.

"Yeah. She called me...said she'd found the perfect property for Bristol."

"Um, that sounds a little coldhearted," Ethan said with a frown.

Rocky shook his head. "Actually, I don't see it that way at all. She apologized and told me how worried she's been. I've seen her on a few searches too. She told me when she saw the property, she immediately knew Bristol would love it, even after only knowing her for a short while. I wasn't interested in seeing the house, mostly because I'm too consumed with worry. But also because I guess it needs considerable work. She told me that when we find Bristol, maybe having this house would give her something to concentrate on. Something to help put what happened to her in the past."

"She said that?" Ethan asked. "Straight up? That's kind of fucked up."

Rocky shook his head. "Yeah, I wasn't too thrilled...but then I thought about it for a bit. She's kind of not wrong. So I said I'd meet her and go look at the property."

"You want company?" Ethan asked.

Rocky shook his head. "No. Thanks though."

"You need to eat more," Ethan said after a moment. "You aren't looking after yourself. Bristol would be pissed at you, and probably *me* for not making sure you eat...and sleep."

Rocky's lips twitched. His brother was right. But the thought of eating made him nauseous. "I'll grab something before meeting with the realtor."

"Right," Ethan said, obviously knowing he was lying. "Call me later about the property?"

"I will. You gonna give Simon a head's up about what's coming his way?"

Ethan sighed. "Yeah. I'll head over there now."

"Thanks. Give Lilly my love."

"I will."

The two men hugged, not ashamed in the least about the display of affection. Ethan pounded Rocky on the back before he turned to walk toward the police station.

Rocky felt guilty for a moment, knowing his brother—hell, their entire team—had been spending every spare minute of every day, for the last two weeks, doing all they could to find Bristol.

Raid had taken Duke out every day, hoping against hope to catch Bristol's scent, with no luck. Zeke had left the running of On the Rocks to his bartenders and Elsie, who were all working extra hours to cover for him. Drew, Brock, and Talon had been doing everything in their power to use their skills to find any small sign of Bristol's whereabouts.

Her disappearance had brought them all even closer, but it was bittersweet...since she was still missing.

Rocky could hear people chatting as they walked along the sidewalks around the square, saw cars driving slowly, smelled bread baking at The Sweet Tooth...everyone was going on with their lives as normal. While his life had completely stopped.

Sighing, and praying that today would be the day they got any sort of clue regarding Bristol's whereabouts, Rocky walked across the grass toward his car. He had mixed feelings about seeing the property and house the realtor thought Bristol would love, but the last thing he wanted to do was go back to an empty apartment.

* * *

Simon ran a hand through his hair in frustration. It wasn't as if he didn't agree with what Rocky had told the townspeople who'd come out to help with the search this morning, but it certainly made his life a lot busier. The phone had been ringing all morning, with people telling him all the strange things they thought their friends, neighbors, and even strangers in the grocery store were doing. He was obligated to check them all out. Right now, he was alone in the station because all four of his officers were chasing some of the leads that had been called in.

He'd finally found a minute to sit and eat his lunch—even

though it was two in the afternoon—when the bell over the front door of the station chimed.

Sighing, Simon put down the sandwich before he'd even taken a bite. Since they were a small department, they didn't have a full-time admin assistant to greet people who came in. So he walked to the front of the office, where he saw Davis Woolford waiting.

"Davis. Good to see you. Everything all right?" Simon asked.

Davis fidgeted as if he wasn't comfortable inside the building. "We were told to come to you if we saw anything off," Davis said.

"That's right. Are you hungry? I was just sitting down to eat lunch."

Davis shook his head. "Sandra gave me something a while ago."

Simon nodded. He wasn't surprised. The business owners of Fallport did their best to take care of the man. "Would you mind coming to sit with me as I eat then? I'm starving."

Davis nodded, and Simon held open the door to the back offices. The stench of the man assaulted his nostrils, and he immediately regretted asking him to sit with him while he ate. Mentally shrugging, and doing his best to breathe through his mouth and not his nose, Simon led them to the small conference room where his sandwich was waiting.

Davis sat on the very edge of a chair across the table from Simon, looking everywhere but directly at him.

"Why don't you go on and tell me what you came to tell me," Simon urged gently.

The homeless man nodded but it took a minute before he began to speak.

Before he'd gotten even two sentences out, all thoughts of eating flew from Simon's head.

"You know how I like to look in dumpsters for stuff. Well, I was at Rocky's apartment complex, going through the trash in the back, and a man came rushing around the corner, screaming at me. He scared me, and I immediately backed away. He told me I was trespassing and had no right to be there. Everyone knows me, they know what I do...look for stuff I can sell and use. I don't mean no harm. Anyway, his face got all red and he was real mad. He reached into the dumpster and pulled out a bag of trash. He yelled at me some more, then took the trash bag with him, up to his apartment."

"Who was it?"

"Don't know his name. He's new in town though. Was a jerk to me at the festival. Haven't seen him around much."

"And he took his trash back up to his apartment?"

"Uh-huh. I didn't get a look inside before he grabbed it. But Rocky said to tell you when we saw things that were out of place, and I thought maybe that qualified."

"It definitely does. When was this?"

"A few days ago. I didn't think too much about it at the time, other than the guy was an ass, but now, after what Rocky said, I'm wondering about it. Especially because he lives in the same complex as Rocky and his woman.

"I don't like to gossip. It's just not in my nature. I know people talk about me, and that's fine, I don't much care. But I don't like to do it to others. I see a lot of what goes on around here and have always kept my mouth shut. But Bristol's nice. She smiled at me all the time and met my eyes. Most people don't do that. They think if they don't see me, I won't be there, and they don't have to worry about me none. But she saw me. If I can help, I want to."

"I appreciate you coming in, Davis. And no matter how much you think people don't see you, you're wrong. They do, and they worry. Anytime you want to try getting off the streets, you've got lots of people who are ready to help."

Davis nodded. "We done?"

"We're done," Simon said. "I'll walk you out."

The two men walked back to the front of the station, and Simon shook Davis's hand. "Thank you for coming in and talking to me."

"I hope she's found soon."

"Me too," Simon agreed.

He didn't wait to watch Davis walk away. He immediately went to his office to do some research, his lunch forgotten.

* * *

Rocky sat in his vehicle in the parking lot of his complex, staring off into space. He didn't want to go upstairs to his empty apartment, but he couldn't think of anywhere else to go. He'd met with the realtor and she'd driven him out to see the property she thought would be perfect for Bristol.

She wasn't wrong.

Rocky knew instinctively Bristol would love it. He could see immediately why there hadn't been a lot of interest in the place; it definitely needed work. But it had great bones and the charm of the house, built a hundred years ago, was undeniable. There was a large red barn on the property that he could easily turn into a workshop for Bristol. The detached garage needed to be torn down and rebuilt, but that wouldn't be difficult. He wanted to have an attached garage for her anyway. It was safer.

He could imagine him and Bristol sitting on the wraparound porch, talking about their days after work. He was already thinking about which walls could be knocked down inside to open up the place, and the kitchen was large, especially for the year the house was built. He'd get all new stainless-steel appliances, and they could refurbish the cabinets together. There were plenty of bedrooms, and the forest surrounding the backyard would be an amazing playground for children.

All in all, the property was close to perfect.

If only Bristol was here to see it.

His ringing phone scared the shit out of Rocky, and he jerked in surprise before reaching for it. Praying it was one of his teammates telling him they'd found Bristol, or Simon saying he had a lead, Rocky was disappointed to see Finley's name on the screen.

She and Bristol had gotten close in the short time they'd known each other, and he genuinely liked the shy owner of the bakery. But he wasn't sure he was in the mood to talk. To hear one more time how sorry someone was.

Ultimately, Rocky clicked on the green button to answer the phone. Anything would be better than going upstairs to his apartment.

"Hello?"

"Hi. This is Finley Norris. Is this Rocky?"

"It's me," he said.

"Good. Um...I heard what you said this morning, and I think it was really smart."

"Thanks," Rocky said absently, wondering if she'd just called to pay him a compliment.

"I've been thinking about Bristol, and worrying about her. After the morning rush, I wasn't in the mood to bake and was futzing around on the computer, killing time, you know? And I got to thinking about the Pickleport Festival, and how awesome the jewelry was that Bristol had made. I'd been kicking myself for not buying anything before she sold out. So I went to her website, thinking maybe I could buy something to—" She stopped abruptly. Then sighed quietly and finished, "Well...to

293

remember her by. You know, like a bracelet that would remind me of her every time I saw it."

Rocky closed his eyes. He didn't like where this was going, not at all. If she was going to suggest making some sort of memorial bracelet people could wear, he just might lose it.

"I'd gone to her site one other time, just because I was curious. But this time I was surprised...because there's a bunch of new stuff listed since the last time I looked."

Rocky immediately sat up straighter in his seat. "*What?*"

"Yeah. There's a bunch of new earrings and bracelets and necklaces. I looked at the bottom of the site, and it said it had last been updated *this morning*. Which I thought was weird. I mean...right? Isn't it?"

He couldn't speak with the adrenaline suddenly pumping through his veins.

Finley kept talking. "Why would there be new stuff on her site if she's been missing for two weeks? And I'm almost positive she hadn't put up anything new since she came here. She told me she was enjoying her time off. So that got me thinking, and I went to the reviews page of her site.

"Rocky...there've been three reviews left in the last *week*. They were gushing about how beautiful the jewelry was—I mean, of course they were—but they also said they were thrilled she was posting new stuff again. One of the ladies who posted said she got her earrings yesterday, that she couldn't be happier to have an original Bristol Wingham design in her collection."

"Holy shit," Rocky whispered, energy all but drowning him.

He knew it! Bristol was alive!

Yes, there was a chance someone else was posting on her site and using it to make money...but he knew to the marrow of his bones it was Bristol. *No one* could make jewelry like hers.

She was out there—and he was going to find her if it was the last thing he did.

"Thank you so much for calling, Finley," Rocky finally said, his voice thick with emotion.

"Of course. I just thought it was so strange. And I've been praying every night that she's found."

"Can I have Simon go and talk to you if he needs to?" Rocky asked.

"Absolutely. I'll do whatever I can to help. Although he can visit her site and see for himself the same things I did."

"Right, of course. You did good, Finley. Thank you. I'll be in touch." He hung up without waiting for her response. It was rude, but Rocky was too excited to worry about that at the moment. This was the first solid clue they'd received that Bristol was still alive. She was out there somewhere, making jewelry.

A momentary thought hit him that maybe she *had* left voluntarily. Maybe she'd gotten sick of Fallport, of him, and had started her life over somewhere.

Rocky immediately dismissed the thought. No, Bristol wouldn't do that. Wouldn't disappear without a trace, not without telling someone where she'd gone. She certainly wouldn't leave without a single one of her possessions, including her phone and purse.

She wasn't in Kingsport. The police there had said no one was at her house, and they'd even staked it out. No one had come or gone during the last two weeks.

He didn't know where she was...but for some crazy reason, someone was forcing her to create jewelry, and then selling it online.

And if they were selling it, they had to be mailing it.

With that thought, Rocky turned the key in the ignition and

backed out of the parking spot. He needed to go to the post office and see if Guy or the postmaster could help.

They were getting closer to finding her. Rocky felt it in his bones. This was it. The break they needed.

"Hang on, Punky," he said out loud as he drove a little too fast toward the square. "Just a little longer."

CHAPTER EIGHTEEN

Rocky hadn't realized how late it was when Finley called, and by the time he arrived at the post office, it was closed. The last thing he wanted to do was go back home, but he had no choice. Having to wait for the post office to open in the morning was exceedingly frustrating. There was no guarantee that whoever had taken Bristol had mailed packages from *this* post office, but for some reason, Rocky had a feeling he was on the right track.

After another sleepless night, Rocky called Simon and asked if he would meet him at the post office as soon as they opened. He didn't say why, not wanting to do anything that might jeopardize this lead. He also didn't want Simon to try to talk him out of talking to the employees at the post office, to insist he was just desperate for any kind of clue, or to tell him to let the police handle the investigation.

Rocky pulled up to a spot right outside the post office on 12th Street. It wasn't until he was out of his Tahoe and walking toward the entrance that he realized only Silas and Otto were sitting in their usual places around the circular table where they always sat.

"Where's Art?" he asked as he approached.

Silas frowned. "We don't know. He's usually here by now."

Shit. The last thing Fallport needed was another missing person.

"What's Simon doing here?" Otto asked.

Rocky turned and saw the police chief walking across the square, toward them. "I asked him to meet me here. Finley called me with a clue yesterday, and we're following up on it." Rocky shook Simon's hand when he approached.

"Where's Art?" Simon asked.

"That's what I asked," Rocky told him.

"He hasn't shown up yet," Otto said.

"That's odd. Maybe I'll go check on him after we're done here," Simon said, then turned to Rocky. "So, why did you want to meet here this morning?" he asked.

Rocky quickly told the police chief and the other two men what Finley had discovered. Hell, he probably should've thought about going to see Silas and Otto last night; they might've seen whoever it was who'd brought the packages to be mailed, since they were literally here all day, every day...if indeed they'd been mailed from Fallport in the first place.

He turned to the two older men. "Have you seen anyone coming in frequently with small packages? I'm assuming they were small, since the items people were reviewing online were jewelry."

Silas's face paled—and he shared a long look with Otto.

"What? What's wrong?" Rocky asked.

"Maybe nothing. But yesterday, we were sitting here minding our own business, like usual..."

Rocky resisted the urge to snort. These men never minded their own business. Ever.

"...and Art suddenly said he needed to do something."

"What did he need to do?" Simon asked.

"I don't know. He wouldn't say. Just got a determined look on his face and got up and left. It was strange. Very strange," Silas said.

"What happened right before he left?" Simon asked.

"I'm not sure. I mean, it was a normal day. I was beating his butt in chess and we were taking a break. A few people came by, we chatted a bit, then he just up and decided to leave."

"Who came by?" Simon asked in a harsh tone. Then he took a breath. "Sorry. But it's important."

"Well...the mayor was one," Silas said.

"Pompous ass," Otto muttered.

"The principal of the high school. Then Hank Blackburn. Grogan came to pick up some packages for his store, said they were the samples of some of the Bigfoot stuff he ordered and he was too impatient to wait for them to be delivered. Let's see... Agatha, Clara, Thomas. And Lance something or other...you know, that guy who looks a bit like that famous actor...you know which I'm taking about, Otto, right?"

"The guy in that *Jurassic Park* movie? Chris something?"

"Yes! That's the one," Silas said with a smile.

Rocky was stunned. These guys were better than any surveillance system, that was for sure. They might be old, but that didn't mean their minds weren't as sharp as ever.

Simon nodded. "And all the men you saw...what were they doing here?"

"What everyone does. Mailing stuff," Silas retorted.

"Did you see how big any of the packages were that people brought by? Or see who they were addressed to?"

"Sorry, I didn't. Did you, Otto?"

The other man shook his head. "No, but I think Art might've seen at least a few of the packages. He said something to someone, but Silas and I were arguing about the move he'd just made in the game and we missed it."

"But come to think of it, Art left not too long after that," Silas said.

"Come on," Simon said abruptly to Rocky.

"But we need to talk to Guy or the postmaster."

"No, we don't. Trust me on this," Simon retorted.

Without another word of protest, Rocky nodded.

"Stay put," Simon told Silas and Otto. "Do not move from this spot. Hear me?"

Both men looked confused, but nodded.

"We're going to go check on Art. I'm sure he's fine...probably just overslept," Simon said.

The hair on Rocky's arms was standing straight up. The police chief knew something. He wasn't sure what was going on yet, but if he thought it was more important to talk to Art than check with the postmaster, that's what they were going to do.

"You drive," Simon told Rocky as they headed for his Tahoe.

Rocky jogged around his vehicle and climbed in. "Want to tell me what's going on?" he asked.

"No. I need you to stay calm and not lose your shit."

And just like that, Rocky had a feeling Simon knew who'd taken Bristol. "Who is it?" he bit out.

"I'm not completely sure yet."

"Bullshit. You know. I can't believe you haven't fucking told me before now."

"That's because I *didn't* know. But after talking to Art, I'm guessing I'll know for sure. My deputies are busy this morning.

Bo got a call about a car window being broken last night, Robert's checking up on some of the leads people have called in, Chad's camping with his family, and Miguel just got off shift. I'm going to call Bo, Robert, and Miguel, but I don't know how long it'll take them to get here. I need some backup. I know everything in you is telling you to find Bristol, and we'll do that as soon as we have more information, but in the meantime, I need you to have my back. Can you do that?"

Rocky glanced over at the police chief as they drove toward Art's house. It was a small two-bedroom place not far from the square. Rocky was more sure than ever now that Simon knew who'd taken Bristol, but he wasn't the kind of man to leave someone's flank vulnerable. "Yes," he said simply.

"Thank you. I swear on the badge I wear that I'll tell you everything I know, as soon as we talk to Art."

Rocky nodded. "Do I have time to call Drew or one of the other guys?" he asked.

"After we talk to Art," Simon said again. "If he tells me what I *think* he's gonna tell me, we'll need everyone. All of your military experience will be appreciated."

Rocky's stomach rolled as he pulled up in front of Art's house just two minutes later. Nothing looked out of place. The door was closed and no lights were on. It looked just like it always did.

Simon and Rocky walked up the sidewalk to the front door. Simon knocked. When there was no answer, he knocked again, harder.

When there was still no sound from within the house, Simon pulled his weapon from the holster at his side. "Stay behind me," he said.

Then he backed up, raised his leg, and kicked the door.

Rocky couldn't help but be impressed. Simon was in his mid-fifties and a bit soft around his middle, but there was enough power behind that kick to bash the door open in one blow. The fact that Simon hadn't bothered to walk around the house, looking for another way in, told Rocky that whatever suspicions the chief had about why Art was missing this morning...they were serious.

The two men crept into the house, Simon's pistol at the ready, with Rocky at his back. He felt naked without a weapon, but there hadn't been time to go back to his apartment. They cleared the living area and a small galley kitchen. They made their way down a hallway, toward the two bedrooms—and a familiar smell reached Rocky's nostrils.

He'd never forget that coppery scent. It had been burned into his memory after so many missions.

Blood.

"Art?" Simon called out. "It's Simon. Are you all right?"

There was no answer.

Simon pointed to his eyes, then to the space in front of him and Rocky nodded. They crept forward, and Simon slowly pushed the bedroom door open.

The sight that greeted them made too many bad memories flash through Rocky's brain.

There was a trail of blood from the doorway to where Art was now lying motionless in the middle of the bedroom. Rocky assumed he'd attempted to crawl to a phone he could see on the table next to the bed. He hadn't made it.

"Fuck," Simon swore. "Stay with him while I clear the other bedroom."

Rocky nodded and went to his knees next to the old man. He gently rolled Art onto his back—and was shocked as hell when the old man's eyes popped open and he threw an arm up, clearly trying to protect his face.

"Easy, Art! It's me. Rocky Watson. You're okay."

Art's mouth opened and closed as if he was trying to speak.

"Shhhh, don't talk. Save your energy," Rocky told him. He lifted the man's shirt and saw where the blood was coming from. There was a large stab wound to his upper right chest. He immediately put his hands over the hole, even though the bleeding had mostly stopped, making it obvious that he'd been hurt quite a while ago.

Anger threatened to overcome Rocky. Who the hell would stab a ninety-one-year-old man? And why? It made no sense. Art could be ornery, but he was completely harmless.

Simon arrived back in the room and Rocky heard him talking to someone on his phone. Most likely calling for the paramedics. Then he knelt down next to Rocky. "How's he look?"

Rocky shook his head. "Not good. I've only found one puncture wound, but there could be more. I'm shocked he's still conscious."

It was obvious Simon hadn't realized Art was awake. His gaze turned to the older man's, and he leaned close. "Who was it, Art?"

Art's mouth once again did what it had before. Open, close, open, close.

"You knew, didn't you?" Simon asked. "You knew and confronted him instead of coming to me, or Rocky, or hell...any of Rocky's friends."

Art shook his head. "Saw...package. Bristol's name. Came back home to call... Followed me."

"Shit," Simon swore. "He attacked you to keep you quiet. I'm guessing he thought he'd covered all his bases, but he was wrong. He didn't know how strong you are. I think I know who it is,

Art. But I need you to tell me so I have probable cause to go get the son-of-a-bitch," Simon said firmly.

Rocky held his breath. There was no way he wasn't going after whoever had done this to Art—and who'd likely kidnapped Bristol. He didn't give a shit what proper procedure said.

Art's lips moved, and the sound that came out was barely a whisper. In the background, Rocky could hear sirens approaching and knew the small house was about to be over-whelmed with people. He leaned down to make sure he heard the name Art was struggling to tell them.

"Lance."

Son of a fucking bitch.

Rocky started to stand. He needed to go. To hunt down the animal who'd done this.

But Simon grabbed his arm with a hold that was surprisingly strong. "Keep your damn hands where they are," he snapped. "You let go, he could die."

Rocky wasn't sure about that. Art's wound wasn't really bleeding all that much anymore. But he took a deep breath in through his nose anyway. Everything in him was screaming to go find Lance Zaun. To beat him to a bloody pulp. To force him to confess where Bristol was. But if he saw him right now, he'd kill him. And if he was in jail, he couldn't help Bristol.

"I'm gonna get him," Rocky told Art, whose gaze was fixed on his now. "He's going to pay for doing this to you...and for whatever he's done with Bristol."

"Packages," Art wheezed again.

Rocky nodded. "Finley called me last night, told me she saw new reviews on Bristol's website. I was at the post office this morning to check on it. Looks like you beat us all to this lead. I'm not surprised. You and your cronies always seem to know everything going on in this town."

Art's eyes closed.

"You are *not* going to die," Rocky said fiercely, not knowing if his words were true or not. "You're too tough to let some asshole like Lance Zaun take you out. Besides, Otto was telling me all about how far ahead he was in your chess game wins."

With that, Art's eyes opened again and he said, "Lie..."

"I'm gonna call your granddaughter. Is there anyone else you want me to contact?" Simon asked as they heard people enter the house.

Art shook his head slightly and his eyes closed once again.

Rocky was never as glad to see anyone as he was the two paramedics who burst into the room at that moment. He listened with half an ear as Simon gave them a rundown of what he knew. Then Rocky stood back and let the professionals do their job. He heard one calling for a chopper, and knew Art was in good hands. He backed out of the room before turning and heading for the door.

Simon had a hold of his arm before he got too far.

"Stay with me, son."

"That son-of-a-bitch has Bristol!" Rocky growled.

"Yeah, he does. And if you go off half-cocked, there's no telling what he'll do to her. She's stayed alive for this long, don't make him panic and kill her."

Simon's words stopped Rocky in his tracks. The police chief was right. Lance hadn't hesitated to try to kill a harmless old man. If Rocky screwed up in his desperation to find her, Lance would do the same to Bristol. Even though he hated thinking of her under that asshole's thumb for even one second longer than necessary, the thought of the guy stabbing her, like he'd done to Art...

"What's the plan?" he asked.

"We need to find Lance. Watch him. When we're sure he's

alone, we'll take him down and get him to tell us where he's got Bristol."

Rocky nodded and pulled out his phone. Some of the deadliest men he knew were right here in Fallport. If there was ever a moment to use what they'd learned in the Armed Forces, *now* was that time.

CHAPTER NINETEEN

An hour later, the Eagle Point Search and Rescue team had fanned out all over Fallport, looking for Lance Zaun. And they weren't the only ones. The entire town was on the lookout, especially after hearing what had happened to Art. No one took kindly to one of their own being attacked. And because it was Art, everyone was twice as fired up.

Then, five minutes ago, Davis had walked into Grinders and asked to use the phone. He called the police station and asked to speak to Simon. He'd been patched through to the chief's cell phone—and told him he'd seen Lance at his apartment a few minutes ago. He'd been carrying a large box to his car...and it looked as if he was packing to leave.

Rocky had stuck close to Simon, knowing the police chief would be at the forefront of the investigation. How the man could've gotten out of his apartment and to his car without being seen by the officer Simon had assigned to watch for him, Rocky didn't know. Didn't care either. He was just relieved they finally had a sighting.

Simon had thanked Davis, then immediately called his officers and told them to come in without sirens and meet at the apartment complex. To park down the street to avoid tipping off Lance that they were on to him.

Rocky called his team and told them the same thing. All the while, nausea rolled in his belly.

This was it. They'd grab Lance and make him tell them where Bristol was.

As soon as he'd found out Lance Zaun was the one who'd stabbed Art, Rocky had the sickening and incredulous thought that maybe he'd kept Bristol right under his nose the entire time. He tried to dismiss the idea. There was no way Bristol had been three doors down from him for the last two weeks. He'd have known if she was that close.

But the thought ate at him. What if he *didn't* know? What if she *was* there?

Anxiety rose within Rocky and it took every bit of discipline he'd learned as a SEAL to not storm up the stairs and rip Lance's door off its hinges to see for himself.

"How'd you know it was him?" Rocky asked as he and Simon crouched near the apartment complex, their eyes peeled on the stairs, waiting for Lance to make an appearance once more.

"Davis came to see me yesterday afternoon. Said Lance was acting strangely in regard to his trash. You know how Davis looks through the garbage? Well, Lance found him doing it, yelled at him, then took his trash *back* upstairs. I wasn't one hundred percent sure, but I did some research."

"And?" Rocky asked impatiently.

"Lance Zaun has been in and out of psychiatric hospitals for practically his entire life. His own parents were scared of him, and they washed their hands of him when he turned eighteen.

Kicked him out of the house, moved, changed their *names*, in fact.

"I wasn't able to read the medical reports on him, but from the notes different officers have made after his various arrests for public disturbances, threats, and Peeping Tom activities, he's got an obsessive personality. He's calm one minute, out of control the next. When a longtime detective out of Memphis wrote that he was, and I quote, 'one of the scariest men I've ever met in my life,' I was pretty sure I had my man. I didn't have any proof he had Bristol though," Simon said, the apology easy to hear in his tone. "If I did, I wouldn't have waited."

Rocky nodded. He understood. That didn't mean he liked it, but he did understand.

"What's the plan?" he asked.

"When he comes out of that apartment, we rush him. Under no circumstances is he to get back up those stairs."

Rocky closed his eyes for a moment. "You think she's in there." It wasn't a question.

"It's the only thing that makes sense," Simon said. "We've literally looked everywhere else."

Rocky tried to control himself, but he failed. He turned and threw up into the weeds growing next to the brick building.

Thinking about what Bristol had gone through, was still going through, made him throw up again.

"Easy, son," Simon said quietly, briefly putting a hand on Rocky's back.

Wiping his mouth with the back of his hand, Rocky took a deep breath, tears stinging his eyes.

To his surprise, Simon's hand appeared—with a fucking pack of Life Savers in his palm.

"What the hell?" Rocky asked, as he gratefully took them

from the police chief. "You normally carry these around?" he asked.

Simon shrugged. "Yeah. Been around the block long enough to know that shit can hit the fan at any moment, and what bothers me doesn't bother someone else, and vice versa. So I carry some strong-as-hell peppermints around, just in case."

Rocky nodded, but the thought of Bristol being right under his nose just about killed him. He'd failed her. Big time. And if she was all right—*God, let her be all right*—and if she still wanted him after he hadn't protected her, hadn't found her in a timely manner, he wouldn't *ever* fail her again.

"There's movement. Stand by," Ethan's voice said over the radio. They'd all programmed their radios to the same channel. There were currently seven pissed-off SAR team members and three deputies, plus Simon, ready to make their move.

All eyes were on the stairs when Lance Zaun looked around nervously as he exited his apartment. He put down the large box he was carrying and turned to close and lock the door behind him.

Nothing could've told Rocky more clearly that Bristol was behind that door. Who locked their deadbolt when they were just putting a box in their car? No one. Unless they didn't want anyone to see what—or who—was behind that door.

Lance picked up the box once more and made his way toward the stairs. Rocky started a countdown in his head as he waited for him to reach the ground.

Ten, nine, eight...

His heart started beating overtime.

Seven, six, five...

He wanted Lance to fucking suffer, but more, he needed to get to Bristol.

Four, three, two...

Simon and his deputies were going to head straight for Lance, while Rocky and his team would go up the stairs.

One.

"Go! Go! Go!" a voice said over the radio.

Rocky was already on the move, running as fast as he could for the stairs the asshole had just come down.

Surprised by the number of people appearing out of nowhere, Lance froze for a moment—then he spun as if to go back up the stairs.

Miguel, one of Fallport's finest, got to him first. Then Bo and Robert were there. Bo stood back with his weapon pointed straight at Lance, who was now face down on the concrete with three men holding him down, yanking his hands behind his back.

"Lance Zaun, you are under arrest for the attempted murder of Arthur Lever. And I'm reserving the right to add to those charges as soon as we get inside your apartment," Simon told him.

"*No!* No, no, no, no, no! She's mine! She's always been mine!" Lance screamed as he struggled under the officers.

Rocky didn't slow his pace. He didn't need to see Lance go down. He needed to get to Bristol.

He and Ethan arrived at the door at the same time. He vaguely saw his neighbors opening their doors and staring at the spectacle going on around them in surprise and fear. He rammed his shoulder against the door, but it didn't budge.

"Fuck," he muttered as he took a breath and tried again, with the same result.

"Together," Ethan said.

"No. Stand back," Drew ordered.

Turning, Rocky saw Drew and Brock both held battering rams.

"Figured we might need these," Drew said. "Call it a parting gift from my last job," he said with a determined look on his face.

It was obvious Brock also had experience using the tool to break down doors, because he stood at the ready, waiting for Drew's word.

Ethan grabbed Rocky's arm and pulled him back, letting their teammates have a crack at the door. On the count of three, the two men slammed the rams into the door at the same time. The sound of wood breaking was one of the best things Rocky had ever heard in his life.

Pushing his teammates out of the way, he rushed through the door, absently noting that the deadbolt was reinforced and wasn't the same as the one on his own apartment.

"Easy," Zeke muttered. He had a pistol in his hand and he was pointing it into the seemingly empty apartment. For just a moment, Rocky's stomach fell.

Bristol wasn't there. The living area looked almost exactly the same as it had the last time he'd been in here, to help move furniture in for Elsie and Tony.

But then he shook his head. No. She was here. She *had* to be here.

Zeke and Drew cleared the living area and the kitchen. It looked almost scarily normal. The two men walked shoulder-to-shoulder down the hallway toward the bedrooms. The first one was empty. They prepared to enter the master.

The door was locked.

This time, it was Talon who came forward with the ram. He didn't hesitate, and the door smashed into several pieces with his first hit.

Rocky heard Talon's shocked inhalation before he pushed his friend aside.

And what he saw made his heart soar—and broke it at the

same time.

Bristol. She was alive.

Her eyes were huge in her face as she stared at the doorway. She had a ball gag in her mouth and saliva dripped from her chin. Her hands were cuffed to a chain, and her right leg was propped up on a few pillows. The chain circled her ankle as well, running down to the bed frame.

The room smelled musty and had a funk to it Rocky couldn't identify. It was also pitch black. The only light coming into the room was from the hallway behind him. There were what seemed to be blankets hung on every wall, including over the window.

Rocky took in the surroundings in a split second before he was on the move to Bristol's side.

She was making high-pitched whimpering noises in her throat, and it was the most heart-wrenching thing Rocky had ever heard in his life. In the back of his mind, he heard a clicking sound. Vaguely, he registered the sound as a cell phone camera. He knew the scene needed to be documented with pictures in order to be able to prosecute.

He hated it, but he understood. And was grateful to whoever'd had the presence of mind to do what he couldn't.

Rocky fell to his knees next to the bed and frantically reached for the contraption around her head. When the woman he loved more than life itself jerked away from him, he froze.

"Easy, Rocky," Ethan said quietly. "Go easy."

Taking a deep breath, Rocky said, "It's okay, Punky. We're here. You're safe. I'm gonna get this off, okay? Hang on for a second and we'll have you out of here."

The more he talked, the more she seemed to calm.

The sight of her bound in chains made Rocky want to fucking *kill* Lance. Bristol needed him more. She came first.

Always. But that didn't mean he wasn't making plans in the back of his head as to how to end the man once and for all.

He knew people. People who knew people. The kind who could easily get to the asshole who'd done this to Bristol, even when he was behind bars.

It took a minute for him to figure out the straps of the gag, and the second he removed the ball from Bristol's mouth, the most anguished, heartbreaking, pissed-off scream came from her throat. Rocky had never heard a sound like it. It went on and on, as if she was purging all the fear that had been bottled up since she'd been taken.

The sound eventually tapered off and turned into sobs. Drew and Talon were working on freeing her hands from the chains, and Ethan and Raiden were at her feet, probably doing the same with that manacle. Rocky took her into his arms, and when she buried her head against his neck, when he felt her hot breaths against his skin as she cried, Rocky closed his eyes in thanks.

He had no idea what she'd been through, but she was alive. He'd get her the best psychologist in the country to help her deal. Whatever they had to endure, Rocky was just so damn grateful she was in his arms again.

Light suddenly pierced the room when Zeke tore down the blankets that had been covering the window. Dust motes swam in the air, highlighted by the sunlight coming from the window.

Rocky could feel Bristol doing her best to control herself. She pulled back and looked up at him. Someone handed him a towel, and Rocky gently and reverently wiped her chin and face of the saliva and tears that still lingered.

"Water," Brock said as he handed Rocky a glass.

"Please," Bristol whispered as she eyed the liquid. Rocky helped her sit up and held the glass to her lips. She drank it down without pausing to take a breath. When she was done,

Rocky passed the glass backward, not caring who took it from him. He couldn't take his eyes off Bristol. He could hardly believe she was here.

"Her leg's fucked," Talon said in a harsh whisper.

Rocky turned away from her face for the first time.

Finally, Bristol spoke. Her voice was rough, as if it had been a while since she'd spoken. "He smashed it with a hammer after he removed the cast," she said. "He didn't want me to be able to get up, so he went all *Misery* on me."

Horror almost drowned Rocky. He'd never liked that movie. Hadn't been able to stomach watching the entire thing. And to think something like that had happened to his Bristol...it made him want to hurl once more. He controlled himself. Barely.

"He soundproofed the room with the blankets. He gagged me whenever he left so I couldn't call out. Chained my hands down so I couldn't remove the gag. I was literally stuck. I didn't know when it was day and when it was night." She was talking almost frantically now, as if wanting to get all the details out in case something else happened. "When he didn't kill me that first day, and didn't seem interested in raping me or anything, I thought my best course of action was to do whatever he wanted. To be nice to him. I didn't want him to see me as any kind of threat. Or to use that hammer on me again." She used her chin to bring everyone's attention to the hammer sitting on a small table on the other side of the room.

As proud as Rocky was of his woman, hatred burned in his heart.

"All right. She's free," Drew said.

"Nobody touch anything," Simon ordered. Rocky hadn't even noticed the police chief arriving. All his attention had been on Bristol. "We need to preserve the evidence to take this asshole down."

"Oh, he's going down," Talon said, anger making his voice shake.

Delayed reaction began to set in for Rocky. The dark room, the hammer, the chains. He began to shake...and couldn't seem to stop.

"It's okay," Bristol said, putting her arms around him as best she could from her position on the bed. "I'm all right. You found me." It was amazing how calm she sounded. After her initial reaction, she'd managed to pull herself together.

"I'm sorry. I'm so sorry!" he said, burying his head in her hair.

"For what?" she asked.

"For taking so long!"

She chuckled—and Rocky whipped his head up in surprise at the sound. How the fuck could she be *laughing* right now?

She lifted a hand and cupped his cheek. "I knew you wouldn't stop looking until you found me. Doesn't matter how long it took."

She was wrong. It *did* matter how long it had taken him. But he managed to mutter, "Damn straight."

"I was going to fight like hell to keep from being put in that, broken leg or not," she said, motioning to something behind him.

Blinking in surprise, Rocky looked around and saw something else he'd missed before.

A large open suitcase.

"He was freaked out yesterday, for some reason. He started getting ready to leave with me. He was going to drug me, stuff me in that, and carry me out."

Every muscle in Rocky's body tightened.

"Holy shit," Drew muttered.

"I wasn't going to let that happen. I was going to fight, no matter how much my leg hurt. I managed to hide a needle when he wasn't looking. One that I'd been using to make the jewelry he wanted me to create. I was going to stab him in the eye or something."

"Good girl," Zeke praised.

Rocky wanted to tell Bristol how proud he was, but he couldn't get anything past the lump in his throat.

"Coast is clear. He's on his way to the station," Simon said quietly. "We need to get her out of here. I've informed the paramedics that they need to go straight to Roanoke with her. The chopper is still occupied..." His voice dropped off, and the team already knew why the helicopter wasn't available. Because it was still busy taking Art to the trauma center.

"Yes, please," Bristol said with a small sigh, not knowing what had happened to the older man. "I could use a long hot shower, a huge hamburger, and maybe a pedicure while we're at it."

Everyone chuckled at that, but Rocky couldn't bring himself to laugh about this. Not yet, and probably not ever.

"Can I carry you? Or will that hurt you too much?" Rocky asked.

"You carrying me will never hurt too much," she replied.

Rocky wasn't so sure about that, but since he wanted her out of this room and apartment, he was willing to try.

"I'm going to pick you up, but let me know if it's too painful and we'll figure something else out."

She grimaced, letting Rocky know she was probably already in more pain than she was letting on. But she nodded. "Let's do this."

"I'll hold her leg still," Talon said. "Go easy."

As if he wasn't going to fucking go easy. But he didn't snap at his friend. They were all on edge, and seeing Bristol in this condition was eating at everyone.

"Ready, Punky? Here we go." Rocky gently slid his arms

under her and lifted her from the bed. He heard her inhale, but she didn't otherwise let one sound of pain escape her lips. Rocky could feel that she'd lost weight, and it made him want to kill Lance all over again. Motherfucker was going to pay.

Talon gently let go of her leg and nodded at Rocky. He walked carefully toward the door. He let out a small exhale of relief when they exited the prison she'd been in for the last two weeks. He heard the sound of the ambulance arriving when he neared the door, and walked a little faster. It looked as if they would be making another trip to the hospital in Roanoke, but as he'd done the last time, Rocky wasn't going to leave her side.

He wondered if Art would be there too, but decided he'd worry about that once he knew Bristol was going to be okay.

Lance Zaun had caused a lot of pain for Fallport, but Rocky was proud of the way the town had come together to search for Bristol. They'd band together again to help care for both Art and Bristol when they came home to heal.

Rocky carried her down the stairs and toward the ambulance that had just pulled in. As the medics were preparing the stretcher in the back for Bristol, Rocky looked down at her. She was pale, her hair was greasy, she smelled like Zaun hadn't washed her at all...but he'd never seen anyone as beautiful in all his life.

"I love you," he blurted, not willing to wait one second more to tell her.

She closed her eyes for a moment, then opened them and met his gaze without fear or doubt. "I love you too. I knew you'd find me. I *knew* it, Rocky. Just like you found me in the forest a few months ago. I just had to hold on, make him think I was his friend, until you did."

Her confidence in him slayed Rocky.

"If you could put her down here, sir," one of the paramedics said, interrupting their moment.

Rocky moved carefully, doing everything in his power not to jar Bristol more than he already had. He gently lay her on the gurney, but realized he was having a very hard time stepping away.

"Sir? If you can please move so we can do our assessment."

Rocky nodded—and didn't move.

It wasn't until Bristol squeezed his hand and said, "I'm okay," that he was able to force his feet to shuffle to the side.

"Assuming you're going with us?"

"Yes," Rocky said firmly. He wanted to see them try to force him out of the back of the ambulance. It wasn't happening.

"I'm gonna go get Lilly. We'll meet you in Roanoke," Ethan said from the open doors of the vehicle.

"Same. Elsie would raise hell if I didn't bring her," Zeke said.

"We'll see you there too," Drew said.

Looking at the faces of his team, Rocky once again thanked his lucky stars they were there. "Thanks, guys. Just...thanks."

They all nodded as the paramedic shut the doors.

"We've already gotten approval to go straight to the trauma center," the paramedic told Rocky.

He nodded, but still couldn't take his eyes off Bristol. Her eyes were closed and she was grimacing as the other medic in the ambulance began to check her over. He wanted to yell at the man to be careful, but he kept his mouth shut. The less he interfered, the sooner Bristol could get the medical care she needed.

He couldn't stop himself from leaning forward and putting his hand on top of her head. A small smile formed on her face, but she didn't open her eyes. Just knowing that she was aware he was there was enough...for now.

CHAPTER TWENTY

Bristol was more than ready to go home. She'd been in the hospital in Roanoke for a week. She'd had surgery to replace the pin that Lance had knocked free when he'd re-fractured her leg. She had an infection from the wound that was being stubborn, she was dehydrated, and her blood pressure was a bit wonky. But she was alive, and so thankful for that.

She'd been devastated to learn about Lance stabbing Art. Apparently, he'd seen the shock on Art's face when the older man saw the package Lance was carrying into the post office, and had followed him home. When Lance broke in and confronted him, Art denied knowing anything about seeing the package, but the kidnapper couldn't risk Art alerting the author-ities. Lance had stabbed him, probably assuming he'd bleed out and die.

Bristol hadn't been able to see Art in the hospital, but as soon as they were both released, he was going to be the first person she went to visit. Rocky assured her that Art was doing well, and his granddaughter had taken a leave of absence to help him recuperate.

Rocky had been amazing. Now that she was free of Lance, Bristol was suffering nightmares and flashbacks. He stayed in the hospital with her, and when she woke up during the night, confused about where she was, the first thing she saw when she opened her eyes was him. He refused to let anyone turn off the lights in the room, so she never had to be in the dark.

The last three days, he'd left for a few hours during the daytime, telling her he had some things he needed to take care of back in Fallport. She hated to see him go, but she also didn't want to be clingy. He didn't elaborate on what he was doing, but Bristol figured he'd tell her if it was important.

She'd had a steady stream of visitors when Rocky wasn't there, so at least she was never bored or lonely. Bristol had cried —hard—when she'd seen Finley. Rocky had told her all about how she'd been the one to visit her website, and figure out that people were leaving reviews on stuff they'd received very recently. When Bristol had expressed concern that her friend had closed the bakery to visit, Finley had shrugged and said she'd put a note on the door that she was in Roanoke visiting Bristol, and if anyone had a problem with that, tough.

It was wonderful to see Finley gaining some confidence. But it seemed she was still just as shy around Brock...because when he'd shown up to visit with Bristol, Finley had stayed for only a few more minutes. Then said she had stuff she needed to get done, leaving quickly. Bristol *so* wanted to say something to Brock about her, but she didn't want to embarrass Finley.

It was currently mid-afternoon a full week later, and Bristol was more than ready to get out of the hospital. She was grateful for the amazing care she'd received, and for everyone who'd driven out of their way to visit, but she wanted to go home with Rocky. Wanted him to be able to sleep on something more comfortable than the hospital cot next to her bed or the chair.

"How are you doing, honestly?" Rocky asked. He'd just returned an hour earlier after another trip to Fallport.

"I'm okay."

"I know you talked to Simon about the facts of the case, but I'm more interested in where you're at here," he said, brushing his thumb against her temple gently.

"Honestly? I'm all right. I can't deny I was scared to death, but as long as I did what he asked, it was almost as if he was...a roommate." The first time Bristol had said Lance's name, Rocky'd had a visceral reaction. His face got red and his fists clenched as if he couldn't even bear to hear the name of the man who'd kidnapped and held her captive. So Bristol did her best to not say it in Rocky's presence again.

"He was *not* a roommate," Rocky bit out.

Bristol put her hand on her man's cheek. "I know," she said softly.

"I can't get over that you were so close," Rocky said miserably.

She hated that he was beating himself up over that. "I shouldn't have opened the door."

Rocky shook his head. "No, don't do that. Fallport's not exactly the big city. Besides, you recognized him. You were minding your own business and evil came knocking. This wasn't your fault. None of it was."

She nodded.

"But I'm struggling," Rocky admitted.

Bristol's heart broke. His words weren't a surprise. She could see it in the lines of his face and the way he held onto her almost desperately.

"It's going to take some time for both of us to get over it," she said.

Rocky nodded. "Please know that when I get overbearing and overprotective, it's because I spent two weeks in hell. Nothing near what *you* were going through. But not knowing where you were or if you were suffering...I never want to experience anything like that again. Ever."

"I understand." And she did. While her time chained to that bed certainly wasn't fun, she had a feeling Rocky had suffered more than she had, even with her injured leg.

"You ready to get out of here?" a nurse said cheerfully as she entered the room.

Rocky stood, moving to the end of the bed and giving the nurse space to check Bristol out once more before she was officially discharged. His fingers rested on her left foot, keeping the connection between them.

Bristol's stitches had been removed that morning and another cast had been put back on her leg. At this point, it was all familiar to both Rocky and Bristol, and they knew what to expect for the next month or so when it came to her recuperation.

An hour later, she was sitting in Rocky's Tahoe as they headed south on the interstate.

"What's that smile for?" Rocky asked at one point.

Bristol looked over at him. "I'm just happy. I know that sounds crazy, but after two close calls, I'm so grateful to still be here. The sun is shining—oh my God, I'll never bitch about it being too sunny again after being in that tomb of a room—and the fresh air feels awesome. I'm with the man I love and going back to the town where everyone went out of their way to do whatever they could to find me. What's not to smile about?"

Rocky reached over and took her hand in his. Bristol had

never felt so content. Some people might not understand how she could still be so upbeat and positive after everything that had happened. But she was alive. Rocky loved her. She had amazing friends that she'd never take for granted. So yeah, even after two weeks of hell, she was happy.

Rocky pulled onto I-480 and it felt like coming home to Bristol. She hadn't lived in Fallport for long, but she couldn't imagine living anywhere else now. They talked a bit about what was happening back in town. Rocky mentioned that Drew and Art's granddaughter had met in the hospital, and it hadn't gone well.

"Why? What happened?" Bristol asked.

"They just rubbed each other the wrong way. I guess Caryn is a firefighter in New York City and is used to being in charge with just about everything in her life. She's tough as hell, and maybe a little rough around the edges. She was upset because Art was having a bad day, and I guess she took it out on Drew, who was visiting him."

"Oh, poor Art. But he's doing better, right? You told me he was supposed to come home soon."

"He is. I checked on him before we left today. He sends you his love and said that you better be the first person who comes to visit him when he gets back to Fallport."

"Of course I will!" Bristol exclaimed. "Anyway, so Drew and Caryn butted heads?"

"Yeah. She'll be in town for a while, staying with Art until he can be up and doing things on his own again."

"That's awesome. He'd hate being in a rehab center or nursing home."

"That's what Caryn said."

"So what was the problem between her and Drew? He's one

of the nicest people ever. I can't imagine him not getting along with someone," Bristol said.

"He was a cop. She's a firefighter," Rocky said.

"So? I thought those two professions got along?"

"They do, but there's also a natural competitive thing, I think. And apparently Caryn doesn't think highly of officers because her ex was a cop in New York. So when she heard that's what Drew used to do, I'm guessing she immediately got defensive."

Bristol couldn't stop the small smile that formed on her face.

"What are you smiling about *now*?" Rocky asked.

"Just how much you know about the woman. Good ol' Fallport gossip network, hard at work. Caryn used to spend summers in Fallport, right?"

"From what I understand, yeah."

"So she's practically a local."

Rocky shrugged and nodded.

"I'm thinking Drew's gonna have his hands full," Bristol said.

"What does that have to do with Caryn sort of being from Fallport?"

"Everyone's gonna take sides. And make bets."

"Bets?"

Man, her guy was clueless sometimes. "Yeah. On how long it'll be until they hook up."

Rocky stared at her for a moment, before chuckling. "Okay, I can see that. But Drew's kind of standoffish. And I'm not sure this Caryn woman is his type."

"So...you want to bet?" Bristol asked.

His lips twitched. "Sure, why not. What do you want to bet?"

"Hmmm." Bristol brought her free hand up to her mouth and tapped her lips. "How about this. If Caryn and Drew get together while she's in town looking after her grandfather, you'll let me make a life-size stained glass of you in the forest, doing your thing."

Rocky rolled his eyes. They'd talked about this at some point in the last week, and he'd been adamantly opposed to the idea. He'd said the last thing anyone would want to look at, himself included, was a glass rendering of him. He claimed they'd mistake him for Bigfoot or something. That the idea of her making a stained glass of Bigfoot, like she'd originally planned, would be much better. Bristol disagreed wholeheartedly.

"Fine. And if they don't, you'll marry me before the end of the year."

Bristol stared at him in surprise. "What?"

"You heard me. I want you to be mine officially. And I want to be yours. Man and wife. Married. Hitched. The whole nine yards."

Suddenly Bristol was having a hard time breathing.

"Will you marry me, Punky? I can't imagine my life without you in it. Without you by my side."

Holy shit. "Yes! Of course I will!" she exclaimed.

"Hadn't really meant to do that while I was driving," Rocky complained.

"But, when *I* win that bet...does that mean we aren't getting married by the end of the year?" she asked.

Rocky grinned. "Nope."

Bristol rolled her eyes. "Then what's the use of the bet?" she asked.

"Tell me honestly that you don't already have that stained glass of me in the forest already all planned out in your head," Rocky said.

Bristol bit her lip.

He laughed. "Right, so your end of the bet is bullshit, and so is mine."

Bristol couldn't help but smile. He was absolutely right.

"So your brother is having a Halloween wedding, and we're having a Christmas one?"

"Looks like it," Rocky said. "You okay with that?"

"Yes."

"Good."

"Am I gonna get a ring?" Bristol asked after a moment.

"Oh, you want a ring too?" Rocky asked.

For a second, Bristol thought he was serious, but then she saw the grin on his face.

"You're mean," she complained with a pout.

Rocky brought her hand up to his mouth and kissed the back of it. She relaxed against the seat as they headed into Fallport. Seeing Rocky relax enough to smile was one of the best gifts she could get. The last week in the hospital had been just as hard on him. Hell, the last few *weeks* had been extraordinarily hard on him.

Bristol couldn't help but tense as they neared the apartment complex. The building held some of her happiest moments, and some of her worst memories as well.

But instead of slowing down to pull into the parking lot, Rocky drove right past it.

"Um," Bristol said, turning to see the large brick building disappearing behind them. "You missed the turn."

"No, I didn't. I want to show you something."

"Oh, okay," Bristol said. She was confused and her leg was throbbing, but if Rocky wanted to show her something, she'd hang in there a little longer. She also couldn't deny that she was glad for a delay from going up those stairs to the second floor. Having to pass the apartment where she'd been kept hostage wouldn't be fun, but she was determined not to let Lance Zaun take any more from her than he already had.

They drove past the square, past the Chestnut Street Manor Bed and Breakfast, until they were on the outskirts of Fallport. Rocky turned down a dirt road. It looked as if they were just driving straight into the forest surrounding them, but at the last minute, the road made a sharp turn—and then a large colonial house was sitting in front of them. A huge, dilapidated red barn stood off to the left. The grass was at least knee length and the property looked neglected and forgotten.

Bristol turned to look at Rocky in confusion.

"Welcome home," he said quietly.

* * *

Rocky was nervous. He'd already fucked up his marriage proposal by blurting it out like he had, he didn't want to mess this up too. But then again, buying a house for a woman without her laying eyes on it wasn't exactly the smartest thing he'd ever done.

The second he'd seen this property, he'd known it was home. There was a lot of work needed but he was a damn good contractor, and while it might take a while, he'd fix it up exactly how Bristol wanted it.

He waited with bated breath for her reaction to his words.

"What?" she asked, turning her gaze from him back to the house, barn, and land.

"Your realtor called me while you were missing, said she'd found what she thought was the perfect place for you. You and her had talked a lot about what you were looking for. As soon as I saw it, I knew you were meant to live here. This is what I've been doing while you were in the hospital. I had to come back and sign some papers, finalize the finances, things like that. But it's a done deal. It's yours. Ours."

"I...I don't know what to say," Bristol said.

Rocky swallowed hard. He couldn't tell what she was thinking.

When she looked back at him, there were tears in her eyes.

"If you hate it, we'll—"

"I love it!" she said, interrupting him. "I want to jump out of this car and go look at it, but I can't and that pisses me off! It's perfect, Rocky! I can already see myself in the barn, making my stained glass. And that porch is to die for. Can we get a porch swing? It looks like it goes all the way around. Does it? I hope it does! We can sit out there and have dinner and stuff when it's nice out. And the yard is huge! We can have everyone over. Oh! Can we get married here? It might be cold in December, but we can use the barn to have our reception and—"

It was Rocky's turn to interrupt. He reached over and put his lips over hers, halting her rambling with a deep kiss.

When they were both breathing hard, he pulled back, keeping his hand behind her neck—he wasn't even sure when he'd put it there—and said, "I love you, Bristol. So much. I want to make this our home. Raise our children here. Watch you create your art. I'm gonna put floor-to-ceiling windows all along the back of the house. Our bedroom will have a balcony so we can open the doors and let in the breeze. I never want you to feel cooped up or be in the dark, ever again. I promise to always find you, even when you run away because I've pissed you off. Of course we can get married here; it's a great idea. Maybe we can even practice with Ethan and Lilly's wedding...it shouldn't be too hard to get at least the barn all fixed up, even though October isn't that far away."

Bristol smiled at him. She leaned forward and rested her forehead against his. "I love you so much. Although..." She lifted her head and frowned. "This place couldn't have been cheap. I've got more money than I know what to do with. Will you let me pay off the mortgage?"

He smiled. "There's no mortgage, Punky. I bought it outright. Cash. No inspection or anything. You picked a great realtor. She played hardball. Their list price was way too high for all the work that needs to be done with this place. We offered a low but fair price, and the owner agreed. He was ready to be done with it."

Bristol frowned. "I don't mean to bring this up, but since we *are* getting married...you had that much cash lying around?"

Rocky didn't take offense. "Don't ever hesitate to ask me anything. And yeah, I did. I made decent money as a SEAL, and it's not like Fallport has a lot of things to spend money on."

"Right. Well, I'm paying for all the renovations then."

Rocky opened his mouth to protest, but Bristol covered his mouth with her hand. "No, no arguing. If we're gonna have a partnership, you're going to have to get used to me spending money. I didn't plan to become rich. And I want to spend my money—*our* money—on us, Rocky."

He kissed her palm and she dropped it slowly. "Okay."

She gave him some side-eye. "Okay?"

"Yup."

"I thought alpha men got weird about women spending money on them."

He chuckled. "Hey, I don't mind you being my sugar mama if you don't."

She grinned.

"I don't see this as spending money on me, but like you said, on *us*. We're investing in our future. We're building a home for our children. A place where hopefully years and years from now, they'll bring *their* children to visit their grammie and grandpa. Eventually they'll inherit, and the circle of life will continue."

Bristol's eyes filled with tears. "I like that thought."

"Me too," Rocky said, then kissed her softly. "You want to go see it?"

"Yes!" Bristol said, excitement lighting up her eyes.

Rocky knew there would be tough times ahead. They both had some demons to conquer, and the work that had to be done on the house would be difficult to live with for a little while, but he had no doubt that together, they'd make this work. He wasn't willing to have it any other way.

"Stay put," he said as he opened his door.

"Funny guy," Bristol muttered before he left the Tahoe. "It's not as if I could go anywhere on my own anyway."

He was still smiling when he opened her door and reached for her. Rocky carried her into the barn first, telling her what he had in mind for the huge space. Then he carried her to the house...and an even bigger surprise.

The second they walked in, Rocky sighed in relief.

Their friends had come through big time. They'd completely moved them out of his apartment, bringing all their stuff to the house. It didn't even start to fill the space, but it was a start. And once they moved Bristol's things from her house in Kingsport, it would start to look even more like a home.

"How...what?" Bristol stuttered when she saw his couch sitting in the middle of the living room.

"It's gonna suck to live here while I do all the renovations, but there's no way in hell I was bringing you back to that apartment complex," he explained quietly. "If I had my way, it would burn to the ground, but the people who currently live there wouldn't like that much, I'm guessing. So I did the next best thing."

"You bought us a house and moved us in within a few days?" Bristol said with a small shake of her head.

"Pretty much." Rocky bent over and placed her gently on the couch. "I love you, Bristol. So much, you'll never know."

"Wrong. I do know, because I love you the same way."

She reached up and grabbed his beard and pulled him down so she could kiss him.

"Hey! Is it safe to come in?" a female voice called out from the doorway.

"Oh...and we're having a welcome home party too," Rocky told her with a grin, still bent over, her hand still holding his beard. He'd never liked people touching his facial hair, but with Bristol, he couldn't get enough of her hands on him.

"Love you," she said softly.

"Love you too," Rocky returned, kissing the top of her head. "Welcome home, Punky."

Then he stood to greet the people currently filing into the house. His brother, Lilly, Zeke, Elsie and Tony, Drew, Brock, Talon, Raiden and Duke, Finley, Khloe, Otto and Silas, Doc Snow and his partner Craig, Sandra, Whitney...even Edna and her husband had shown up. The house quickly filled with people.

Rocky kept his eye out for the one person he'd personally invited...and he hoped like hell would show up.

Bristol was holding court from her spot on the couch because she couldn't exactly get up and walk around, but no one seemed to mind. People had brought food and drinks, and everyone was smiling and laughing. This was what Rocky loved about Fallport. The community.

"I take it she likes the house," Ethan said, coming up behind his brother.

"Yeah. Thank fuck," Rocky said. Then he added, "And you should know, you and Lilly are getting married here."

Ethan laughed. "We are?"

"Yup."

"Cool. Reception in the barn?"

"Uh-huh. It'll be a dress rehearsal for *our* wedding around Christmas."

"Then you'd better get to work, because Lilly and I aren't pushing our date past Halloween," Ethan said.

"Whatever. You won't have to," Rocky said, giving his brother a shove with his shoulder. "It'll be done."

Ethan turned then, pulling Rocky into a hard embrace. "Happy for you, bro. So glad things worked out."

Rocky closed his eyes and thumped Ethan on the back. "Love you, man."

"Love you too."

They broke it up and smiled at each other.

The door opened then, and Rocky turned to see who'd arrived. He beamed at seeing the two men in the doorway. "Excuse me," he told Ethan, and went to greet them.

He shook both men's hands. "Bristol is gonna want to have a word with you," he told Davis.

The man looked as if he'd made an attempt to clean up for the visit. His hair was combed and his shirt and pants didn't look as dirty as usual. But he didn't exactly look thrilled to be there.

The second Bristol saw who was with him when Rocky approached her spot on the couch, her eyes filled with tears. She put her face in her hand as she tried to hold onto her composure.

When she looked back up, Rocky could see tears on her cheeks. "Davis," she whispered.

"Bristol," Davis said.

"Please, come here," she requested. Davis shuffled over, and she gestured to the empty spot next her. "Sit?"

"I'm...I'm not really dressed for that."

"Whatever. *Sit.*" This time it wasn't a question.

Davis sat.

Bristol leaned over, being careful not to jostle her leg, and hugged the homeless man. Davis sat stiff in her embrace, but he did bring one hand up to awkwardly pat her back.

She pulled back, but didn't let go of his arms. "Thank you."

Davis shrugged.

"No, seriously...thank you. Rocky told me you were the first person to go to Simon to tell him what you saw. And you were absolutely right, it was very weird that he didn't want you looking through his trash. There were some beads, business cards he'd made on his computer back in Kingsport, and probably other things in there that totally would've given away the fact that I was in his apartment."

Davis shrugged again, but Rocky saw him sit up a little straighter.

"As far as I'm concerned, you're the eyes and ears of this town," Bristol went on. "You see everything. I hate that you're sleeping on the streets though. Won't you at least consider letting me...us, your friends...give you at least a tiny home? We can put it near the square. Maybe behind the diner, in the corner of the parking lot. Sandra and I talked about it a while ago, and she agreed."

Davis looked anywhere but at Bristol.

Rocky held his breath. Many people had tried to get the homeless man to accept their help, but he'd been very stubborn so far.

"I'll think about it," Davis finally said.

Bristol beamed, as did everyone within earshot.

"Yay! Thank you!" she said excitedly, and hugged him once more.

Davis had obviously reached his limit of affection, because he stood up from the couch.

"Help yourself to food and whatever," Bristol told him, still beaming.

Davis shuffled off, and Rocky stood back and watched as the strongest woman he'd ever known thanked Simon. Then continued to make everyone around her feel as if they were the most important person in the world as she talked to each of them.

His Bristol was amazing. Looking at her, no one would ever know the hell she'd experienced only a week ago. She made him want to be a better man, every single day.

Rocky made sure to thank each and every person as well, not only for helping to get him moved and for setting up the house, so he could bring Bristol back here, but for being such good friends. Everyone was giddy with relief that Bristol had been found and that she was going to be okay.

She wasn't quite there yet, but she *would* get there. As would he.

The evening wound down, and people trickled out, and soon it was just he and Bristol in the house once more. He sat next to her and palmed her cheek. "You're tired."

She gave him a wan smile. "Exhausted. But happy. I wouldn't have missed this for the world."

"I probably should've told them all to go away after an hour and come back tomorrow, when you've had a chance to sleep."

Bristol shook her head. "No, this was perfect."

"You want to see the rest of the house? Hell, I didn't even get you past the living area before everyone descended."

"Yes, please."

Rocky picked her up gingerly and gave her a quick tour of the rest of the house. He hadn't lied about it needing a lot of work, but she didn't seem to notice the warped floors or the drywall that needed replacing. The bathrooms were especially atrocious, with pink appliances in one and green in another.

"I love it," she told him as he lay her on their bed in the master bedroom. The room was too dim, and Rocky couldn't wait to knock out the wall and put in a balcony and floor-to-ceiling windows. He never wanted Bristol to feel hemmed in again. Especially not in a space that would become their sanctuary from the world.

"I'm glad."

"And I love you. So much, it's almost scary."

"It's not scary...it's right. I felt it from the first time I saw you crawling on the forest floor. I instantly knew you were someone I had to get to know. If I didn't, I knew I'd be missing out."

"That's sweet," she whispered.

"Not sweet. Truth," Rocky said. "Now, you want to take a bath?"

"Oh my God, yes."

"The hot water works, but there's no guarantee how deep the water will get before it runs out."

"Don't care. A bath sounds heavenly."

An hour and a half later, Rocky pulled Bristol into his arms. She smelled like the vanilla bubbles he'd poured into her bath. Her hair was still damp, but he didn't care. Being able to hold her like this was literally every dream come true for him.

"This is what kept me going," Bristol whispered.

All the lights were still on in the room, and would stay on until Bristol's demons were chased away. He didn't care in the least. As long as she was with him, he could sleep anywhere. He tightened his arms around her, emotion overwhelming him and not letting him speak.

"I swear I could feel your arms around me, telling me to be

patient. That you were coming for me. Not to piss him off, to stay calm and do what he said."

"I'm so damn proud of you," Rocky said when he'd gotten control of his emotions.

"You know what?" she asked.

"What?"

"I'm proud of myself too."

Rocky smiled. He loved that for her. "Good. You should be."

"I can't wait to live my life with you."

"Same," Rocky said.

Silence descended on the room. Contentedness spread throughout his body. This was what he'd dreamed about while she'd been missing. Having her back in his arms. Safe.

Lifting his head, he saw Bristol was already fast asleep. She'd never fallen asleep this fast back in the hospital. It was good to know she felt as safe with him as he did with her.

Rocky kissed her temple and settled next to her with a small sigh. This was what had been missing in his life.

No, *she* was what had been missing.

He fell asleep with Bristol's scent in his nose and the knowledge that no matter what bumps might be in the road for them, after the last two weeks, they'd be able to weather anything.

EPILOGUE

Drew Koopman hated this time of year. He didn't like the heat. Didn't like the humidity. Didn't like that tax season was over and he had too much free time on his hands.

He was restless and needed to do something. Sitting at home thinking about all the cases he hadn't been able to solve, all the people who'd hated him simply because he wore a uniform, the men and women he'd worked with who had given their all to the job, literally. As well as the assholes who wore a uniform and gave every single officer out there a bad name.

When he'd retired, he was more than ready to give up his badge and come to Fallport.

Drew was more than aware he was standoffish and hadn't made many friends in town, outside of his team. It was hard for him to trust, and his previous job in law enforcement didn't help any. He was working to try to loosen up, but it wasn't as easy as he thought it might be.

Deciding he was getting morose and needed to get out of his small house, Drew headed out the door. A walk would do him good. It was still early enough that the heat and humidity weren't too bad yet. He walked toward the square, thinking about his friends...and how happy they were with their women.

Lilly, Elsie, and Bristol were really great. Drew liked them a lot and was pleased his friends had found people they could spend their lives with. He wasn't sure he wanted that for himself. Drew enjoyed being alone. He wasn't someone who liked long conversations, he didn't watch a lot of TV, he preferred the silence to a lot of external stimulation.

Maybe it was because he was an only child whose parents didn't have a lot time for him when he was growing up. He was used to entertaining himself. Maybe it was because of the time he'd spent alone in his patrol car. Whatever the reason, Drew had no problem being by himself, and after forty-five years, he assumed that was just his lot in life.

Hiking was something he did for his job with the Eagle Point Search and Rescue team, but he also went out into the woods on his own a lot, as well. He knew the trails around the town like the back of his hand because he'd spent so much time on them. He felt freer when he was surrounded by nature.

The walk to the square didn't take long, and Drew headed for Sunny Side Up. He debated whether to go to The Sweet Tooth and get one of Finley's mouthwatering pastries or to the diner for a proper breakfast. Because he had absolutely no plans for the day, he decided the sit-down breakfast would kill more time.

As soon as he opened the door to the diner, Sandra called out a welcome. Smiling, Drew gave her a chin lift and headed to an empty booth along one side of the restaurant. Even though it was early, the place was fairly busy. It took a couple of minutes for Karen, one of the waitresses, to come over to his table.

"Morning, sweetie. Coffee?"

"Yes, please," Drew said eagerly.

She filled a cup and said, "Do you need some time? Or do you know what you'd like?"

"Can I get two eggs over easy, hash browns, sausage links, a cup of whatever fruit you've got, and a large glass of orange juice?"

"Of course. We're running a little behind, since Carl had a family emergency and we've only got one cook. But I'll get your OJ and the fruit right out to start you off."

"Everything all right with Carl?" Drew asked.

"Yeah. His wife's pregnant and having a hard time of it, as you might know. I guess their three-year-old woke up with a fever this morning, so he's staying home to take care of everyone."

Drew nodded. He did know about Carl's wife. Doc Snow had put her on bed rest and told her that if she wanted to deliver a healthy baby, she needed to take it easy. It was amazing how much everyone knew about everyone else in small towns. "No problem on the wait. I've got no plans today."

"Thanks. I'll be back with your drink and that fruit," Karen told him.

Things always picked up in Fallport in the summer. Tourists came to town to hike the trails in the Appalachian Mountains, and now that word had gotten out about the paranormal investigations show that had filmed there—and the first episode had debuted on TV—more and more of the tourists visiting were doing so with the hopes of catching a glimpse of the elusive Bigfoot. It would only get worse once the Bigfoot episodes actually aired.

He was sipping his coffee and eating the fruit Karen had dropped off when the little bell over the top of the door tinkled and someone entered.

Looking up, Drew couldn't explain the uncomfortable feeling in his chest when he saw who it was. Caryn Buckner.

She was Art's granddaughter, who'd come to town to help him get back on his feet after he'd been stabbed. Drew didn't understand why she made him uneasy. She was nice enough—he'd cut her some slack for their rough introduction at the hospital, since she'd been stressed out—and everyone in town seemed to genuinely like her.

She was a few years younger than him, was the same height, around five-ten. She had short blonde hair and blue eyes. She wasn't exactly overweight, but she was definitely solidly built. Muscular and strong. Drew had seen her lift her grandfather without help when he'd popped into the older man's hospital room in Roanoke, while he was there visiting Rocky and Bristol.

It didn't turn him off. Quite the opposite. Drew had always been attracted to women with Caryn's build. There was nothing wrong with Bristol, but since she was an inch or so under five feet, Drew felt like the hulk around her.

Unfortunately, he and Caryn hadn't gotten off on the best foot. All he knew was that she made him uncomfortable, and apparently the feeling was mutual.

He watched as everyone greeted her as if she'd lived in Fallport her entire life. From what Drew understood, the woman had spent some summers here, and that apparently was enough for her to be treated as a local.

Sandra came out of the kitchen and gave her a huge hug. He could hear the two women talking about how Caryn was there to pick up a meal for Art, who was grumpy that he was still confined to his bed for another couple of weeks. His friends, Silas and Otto, were spending the afternoons with him, updating him on the gossip he was missing by not sitting outside the post office like usual, but he was still going a bit stir crazy.

Drew wasn't upset that he'd spent almost five years trying to be accepted into the tight-knit town, and yet this woman came back after not being here for years and everyone treated her as a long-lost daughter or something. It *did* make him wonder what had kept her away, given the warm reception. If he'd had a place to go where he was embraced and accepted without reservation, he definitely would've gone there after getting out of law enforcement.

A loud noise to his left caught his attention. Glancing at the family sitting a few tables down from his booth, Drew saw the father standing next to his chair, looking panicked.

He moved without conscious thought. The man's hands, grasping his own throat, told him loud and clear what was happening. The guy was choking—and everyone was just sitting there, staring at him in shock.

When he got to the man, Caryn was right on his heels.

"I've got this," he told her.

But she shook him off. "*I've* got this," she countered, putting her hands on the man and pulling him away from the table he was leaning on. She easily turned him and wrapped her arms around his chest.

Drew watched with a frown of concentration. He was trained in first aid, had always had to be as a Virginia State Police Officer. And his training had come in handy in the field since moving to Fallport, as well. But it was more than obvious Caryn had the situation under control.

After two hard thrusts of the Heimlich Maneuver, a piece of food flew out of the man's mouth and landed on the floor. Caryn dropped her arms from around the guy, but kept a hand on his arm, steadying him.

Drew moved a chair behind him, and Caryn helped him sit,

telling him softly and reassuringly that he was going to be all right.

Drew might've been annoyed with the woman, and the way everyone in the diner was congratulating and thanking her for moving so quickly—it was almost amusing how everyone conveniently hadn't noticed that he'd actually gotten to the choking man first—but he'd never been a person who craved the limelight. He was more than happy to let Caryn have it as he stepped toward his booth.

However, as he watched her interact with the locals, he realized *she* wasn't comfortable with the attention she was getting.

Their gazes met, and for a second he saw a lack of ease there that spoke deeply to him. He thought maybe he was seeing a part of the woman she didn't let out very often, a part that she kept behind a very thick wall.

But a veil fell over her eyes with a blink, and the bravado he was already used to seeing was back. After checking to make sure the man was truly all right, Caryn sidestepped away from the table, giving the family some privacy, and moved toward Drew.

"You totally wanted to push me out of the way, didn't you?" she asked Drew quietly.

He chuckled in surprise. "Yeah, kind of."

"Good thing you didn't. I would've taken you to the ground," she said confidently.

"You think you could?"

She eyed him up and down, then said with a shrug, "I *know* I could."

She sounded rather conceited, but Drew actually admired her confidence. He simply raised a brow at her in response.

"You have any training?" she asked, motioning to the man behind her.

"In first aid? Yeah. Assuming, since you're a firefighter, you're at least an EMT?"

"Paramedic," she corrected.

Drew was impressed. Not that it mattered. This woman was leaving. Going back to New York City. She probably hated being here in this sleepy little town. She obviously hadn't missed it enough to come visit anytime recently. He approved of her coming to look after her grandfather, but she'd probably be gone as soon as Art was back on his feet.

"When are you leaving?" he blurted, immediately embarrassed at how awful his question sounded.

"Why? In a hurry to see me go so you can play hero without interference?" she asked.

Brows shooting up again, Drew opened his mouth to answer, to both apologize for his rude question and deny her accusation, but Sandra interrupted them.

"Caryn! That was amazing. Thank goodness you were here!" The diner owner looked at Drew and said hurriedly, "Not that you wouldn't have been able to help too." She shrugged apologetically then turned back to Caryn. "Your order's ready and it's on the house."

"Oh, no it's not," she countered. "I'm not taking free food from you."

"It is, and you are," Sandra countered.

The two women headed back toward the front of the diner and the bag that was sitting on the counter, waiting for Caryn.

At the last minute, she stopped and turned back to Drew. "I shouldn't have said that. I'm sorry."

Drew nodded once, accepting her apology. He didn't want to be at odds with the woman, and he actually liked that she wasn't afraid to stand up to him. To backtalk him. He realized with a start that it had been a long time since anyone had stood up to him like she had, other than his teammates.

There was a lot more to Caryn Buckner, and for the first time in a very long time, Drew found his curiosity had been piqued.

She turned back to Sandra and they continued their walk to the counter. Drew sat back down, but didn't take his gaze from Caryn. She intrigued him.

He realized that she hadn't answered his question. He had no idea how long she was going to be in Fallport. It was likely she'd be leaving sooner rather than later, since Art was well on the mend.

That being the case, it was ridiculous to want to get to know what made her tick...but the longing was there just the same.

It had been years since Drew had felt anything for a woman. He wasn't sure he liked it. Thank goodness she'd be gone soon, and he could forget the way she looked at him with a mixture of censure, curiosity, and vulnerability.

* * *

Whew! Such sparks between Drew and Caryn (and you KNOW she's staying! lol) Read on to find out how Drew feels about that and what trouble is brewing in *Searching for Caryn!*

Want to talk to other Susan Stoker fans? Join my reader group, Susan Stoker's Stalkers, on Facebook!

Also by Susan Stoker

Eagle Point Search & Rescue
Searching for Lilly
Searching for Elsie
Searching for Bristol
Searching for Caryn (April 2023)
Searching for Finley (Oct 2023)
Searching for Heather (TBA)
Searching for Khloe (TBA)

SEAL Team Hawaii Series
Finding Elodie
Finding Lexie
Finding Kenna
Finding Monica
Finding Carly
Finding Ashlyn (Feb 2023)
Finding Jodelle (July 2023)

The Refuge Series
Deserving Alaska
Deserving Henley (Jan 2023)
Deserving Reese (May 2023)
Deserving Cora (TBA)
Deserving Lara (TBA)
Deserving Maisy (TBA)
Deserving Ryleigh (TBA)

SEAL of Protection Series
Protecting Caroline

Protecting Alabama
Protecting Fiona
Marrying Caroline (novella)
Protecting Summer
Protecting Cheyenne
Protecting Jessyka
Protecting Julie (novella)
Protecting Melody
Protecting the Future
Protecting Kiera (novella)
Protecting Alabama's Kids (novella)
Protecting Dakota

SEAL of Protection: Legacy Series

Securing Caite
Securing Brenae (novella)
Securing Sidney
Securing Piper
Securing Zoey
Securing Avery
Securing Kalee
Securing Jane

Delta Force Heroes Series

Rescuing Rayne
Rescuing Aimee (novella)
Rescuing Emily
Rescuing Harley
Marrying Emily (novella)
Rescuing Kassie
Rescuing Bryn
Rescuing Casey

Rescuing Sadie (novella)
Rescuing Wendy
Rescuing Mary
Rescuing Macie (novella)
Rescuing Annie

Delta Team Two Series

Shielding Gillian
Shielding Kinley
Shielding Aspen
Shielding Jayme (novella)
Shielding Riley
Shielding Devyn
Shielding Ember
Shielding Sierra

Badge of Honor: Texas Heroes Series

Justice for Mackenzie
Justice for Mickie
Justice for Corrie
Justice for Laine (novella)
Shelter for Elizabeth
Justice for Boone
Shelter for Adeline
Shelter for Sophie
Justice for Erin
Justice for Milena
Shelter for Blythe
Justice for Hope
Shelter for Quinn
Shelter for Koren
Shelter for Penelope

Ace Security Series

Claiming Grace

Claiming Alexis

Claiming Bailey

Claiming Felicity

Claiming Sarah

Mountain Mercenaries Series

Defending Allye

Defending Chloe

Defending Morgan

Defending Harlow

Defending Everly

Defending Zara

Defending Raven

Silverstone Series

Trusting Skylar

Trusting Taylor

Trusting Molly

Trusting Cassidy

Stand Alone

Falling for the Delta

The Guardian Mist

Nature's Rift

A Princess for Cale

A Moment in Time- A Collection of Short Stories

Another Moment in Time- A Collection of Short Stories

Lambert's Lady

Special Operations Fan Fiction

http://www.AcesPress.com

Beyond Reality Series
Outback Hearts
Flaming Hearts
Frozen Hearts

Writing as Annie George:
Stepbrother Virgin (erotic novella)

ABOUT THE AUTHOR

New York Times, *USA Today* and *Wall Street Journal* Bestselling Author Susan Stoker has a heart as big as the state of Tennessee where she lives, but this all American girl has also spent the last fourteen years living in Missouri, California, Colorado, Indiana, and Texas. She's married to a retired Army man who now gets to follow *her* around the country.

She debuted her first series in 2014 and quickly followed that up with the SEAL of Protection Series, which solidified her love of writing and creating stories readers can get lost in.

If you enjoyed this book, or any book, please consider leaving a review. It's appreciated by authors more than you'll know.

www.stokeraces.com
www.AcesPress.com
susan@stokeraces.com

facebook.com/authorsusanstoker
twitter.com/Susan_Stoker
instagram.com/authorsusanstoker
goodreads.com/SusanStoker
bookbub.com/authors/susan-stoker
amazon.com/author/susanstoker